The Works of John Gordon Davis

Hold My Hand I'm Dying (1967)
Cape of Storms (1970)
The Years of the Hungry Tiger (1974)
Taller Than Trees (1975)
Leviathan (1976)
Typhoon (1978)
Fear No Evil (1982)
Seize the Reckless Wind (1984)
        aka Seize the Wind
A Woman Involved (1987)
The Land God Made in Anger (1990)
Talk to Me Tenderly, Tell Me Lies (1992)
Roots of Outrage (1994)
The Year of Dangerous Loving (1997)
Unofficial and Deniable (1999)

Non Fiction
Operation Rhino (1972)

Hold My Hand
I'm Dying

John Gordon Davies

This edition published in 2015 by House of Stratus, an imprint of Stratus Books Ltd., Lisandra House, Fore Street, Looe, Cornwall, PL13 1AD, U.K.
www.houseofstratus.com

Typeset by House of Stratus.

A catalogue record for this book is available from the British Library and the Library of Congress.

ISBN 07551-5402-9
EAN 978-07551-5402-9

Part One

Chapter One

It is hot in the Zambezi Valley. In the spring it is pregnantly hot, feverish, and the loins of all the valley's creatures itch for the new season. In the spring the bull elephants trumpet and seek out and mount their cows again, the lions rumble over their slinky lionesses, indeed all living things snort and chase their willing womenfolk. In the springtime, more than other times of the year, the young men of the Batonka tribe woo their bare-breasted black maidens and, according to the custom, drag them off into the bush and rape them, so that their fathers may claim both damages and bridal price. In the spring the Sikatonga witch-doctors begin their ritual to make the rain come, and the tribesmen watch the sky and wait for the Sikatongas' orders to begin to hoe the hot dry soil. Then comes the summer with thunder like cannon, and the rain rushes warm and fat and straight down upon the valley, the great Zambezi river swells and roars and the valley is full of steam and slush and sog, the valley jungle turns a reckless riotous green, and the Sikatongas know they have done their work well and that the ancestral spirits have not deserted them.

But this springtime the tribesmen of the Zambezi Valley were uncertain whether they should plough their clearings in the jungle, although the Sikatongas had begun their ritual to summon the rain. There was gloom in the valley. For the past year the Native Commissioner had been warning them of a great flood that was to come to the valley, a flood which would stay forever and drown the whole valley and its huts and animals and jungle gardens. The white men, the Native Commissioner had explained over and over again, were building a great wall across the river where it flowed through a great gorge called Kariba. The wall would stop the mighty river and cause it to flood the valley and turn it into a sea two hundred miles long and twenty miles wide. And all the people would be moved to new lands which the Government was providing for them above the escarpment of the valley. The Batonka people were unconvinced. They trusted the Native Commissioner and called him Elder Father, but how could the white men build a wall across the mighty river? Every man knew that the mighty river was the home of Nyamayimini, and the gorge called Kariba was his den. No man could stop the river. And there were some strange men who came to the valley, black men in city clothes who said that they were going to rule the country, and these men said that the story of the flood was a white man's trick to steal their land, that the Batonka people should refuse to move and that they should gird themselves for war.

This springtime a strange young black man walked down the escarpment and through the jungle of the southern bank of the Zambezi Valley. He was tall and broad and handsome and he wore long baggy trousers with bright patches upon them, he wore miner's boots and he carried three spears, and an axe and a knobstick. He was a Matabele man from far above the escarpment and he had no rightful business in the Zambezi Valley. He was hunting elephant illegally for their ivory, which he proposed to sell to the white traders in Bulawayo.

He watched the ground for spoor of elephant and he walked noiselessly down the hot white sand of the river-bank and then he came upon a naked girl washing in the river. He sat down on the sand and watched her.

She had her back turned to him and she did not hear him. The water came up to her knees and she bent her supple back and hips and threw water over her shoulders and she rubbed her wet-black skin with white river sand. Her legs were long and strong and her buttocks were round and firm and as she bent to scoop water over herself he glimpsed that part of her which will always hold strong men captive. The elephant hunter was a stronger man than most.

'Eeeeh!' she cried when she saw him. Both her hands shot down to cover her nakedness.

The hunter did not move but he smiled.

'Your breasts are very beautiful to see.'

The girl did not worry about her breasts. All women had breasts and they were never covered in the Zambezi Valley.

'Who are you?' she cried, still clutching herself.

'I am a crocodile,' the hunter said happily, 'and if you try to escape I will devour you.'

'Go away,' she said, 'or my father will come with his spear and kill you.'

The hunter lifted his three spears and showed them to her.

The girl looked very upset. 'I want to come out of the water,' she said.

'Come out then,' the hunter said. 'You will find that I have not only the jaws of a crocodile but also the testicles of a lion.'

The girl looked up and down the bank.

'And I have the feet of an antelope,' the hunter said leisurely.

The girl tried again. 'My lover will come soon.'

'Pah!' said the hunter. 'He is a Batonka, I am a Matabele. The Batonka always paid tribute to the Matabele before the white man came.'

'I will complain to the white man Native Commissioner, and he will place you in his jail,' the girl said.

The hunter looked unperturbed. 'He is far away above the escarpment.'

Her hands still covered the apex of her plump thighs. Her skin shone in the sun. She liked the hunter.

'If you are a Matabele,' she said, 'how is it you speak my language?'

The hunter puffed his chest a little. 'I have just come back from Johannesburg,' he said, 'where I was digging for gold on the mines. There were two of your tribe working there. We talked because we came from the same country. On the mines, they emptied the latrine buckets,' he added.

The girl was impressed.

'So you are rich, because you come back from the mines.'

'Very rich. I have fifty pounds in my kraal.'

'How are you called?'

'My name is Samson.'

'Samson?' the girl said. 'That is a strange name.'

'It is a white man's name. It is the name of one of their great forefathers. He once pulled a big hut down upon his tormentors.'

The girl was impressed, for it is very important to have a white man's name.

'What is your totem?' she asked.

'My totem is Ndhlovu, which in my language means Elephant. I am as strong as an elephant,' he added.

'What are you doing in our valley?'

'I seek another bride,' the hunter said easily and untruthfully, although he liked brides.

'How many wives have you?' the girl asked.

'Three,' the hunter said, 'one in Johannesburg and two at my kraal. I have many children.'

'You must be rich indeed,' the girl said seriously.

'I am,' the hunter said.

'Then why do you trouble me?'

The hunter looked at her. 'Because I love you,' he said from the hot white river-bank. 'I think I want you to be my junior wife.'

The girl was not displeased, but it would not do for a Batonka girl to appear too pleased. She hung her head a little coyly and scratched the river bed with her toes.

'You cannot love me,' she said, 'because I am already betrothed. My lover has already begun to pay the cattle for the bridal price to my father.'

Such formalities did not bother the hunter.

'Where is your lover now?'

'He has gone to work far away in the white man's town of Bulawayo,' the girl said proudly, 'to earn some money to buy more cattle to pay my father.'

The hunter was unimpressed.

'He is working for the Municipality emptying latrine buckets too,' he said.

The girl did not deny it. Most of the Batonka men who left the valley for Bulawayo did this work, she had heard.

'Do you love me?' the hunter said.

For reply the girl dashed for a corner of the bank and ran up it and into the bush. She cried 'Eeeh – Eeeeh – Eeeeh – Eeeeh' as she ran, and she cried 'Oh – my mother – my mother,' but she did not cry it too loudly, nor did she run as hard as she could.

Samson let her get a little distance then he climbed to his feet and loped through the bush after her. He grabbed her arm and he spun her round and thrust his hand on her breast.

'Today you will love me,' he announced.

The girl pulled against his hands and wriggled and tried to cry tears but none came.

'Eeeh! Oh my mother! Today I am killed at this place by a bad man. Today I am dying. Oh my mother—'

She stuck out her buttocks and made to dig her heels into the sand and she cried out but the hunter pulled her along easily enough.

'Oh my mother—'

The hunter got her to a place of his liking, a clearing with warm dry grass upon the ground and he spun the girl round to him again and slapped her softly on the side of the head and he put his heel behind her ankle and pushed her. She tumbled back on to the ground, and he fell on top of her.

She wriggled and cried 'Oh my mother' and crossed her legs, but the hunter put his knee between her thighs and forced her legs apart and he unbuttoned his trousers. The girl beat him on his shoulders with her fists, but not very hard.

She still struggled a little as he began to find his way inside her, but then her wriggles grew less and her cries turned to moans and she stopped beating him and her arms went around his shoulders and held him and her body began to move with his.

Her father was not displeased, for now he could claim damages, but he pretended to be.

'How did he do this bad thing to you, my daughter?'

'I was washing my body in the water and he came up to me and caught me and did this bad thing,' the girl sniffed.

'And who is this bad man?' her father asked, very indignant.

'He is called Samson.'

'From whose village is he?'

'He is a Matabele from over the escarpment,' the girl snivelled.

Her father was genuinely angry.

'What! No Matabele will have my children!'

He set off with his elder sons to find the hunter to claim his damages. But he had some difficulty capturing the hunter and he was very angry because he was a Matabele and when they overpowered him they took him up the long jungled footpath of the escarpment to the post of the Assistant Native Commissioner at Nyamanpofu.

Chapter Two

Hot. The sun was behind the thunderclouds, but they refused to rain. Heat hung motionless, moist hot over the vast brown bush, and in the old courtroom it stank, the heat wettened with old sweat on black people sharpened up with new sweat. Joseph Mahoney slid a fresh piece of blotting paper under his writing hand to stop his sweat smudging his notes of the evidence and he flicked the sodden piece on to the floor. His hair stood up, spiky from running his sweaty hand through it. He took hold of the lapels of his black gown and flapped them to try to cool his wet shirt and said: 'Yes, next case, Mr. Prosecutor.'

The fat sergeant was pink with moisture.

'May it please Your Worship to proceed with case number four on the roll. Regina versus Tickey—'

The black constable was leading the little black man into the dock. Tickey saluted Mahoney anxiously.

'Regina versus Tickey, indeed?' Mahoney said.

Big deal, he wanted to say – big deal, and I'm drunk with power. Elizabeth the Second, no less, By the Grace of God, of Great Britain, Northern Ireland and the Colonies and Dominions beyond the Seas, Queen, Defender of the Faith, versus—?

Versus Tickey. That's who.

'And what's Tickey done?'

'Drunk whilst riding a bicycle on a public road, Your Worship,' Sergeant Sheerluck Holmes said pinkly.

Drunk in charge of a bicycle, was he? Why that's a hideous crime, terrible, scandalous. The Queen just won't put up with that kind of stuff in Her Colonies. She told me so Herself.

'Yes?' he said tiredly.

Tickey had been drunk all right. Weaving down the Nyamanpofu road after thirty-six convivial hours drinking beer at Jonah's huts, he crashed at the feet of African Constable Tobias. Tickey had nothing to say for himself.

'This,' said Mahoney most heavily, 'is a most serious case indeed. The Nyamanpofu road is a road in Law, even if it is not one in fact. You might have injured somebody. And you might have ridden into one of those potholes and never been seen again.'

He paused between each sentence to allow the interpreter to translate to Tickey. Tickey looked very worried and very sorry.

'Fined one shilling,' Mahoney said. 'Next case.'

Christ he said to himself.

It was not that Joseph Mahoney disliked the natives. Joseph Mahoney knew kaffirs. He *knew* kaffirs. Old man Mahoney had been a Native Commissioner, Joseph had been born on a bush station like Nyamanpofu, and when he was an infant his mother had put mustard on his tongue to break him of the habit of speaking Sindebele in the house, instead of English. His earliest memories were the warm sweet sweaty smoky smell of the inside of the mud huts of the servants' compound, the fire flickering on the black faces squatting' round the cooking pots, stories of the jungle and warriors and ghosts and witches. The first fairies he learned about were black ones, the first tales of might and glory and chivalry he heard were about black warriors, indunas of the mighty Lobengula who swept all before them from the Limpopo to the Zambezi, the first games he played were with wooden spears and ox-hide shields, screaming Matabele battle cries with black boys also brandishing spears and shields and battle cries, the first heroes he worshipped were the black men who worked for his father, who taught him to stalk and hunt with stick and spear long before his father gave him his first .22 rifle for his tenth birthday. And now, at twenty-five, Joseph Mahoney, Bachelor of Arts in Anthropology and Bantu Languages (Cum Laude) and holder of the Civil Service Law Certificate (third class), had been working in the Native Department of the Southern Rhodesia Government for five years. He knew kaffirs, he liked kaffirs and he was good at administering them: it was not because of the heat and stink in the courtroom, nor the tedium of recording the evidence in longhand, nor the delay in interpretation when he could understand everything perfectly in the vernacular: Joseph Mahoney was beginning to say Christ rather frequently because down there a valley was dying, a way of life was dying, and there were more important things for a man to do than try the case of Regina versus Tickey.

'... Regina versus Samson Ndhlovu,' Sergeant Sheerluck Holmes was saying, 'a preparatory examination into an allegation of rape.'

Samson Ndhlovu sat big and sweating and patient in the dock and listened woodenly to the evidence. He kept his eyes fixed on the wall above Mahoney's head and only looked at the girl when a new exaggeration came out. Once he caught Mahoney's eye, and brown eye held blue eye as Mahoney tried to sum him up professionally and as Samson tried to sum him up as a man. They stared each other out for twenty seconds, then simultaneously Mahoney reverted to his notes and Samson looked down with embarrassment.

The girl lied in the witness box. Dressed in her best loin cloth and a pouch for her breasts made of a flour bag – for she had heard that the Matabele people above the escarpment considered it a curious thing for a woman to bare her breasts in public unless suckling – the girl was a confusion of pride at being the centre of attention, the necessity to put up a good show for her relatives crowding the public benches and squatting outside the Court, the injured virtue she had had drummed up in her, and the lies that it all necessitated. She cried in the witness box. She cried and lied in confusion, the sergeant had to coax the story out of her. She had not tacitly consented to the sexual intercourse, oh no, she had cried out and struggled as hard as she could. The accused had run up to her as she stood washing her body in the water and he had seized her and thrown her to her back in the water and there and then he had raped her. It looked as if her tears were tears of distress at the memory of what had happened to her. There were only two people in the Court who knew she was lying: Samson Ndhlovu and Joseph Mahoney. Mahoney called rape the National Sport of the Natives.

'Does the accused have any question to put to the witness?' Mahoney asked drily.

Samson Ndhlovu stood up. He cleared his throat quietly and looked his judge in the eye. Yes, he had a question, only one.

'Yes,' Mahoney said. 'Ask it.'

Samson Ndhlovu squared himself.

'Am I a duck?' he asked.

Mahoney dropped his pen and threw back his head and laughed.

At four o'clock he discharged Samson Ndhlovu.

Solomon Otto Berger, Warder in charge of Her Majesty's Gaol at Nyamanpofu, threw the tennis ball in the air and then hit it over the net. It was a good service but it was not irreturnable.

Solly leaned on his racquet and looked at the black prisoner peevishly. 'Now listen to me,' he said in Sindebele, 'you should have been able to hit that ball back. You are not doing your best.'

The prisoner fiddled with his old racquet sheepishly and picked his nose. 'Sorry, Nkosi,' he mumbled.

Solly shook his head. 'First thing tomorrow morning,' he ordered, 'you must go to the garage wall and practise. Especially your backhand, your backhand is very bad.'

'Yes, Nkosi.'

The prisoner did not like tennis. He would rather dig gardens or roads any time. When a man digs gardens or roads he does not have to work hard but all this running about on the tennis court trying to hit the ball over the net nicely! The white men were very strange people to torment themselves so. But the prisoner was learning. 'He's got potential,' Solly Berger had said to Joseph Mahoney. 'Pity, he isn't staying with us longer.'

Solly looked at his watch. 'Okay, five o'clock,' he said in English. 'Time to knock off.'

He walked off the home-made tennis court and down the dirt track to his small gaol. Two tame bandits were walking ahead of him, unguarded, carrying sickles, returning from their hard labour in Mahoney's garden. A black prison corporal in a green uniform stood at the gate. He saluted Solly.

'Is the class ready?' Solly asked.

'Yes, Nkosi.'

Solly Berger gave literacy classes to whoever of his prisoners was interested and he paid for their pencils and exercise books himself. It was his contribution towards the new Policy of Partnership Between the Races that was swelling the breasts of the Rhodesian politicians.

'Nkosi?' the corporal spoke.

'Yes?'

'The road gang is not back yet, Nkosi.' Solly jerked his head round.

'Not—? They should have been back an hour ago.'

'Yes, Nkosi.'

Solly glared at him. 'Well why didn't you come and tell me?'

The black corporal flicked his eyes down and shuffled.

'I was waiting to see if they came back first,' he murmured.

'You were waiting—!' Solly cut the sentence with exasperation. He glared and the nostrils of the old Jew nose were dilated. 'Christ,' he ended.

He thought: *Munts* ...

The road gang were Nyamanpofu's hard cases. There were eleven of them under First Class Prison Corporal Amos. Every morning they set off down the road into the sunrise, armed to the teeth with picks and pangas and sickles. First Class Prison Corporal Amos guarded them with one pioneer model shotgun.

Solly turned to a tame bandit.

'Run to the house of the Mambo Native Commissioner and ask him to come. And tell him to bring his gun,' he snapped.

The prisoner jumped and started running. Solly turned into the prison office, then turned and shouted after the prisoner: 'And tell him to bring some beer!'

Solly hurried into the office and picked up the telephone and whirred the handle twice. A tired African voice answered: 'African

Constable Toby here-ah.'

'Gimme Sergeant Holmes, Toby.'

'Ah!' Toby beamed into the mouthpiece. 'Sujenti Holm-is not ini station, sah.'

'Where is he?'

'Out-i, sah.'

'Christ!'

Solly hung up. He whirred the handle again, a long, a short and two longs. On a farm forty miles away a heavy Dutch accent said: 'Frikkie van der Merwe, here.'

'Frikkie, Solly Berger here. It looks as if some of my prisoners have done a bunk. Tell your natives to watch out for strangers. And will you stand by for a manhunt? I'll phone you back later. Meantime can you please get on the phone and ring up your neighbours, Johnny and Klaus and Steve and the boys and tell them to do the same and to stand by—'

The three black prison corporals and the three black police constables squatted round the front gates of the prison, awkwardly, holding for the first time in their lives the prison shotguns that Solly Berger had issued for the first time in his prison service career. The prison was quiet, all the prisoners were locked up. Solly Berger and Joseph Mahoney sat in the front seat of Mahoney's old Chevrolet parked outside the prison, their rifles leaning against the seat beside them. They were quiet. They drank beer out of bottles and they stared pensively through the windscreen into the gloom down the road the prisoners had gone. Solly shifted his buttocks.

'Give them ten minutes,' Mahoney said, without moving his eyes. 'Then you better press the panic button.'

Solly grunted. 'If they've done a bunk they're sure as hell not going to walk down the road. They'll have melted into the bush and we sure as hell won't catch up with them tonight.'

Mahoney grunted. 'Good thing Tennis wasn't with them. What would we have done for a fourth?'

Solly opened his door, climbed out, faced the direction of his house and shouted: 'Joshuah!'

From Solly's kitchen: 'Nkosi?'

'Beer please.'

'Nkosi.'

The cook came trotting through the gloom with two cold bottles of beer. Solly and Mahoney sat silently drinking and waiting.

'God, I'm sick of this,' Mahoney said suddenly.

Solly looked at him. 'Sick of what?'

'This life. This life of Native Commissioner,' Mahoney said tonelessly to the windscreen.

Solly's eyebrows went up. 'I thought you liked it?'

'I do.' Mahoney did not seem about to expand on his contradiction.

'But?' Solly prompted.

Mahoney sighed and took a slug out of his bottle, opened his mouth and then said nothing.

'You've done well,' Solly said slowly. 'You're your own boss at twenty-five, boss of this whole district.'

Mahoney shook his head. 'Boss of the natives, chum. Big deal.'

Solly nodded wisely. 'You're just bushwhacked,' he said. 'You need another trip to the liquorish lights of Bulawayo.'

Mahoney snorted softly. 'Two hundred and fifty miles,' he said, 'over hell's own roads. You get there and what happens? You spend the week-end frantically combing the bars looking for something to screw, fail, and then come Sunday you drive the two-fifty miles back.'

Solly nodded. 'I know.' He paused. 'What you need is to get married,' he said.

'And how does a nice guy like me find a wife stuck in the bush?'

'Advertise,' Solly said.

Mahoney snorted softly again. He leaned over and looked at Solly's watch. 'Well,' he said, 'I don't see your bandits.'

Solly nodded. He climbed out of the car, looking worried. 'I'll call Frikkie again and ask him to get his pals together.'

Solly walked into the prison office and picked up the telephone. Mahoney climbed out of the car and looked at the black men.

'Now then, you men—'

He stopped. He turned his head and listened. He peered down the road into the dusk and held up his hand and listened again. Then he jerked round and hurried to the office window and rapped on it and motioned Solly outside. The black corporals and constables were saying ah! ah! and listening.

'D'you hear it?'

'Yes,' Solly whispered.

'Do you recognise it?'

'I'm not sure.'

'It's a Matabele Warrior marching song.'

Ah! Ah! from the blacks.

Mahoney turned to them.

'Get into riot drill formation,' he hissed.

The black men scrambled into a line. Mahoney wished Sheerluck Holmes were there. This was his department. Solly and Mahoney cocked their rifles and stood poised, peering down the road.

The chanting was drawing closer but they could only see a hundred yards in the last dark twilight. Mahoney suddenly turned to the nearest policeman.

'Get into the car, when I shout, switch the lights on bright.'

The only sound in the blanket of evening was the deep chant. It was a thrilling, frightening noise. Mahoney had not heard it since he was a boy. It was a song indunas had sung as they loped into battle, a savage virile old old sound of battles long ago. It gave Mahoney gooseflesh, he loved the sound, the sound of Africa, and he feared it.

Then they saw in the gloom, sixty yards away, a blur of movement. The blur began to take shape. A body of men marching. Mahoney and Solly lifted their rifles to their hips.

The group took better shape. They were marching close together, beating their feet on the ground hard, chanting. 'Zhee – Zhee – Zhee—' Mahoney lifted his rifle higher.

'Lights!'

The headlights flashed bright.

Two lines of prisoners were marching, squinting into the headlights, marching side by side. Next to the column marched a prisoner, carrying a rifle. He carried the rifle on his shoulder, and they were all in step. They swung their arms to shoulder height and looked straight in front of them. First Class Corporal Amos was conspicuous by his absence. The column of marchers was carrying something between them. It was a home-made litter. And lying in the litter, very drunk and incapable, was First Class Prison Corporal Amos.

'Skw-a-a-a-a-i—Ha!'

They came to a smart halt in front of the headlights.

Mahoney and Solly slid their rifles to their sides. The riot squad lowered their batons.

The rifle carrier, one Shadrek Kumalo, presently doing a three-year stretch for six counts of Assault with Intent to do Grievous Bodily Harm – Shadrek had sorted the men from the boys with a knobstick at a beerdrink – Shadrek Kumalo marched forward to Solly Berger, ordered himself to halt at the top of his lungs and saluted. On behalf of the gang he apologised for being late, Nkosi, and expressed the hope that they were not too late for supper. It had, he explained, taken them a long time to find the corporal in the bush, because very many people were holding beerdrinks today to appease the ancestral spirits and to exhort them to make the rain to come.

Joseph Mahoney was a little drunk. He paced slowly up and down the long red cement verandah of the Residency in the dark holding a glass of beer, smoking.

Bushwhacked and sex-starved, maybe, he thought – certainly I'm sex-starved. Maybe Solly is right, maybe that is my only trouble. Bushwhacked and sex-starved – you get unstable in the bush. Woman, you cry out for the softness of woman, the love of woman. You feel you could go crazy for the soft sweet secret sticky slimy hot beautiful depths of woman, the in and out and the suckiness of woman, you keep thinking of those thighs, the marvellous round soft warm smoothness of thighs, the feel of the flesh of her buttocks in your hands as you ride her, the softness under your chest, and you feel you will go mad if you don't have a woman. When you get that feeling after too long in the bush you get that seethe in your loins, that pressing tingling hotness, that pressing, and you feel you must walk out of the bush, get up and walk out of Court and jump into your car and drive the two hundred and fifty miles to town and bloody well find yourself a woman, as is your right. And you feel you would love that woman, adore her, fight fiercely for her, because she answers that hot pressing feeling, you feel that you would never be unhappy again just so long as you always had her, you would never get tired of her. Unstable, you get unstable in the bush. Like that girl, that nurse, Jean Whatshername. She was nothing much, nothing much to look at, why else did she come out with him on a blind date, only the desperadoes go out on blind dates. She had very little breasts and she was plump and her legs were too fat although they looked all right in high heels; but she was a woman, she looked at him with woman eyes from woman body, and her mouth was warm and wet inside and she had moaned in her throat and pushed her tongue into his mouth when his hand went up her skirt, up between her smooth warm plump thighs, that smooth flesh – and he had felt that he loved her, there and then he felt he was crazily in love with her, he felt he would never be unhappy again just so long as he had her always, her soft smooth warm thighs to have as his own, to splay them and mount her and ride her, he had almost told her there and then that he loved her. They had been unable to do anything in the front seat of the old Chev, parked outside the Nurses' Home, and he had not had her, and for nights afterwards back in the bush at Nyamanpofu he had thought of her and thought he loved her. Unstable, he realised – a man gets unstable in the bush. And you have these dreams, these women who come to your bed in your dreams, Marilyn Monroe had come and Lauren Bacall and this girl Jean and the faceless ones too, the ones only with stockinged thighs and crotches, and you made love to Marilyn and Lauren and Jean and the faceless ones, sometimes it was very good and sometimes it was spoilt because you finished before you had gone inside her, and sometimes you wake up too soon and then she never comes back that night, no matter how hard you try. And in the morning you wake up and you think: *I must get out of the bush, I must get a job in town, what kind of life is this, I'm not a full man like this.* And you get to hate your job in the bush and you say to yourself: What good am I doing anyway, playing white chieftain over a few thousand munts, sorting out their miserable little problems and disputes, you're worth more than that, you could do more for the country and more for yourself doing a more important job in town, a real job, where you come to grips with real problems, real life, not this artificial kingship in the bush, you aren't in *competition* in the bush, you aren't proving yourself in society, you're just a tin god, a puppet of the Head Office. And you thought of all the exotic things and places too, London and Paris and New York and Tokyo and Hong Kong, crawling with women and you thought of all the adventures you'd missed, all the beautiful sights you hadn't seen and the experiences you hadn't experienced and the thoughts you hadn't thought and the feelings you hadn't felt, and you thought: I must get out, life passes you by in the bush, one part of you *can't* develop in isolation like this, *I must get out*. And then you thought of the actual leaving, leaving behind the only work you knew, the only people you really knew, and you thought of the land husbandry scheme you were developing and the indabas and the black faces turned up to you and waving to you from the fields and saluting you from the roadside and you knew their latest problems, whose daughter had given birth to twins, who was paying lobola for his bride, who had gone off to the mines, who was seeking a divorce and why, whose crops were endangered by elephant, you thought of the drums in the sunset and the smell of the woodfires and the elephant crossing the road, you thought of all these things, and you felt you could not leave, because they were your people and the land was your land and … And you thought: I must get a wife to come to live with me in my house in the bush. A wife.

And Joseph Mahoney sat down in a chair on the verandah and pulled deep on his beer and breathed into the glass so it made a sad lonely tired sound, and he thought about how much he wanted a wife, and he thought of the girl with the thick, long golden hair and wide mouth and the jutting breasts and the sad, slanty eyes.

'Here comes Jake Jefferson and his tart,' Mrs. Smithers had said.

Sitting on a barstool in the Salisbury Country Club last week-end, having his eighth beer, wondering where to try for his blind date seeing the Nurses' Home had not been forthcoming, a girl with long gold hair coming in with a man a good bit older: the girl caught at his heart, a beautiful unhappy girl, a girl of mystery and secrets, he had thought he was in love with her then and there. Jake Jefferson's tart? On her back in some secret flat: it could break your heart, a smashing girl like that, break your heart, she belonged in his house here in Nyamanpofu.

'Why is she a tart, Mrs. Smithers?' too loudly.

'Hush, dear boy!' leaning close, her aging hand on his arm, lingering there. 'Jake Jefferson is married, you see. To such a sweet woman, and Jake and this girl have been mooning around together for years – Hello Jake, hello Suzie, so nice to see you' – Mrs. Smithers twiddling her fingers.

Jake Jefferson and his tart pausing to say hello, Mahoney's heart beating wildly.

'Joseph Mahoney, he's a Native Commissioner near the Zambezi Valley somewhere.'

'The Kariba Valley?' Jake Jefferson, tired-looking, good-looking, speaking. 'I'm going down there myself next month.'

'There's trouble on the north bank—'

Keep the man talking.

But they had moved on, preoccupied with each other, and she had not said anything except How do you do, an unhappy beautiful girl with jutting breasts and long gold hair. Wanting to put out his hand and hold her:

Don't be unhappy, beautiful girl, leave him and come live with me and be my love—

Mahoney sat slumped in his chair on the verandah of the empty womanless Residency; he stood up, embarrassed at his own foolishness. Unstable, you get unstable in the bush. He started pacing off down the verandah again. Forget about it, he told himself, stop thinking about a girl with long yellow hair and sad blue eyes or about any other woman, if you're going to brood try to brood constructively. Why are you restless, apart from your goddam hormones? I am unhappy – he stopped and looked out into the night – I am unhappy because I consider that there are more important things for me to do in this country, this landlocked country which our leaders are trying to preserve by reform, to preserve by the new ideal, Partnership. Partnership between the Races. Equal Rights for All Civilised Men. Trying to stop it going black like Ghana, trying to stop it going berserk and bloodstained like Kenya, by timeous reform, Partnership. Okay, it's probably a good plan. I don't know what chance it's got, what chance a mere three hundred thousand whites have got trying to civilise up to eight million savages in a jungle ten times the size of England – but if it's got to be done there is so much to be done, so much work, a handful of whites trying to spoon-feed eight million wogs, for Christsake, and most of them don't want to be civilised, they want to sit on their backsides in the sun drinking beer, and then there are going to be the wide boys, the black politicians stirring them up like they're doing in Kenya, murder and rape, and genocide, like those wide political boys from the Black North are doing right now down in the Zambezi Valley, telling the Batonka to refuse to move, that the story of a flood is a white man's trick; and there're going to be the long-haired gentlemen overseas shouting the odds – Christ knows it's going to be difficult, so bloody heartbreaking, that—well, that I get sick of sitting on my backside in the bush being the local king, presiding as magistrate over the case of Regina versus Tickey, charged with the crime of being drunk in charge of a bicycle, for God's sake. *Do* something, *teach* them something – I should be a missionary, he thought. Yes, a missionary, an agnostic one so it doesn't interfere with my sex life, be a missionary and teach them cricket so they grow up black Englishmen, like the Jamaicans. Black Englishmen – Christ. What a tragedy it all is. No more jungle, no more lions' roar, no more thatch villages with tendrils of smoke rising in the sunset, no more elders holding their indabas – just civilisation, progress, neat rows of concrete semis with galvanised iron roofs.

Oh God, the heartbreak. That is why I am restless – the heartbreak of Africa, the bewilderment of change, of civilisation, of progress, of partnership. Of Africa dying. Yes, dying. Africa, my Africa is dying, like that Zambezi Valley down there, that mighty magnificent violent valley. It's dying. It's going to be drowned by progress. By partnership. And not only is the hot soil and that feel and that smell of the valley going to be drowned, but so are the animals, the lion and the elephant and the buck. There'll be no more lions roaring in the valley, no more trumpet of elephant, no more calves hanging on to their mothers' tails with their trunks, Solly, in the valley. There's going to be no more sunset silhouettes as the animals come down to the mighty river to drink, no more stamp of hooves and clouds of dust and the smell of dung. There's going to be no more deathscreams in the night as a leopard catches its prey. There's only going to be the screams of the animals drowning. And there's going to be no more sounds of the drum being beaten in the valley. There's going to be no more Batonka living in their mud and thatch villages and worshipping their ancestral spirits and smiling all over their black faces and clapping their hands when they see you, in fact there's going to be no more Batonka tribe. They're going to be taken far away out of the valley, and they're going to be scattered far and wide so they'll probably never see each other again, in nice new neat little concrete townships with shiny new tin roofs and running water in their kitchens and flush latrines. There's going to be no more river god for them, no more Nyamayimini, no more Sikatongas to make the rain for them, no more ancestral graves to worship at because the ancestral graves will be drowned along with the valley and the animals and their villages. The people from one village may never see the people from the next village again, friends and relatives and even lovers. There will be no more Batonka. They will just become bewildered Rhodesians. That's why it's sad, why progress is sad. That's why Africa is dying, because the same sort of thing is going to happen everywhere.

Mahoney sat alone on the verandah in the dark, smoking. There was the pad of bare feet in the house and then the old skinny form of the cookboy appeared in the French doorway. 'Mambo?'

Mahoney did not look around. 'Why are you not asleep, old gentleman?'

Sixpence came out on to the verandah and stood awkwardly, embarrassed, 'I wish to speak to the Mambo.'

'Speak, then, old gentleman.'

Sixpence coughed and shifted uncomfortably. 'Mambo, I wish to go home.'

Mahoney turned and looked at the old man. 'Why?'

Sixpence shuffled. 'Because, Mambo,' he said, 'I hear the white men are going to cause a flood in the valley.'

Mahoney looked at the dark form and then he nodded. 'That is right, old man.'

'My heart is troubled, Mambo. I wish to speak to my people in the valley.'

Mahoney nodded. *You poor old bastard.*

'Where in the valley is your home, old man?'

'Chipepo, Mambo.'

'Ahah – Chipepo. On the north bank.'

'Yes, Mambo,' the old man said.

Mahoney thought. 'Old gentleman?'

'Mambo?'

'There is trouble in Chipepo's chiefdom. Have you heard?'

Sixpence looked down at the cement as if Mahoney could look into his eyes in the dark. 'I have heard, Mambo, but I have not seen.'

'Old man,' Mahoney said slowly, 'the people of Chipepo's chiefdom refuse to believe the flood is coming. They refuse to leave their villages. This is because strangers from the cities have poisoned their minds by telling them that the story of the flood is a white man's trick.'

Sixpence said nothing.

'Old man, many of the people on the southern bank of the great river have already been moved, and the others are preparing to move. But in Chipepo's chiefdom they think the warning of the flood is a trick to steal their land.'

The old man kept his head down and looked at the floor. 'Old man?'

Sixpence looked up. 'Mambo?'

'Old man, the story is not a trick. It is the truth that the flood will come. And many of Chipepo's people will be drowned and their property carried away by the water if they do not move soon.'

Sixpence looked down again.

'Old man, you may go home to your village, and you must prepare to move so that when the District Commissioner on your side of the river comes for you, you are ready. Do you believe me that the flood will come?'

Sixpence nodded once. 'I believe the Mambo, when the Mambo tell me,' he said sadly, 'but when I see the valley and the great river, I do not know.'

Mahoney sighed. 'When do you wish to leave me, old man?'

'When the sun rises, Mambo.'

Mahoney was irritated. 'Tomorrow! You cannot leave until you have found a man to replace you, you cannot leave me without a cookboy!'

The old man nodded.

'I would not leave the Mambo without a cookboy,' he said. 'Already there is a man here who wishes to work for the Mambo.'

Mahoney was suspicious. 'Can he cook?'

Sixpence nodded. 'I asked him and he says he can do everything and anything,' he said.

Mahoney grunted. 'Who is this witch-doctor?'

Sixpence was uncomfortable. He wanted to be gone to his home in the Zambezi Valley, for he had heard the war was coming. He was an old man but his spears were ready and he still knew how to throw them.

'He says he knows the Mambo. He says his name is Samson Ndhlovu.'

That night the rain came to the Zambezi Valley and to Nyamanpofu.

Chapter Three

'Go north, young man!' was the saying in those days. 'It's a young growing country with wide open spaces, and there're fortunes to be made.' It was Federation did it, Partnership, the new hope in rumbling Africa, the grand Federation of Southern Rhodesia, Northern Rhodesia and Nyasaland, partnership of the black copper-rich north with the white go-ahead south, political and economic partnership, Equal Rights for All Civilised Men, brainchild of Britain to beat the winds of change. 'Go north, young man!' And north they came from South Africa in droves, in trains and cars and lorries and on their thumbs, to the hot bushland of Rhodesia north of the Limpopo, the land of Monomotapa. And there were fortunes to be made: Jesus, you could sell anything. The old five bedroomed houses on five acres five miles from town, with wide red cement verandahs all round, found new two bedroomed houses on half-acre stands pushing out to meet them; the old red respectable houses round Fort and Main streets in town found themselves squeezed between blocks of flats that looked down into their back yards. The old houses were no longer respectable old houses, but poor old houses where only the poor immigrants went to live.

'Rhodesia is Lion Country,' said the adverts; 'Always Drink Lion Beer,' and there's the picture of the lion licking its chops. And the young men forgot about the lions and drank the beer. 'Rhodesia is a man's country' and the men lived like gentlemen, and the women liked it that way and they left the kids to the nannies and the house to the houseboy and the cooking to the cookboy and the garden to the gardenboy and went into town to the offices to keep it up. And in the evenings they sat on their lawns and drank gin-slings or went to the Club and drank gin-slings and looked around.

And Rhodesia is Club country. You really should belong to the Club. It is the Club which sets the social pace and standard, it is through the Club that you get invited to the sundowner parties and the dinner parties and the bridge parties and the tennis parties and the swimming parties and the sundowner parties and the dinner parties and the bridge parties and the tennis and the swimming and the dinner and the bridge.

'And the occasional wife-swapping party,' Jake Jefferson said drily.

The Club is a very pleasant place. Many green acres, big Dutch-gabled clubhouse, red cement verandahs, cocktail bar, sedate dining-room.

Saturday night at the Club. Jake Jefferson stood with his back against the bar, holding his sixth Scotch. He looked at his company. Twelve people in his party. *His* party. Sundowners at his house, adjournment for sundowners at the Club, dinner at his expense for the whole damn lot of them at the Club.

'It won't hurt you irreparably to put on a façade of domestic felicity for one night, Superintendent,' Sheila had said.

'It'll hurt like hell,' Jake Jefferson had replied. 'Who are these people I've got to entertain, anyway?'

'*We've* got to entertain, sir,' Sheila had said. 'They're people to whom as Superintendent and Mrs. Jefferson we are socially indebted. You mightn't have noticed, in the rosy glow you succeed in walking about in, but we have, as Superintendent and Mrs. Jefferson, been to their homes and eaten their dinners from time to time over the last six months.'

'Well, why the hell must we dine at the Club?' he had said. 'Isn't it more suitable, and less expensive incidentally, just incidentally, to eat at home?'

Sheila Jefferson had shrugged. 'It's easier.'

Jake Jefferson had got angry. 'Easier! What do I employ a cookboy and a houseboy for!'

So Jake Jefferson stood against the bar playing host as amiably as he could. He tuned in to the conversation, and he took a long suck out of his glass. God! did he have to choose this in preference to Suzie?

'There's Iris. Loves her pink gin, doesn't she?' Nancy Smithers said.

'Don't we all, Nancy?'

'Hello, Iris!' Nancy's face crinkled up in bright greeting and she twiddled her fingers in a wave across the verandah.

'Of course, we do, Jake. I simply said she loves her gin.' Nancy Smithers on the defensive. 'She does knock them back rather. Were you here the other night when she got a bit tight?'

'If I was, I didn't notice.'

'Well, she did. And she was dancing cheek to cheek with Mike.'

'So?'

Nancy blinked at him. 'Well, it's hardly done.'

Jake Jefferson lifted his glass. 'My dear Nancy, it is all too frequently done. If I cast my mind back I remember you doing it. With me.'

Nancy Smithers fluttering her aging eyelids. 'Well really, Jake!'

'Well really what, Nancy?'

'Hardly a thing to say to a friend!'

'Isn't Iris your friend?'

'Of course she is! I think Iris is a dear sweet girl. But for you to stand there and remind me that once upon a time five years ago you and I had a little flutter on the dance floor—'

'Two years ago, Nancy.'

'Two years ago then! At least I didn't have an affair with you!'

'Only, Nancy,' Jefferson said quietly, 'only because you couldn't find your car keys and Sheila had mine.' If you go to the Club you get to know everything. 'Have you heard about Cynthia and Paul?'

'No, do tell me!'

'Well,' cigarette lit, puffing it up into the night air, 'they're separating.'

Disappointment.

'Oh, that again! They've been separating for years and never done it. Paul tells me they haven't slept in the same room for years.'

'Not surprised, Paul's never home!'

'Oh, really! Not a nice thing to say about poor old Paul. He's such an old sweetie.'

Cultured giggles.

'Anyway. No, this time I hear it's the real thing. He's officially moving out and taking a flat in town.'

'No!'

Something new.

'Yes.'

'How d'you know?' Another puff of the cigarette.

'Well my dear – my cookboy. You know what servants are, see everything. Anyway, my old Moses is great pals with Cynthia's cookboy. And Moses told me this morning – he's such a sweet old thing is my Moses, but honestly he's got no brains—'

'None of them have, my dear ...'

'No. Well, old Moses told me there was a hell-fire row the other night at dinner and he was accusing her of all sorts of things—'

'Probably quite accurate, if I know Cynthia.'

'And old Paul packed a suitcase and stormed out and drove off.'

Reflection.

'Well, he's done that before.'

Disappointment.

'But has he come back yet?'

'Moses says not.'

A point to ponder then: 'Shame, poor Cynthia. I must look her up.'

'Poor Paul, I say. She's led him a hell of a dance.'

'Yes, Paul's a sweetie.'

'But a bit of a lad with the ladies.'

Savouring it, rolling round the tongue kindly.

Jesus, thought Jake Jefferson.

The oak-panelled bar was full. Women still in tweed golfing skirts, women in tennis frocks, women in cocktail dresses, men in suits, in white bowling flannels and blazers, men in plus-fours, tanding in groups talking and joking and laughing and putting up drinks. Michael Fox-Smith, the real estate man was there, telling how good business is. Property values sky-high and still you can sell anything. You could even sell the sewage farm, ha ha ha. Houses, Jesus, he just couldn't get enough houses. Rent, buy, anything. Immigrants pouring in. And flats? He had waiting lists a mile long for flats, high rentals too. One month's rent key money – quite a thing. I tell you, Hamish, real estate's the thing. The country's booming, spreading like a bloody epidemic, old boy. Buy, if you can get it – anywhere. In two years you'll treble your money. Hamish is nodding his fat grey head and thinking it's time he put up a round of drinks and figuring out how he can avoid it. He has no intention of buying any land. He's busy mortgaging sections of his present property to pay for the maintenance of his house, his wife and his liquor account. Sundowner parties, tennis parties that turn into sundowner parties, people dropping round for drinks at midday – hell of an expense. But what can you do, you've got to do it.

At the other end of the bar Monica Pryce was saying to Winnie Constance: 'There's Jake and Sheila. Must've got a late pass from his mistress.'

'Jake's making an ass of himself.'

Jake Jefferson looked at James Forsythe. What the hell was he doing in his party? He didn't suppose he had exchanged a dozen words with the young V.I.P. from England since he arrived two years ago. What did V.I.P. stand for – Very Indifferent Prick? Forsythe was coming over to be sociable.

'Well, Jefferson, how's tricks in the police state?'

The policeman took a long sip out of his ninth Scotch.

'Regimented,' he said.

Forsythe laughed.

'Sheila tells me you're due for a promotion to Assistant Commissioner, congratulations.'

Jake Jefferson looked at Forsythe sharply, then glanced at his wife. What did the woman think she was doing? And why tell this slob, of all people?

'Sheila jumps to conclusions,' was all he could think of saying. Then, 'Excuse me a moment,' and he left the bar.

He walked down the passage and into the door marked Gentlemen.

He turned the light on. The noise from the cocktail bar was mercifully cut off. He leaned his back against the door and sighed.

Did he have to choose this for the rest of his life instead of Suzie? That aimless, soulless bunch instead of sweet genuine Suzie?

He left the door and walked heavily over to the wash-basin and splashed cold water up into his face. He looked at himself in the mirror.

It was definitely a forty-year-old face that looked back at him. 'You're old, Jefferson,' he said aloud, 'you've almost had it.' Weight, he could see the weight in his face. 'Whisky, Jefferson, too much bloody whisky.' Lines round his eyes. No longer the light handsome lines of eyes that smile a great deal, but webs now. And on his brow, permanent lines. At his temples, turning grey. Forty. 'The great Jake Jefferson – what's happened to you, you stupid bastard?' Forty. And what have you got to show for it? A wife who lives it up and runs up accounts all round town. A monthly liquor bill two feet long. Dress accounts at Meikle's and Greaterman's. Dinner parties you don't want and can't afford. Debt. But worse than all that, you're gutless.

'Gutless, Jefferson.'

He looked at his face. You got to have guts to be happy. You got to have the guts to kick over the traces and grab happiness. Grab it, Jefferson, get a divorce, tell the Board to stick their promotion up their jersey. Quit the job, get back your pension money, pay your wife's debts off once and for all, take Suzie and your daughter with you and take up that Narcotics job that's going in Hong Kong and start your life again. Stuff the Board and their bloody blackmail. Blackmail: Assistant Commissioner or Suzanna de Villiers. 'We cannot have our top men involved in open scandal, Jefferson. You will lose the respect of your men.'

Jake Jefferson shook his head. Assistant Commissioner, almost top man. Superseding others. Just the right age, it was clear he was being groomed for the Commissioner's job when the Old Man retired. Commissioner. His own police force. The job he'd been working for since he was a trooper. And he need not centre his life round the Club, he could carry on with Suzanna secretly—

But oh sweet Jesus, what kind of a man are you, Jefferson? What kind of a life is that? What about children for her, and a home? Forty – how much youth have you got left to give her? It must be all or nothing, for her. The bloody Board is right.

But—oh God, the divorce. 'Try to sue me, Jake,' she had said, 'and I'll contest it, it'll be the dirtiest divorce suit in the history of this colony, darling. And I'll cite your precious Suzanna de Villiers as your mistress, and don't expect the judge to believe you haven't slept with her after the evidence he'll hear. The police force will love that, reading all the juicy bits about their Assistant Commissioner in the paper. *And* I'll see to it that I get awarded the custody of Helen, the wife always gets the custody of children, I've seen a lawyer too, darling—' Exactly what his own lawyer had said. Christ – Suzie. She wasn't going to drag Suzie into this. And Helen – oh Jesus, his own sweet Helen, the only sweet clean thing that had come out of their rotten set-up. The bitch using Helen as her trump, it suited her to be Mrs. Jefferson, Mrs. Superintendent Jefferson. And she was right, the bitch, the wife always gets the custody of a daughter fifteen years old, his own lawyer had told him that too.

Jake Jefferson looked at his face in the mirror. He took a big breath. 'Fuck the Board,' he said.

He would bloody well send Suzie away first, far away so she could not be dragged into the witness box. And Helen too, send her away too with Suzie, send them both far away first so they couldn't be dragged into the case – Christ. It filled him with elation.

He walked out of the toilet back to the bar, up to his wife. 'Yes, darling?' Sheila turned her bright brown eyes up at him.

'H.Q. has just phoned,' he said, 'and there's been a development. I'm terribly sorry, I'll have to go.'

'Poor darling.'

'Sorry folks,' he said. 'But don't rush off, Sheila will be staying—'

'Poor Jake.'

'Hell of a life being a police officer,' Forsythe said.

Jake Jefferson got into his car and drove out of the Club yard. He did not drive to Headquarters. He drove to Suzanna de Villier's flat. She came to the door in her dressing-gown with a book in her hand.

'Jake! What a lovely surprise!'

He stepped into the room and took her shoulders and looked at her.

'Jake – what is it, you look haggard. What is it, darling?'

He opened his mouth to say it.

'Suzie … We're—'

She waited. 'What?' she whispered. 'What were you going to say?' He closed his eyes and pulled her to him.

Sheila Jefferson said goodnight to her guests on the front steps of the Club and walked over to her new Zephyr. She waited till the Humber parked near the gate started, then she started her engine and followed the big car at a distance. She followed it all the way through the avenues of Hillside and up into the drive of the big house. The lights in the lounge were burning by the time she stopped. She walked through the French windows.

James Forsythe turned from the liquor cabinet and smiled and passed her a glass of Scotch.

Chapter Four

Suzanna de Villiers was not a tart. It is correct that she was not a good Dutch Reformist, not any more. She had lapsed, as it is said, which meant, for practical purposes and language, which was Suzanna's language, that she was doomed to hell-fire and damnation: there is little place in heaven for Dutch Reformists who were prepared to marry a man already married in the eyes of God. Hell-fire and brimstone. Suzanna de Villiers, of old Dopper Kerk stock, was prepared to do it. Suzanna was afraid, she verily believed she would pay the price in due course, but she did not care. She cared for Jake Jefferson.

Suzanna de Villiers did not go to kerk any more. She did not go to church because the Dominee had told her she was a wicked woman and she was doomed.

'See no more of this man!'

'Dominee,' she said. 'I will see this man again.'

'What! Do I understand that you are unrepentant for your sin?'

Suzanna hesitated. 'Dominee, I have done nothing bad!'

'Who are you, child, to decide what is bad? You know the law: "Those whom God hath joined together, let no man rend asunder!"'

'They are already asunder. And I am not sleeping with him!'

'I should hope not!' the priest snorted. 'See him no more.'

'And if I do, Father?' she whispered.

'Hell.'

That was a year before. Instead of going to kerk she worked three evenings a week for no reward as an assistant nurse at the Dutch Reformed Church Mission Hospital for non-Europeans.

Suzanna de Villiers was no coward. But still she blanched when the young Predikant accosted her in the Female Ward at six p.m. She was on her way to the sluice-room to dispose of a pan of vomitus.

'Are you Suzanna de Villiers?'

Automatically she gave a little bob, a quarter curtsey. 'Ja, Vader.'

'I want to talk to you,' the Predikant said. 'Come with me.'

She followed the dapper priest down the passage and into a little alcove. She was still carrying the pan.

'Get rid of that,' he pointed testily, 'and come back here.'

She went to the sluice-room with a pounding heart, and disposed of the vomitus. She washed and dried her hands and returned to the alcove carrying the clean bedpan.

'What's this?' the priest said angrily: he flicked his fingertips over her working smock. 'Wearing the trappings of the servants of God?'

Suzanna was unnerved.

'I've heard about you,' the priest said softly. 'And if half of it is true you have no right here in this house. Now I want to know. Is it true?'

'Is what true, Vader?' she said in Afrikaans.

'That you are responsible for breaking up a home! That you are the mistress of one of the high ranking police officers who lives in this city.'

She was too nervous to be angry.

'No,' she whispered. 'It isn't. Who told you?'

'No,' he said, 'it isn't! Who am I to believe then? I've got ears, I've heard from other voluntary organisations that work in conjunction with this hospital, you know, and some of the members are prominent and trustworthy members of the circles that you seem to have the audacity to move in. And I've heard you no longer attend the kerk. Don't think that working here is any substitute!'

As suddenly as she had been unnerved, her temper rose.

'Is that so, Father? Then you better restore that to its rightful place!' And she thrust the bedpan into his hands.

She wept in the taxi. Her hands shook, but in remorse now. After all, he had only been trying to save her soul, *her* soul. And thrusting the bedpan at him! She had not wished to leave the hospital in that way. She liked them all and she had felt deceitful going there this evening knowing it was to be her last time, but without even telling them so. But how much worse to leave in a rude temper. And in her regret she saw the streets of Salisbury anew, suddenly she loved them all, and she did not want to leave the town and her friends in it. She was still thinking in Afrikaans.

She reached her flat. Everything was packed, ready, her two suitcases in the middle of the floor. The windows, the sills, the occasional tables were stripped of all their things. The flat was bare, abandoned. And suddenly the flat which had meant little to her before and which she had considered a rather poky little place was a lovely flat, home, and the memories of all the happy things that had happened in it were crying out from the walls. She closed her eyes and sat down on the couch. This wasn't the way she wanted to start her life: sneaking off, pretending to everybody she was just going away for a month's holiday and then never coming back. Then when the divorce was all over and Jake joined her, how Salisbury would talk.

'I always said she was a tart—'

'Hasn't the guts to face the music—'

'And there was Jake Jefferson in the witness box, under oath, mind you, and denying adultery.'

Suzanna de Villiers shook her head and dried her eyes. What was she crying for? She was the happiest girl in the whole world. And Jake knew best. He was the boss. Why, they'd live happily ever after—

She got up off the couch, still sniffing, and scratched around in the big cardboard box. She found the half bottle of whisky she kept for Jake. She looked around for a glass, said 'oh damn' and scratched in the box again and produced a tea cup. She was thinking in English again now. She was fluent in English, she only thought in Afrikaans at the hospital these days, and when she wrote home to her father in Cape Town. Poor Pappa! He was very much Dopper Kerk. Godsdiens with the farm labourers every night, whether they liked it or not. He would have a fit when he knew, and Jake an Englishman at that! A *Rooinek!* Pappa was still fighting the Boer War. *Ag, liewe Pappa! Verskoon my, Pappa, ek het horn lief, I love him, Pappa—*

She half filled the tea cup with whisky, sniffed again, then went through to the naked kitchenette and squirted some water into it. She returned to the couch and sipped it. She pulled a face – how people could drink the stuff!

But it warmed her, warmed her belly. She sipped it doggedly, like medicine, and she began to feel better. Her sniffing stopped. It was cold in the flat and cheerless with the lampshade gone. Why, it would be lovely in Hong Kong! Warm and bright and sunny all year round and from their flat they'd have a lovely view of the great sparkling blue sea with ships and sampans and junks on it. The streets below would be bustling with colourful life and there'd be the tinkling singsong sound of the Orient that you always hear on the flicks. And at night, they'd look out from their lounge on to a great sweep of harbour lights and the bright neon lights that she'd seen in the magazines and on week-ends they'd go round the islands to those beautiful palmy beaches, Big Bay or Tiger Water Bay or something like that. And they'd lie in the sun and swim in the blue salt water and have their picnic lunches. And Jake said they'd buy a junk and fit a motor into it and they'd spend their week-ends on it cruising round the bays and Jake wold fish and get brown and fit again. And he'd get long leave every three years and they'd go to—

The door swung open and in walked Helen followed by Jake Jefferson. She was looking pink and excited and nervous. Jake was looking big and crumpled and worried.

'Hullo, Suzie.'

'Hullo, Jake.'

Helen stood with her hands clasped in front of her. 'Hullo, Miss de Villiers.'

'Suzanna!'

The girl looked embarrassed. 'Suzanna, sorry, I keep forgetting.'

'Why, you've been crying!'

Suzanna bit her lip and turned away and shook her head and dabbed her eyes. Then she blew her nose loudly on her hankie. 'It's nothing.' Then she tossed her head and turned around to them with a big sniff and a gay forced smile.

'All set!' she said too loudly.

Jake put his arm around her and he pulled Helen to them.

'You're a fine pair! Helen had a good cry too.' He grinned at his daughter and he pulled her head to him and planted a kiss on her forehead. 'And you too!' He kissed Suzanna's wet eyelids and squeezed them both. Suzanna smiled sheepishly at Helen and Helen smiled sheepishly back. 'Anyway it's good for you to have a good old cry. Takes the wrinkles out of your face! Why d'you think I've got such a beautiful skin!'

Suzanna said: 'Yes, Mister Max Factor,' and they all laughed, a little shrilly.

'Anyway,' Jake said with forced joviality, 'I don't know what you're crying about! When you're languishing on the white beaches of Hong Kong, think of me sweating it out here in dirty old Rhodesia!'

'Sit down,' Suzie said. She dabbed her eyes for the last time. She went to her handbag and took out her powder compact. 'God, I look horrible,' and she put the hankie and compact away without attempting any repairs. She looked at Jake.

'How much time?'

'No rush,' Jake said. 'We haven't got to be there till elevenish.'

She smiled brightly. 'Well, let's have a drink! Only whisky in tea cups, I'm afraid.' When she spoke English there was only the slightest trace of her Afrikaans accent, very soft and mellifluous.

'Suzie, you're a genius.'

'That's what they all say.'

Jake poured whisky into two tea cups. 'Nothing for you, I'm afraid, my girl,' he said to his daughter.

'That's all right, Miss de Villiers,' Helen smiled shyly, her hands folded on her knees.

'Suzanna!' Suzie said.

'My first drink today, I might tell you,' Jake Jefferson said. 'I've been rushing round like a blue-tailed fly.'

Suzanna took her tea cup of whisky from Jake. Helen said, 'Excuse me,' and tiptoed out of the room to the bathroom and closed the door. Suzie looked up at Jake.

'Jake, is everything okay?'

Jake nodded with a mouth full of whisky and sat down.

'Yes,' he said with forced carelessness, 'everything's okay. She's flown down to Jo'burg for the week-end, and she thinks I'm just driving Helen to Bulawayo to spend a couple of weeks with her schoolfriends. By the time it breaks you'll be safely installed at the Capitol Hotel, Kowloon, Hong Kong, you lucky devils.'

Suzanna nodded to the bathroom door. 'And she understands?'

Jake nodded. 'She worships you,' he said, 'and so do I.'

'I wish you were coming.'

'I will be soon. I've given my daughter as a hostage.'

'Jake – d'you think you're wise to come out to the airport? You're compromising yourself – heaven knows who'll be there.'

Jake shook his head impatiently, nervously. 'It'll be all right. I'm coming to see you off – you might run into immigration snags or anything. Especially taking my minor daughter out of the country. Besides I want to see you off.'

'You're the boss,' she said.

The bathroom door opened and Helen came out. He sat back in the armchair guiltily and smiled up at his daughter.

'Everything's fine,' he insisted irrelevantly. Helen sat down on the edge of the couch next to Suzie.

'You look pretty,' Suzanna said lamely.

Helen smiled and blushed and smoothed her skirt. 'Thank you, Miss—Suzanna,' she corrected herself. 'Dad let me wear lipstick tonight,' she added, equally lamely.

'I should hope so, you're almost sixteen.'

'I always let her wear lipstick when she goes out to a party,' Jake said defensively.

And so they talked for half an hour, generally, with frequent silences, trying to keep the girl in the conversation, avoiding the subject of separation. Jake filled the tea cups again with whisky, his hand shaking a little, his mind on the problems and he kept wanting to blurt out his uncertainties. Once his mind shrieked at him, 'You're crazy! Arnold said you were crazy!' and he wanted to start a discussion with Suzie justifying his action, but he took a slug of his whisky and quickly talked about something else. And he looked at his two women sitting on the couch and the whisky was beginning to go pleasantly to his head. And he was joyously glad about what he was doing and he wanted to go over to the couch and hug them and say: You're the only goddam things that matter in this world! It was a relief when Suzanna looked at her watch and said:

'Well, hadn't we better be going?'

Chapter Five

Salisbury's international airport was almost deserted this Saturday night. A few people to meet the few Bulawayo passengers, a dozen black porters in khaki uniform.

They entered the high concourse, and found the Immigration counter down the hall. Suzanna and Helen filled in forms.

They moved on to the weigh bay, checked the baggage through and got their boarding passes.

'Well,' Jake breathed. He looked at the concourse clock. 'Ten forty-five. It's felt as if it took hours.' He smiled weakly at Suzanna. 'Well,' he said, 'I know what we do next. Find a drink!'

The big bar was almost empty. They sat at a table. They looked through the glass doors out on to the runway. There was seldom a sound in the bar, except an occasional murmur from a customer across the room. They drank in silence, tense, heavy with departure, strained with guilt. 'Wish that damn plane would come,' Jake said. He imagined the immigration officers below putting their heads together, suddenly having second thoughts, making a phone call, setting the machinery in motion. 'Don't be a fool,' he told himself, 'what on earth can they do? Phone Sheila in Jo'burg? Hell, even I don't know where she is. I haven't committed any offence, I can send my daughter to Alaska on a sealing expedition if I want to—' At every moment he expected the immigration officer to enter the bar. Or the sheriff with a bloody interdict or whatever Arnold called it. Oh for Chrissake, Sheila's a thousand miles away. The time passed slowly. He looked at Suzanna, sitting rigid, her eyes pent. He leaned across and squeezed her hand and she gave him a tight smile and immediately tears began to bum. The bar began to fill up as passengers for the jet began to arrive.

'British Overseas Airways Corporation announce the arrival of their flight B.A. 248 from Johannesburg,' said the soft-hard female voice of the loudspeaker.

Suzanna stiffened. 'Well, here it is,' she said in a tiny voice.

Quarter past eleven.

'It's got to refuel and so forth yet,' he said.

'Dad, I'm going on to the verandah to see it come in.'

'All right, Helen.' He turned back to Suzie and took her hand again. 'Relax. This is the beginning of a new life together.'

'Jake, it's so sad,' tears back in her eyes, 'and I feel such a cheat.'

'Well look,' he wanted to pour forth self-justification again, as much to console himself as convince Suzanna. He checked himself: 'Suzie, you're not cheating anyone, you're simply doing what I've considered best. If there's been any cheating, I'm the one who's been cheated for years. Now relax, look on the happy side.'

She closed her eyes and nodded and sniffed.

'I could do some relaxing myself,' he breathed. 'Let's have another drink.'

The bar was full now. There was a long low gathering whine and the big jet came screaming in. It ran the whole runway, then laboriously turned and came crawling back over the tarmac with a high-pitched scream. It crawled up in front of the building and then the screaming suddenly descended through a dying whine into ringing silence. The people on the verandah began to mill and then wave. Jake came back with the drinks.

'Our last together for three months,' he said trying to sound cheerful. 'The next time it will be champagne in the smartest damn hotel in Hong Kong!'

'It won't,' Suzie smiled tearfully, 'the next'll be in the taxi cab from Hong Kong airport. I'm bringing a big bottle in an ice-bucket to meet you!'

They laughed.

'On the way to the Magistrate's Court to get married,' Jake amended, 'straight from the airport to the Courthouse—'

'This is the first call for British Overseas Airways Corporation's flight BA 248 …'

Suzanna looked at Jake. 'Hadn't we better go to the Departure Lounge?'

'Relax and finish your drink. There'll be two more calls yet.'

Helen came threading her way back from the verandah. 'Daddy—'

'Yes, I heard it, my love.' He put his arm around his daughter's shoulders.

'Now you two look after yourselves.'

'You too, Jake. You look like death warmed up—'

'I'm fine. And if there's anything you need just cable. And for godsake don't skimp on food, we're not that hard-up.'

She nodded.

'Helen, take those tablets I gave you – Suzie, see she takes her tablets. I want you both blooming when I get there—'

'Yes, Daddy.'

'This is the second call for British Overseas Airways Corporation's flight BA—'

'Well, we'd better go.'

People were moving out of the lounge, down the passage and then down the stairs to the Departure Lounge. It was a relief to move, to merge with the others. He had forgotten his worries in the last minute advice, now he was worrying again, looking around for stationary people who were looking around. There were none. They moved down the stairs in single file and in the concourse he saw a young policeman, and his pulse tripped. God, he thought, I would make a hopeless criminal. They moved through the concourse, it was full of people. The clock showed a quarter to midnight. Suzie squeezed his arm. The crocodile of people were making for the Lounge, bottlenecking now at the glass doorway, kissing and taking farewells, then thinning out as the passengers went through the door. There was a ground hostess at the doorway, nodding and smiling and checking on a list. Jake pulled Suzanna and Helen to one side, against the wall.

'I can't go in, it's passengers only.'

They looked up at him.

'Well, this is it. Good-bye, my two loves. No, it's only au revoir—'

There were people milling round the glass doorway, standing back, waving and signalling through the glass doors. Jake Jefferson's eyes were burning. Suzanna's eyes were bright with tears but her chin and her smile were firm.

'Jake, when you're miserable, just think of those week-ends on our junk and that big fish striking and that salt air in your handsome old face—'

'*Old!*' It was a relief to find something to pick on. They laughed brittlely.

'And you two girls lounging on the deck in your bikinis feeding me beer!'

They laughed again. The tears were hot behind their eyes.

'This is the third and final call for passengers on British Overseas Airways—' the loudspeaker said emotionlessly.

'Dad, I think we're the last ones!'

There were no more people going through the doorway. The crowd around the glass doors was stationary, in a horse shoe, waving and smiling and signalling and chattering. The ground hostess was looking at them, cool, benign, businesslike.

'All right.'

'Good-bye—'

Suzanna stood on tiptoe and kissed him quickly on his mouth. 'Keep a stout heart, Jake.'

'Suzanna.'

She was gone through the doorway with tears welling, pretending to be engrossed in a broken fingernail. There was a man standing inside the doorway, waiting to pass through; she bumped into him. 'Sorry.' She skipped around once to wave again, then she disappeared round the corner of the Lounge. Jake watched her go. Then he turned to his daughter. The girl had tears in her eyes unashamedly.

'Good-bye, Daddy.'

He took her in his arms. 'Now, what's all this nonsense?' he said. 'We're going to be grand, all of us, and just you look after Miss de Villiers.'

'Excuse me, sir.'

43

It was the fat man trying to get through the doorway.

'Sorry.' Jake moved Helen aside: 'We're going to be the best three people in the world.'

'Excuse me, sir!'

It was the fat man again, out of the doorway now. Jake glanced at him irritably.

'Excuse me, sir – are you Jackson Jefferson of …'

There was a ringing in his ears, a ringing that started up from his stomach and flooded his chest, his arms and shoulders and his head, then a dropping sensation. He looked down at the short fat man.

'Yes,' he said. 'Yes, I am.'

The fat man looked relieved and hastily unfolded a paper in his hand.

'I'm a deputy Sheriff of the High Court,' he said fatly, apologetically, 'and I hereby now serve upon you an order of the High Court duly signed by the Registrar of the High Court. This here is called an Interdict and it says: "It is ordered: that Jackson Brian Jefferson be and is hereby interdicted from removing from the jurisdiction of this Honourable Court the person of Helen Stephanie—"'

The concourse was blurred, the faces of the crowd round the doorway a mass of jeering pink, the fat apologetic voice of the sheriff reading the Order. Jake Jefferson moved forward, the weight of Helen on his arm, he took the sheriff by the elbow and pulled them off behind a pillar.

'Now do you understand that?' the sheriff was saying kindly. 'If you don't I'll go over it all again.'

Blindly Jake took the paper. He focused on the official document, stumbled through it and read the date. It was dated today! Why, the bitch had known all along, the bitch, the filthy cruel bloody bitch. Of course, the bloody bitch had smelt a rat and checked.

The Sheriff looked very sorry. 'Now sir …'

An arm pushed the Sheriff aside. 'Jake!' Suzanna said. 'What is it, what is it—?'

'Sheila—'

Suzanna turned on the sheriff like a shrew. He stepped back from her.

'Get away, you!' she hissed. 'Leave him alone!'

The loudspeaker said: 'British Overseas Airways Corporation announce the departure of their flight …'

Jake straightened up. 'Get aboard, Suzie—'

'Will I, hell!'

Chapter Six

Every day Jake Jefferson used to fetch Suzanna de Villiers at her flat in time to drive her to work, and almost every evening he used to fetch her from work, parking outside the tall building in Main Street and waiting for her, giving a short toot on his hooter when she emerged to attract her attention. She used to come smiling over to his car and hop into the front seat and they would drive happily back to her flat for tea and maybe for a drink and supper. Sometimes they went straight for a drink in a bar when he picked her up from work, to the roof garden where they sat high in the open and watched the homeward bound traffic and watched the sunset while they drank cold beer; sometimes to the cool air-conditioned Long Bar which pretended to be nothing but a pleasant bar, sometimes to the Can Can Room, which was all colours and pretended to be in Paris with murals of girls kicking their legs all over the place; and sometimes he took her to the Club where they played golf or tennis before having their sundowner. If Jake Jefferson could not fetch Suzanna at her doctor's rooms he used to telephone her. On Sundays he fetched her from her flat too, particularly on Sundays, and sometimes with Helen, they used to go for picnics into the bush, to Lake McIlwaine and cook sausages and chips and potatoes in their jackets in the live coals and drink beer and he used to fish, and sometimes they spent the day on the farms of his friends around Salisbury. There had to be a riot to keep Jake Jefferson away on a Sunday.

But on her third day back at her employer's consulting rooms Suzanna de Villiers emerged from the tall building on Main Street at five o'clock and she looked up and down the parking bays and she waited again for the toot but none came. She waited for a while, looking at books in a shop window, and then set off back to the private hotel where she had a room. And she asked at the gloomy reception desk if there were any messages for her, and there were none, and she went upstairs and let herself into her small room. She was too late for the hotel tea, so she took her small kettle out from her suitcase on top of the wardrobe and filled it in the handbasin and plugged it in and she sat down on her bed and lit a cigarette and tried to read a magazine story and she waited for the sound of his footsteps or the knock of the hotel boy on her door telling her there was a boss on the phone for her. She drank her coffee and smoked her cigarettes and looked at the same magazine page for two hours and chewed her fingers and her knuckles, but there came neither the footsteps nor the hotel boy. And at seven o'clock she went downstairs and tried to pick through a mean boarding-house meal at a table by herself in the centre of the dining-room, and afterwards she went upstairs and made more coffee and turned the radio on loud to fill the poky room and she smoked cigarettes and waited, but nobody came. Nobody came the next night, nor the next, nor the next, nor the next and Suzanna de Villiers seemed to grow old and thin and shaky.

On the thirtieth day Suzanna de Villiers succumbed to a nervous breakdown and the doctor who employed her put her on a train to the faraway seaside to recuperate. Then she went to live in Bulawayo, in the flat hot dry cattle country of Matabeleland, where she was a stranger to everyone.

Chapter Seven

Spring is a hot ripe virgin moaning out loud, summer is a whore.

In spring you cannot bear to wait for it. In spring you lie awake wishing it, the plunge that will blast the heat from your body in her wet loins, the wet pounding that will make your frustrations burst out free. She will wash it all away when at last she comes to you, and renders you soft again, and calm and content.

Then at last she does come to you in all her tempestuous beauty. She throws herself wildly down upon you, she pounds you with all her fulsome wetness, you open your arms and your mouth and your whole body to her, and she makes you burst.

But when you wake up, she is still there with you. You grow accustomed to her, you no longer need her, and then you begin to dislike her, then to hate her.

It rained for ten days, without ceasing, warm and fat and straight down.

Joseph Mahoney sat on the verandah of the Residency every afternoon and drank beer and watched the curtains of water.

'I'm bushwhacked,' he said aloud – 'bushwhacked.'

The telephone lines were washed down on the Nyamanpofu Road, and atmospherics drowned any ordinary radio. The only communication with the outside world was the two-way radio in the sergeant's police station. If there were any messages for the Assistant Native Commissioner, the sergeant relayed them to him in the morning at the office. Otherwise the Assistant Native Commissioner and the sergeant seldom spoke to each other.

Mahoney sat on his verandah and looked at the garden.

'Looks like a paddy-field,' he said aloud.

He tossed his empty beer can as far as he could into the garden and he picked up his .22 rifle. He sat in his deckchair and sniped at the can. Every evening he sat in the deckchair drinking beer and sniping at the empty cans. He became very accurate. He put his bare feet on the low verandah wall and cradled the barrel of the rifle between his big and second toes, and he could hit the can every time.

After a week he was hitting the can every time holding the rifle like a pistol with only one hand. Then he had Samson drag his dressing-table which had a mirror on to the verandah. He sat in the deckchair facing the dressing-table. He pointed the rifle backwards over his shoulder and sighted down the barrel through the mirror. After a while he could hit the can every time that way too.

He wondered what else he could do with the rifle. 'Short of taking a pot-shot at Sheerluck for kicks or blowing my brains out.'

Down in the valley it was very bad.

The rain fell in a blue-grey curtain and turned the hot dry jungle into a bog. The water ran down the sides of the escarpment in tumbling rivers into the huge trough of the valley and the great river swelled and surged and roared and climbed up its banks. And from the hydrological stations up north in Angola and the far northern parts of Northern Rhodesia there came reports to the engineers building the wall at the faraway gorge called Kariba that more rain was falling there than ever before, that the water was tumbling into the Zambezi's tributaries, that the tributaries roared and were swollen as never before, and that soon a great wall of water would hit the valley and swamp it and tear away the beginning of the dam wall.

At Kariba hundreds of Italians and black men worked in a frenzy in the steep gorge to reinforce and heighten the coffer dam in which the foundations of the wall were being laid. Night and day the trucks slithered and ground through the rain down the sides of the gorge, night and day the drills hammered at the rock and at the concrete, through the night and the day the shifts worked pouring concrete into the gorge. The great Zambezi leapt and tore through the gorge in black and brown fury. It mounted higher and higher up its steep rock sides, higher and higher up and round the walls of the puny coffer dam. Each day a new high water mark went under. But the flood waters from the north had not yet arrived. And even the Italian engineers began to believe in Nyamayimini, the furious river god.

Down in the valley only Chipepo's people refused to move. They refused to believe in the floods, either the temporary one they were told was coming because of the faraway rains, or the great flood that would come next year when the white man's wall was finished.

It took the old man a long time to walk through the Zambezi Valley, because his bones and sinews were no longer as strong as a lion, as they had once Leen, and his cardboard suitcase was heavy for him, and the ground was very wet. It rained all the time – Ah! Never had he seen such rain! It was very troublesome for a man to make a long journey in such rain. But it was good, the Sikatongas had done their work very well and next year the crops would be very big and green and his cattle and his goats would be very fat and his wives and his children and all the people would be fat and happy.

His old black wet brow scowled as he thought about the people and his gardens and his cattle and his goats.

Ah! but what were these bad things the white men were telling him? Even the Mambo Joseph-i was telling him these bad things and the Mambo had never told him a bad thing before, he had never even been cross with him except maybe sometimes when the Mambo's head was sore from the beer and he wanted a wife. Ah! the Mambo drank plenty beer sometimes. And then he would sit on the verandah of his house and look straight ahead for a long time and sometimes he would sit at the table and write many words on paper while he drank too much beer. And then in the morning he would screw up the paper and throw it away. Ah! he was a strange one, the Mambo Joseph-i.

But the Mambo had never told him a bad thing before. Maybe if the Mambo says the flood is coming it is a true thing.

Then the old man shook his head as he walked through the wet jungle.

Ah! that was foolishness to think like that! How can any man stop the river? Not even the white men who are very rich and clever can stop Nyamayimini. Nyamayimini was very fierce and strong. Nyamayimini was there, real, like the valley itself, like the sun itself, like the night, the thunder and the rain. No man can stop the sun from rising, nor the night from coming, nor the thunder, and likewise no man can stop Nyamayimini. And the valley, the valley was real and it had always been here. The valley was like Nyamayimini.

The old man scowled angrily. No, it cannot be a true thing. The wise men from the city said it was a trick. The Mambo Joseph-i had never told him a bad thing, but the Mambo was young, maybe he also had been tricked. Only the young and the foolish would believe a story like that.

The old man lifted up his spears and shook them. The white men were strong but the Batonka people were many and they still had their spears.

For ten days the old man walked through the valley. Some nights he slept in the villages he came upon and the people gave him food and beer and fire and they talked of the story of the flood. But sometimes when darkness fell through the rain there was no village and the old man could not make a fire to warm his wet body, for all the forest was wet. Then the old man slept in a tree so that if a lion or an elephant came it would not catch him very easily. And as he drew nearer his part of the valley he came upon villages but they stood deserted in the rain, for the people had harkened to the Government's story of the flood. When he came upon such villages it made him very angry, and he did not take shelter in any of the deserted huts because the deserted ancestral spirits would still be there and they would be angry and maybe they would trouble him.

On the tenth day the old man came upon the south-em bank of the river opposite Chipepo's chiefdom. The water was higher than he had ever seen it, nearly to the top of the banks. Across the swollen rushing river he could see his village, called Chisamu, and he could see the smoke of the cooking fires coming from the huts. He could just make out his own huts on top of a small, hill, the highest and best huts in the village, and he saw firesmoke coming from his huts and his heart was very glad.

But the village on the south bank was empty, the huts stood wet and rotting in the mud and the rain beat in the doorways. And the old man knelt down and wept for his own neighbours, his friends and his own kith and kin of this side of the river, his own people who had deserted. He prayed to the ancestral spirits not to be too angry with them, to forgive them. And he prayed that the Government had not taken them too far away, so that they would be able to return when they discovered the trick.

Then the old man went to the banks of the river and he called across the hundred yards of swollen water until a man heard him and fetched him in a dugout canoe.

That night the old man sat around the fire in the kitchen hut of his senior wife and his three wives and all his children, and they drank home-brewed beer and feasted, and many of the tribesmen came to greet him and welcome him home. They talked of the story of the flood.

'Our District Commissioner has told us that before the big flood there will come a smaller flood,' said the senior wife, 'caused by the great rains. And he has been urging us to move now to the new land he is providing us beyond the mountains.'

'Pah!' said the old man. 'The story of the little flood is also part of the trick of the big flood.'

'But the river is very full, my husband,' said the third wife, 'and still the sky opens.'

'Pah!' said the old man. 'It is true the river is very angry. But it is angry at the white man for his trick he tries to play upon us. The river will defeat the white men now, and there will be no big flood.'

'But maybe the river will flow over the banks, my husband.'

The old man grew angry. 'The river has flowed over the banks before, old woman,' he growled, 'and we have never been killed. When the river has broken its banks before we have run to higher ground for a little time, and then it has gone away and we have returned. If the river breaks its banks again, then we will move to higher ground until it is gone again. Not before.'

'It is true,' the second and junior wives said, 'it is true.'

Later that night the old man went to his ancestral graves and knelt before them. He greeted all his ancestors whom he could remember.

'I swear I will never leave you, my ancestors,' he said aloud, 'for that is a shameful and a foolish thing.'

And, like the wise men from the north, the ancestral spirits told him that the flood would not come.

In the valley the Zambezi river had high banks of white sand. At Chisamu, in Chipepo's chiefdom, the village and the gardens were below the banks and the high water mark of the river. In the rainy season the river rose to the top of the banks but it seldom flowed over into the land below. It had happened only a few times in the memory of Sixpence, and it had overflowed only a little.

The flood from the north came to the valley with a murmur and then a rumble that could be heard from far away. The people in Chisamu village paused and listened to the noise and wondered. The river was already at the top of the banks and already the gardens below were like paddy-fields from the rains.

It came, came in a low wave down the valley, thickly, quickly, a layer of water running over the swollen river. The wave had an angry froth to its nose and it carried great trees and branches and dead animals. It slid over the banks like pus sliding over an eyelid, then it tumbled and cascaded over and threw itself and its debris into the gardens of Chisamu. Then the wall of water built up to a torrent, thicker and thicker and higher and more angry. It roared down the valley like a great flat fat snake, hissing, carrying all before it. It filled the air with the noise of its rush, it drowned the river banks and they were gone, it ran over the fields below faster than a man can run. And it swilled up the footpaths and tracks of the village and ran in the doorways and doused the fires in the kitchens with a swallowing hiss, it tumbled into the goat and cattle pens and rose up around the animals' bewildered milling legs, to their bellies and upwards. It ate up the grain bins and carried pots and knobsticks and firewood and chickens with it.

The air was full of the shouts of men and the running, of feet and the clatter of the scramble for possessions. The air was full of the bellows of fathers and the shrieks of mothers and the screams of children and the bellows of cattle and the squeals of goats and pigs, and it was full of the screams of insects that had never before seen the light of day as they scrambled over each other for safety, and it was full of the excited cries of the birds that clouded the air and fed upon them as they had never fed before.

And still the brown water kept coming. The river was gone. It was a wicked frothing lake such as the people had never seen.

Many of the people kept running for many miles until they reached the sloping ground, until they had outstripped the running water. They looked back and saw the water rising up the walls of their huts, over the brushwood fences of their goat and cattle pens; they saw men and animals swimming.

But many of the people, many women and children ran for the small hills and kopjes on which the higher huts stood and many climbed the trees and they clambered to the roofs of their huts.

Many people ran to the hill upon which the huts of Sixpence stood.

Sixpence stood in the rain outside his huts on the peak of the kopje and he watched the water. He had run down the hill when the pandemonium first started and he had rounded up his six goats and his four cattle and chased them back up the hill to his huts. They, and his three wives and his nine daughters who were worth six head of cattle apiece in bridal prices, they were his life's work. The cattle and the goats saw and smelt and felt the water and they had stampeded to the high familiar safety of Sixpence's kraal. One nanny goat had fallen down an antbear hole in the excitement and snapped her front leg. Sixpence had gathered her up in his old arms and carried her up the hill.

Many people had run up the hill with them, husbands without their wives, women without their children, children without their parents, the men and women shouting, and the children shouting and scampering in glee and screaming in horror.

Now they stood five deep outside Sixpence's huts, the men and the women and the children and the animals and their young, and the air was full of their weeping and their lamentations and their bleating and their milling.

Sixpence watched the water rise. He was astonished. Never, never had he seen such water, never. The Mambo Joseph-i had once told him about the faraway sea which he said was very big and dangerous, but the sea could never be bigger nor more dangerous than this water. Nothing more terrible had ever happened in the world. He could see the water rise before his eyes, inch by inch. There was a watermark, the stick on Chipunza's cattle pen. Look away at the water, and when you look back the stick is shorter. The water is under Chipunza's good cow. It is at her udder. You look away at Marombi's huts, then you look back and already her teats are under the brown water. This was terrible water.

The people were lamenting behind him.

'It is true, the flood has come, what the white men told us is true—'

'Silence! You foolish people!' he roared. 'Can you not see that the river is angry with the tricks of the white men. This is but an omen – silence, I told you!'

But the silence did not come. Even the womenfolk could see that the long low hill had become an island. And if what the white men had said was true—?

The shriek of a goat pierced the wet noise. They all searched the muddy running water. Then they saw them nosing their way, big and brown and sinuous and treacherous and greedy through the rising scum, the crocodiles.

It started raining harder.

High up on the escarpment Joseph Mahoney sat on the verandah of the Residency. The rain had let up to a heavy drizzle. Through his garden he could see the corner of the verandah of the sergeant's house, seventy-five yards away. He could see the sergeant sitting on the verandah with his feet up, drinking a can of beer. The sergeant lifted the can to his mouth and took a long slug out of it, then he rested the can upon the wall of his verandah. It stood in a row with several other cans.

Seventy-five yards away Mahoney lifted his can of beer to his mouth and put it down on his verandah wall.

It stood with several other cans. Mahoney watched the sergeant for a long time and he looked at the row of cans on the sergeant's wall for a long time.

After a long time Mahoney picked up his .22 rifle. He raised it slowly to his shoulder and drew a long careful bead on the full can of beer resting on the sergeant's verandah wall. He held the bead for a long time, too long. The sergeant's hand came down and picked up the can. Mahoney lowered his rifle.

The sergeant's arm came out again and replaced the can on the wall again. Mahoney raised his rifle again and he drew his bead and he squeezed the trigger.

The sergeant jumped. His can of beer was gone. He stared down at the wall. Then he turned and stared in disbelief at Mahoney's house. He could see Mahoney crouching behind his wall. Then three more shots rang out, crack – crack – crack, and the sergeant's three empty cans were gone too.

And from Mahoney's house came his howl of laughter. It was the first time he had laughed in ten days.

Sergeant Sheerluck Holmes stood there, his mouth open, staring in disbelief and indignation. Then an angry smile broke across his face. He turned and ran into the house for his own .22 rifle.

The shooting match lasted for two hours, with ceasefires only to allow Samson and the sergeant's batman to bring on more beer.

It ended when the Provincial Native Commissioner's message from Bulawayo came crackling over the police two-way radio. It ordered the Assistant Native Commissioner at Nyamanpofu to get down into the valley with his boat and try to lend a hand to the Northern Rhodesia authorities at Chipepo.

Chapter Eight

It took them twenty-nine hours to get down the escarpment in the police Land Rover. There were chains on the wheels and they slid and they churned and they slipped down the escarpment and they stuck seventeen times in the mud and Mahoney and the four black men climbed out up to their calves in mud and crouched down behind the back bumper and shoved and heaved and dug and swore and laid branches under the spinning wheels and the rain beat down on their backs and their hair hung in their eyes and the windscreen wipers went slosh-slosh, slosh-slosh, and the water poured in and their breath steamed up the glass and they were very wet and very tired and they smelt dank and steamy. And when they got to the bottom the mud was deeper, for the water was running off down the sides of the escarpment, and they dared take the Land Rover no further and they climbed out and they dragged and carried the boat the last five miles through the mud and the rain, and they had to leave a constable in the Land Rover to blow the horn every quarter hour, so that the policemen would find their way back to it because they could not see more than fifty yards in the rain. And when they found the water they saw that the river had gone and there was only a new brown swirling rising lake eating up the trees. They fitted the outboard to the boat and Mahoney and Samson climbed in and they shoved off for the north and they disappeared through the curtain of water amongst the treetops, and the noise of their outboard motor was swamped with the noise of the rain.

'Bail,' Mahoney said.

The river had gone, but out in the middle where the river had been the current tore at the boat and the water twisted and spun. They charged the current and were swept down with it, but they swung out beyond it and then they were back amongst the bending straining treetops again, and here and there they ploughed through the roof-tops of villages, the water tearing through the conical thatch and washing by were dead dogs and chickens and goats and cattle.

It took three hours to find the new north bank, and then they turned with the current and churned east down through the trees towards Chipepo. There was a crack of thunder and the sky opened wider and down it came, harder than ever before.

Samson's brown arm pointed. 'Nkosi!'

Then Mahoney saw him, too, through the rain, dead ahead, a single wet white man clinging in a tree. His hair hung over his face and he was very white but he was grinning.

Mahoney waved.

'Okay!'

Mahoney cut the throttle down. The tree was twenty yards ahead. The water tore around the trunk in two deep channels. The current carried the boat. He cut the throttle right down, it made no difference. The tree loomed up, the boat skewered in the water, the water rushed on. Mahoney cursed and ducked. He opened the throttle to capacity and swung the handle aside. The boat roared and surged to the side. They swept under the tree, the branches tearing at their heads and at the boat and the boat rocked and skewered. Then they were out the other side, sweeping downstream with the current, their faces gashed from the branches. The tree and the man were far behind.

Mahoney cursed again.

'All the river to choose from …'

He swung the boat into an arc and got clear of the channel. The boat had taken in water and he told Samson to start bailing. He headed the boat back up-river. He opened the throttle right up but it was slow going. The water curved up the prow. He ordered Samson down aft but it made little difference. The old outboard just did not have enough guts for this kind of work. He pushed the boat far up-river of the tree and the man came back into view. Then he turned the boat and cut across at an angle with the current. It was no good. As soon as the boat hit the current it got caught up in it and was carried past the tree. They tried again. They went into the arc and came back down on the tree. Samson knelt in the prow to try to catch a branch. The man shouted and waved his free hand and shook his head vigorously. The current tore at the boat. Mahoney turned it full throttle towards the tree. Samson leant out and grabbed at a branch. He caught and the boat rocked and swung in the current. He grabbed for a bigger branch and caught it, the boat rocked, its gunnel dipped under and the water poured on. Samson staggered and let go. The boat was swept on, stem first.

'Bail,' Mahoney said.

He turned her round, and out of the current. He took her back up-river. As he turned the boat downstream again the man started shouting and waving again. Mahoney made for a clump of trees and told Samson to catch one. He cut the engine.

'What?' he shouted.

The man shouted again and pointed into the branches.

'Oh,' Mahoney muttered. 'Charming.'

'What's he say, Nkosi?'

'He says there's a snake in the tree with him,' he said. 'In the branches you caught last time.'

Mahoney had an idea. He wondered why he had not thought of it before. Though he wouldn't fancy it himself. He signalled to the man. He made diving and swimming motions.

'Jump in!' he shouted through the rain. 'We'll pick you up downstream.'

The man shook his head and waved his arm and shrugged.

'Nkosi?'

'We've really found a winner,' Mahoney muttered. 'He says he can't swim.'

He considered what to do. He took over the branch Samson was holding. 'Keep bailing,' he said. He took a slug out of the brandy bottle. Then he held it up for the man to see.

'Your health,' he shouted and the man grinned.

'Must be a Cockney,' Mahoney said. 'Well, I suppose the only thing is to try again and try to shoot the snake if it wants a lift too.' He took the safety catch off his .22 and kicked the motor into life while Samson held on to the branch.

'Let go,' he said and turned the boat round. The man was watching intently and Mahoney waved again. He tried to hold the boat against the current. The man started shouting and waving again. Mahoney turned the throttle on high and tried to beat the current. The current caught the boat and they were heading straight for the branches at full throttle in full current. The branches loomed up, low and rough and treacherous. The man jumped. Shoulder first he hit the water and he was gone.

Mahoney swung the tiller hard, the boat swept round the tree. He kept swinging hard till it was out of the channel. They swept in an arc and watched the channel for the man.

'Jesus!' Mahoney said. 'That's a gentleman.'

'Ah! Sterek!'

There was no sign of him. Only the swirling fluted corrugated surface of the channel water. Five, ten, fifteen seconds. They began the circle the second time, the engine roaring, the water tearing, the rain beating. Their heads turned against the sweep of the boat, anxiously scanning the water. Twenty-five, thirty seconds. No sign.

'He's a goner.'

Forty-five seconds and Samson shouted.

A hundred yards down from the tree a pair of arms emerged, then a wet head. The arms were beating the water like a child and the face was turned desperately upwards bursting and gasping for air. On he was swept in the current.

Mahoney opened the throttle and screamed after him. Samson pulled him over the gunnel. He slapped the man between the shoulder blades as he coughed and spluttered. Mahoney had the boat out of the channel.

The man finished coughing and looked up, very wet. Mahoney passed him the brandy bottle.

'Dr. Livingstone, I presume?'

The man took a long pull from the bottle then belched.

'No, he smiled wetly. 'Jefferson. Jake Jefferson.'

'Jake Jefferson ...'

The man was coughing.

'Welcome aboard. What were you doing in the Zambezi Valley?'

'Oh,' said the policeman, 'just hanging around.'

It was late in the afternoon before they saw another boat. It was the Northern Rhodesia District Officer's, and he was very glad to see them. He'd been having one hell of a time.

Chapter Nine

Brown water pulling, thatch roof-tops straining, poking through like upturned sieves, water smacking in door frames like it does against jetties, mud walls crumbling, firewood floating, carcasses drifting, cowdung bobbing. Silence, the silence of rain falling and the brown muck rising, rising, ssh-ssh, smack slop plop. A suitcase, an old cardboard suitcase, the hiding place of a lifetime's possessions, an old suitcase sodden, disintegrating, half-drowned, floating by. What treasures it once stored, what frightening journeys it had seen to the white men's cities. All gone, abandoned, floating for a while downstream. Chickens floating by, chickens everywhere, feathers sodden and their heads lolling downwards, water in their wings. Poor birds who had scattered and squawked up on to familiar perches, fled into familiar huts and tried for the rafters. Dogs, quite a few skinny dogs and puppies who had swum around bewilderedly and tried to make it back against the water to familiar ground. And cattle and goats, sodden and drowned. All drowned in Nyamayimini. And still the rain fell and the water climbed. Leisurely, but confidently and maliciously.

Mahoney leaned over the side of the boat and grabbed a dead chicken and threw it into the boat. It fell with a plop among a heap of dead chickens. Then he steered the boat among the trees for the water-logged shoreline. Samson jumped out and held the boat while the old woman and children climbed out. They were wet and cold and shivering and they had lost all their property. He had plucked them from trees and roof-tops and islands.

'These too.' He picked up a chicken by the leg and flung it on to the bank. It plopped on to the shore dead and wet. 'Eat them. It will be a long time before the Government can get food to you.'

The old woman bent and picked up the chicken.

'Bwana, how will we make the fire to cook them?'

'I don't know,' Mahoney snapped. He threw out more chickens. 'The Government is very clever but it cannot make wet wood to be dry nor foolish people to be wise. You should have harkened when you were warned of the flood.'

He was wet and cold and tired and angry. He had not slept for thirty-six hours. Nor had he eaten all day. He looked at the old woman and the children shivering on the bank and appealing to him for dry wood. He felt anger, not pity.

'Where are your menfolk?' he shouted. 'Why is it that you are alone in danger?'

They stared at him dumbly. The children moved to the old lady and one put out a hand and held her rags.

'Old gentlewoman, where are your menfolk?' he shouted.

The old lady hung her head. 'I do not know,' she said. 'They ran with the women and children and they told me to run also. But I was caring for the goats and the cattle and I stayed to try to let them out of their kraals. But the water came too quickly for me.'

She bent her old body and picked up a dead hen. The neck hung down limp and she lifted up the head and examined it.

'This is the hen of my son,' she said quietly, 'and it was a fine hen. It made many chickens and it looked after them well. Even now she was sitting on ten eggs by Gwatadza's big rooster.'

She dropped the chicken. It fell in a sodden heap and rolled over, its neck twisted back. She stood bent and wet and shivering in the rain. The water ran off her old black head and down her creased toothless face.

Her thin legs stood precariously on the slippery bank, trembling, and she clutched her wet rags around her. Mahoney was sorry he had spoken harshly.

'Stay well, grandmother,' he said. 'Take the children over this hill. Some distance to the west you will find other people and soon the lorries of the Government will come there. They will help you and give you medicine. Take also the chickens.'

The old woman raised her hand. 'Stay well, younger father,' she said.

Samson shoved off. When they were fifty yards out Mahoney looked back. The old woman was slowly climbing the rocky slopes with the children straggled about her.

It was much later when the boat came to Sixpence's kraal upon the hill. And still it was raining.

The rain fell in curtains, straight down. All the firewood was gone, the ground outside the hut was mud that sucked at the feet, water and the urine and the faeces of the animals. The people huddled in the sleeping hut of Sixpence at the very top of the hill, and in the sleeping hut of the senior wife a little lower down the slope. Already the water had crept into the doorways of all the kitchen huts of all three wives and the pots and utensils had been moved to the top of the hill. They lay in the open in a heap and the rain ran down the thatch of the huts and fell in a screen to the ground. The goats stood around the walls of the huts under the eaves bleating, and shivering and the last season's kids ducked their heads under the bellies of their mothers. The nanny goat with her broken leg lay down under the eaves. The three head of cattle stood still in the rain with their heads hanging down to keep the rain out of their eyes, and sometimes they stamped their feet and lifted their heads and sniffed the air and lowed. The people were subdued in the two remaining huts, huddled damp and steamy together. The men shook their heads in worry and wonder and told of what they had seen. The children were quiet in wide-eyed agitation at their elders' conversation. A baby cried at its wet discomfort and its mother gave it her long breast to suck. They watched the rain and the water through the doorway.

'Look!' a man's arm pointing out the door.

The people craned their necks forward and looked. Another crocodile squirming brown across the brown water. It nosed its way slowly through the floating flotsam, just its nostrils and forehead and yellow reptile eyes poking above the water, the ridge of its spiny back and the powerful swish of its tail.

'Ayeeeh!' a woman cried softly. 'Today we are dying in this place.'

Sixpence stood alone in the thick rain between the huts. He bent and picked up a stone and threw it at the crocodile.

'Go away, vile one!'

The crocodile lashed around startled, then it turned away and paddled round the island. The old man threw another stone. It landed near the beast but it did not hurry. It knew that it alone was not in trouble. It disappeared from Sixpence's view round the half-drowned kitchen hut of the third wife. It nosed its way through the doorway and looked around, then it turned and swam out again.

Sixpence scowled into the rain. His old shirt and trousers were sodden and he was hungry, but he thought of none of these things. He could see the water rising, swirling inch by inch up his hill. He saw his huts go, one by one, the huts of his junior wife, he could measure the rise of the water against familiar marks on the walls. There was the water lapping around the grinding stone outside the kitchen of his third wife. Together he and his new young wife had gone down to the river and selected the stone and they had carried it between them up the hill to her huts. It was a good stone, an ideal stone with already a natural depression in it for grinding the corn for porridge with a smaller stone. Everybody had admired the stone, and now there was the river rising up over it again. And now it was right over the stone and it was running into her cooking hut. He could note these things. But his mind did not really dwell on that. His mind dwelt on wonder, angry astonishment. The water was rising, surely, but it was unthinkable that it would not stop in time. This hill was his home and here his ancestral spirits lived with him.

All day Sixpence stood alone in the rain and watched the water rising all the time. Then it crept up to the yard outside the doorway of the sleeping hut of his senior wife. The people in the hut watched it with ahs and mutters and then they crept out of the hut back into the rain. And they stood under the eaves of Sixpence's hut with the goats and some of them just stood with him in the rain. They saw the crocodile again and the men threw stones at it but it did not go far away. It coursed around in the muddy rising water, out of range.

Still it rained and the water rose up. There came two more crocodiles and the men threw more stones and the women began to lament and the children cry. But they did not go far away, and the water came in the doorway of the sleeping hut of the senior wife and it covered its hard cowdung floor, and it ran round the sides of the hut and up the slope. The cattle sniffed the wet air and took some steps backwards, facing the water and they stretched out their necks and mooed. Then night fell, inky black and thick and wet, and the sounds settled down to the lap of the water and the intermittent cries of the children, and the mutter of the men in the black rain. But later there came another dreadful sound.

'What is that?'

'Ah! What is that?'

It came again, a stifled snorting, cut off in a splash and gurgle, then a great thrashing splashing in the blackness. Then another splash and the terrified bellow of the cow. Then splashing again and the bellow was cut off in the water into a snort. Then only the muffled noises of bodies straggling in the water then desultory lapping sounds again. The people knew through the darkness what it was, they could see nothing beyond the lengths of their arms and they scrambled closer together and tried to push into the doorway of the hut, trampling and pushing each other.

'Crocodile—crocodile!' and the children began to scream and the men to shout.

Only the old man Sixpence did not scramble in the blackness. He stood under the eaves with his spear raised to his shoulder in the blackness. The tears ran down his face with the rain.

'My cow!' he wept softly. 'My cow, oh vile one, vile one.'

And in the dawn the water was six feet from the doorway of the sleeping hut.

'It looks like Noah's Ark,' Mahoney said aloud.

It did look like Noah's Ark through the rain, the hut standing on a tiny strip of ground, with the people and the goats standing round the hut and crowding at the doorway. You could not see the escarpment beyond the hut atop the water.

He turned the throttle up and headed straight for the island. The people were shouting and clapping their hands.

'Crocs!' Mahoney whispered. The beasts swam away from his wash. The bastards!' He felt for his .22. 'Dammit! Why didn't I bring the three-oh-three?' Still the twenty-two would sting them. He felt for his box of cartridges under the seat. 'Dammit,' he cursed again. 'You fool, you big bloody fool!' The cardboard box was soggy in wash in the bottom of the boat, the cardboard falling apart. 'Dammit and they've been there all night!'

He opened the magazine on the gun. Empty. Just one up the spout. 'You tit! You tit-tit-tit!'

He steered the boat angrily around the rooftop of the cooking hut of the second wife. He snapped the throttle down and the boat swept silently up to the island and grounded on the muddy slope. Willing hands grabbed her. He jumped ashore.

'Women and children first,' he shouted in bad Tonga. 'All women and children come here.'

The women and children huddled in the rain.

'You mother, sit there, you mother over here, you girl of marriageable age sit next to this person. No more adults this journey. Now the children—'

The boat could hold six, nine at a push, low in the water.

'Whose property is this? It can be held in the hands.'

'It is the property of the third wife of Sixpence,' a man said.

'Sixpence?' Mahoney looked around the black faces in the rain. 'Where is this old man?'

'He is here, Bwana.'

'Where?'

The senior wife led him around the side of the hut. The old man stood under the eaves with the goats, his back against the wall and his feet stuck out into the water. He was looking aloofly out over the water.

'Old man!'

Sixpence turned his head to his master and nodded. He put his hands together and clapped them quietly.

'You are welcome in my kraal, Mambo. I am ashamed I have not fire and food for the Mambo.'

'My heart is glad to see you, old man. But come now. I am taking the people to a safe place. I will return shortly for you and your wives and the other people. You must help them to be ready.'

Sixpence nodded. 'Next year the crops will be very good,' he said, 'for the river will have deposited much rich soil in the garden. But my two cows are eaten by the crocodiles.'

'Old man, I go now. We will talk about the crops tonight in a safe place, you and I, and we will make a plan. But make speed now.'

He looked at the old man. The old man just looked ahead into the rain. 'Sixpence!' But the old man did not move. Mahoney turned and sloshed round the side of the hut.

'Who is the senior wife of the old man?' he shouted. 'You, old mother? Then gather his property and be ready when I return. And urge the old man to make haste. Stay well.'

He splashed down through the water to the boat. 'Samson, stay behind and help the people. If the crocodiles come, beat the water with sticks.'

The water had risen almost to the doorstep when the boat returned. The second wife had put a dam of sticks and mud across the doorway. The women were in the hut and the men stood outside to beat the water. Sixpence still stood at his place under the eaves with his spear and the nanny goat. The goat had climbed to its feet, for the water had reached its lying place. It stood on three legs and bleated and sniffed the air.

Mahoney looked around quickly as he beached the boat and jumped into the water. No crocodiles. The water was up to his knees.

'Is every person ready? Let every person come here quickly. Quickly old mother! Pass me your belongings.'

He slung her blankets into the boat. They milled around the boat, the water over their ankles.

'Sit here! No here! Samson, show the people where to sit. You, woman, in here—'

He pushed and bundled them into the boat. They sat huddled in their places in the boat clutching their small belongings, the rain teeming down on them.

He counted. Six adults, plus himself and Samson and the old man.

'Where is this old man?' Mahoney splashed round the hut.

'I am here, Mambo.'

He stood under the eaves with his spear and the nanny goat. The water pushed up over the little dam across the doorway and trickled into the dark hut.

'Come now! The boat is ready and we are waiting for you!'

The old man looked away. 'Go then, Mambo.'

'For Chrissake!' Mahoney took a step towards him and the old man stepped back.

'Do you wish me to hit you, old man?'

'The Mambo cannot hit me in my own kraal.'

'It is your kraal no longer,' Mahoney shouted. He knew it was the wrong thing to say. 'It belongs to the river now. And to the crocodiles who will eat your body!'

He jumped at the old man and grabbed his thin arm. The old man jerked it away and stepped back.

'Fool!'

Mahoney lunged again. The old man stepped backwards into the water. Mahoney caught the arm with both hands. They were up to their knees in the water. The old man's free arm jerked up. He held the spear poised at Mahoney.

'I do not wish to injure Mambo. Let him let me stay in peace.'

From the other side of the hut came Samson's shout.

'Crocodile, Nkosi!' and loud shouts of the men to chase it away.

Mahoney let go the arm and waded up to the eaves of the hut. There the water was well over his ankles.

'Come out of the water, you idiot!'

The old man stood, the water eddying round his knees.

'Samson!' Mahoney shouted angrily. 'Pull the boat round here.'

'Yebo, Nkosi.'

Samson pulled the boat load of people round the hut. 'Three crocodiles other side, Nkosi.'

'Women!' Mahoney shouted. 'Speak to your husband! Tell him to come with us!' The wives began to weep.

'Come, husband. The water and the crocodiles will eat you.'

The old man did not look at them. He just shook his head and said Ah! in disgust.

'Get me the gun,' Mahoney snapped. He took it and pointed it at the old man.

'Do not shoot him!' the senior wife screamed. Sixpence looked at Mahoney steadily.

'If you do not come, old man,' Mahoney shouted, 'I will injure you. I will shoot the hand which raised the spear at the Queen's Representative.'

Sixpence stood his ground. He moved the spear up and down his shoulder.

'Kill me then, Mambo,' he said angrily, 'but I will not come.'

Mahoney sighted down the barrel at the moving hand. He was trembling with a sick anger. He did not want to shoot at the old man. He did not even think that he would be accurate. He wanted to cry for the old man.

'Crocodile!' the women screamed.

And snaking through the water giving the hut a wide berth was the ugly reptile. It was swimming for the old man.

'Eeh!' the women screamed and the old man turned to face the crocodile. He lifted his spear and shouted, 'Aaarh!'

'Oh Jesus.' Mahoney swung the gun round and shot at the hideous head. It missed, but the crocodile jerked and swam angrily away.

Mahoney lowered the gun. 'Now come out of the water, old man.' He was shaking.

The old man turned back to him slowly.

'When you are gone.'

'Jesus!' Mahoney saw the other crocodiles nosing around the water a distance out. 'Get into the boat,' he snapped at Samson. The crocodiles would flush the old boy out, back up to his hut. The boat already had to carry eight, low in the water, without the old boy rocking it.

Mahoney climbed into the boat. It rocked as he pulled the cord to start the engine, and the women jerked and clutched each other.

The gunnel dipped under and she took in water. Mahoney scowled at the women.

'If the boat rocks like that again we will all be food for the crocodiles,' he snapped. 'Now be ready for it!'

He pulled the cord again and again and the boat rocked but the engine did not start.

'Oh no, not wet plugs as well.'

He pulled again and the engine kicked and started.

The old man waded up to the wall of his hut. The water swilled through his doorway.

'Now, will you come, old man?'

Sixpence stood in the water under the eaves. The goat bleated on its three legs, the water touching its belly.

'No.'

'You are a stubborn old fool!'

The old man said nothing. Mahoney put the engine into gear and opened the throttle carefully. He turned the tiller-handle and the boat began to inch through the water heavily. The water came to within two inches of the gunnel.

He turned the boat about and he looked back at Sixpence. The goat was still bleating. The old man raised his hand in a tired salute.

'I will take these people to a safe place, old man,' Mahoney shouted. 'And then I will come back for you.'

The old man said nothing. He just looked at them.

Mahoney opened the throttle and the boat surged sluggishly.

From thirty yards away he looked back at the hut. He saw the old man standing there. The goat was bleating loudly. He saw the crocodile nosing through the water leisurely towards the hut, still a distance away. He saw the nanny goat hobble in the water, its broken leg held up, trying to make its way round the wall of the hut to the doorway. He saw the old man bend and pick up the goat in his arms. It was still bleating. The old man waded through the water round the hut. He ducked his head and carried the goat through the doorway into the dark hut. The old man and the goat disappeared inside the dark hut, and the goat was still bleating loudly.

Mahoney opened the throttle and the boat pushed away into the rain.

The crocodile swam towards the hut and the noise of the bleating. It made a swishing circle outside the hut, then it swam through the doorway of the hut also. And after a few moments the noise of the bleating stopped and there was only a splash in the doorway.

That was the summer. It was to be winter once more before civilisation saw Mahoney again.

Part Two

Chapter Ten

'Go north young man,' was the saying, and north they came, the fitters and the turners and bricklayers and carpenters and the miners and the salesmen and the businessmen and the bright young men to become salesmen and businessmen and to be tomorrow's executives in the Anglo-American Corporation, and the British South Africa Company, and the Roan Antelope Corporation and in the thousand and one corporations that sprang up in the hot flat bushland of Rhodesia, north of the Limpopo. There was a fever in the land, an exciting fever of the opening of the new frontier, of staking your claim and hitting it rich, there was an optimism in the air and the air vibrated with the rattle of pneumatic drills and the crunch of old walls coming down and the new walls going up. Thanks to Federation. Federation of the rich primitive North with the go-ahead South. Partnership of the Black North and the whiter South, wealth shared with know-how, black hand clasped with white across the mighty Zambezi in the new deal handshake on new brotherhood, big white brother shaking hands on the deal with little black brother, big white brother going to be fair with little black brother and teach him the ropes. Progress. A Partnership booming.

And down in the valley, a new link of Partnership was being forged, a link of water, an inland sea.

It is hot in the Zambezi Valley, even in the winter time.

Down in the gorge called Kariba, temple of Nyamayimini, the white man's mighty wall reared up, looking puny from the heights but very big when you climbed down to it, its top jagged and hugely uneven like a giant's battlements poking up out of the deep black scarred rock of the great gorge. It was hot, the ground burned underfoot and the bush was crackling brown. The air shimmered and vibrated with the hammer and thump of the drills and the shouts of the men and the grinding of the truck engines and the clank of steel on cement and rock. The great Zambezi river banked up around the wall, then it swilled bewilderedly round, then found its way through the huge tunnel hewn in the huge rock banks to where the giant turbines lay entombed. Then far downstream below the wall the river swilled out into the sunshine again, masticated by the turbines and humiliated. Then it collected its ruffled self and it began to rumble on down the gorge again, to become the mighty magnificent river again.

Above the wall a long split tongue of blue water reached slowly, quietly up into the mauve haze of the great valley. It wound its way round hills and it crept up into ravines and it disappeared into the vast jigsawed depression of Central Africa, and into its thick primitive mauve haze. It was drowning the great valley. The Batonka tribesmen were gone. Their huts and their gardens and their shrines were all buried under the slowly rising water, or standing empty and waiting to be drowned. The Batonka had left the blood of eight tribesmen to drown in the dust that would become the ocean bed, the blood of eight men who had seen fit to fight it out with the authorities who the strange wise black politicians said were tricking them. All gone, a way of life become an ocean bed. Down in the great valley only the wild animals remained, the huge population to whom the authorities could not explain about the flood. And they were going to drown too.

And Kariba, the little shack township which had planted itself on the top of the gorge in the middle of the jungle – the eyes of the world were on Kariba. There were newspapermen from all over the world hitching rides through the jungle to Kariba with their cameras and their notebooks to take pictures of the animals struggling in the water. Newspapermen jostling and competing to get on to the few boats of the few sunburnt men who were trying to rescue some of the animals. 'Operation Noah,' the newspapermen called it, but there were very few boats and there were very few men.

Chapter Eleven

Joseph Mahoney was ninety miles away from the wall, where the Zambezi was still river.

He stood on a large grey rock. The river ran deep and wide and swift here. He wore only short trousers and his body was thin and hard and very brown. His hair was long and shaggy and his face was matted with beard. He had a stout fishing rod in his hands, fitted with a good Penn Surfmaster reel, and at the end of the nylon line was a wire trace and a bronze spoon the size of a shoe-horn, fitted with a big hook.

Twenty yards upstream a boat was beached. Higher up on the bank lay three big brown scaly bloated crocodiles, dead and beginning to putrefy in the sun and there were flies crawling into the bullet holes in their big carnivorous heads. Samson Ndhlovu was standing astride one of the beasts and he lifted an axe high above his head and he brought it down on to the ridge of the crocodile's spine. He hacked the bony shell open, then he hacked down the length of the spine and the stink of the rotting reptile flooded out. Then he took his big hunting knife and he jammed it down between the hide and the flesh and he pulled back hard on the knife and the hide tore away from the flesh. Further from the bank in a big dry clearing the earth was a jigsaw of crocodile skins stretched out and pegged to the ground, raw side uppermost, covered in coarse salt, drying in the sun. Next to the clearing was a small lean-to of brushwood and inside it were stacked bundles of crocodile skins.

Mahoney swung the fishing rod backwards over his head then swiped it forward. The reel sang and the spoon snaked out high over the river and then it fell into the swift water. He gave it a few seconds to sink a little and then he dipped the tip of his rod down and he began to reel in. The spoon wriggled and flashed through the water until it was back at the foot of the rock. He cast it out again and again a dozen times. Then he got what he was waiting for, the sharp heavy strike on the spoon.

He swiped the rod up and held it and worked on his reel and struck again and reeled and struck again and again. Then the line began to streak sideways across the water against his hold, he gave out line and it streaked tight through the water coming up, up, up to the surface, up, and the big tiger fish broke the surface.

It jumped high in the air in a splash of silver water, and its long yellow and black striped body flashed in the sun. It shook its head furiously, its big mean head with its snapping jaws agape. This was the dangerous part, the time most tiger fish get away, shaking the spoon out of their great jaws.

The tiger fish dropped back into the water in a fury and dived and Mahoney struck again. The fish streaked across against the strain and it broke surface again twisting and shaking and jerking and snapping in the sunlight, then crashing back into the river. Again and again it jumped and shook and Mahoney struck harder and worked on the reel. After fifteen minutes the fish was thrashing near the foot of the rock, straining and dashing round and sideways and back again frothing and churning and shaking.

'Bring the gaff.'

Samson came running with the stick with the sharp big hook lashed to the end of it. Mahoney locked his reel and held the rod on high and he crouched down on the rock. He chased the big thrashing fish through the water, poking with the hook, feeling and chasing for a chance to sink it into the fish. He jabbed, but the hook glanced off the twisting fish. He chased again and got the hook under its soft white belly and he jerked the stick and the hook sunk home up into its bowels. He straightened and lifted the stick out of the water with the heavy fish snaking and snapping on the end of it. He walked up the bank and shook it off the hook. It jumped and snapped with its rows of long razor teeth that could bite off a man's finger. He took a stone and carefully, sharply knocked the fish out with it. Then they crouched down to admire it, as men always do with a handsome tiger fish, and stroked their fingers down the long horizontal black and yellow stripes.

'Beautiful,' Samson nodded.

'Cook it,' Mahoney said in Sindebele, 'and smoke the jaws, I want to keep them. I will go ahead with skinning the crocodiles.'

'Yebo, Nkosi.'

Mahoney went down to the bank and prized and levered and wrenched and slashed the skin off one crocodile. The red stinking flesh of the huge reptile lay naked and dismembered on the bank.

Samson came back.

'Skoff ready, Nkosi.'

Mahoney straightened up, stinking blood on his hands and arms and chest and legs.

'The crocodile meat is nicely rotten,' he said. 'It may make good bait.'

He went to the water's edge and rubbed sand and water over himself. Then they went back to the camp where the fire smoked over the big black cooking pots and the big black frying pan. The tiger fish lay in it with only its head and tail chopped off, fried golden black in a batter of mealiemeal and impala fat. In the pot was a mass of thick dry mealiemeal porridge. Mahoney lifted the fish out, chopped it in half with a bush knife and they sat round the fire on rocks. Mahoney ate with a fork and his fingers out of a tin plate, Samson ate with just his fingers. They put pieces of porridge into their mouths, then a piece of fish. They ate in silence. When Mahoney was rolling a cigarette, Samson spoke for the first time.

'Nkosi?'

'Hmmm?'

Samson smiled his wide smile on his big black face.

'Does the Nkosi not thirst for beer again?'

Mahoney did not look at him. 'Not particularly,' he said, avoiding the issue.

'Beer is good for a man,' Samson said, 'it makes him strong.'

'And foolish.'

'Only if swallowed in excess,' Samson pointed out.

'That is the trouble, you swallow in excess. Last time at Kariba you swallowed so much I had to collect you from the police station.'

Samson laughed deep, white teeth wide in black face.

'It was the fault of those Nyasa men, Nkosi, for trying to fight with me.'

'For trying to save their womenfolk, you mean,' Mahoney said, and Samson's laugh seemed to reverberate across the river.

Then there was silence again. Mahoney fetched a book from his tent and read while he finished his cigarette.

'I thirst for beer,' Samson said, as if to himself.

Mahoney did not look up. 'Well, if you have such a great thirst, why do you not make some beer here? You must know how to make the kaffir beer your womenfolk make.'

Samson nodded thoughtfully.

'That is a good idea, Nkjosi,' he said, 'but alas I have no drum big enough.'

'Use a paraffin tin. Several paraffin tins.'

'Alas Nkosi,' Samson said sadly, 'we do not have enough sugar.'

'Use honey, then,' without looking up, 'go and smoke out some wild bees.'

'Beer is unpleasant without sugar, Nkosi, and I am very afraid of bees.'

'How did we get our honey in those bottles, then?'

'I think those were very sick bees, Nkosi,' Samson said and Mahoney snorted to suppress a laugh.

'What you mean,' Mahoney said at last, 'is that you feel it's time we went to Kariba again and you can go and get blind drunk in the shebeens and squander your pay on Kariba Kate!'

Samson smiled sadly and deferentially. 'Ah! but it is a long time since we went to Kariba, Nkosi.'

'Three months,' Mahoney said.

'Three months, Nkosi?' Samson said mournfully. 'That is indeed a long time. And we already have a full load of skins and we are running short of petrol. And sugar,' he added.

'Ndhlovu,' Mahoney said firmly, 'we have a space in the boat for many more skins. And we have enough petrol to last another four weeks. We are not going to Kariba for at least one month. If you wish to leave me you go with the first other boat we see.'

He knew Samson would not leave him. Had he thought he would, he would have gone to Kariba. Samson looked hurt.

'Ah! I would not leave the Nkosi,' he said and Mahoney grunted and went back to his book.

'No,' he said, 'you're making too much money out of the Nkosi.'

He put his book aside and threw his cigarette into the fire ashes. He got up off the ground.

'Come,' he said, 'let us skin those crocodiles and bait up the hooks.'

Chapter Twelve

In the late afternoon they put out into the big river. The sun shone low down the valley, the tall river reeds were green golden and the African mahogany cast longer shadows and the distant sides of the wild escarpment were gold-tipped but turning blue. It was quiet, jungle quiet, with only the slide of the river and now the throb of the outboard motor. Both men wore only blood-spattered short trousers, but both had shirts stashed away for the winter evening's cool. Samson crouched on his haunches in the bows facing for'ard, his thick arms outstretched holding the prow, his black woolly head turning slowly from left to right, scanning the riverbanks, the sun shining black on his strong back. Mahoney sat at the machine, his left hand on the tiller, the air blowing his thick long hair off his hairy face, a cigarette in his mouth. He was also watching the riverbanks. They chugged down the river slowly, looking for a chance shot. A mile below the camp they saw eight buffalo near the water. There was an old bull and five cows, and their horns curled thick and heavy on their heads and their manes were long and shaggy and there were two half-grown calves with them. They were drinking at the water's edge, the calves in the middle and cows and the bull on the flanks, watching. They looked up as the boat came round the bend and they snorted and turned and stampeded back into the thick bush, the calves galloping beside their mothers and bucking and kicking up into the air with their hindlegs. Another mile, and the river widened out into the lake, twelve miles wide.

The lake disappeared round a twist in the valley twenty miles away. It was studded with islands, hills and ridges that the water was slowly climbing. Tree tops poked through the water in patches, the branches bare and dying, and at the shallow edges of the rising lake the water was creeping through the jungle. An angry high-pitched scream came from the south.

'Listen!'

It came again, a wailing squeal from great lungs.

'Elephant.'

'Look.'

Simultaneously they saw it through the water-logged tree trunks, a big heavy movement of the trees, then a hulking grey body, a mile away. Mahoney veered the boat to the shoreline and opened the throttle. Then he slowed down and manoeuvred the boat through the acres of tree trunks.

The old bull elephant was standing on the edge of the lake, the water covering his great feet and he was milling up and down. He lifted his head and looked shortsightedly up and down the waterline and he lifted his trunk and sniffed the air. He plodded out of the water and bulldozed through the trees for thirty yards and then he plodded experimentally back into the water and sniffed and peered again. Then he flapped his ears bad-temperedly and filled his lungs and let go another anguished trumpet.

'Poor old bastard.'

'He is looking for his wives,' Samson said sympathetically. 'He has been away for the winter and now he wishes to return to them and he finds water where there was none before.'

'So spring has come,' Mahoney said. 'Poor old chap, he will never find them again.'

Samson shook his head.

'No, he will have to stay on this side for ever, now.' They watched the elephant wander distractedly down the lake shore, knocking over trees and bushes in his confusion and irritation and trumpeting his frustration and calling his wives. But no answering trumpet came back. Mahoney turned the boat round and threaded back through the trees to the open water. He opened the throttle and sped down-river on the fringe of the trees. 'Look.'

Samson was pointing out to the open water. Two hundred yards out a line of trees stuck high above the water, a dozen trees on the top of a submerged hillock, and the branches were black and bending under the weight of creatures clustered on them.

'What are they?'

'Birds, perhaps,' Samson said.

'No,' Mahoney said, 'not birds.'

He turned the boat and headed for the thicket of trees. As they drew nearer the trees began to shake and black creatures began to jump and scramble over each other like lice.

'Monkeys?'

He cut the engine and the boat drifted towards them, and the roar of the engine was taken over by the shrill chattering of the little apes, like the applause of an audience.

'Oh, God!'

Every branch, every available piece of the trees was taken up with monkeys. Monkeys clutched the trunk with their arms and legs flung desperately round, monkeys clutched on branches, dangled on twigs, monkeys clutched on to each other, sat on each other's backs, burrowed under each other's chests and between each other's legs. Every monkey that could turn its head was staring at the boat drifting closer to them; twisting their necks they chattered and screamed. The boat drifted closer and there was a great panic and a scramble and some monkeys jumped on to other monkeys and some tried to burrow deeper under others' bellies and some crawled up the backs of others. Monkeys lost their hold and fell into the water and they splashed around feebly and swam for the tree trunks again but when they got there there was no room for them and they reached up and clung to the fur and the feet of the other monkeys and they tried to climb up on each other's backs and they stood on each other's heads, but they could not get out of the water, so they just hung on there. One small monkey that had lost its hold had caught on to the tail of another before it hit the water and it tried to climb up the tail but it found nothing to grip and it just hung on to the tail with both its arms upstretched and it blinked at Mahoney and Samson Ndhlovu and they could see its small heart knocking against the soft fur of its chest. 'Oh God.'

Every leaf, every piece of bark, every soft twig had been stripped off the trees and eaten, and now there was nothing left to eat. And even through their winter coats it could be seen that they were thin and starving. And then Mahoney peered closer at the monkey clinging to the bottom of the trunk, and he could see the monkey had been clinging there for a long time, for its legs and hindquarters were in the water and they were waterlogged and the skin and the fur had started to peel off.

'Oh God.'

The monkeys stared at them and they stared at the monkeys. 'What can we do, Nkosi?'

Mahoney shook his head. What could be done? There were two hundred monkeys in the trees.

'What would they do if we caught some and brought them into the boat?' Samson said.

'Bite,' Mahoney said flatly. 'Monkeys bite, and then you get lockjaw.'

'Shall we try, to see?'

'Yes.'

They leaned over the gunnels and paddled the boat up to the nearest tree.

'I'll try the one who is hanging on to his friend's tail,' Mahoney said.

It tried desperately to scramble higher up the tail, but it could not and it just hung there watching, its heart beating very fast.

'Come on, little fellow.' Mahoney leaned over the stem and stretched his hand gingerly towards the little thumping breast and he made soothing whistling noises. The monkey tried to scramble again but then found it could go no higher and it just hung. Mahoney's hand came within a foot of the breast and the monkey curled back its mouth and bared its little yellow fangs and made an angry noise in its throat. Mahoney withdrew his hand quickly. A great chattering and a scramble resumed in all the trees and more fell off and swam to the trunks.

'Come on, I'm trying to help you.'

He stretched out his hand again and again the treacherous fangs were bared and the scramble on the trees resumed.

'Oh, shut up, you bloody idiots, I'm trying to rescue you!'

Mahoney stretched out again and got very close to the monkey and it tried to bite him. 'It is no good,' Samson said.

'No,' Mahoney said.

They looked at the little creatures sadly.

'Sorry, there's nothing we can do for you, fellows.'

'Sorry,' Samson said, 'very sorry.'

'Except this,' Mahoney said sadly. He picked up the 12 bore shotgun. He opened the breach and put two cartridges in the double barrel. He opened a tin box and brought out a big carton of cartridges and put them on the seat beside him. He passed Samson the .22.

'Shoot any that fall wounded,' he said.

They paddled the boat a little way from the trees. Mahoney pulled back the hammers on each barrel and lifted the rifle to his shoulder. The monkeys all stared at him, chattering softly now. Mahoney felt sick. It was like firing into a crowd of people. He sighted the barrel into the middle of the nearest tree, and he could feel his hands shaking, and the nausea.

'Sorry, chaps,' and quickly he pulled the first trigger.

There was a deafening crack and his shoulder was jolted and the boat rocked. His eardrums sang and the valley was full of the explosion. Immediately, blindly he pointed the barrel into a different position in the same tree and pulled the other trigger. Frantically he lowered the gun and broke the breach and rammed two more cartridges into the barrels and snapped the breach to. Samson was standing up in the bows and firing rapidly into the water with the .22 repeater.

The carnage. The pandemonium, the blood, the screams, the clutching, the jumping. Monkeys were blown to bits out of the trees, blood and fur and bodies flying, monkeys screamed and jumped and fell wounded into the water, monkeys thrashed in the water with blood running from them, monkeys clung wounded to the naked branches and ripped open their wounds with their fingers and pulled out their insides, monkeys made it back to the trunk and clawed their way back up dripping water and blood. And the whole time the screams, the terrified squeals and chattering, and the scramble and clutching in the other trees. Again and again Mahoney fired through the trees, no longer sickened, only frantic to destroy and end the fear and the carnage. Samson stood firing in the bows and the crack crack of their rifles filled the valley.

Then it was quiet. All over. A few monkeys twitched in the bloody water and Mahoney took the .22 from Samson. 'Start the motor.'

Mahoney stood in the bows and shot at the wounded creatures. Then Samson opened the throttle gently and they nosed through the trees among the dead. The water was clogged with little furry bodies and blood and hanging flesh. They went through the battlefield and they leaned over the sides and lifted the dying out of the water and cracked them on the head with their axes.

'This will be a good place for crocodiles, tonight,' Samson said.

'I think it's too far out. Pick out a few big ones, we'll try them for bait.'

'Yebo, Nkosi.'

Clinging to the trunk of a tree only a few inches above the water, shivering and wet was a baby only a month or two old. It was clinging wearily and lost and its head was turned to them.

'Take the boat there.'

The boat inched up to the tree trunk and the tiny monkey turned its head away and tried to bury it into the trunk. It tried to climb up the trunk but it could not. Mahoney stretched out and plucked it off the trunk. It made tiny protesting noises and he brought it into the boat. He held it in both hands in his lap and it shivered.

'Poor little bugger, he'll never play rugger.'

First it wriggled, trying to clamber out of the hands holding it, casting wild anxious glances all round the boat and making its noises. Then it grew accustomed to the hands holding it and it stopped struggling and looked up at Mahoney with big round eyes.

'Have we got anything for it to eat?'

'Only mealiemeal and the buck's meat for our supper, Nkosi.'

'He may eat mealiemeal. Mix a little with water.'

Samson came holding the dough in the palm of his hand. He

pinched some off and held it out to the monkey. It cowered away and he dabbed the dough against its nose. The monkey sneezed and licked its nose.

'Go on.'

He held the dough out to it again. Then the monkey extended a tiny hand and grabbed the dough. It sat back on Mahoney's knee in the cage of his hands and raptly stuffed the porridge into its mouth and then looked around for more. They both laughed. 'Give him some more.'

They sat for ten minutes feeding the monkey. The monkey's mouth was smeared with dough and he leant out and scraped the crumbs off Samson's hand.

'What will you call him, Nkosi?'

'I think a good name would be Little Ndhlovu, after his elder brother,' Mahoney said, and Samson laughed so long and loud with his wide mouth flashing teeth that he rocked the boat.

'Pass me my bush jacket,' Mahoney said.

He put on the baggy tunic and emptied one of the big pockets. He stuffed the monkey in there. It crouched down in the bottom of the pocket.

'Work,' Mahoney said, and stepped over the meat and the carcasses to the stem. He opened the throttle and they churned away from the blasted trees and the bloody carcass-clogged water, heading into the open, then they travelled down the shore line again.

Chapter Thirteen

They chugged up the ravine in the late afternoon. Behind them stretched the tongue of the lake in the trough of the valley, still in the slanting sunlight, but they were in the shadow of a great shoulder of the escarpment and the banks of the tributary were high and left the river in deep shadow. The banks of the river were mottled with white sand beaches and big grey rocks and tall sharp reeds and there were eerie bends. The sun went down.

'Rock ahead, Nkosi,' and Mahoney swung the boat to starboard.

Samson turned and picked up a hunting lamp. He held it up to Mahoney and Mahoney nodded and Samson switched it on and played the beam ahead.

'We'll camp at the next beach,' Mahoney said.

They carried their gear high up the dark sand and dumped it.

'What about the monkeys and the crocodile flesh, Nkosi?'

'Put it in the corner near the rock,' Mahoney said, 'it stinks.' He sniffed his shoulder. 'More than I do.'

Mahoney built a large fire in the middle of the beach and Samson unpacked the gear and brought out the cooking pots. Into one he put mealiemeal and water and into the other he put ribs of venison.

'Wish we had some potatoes and onions and peas,' Mahoney said, watching him. 'I am growing weary of sadza. Couldn't you grow some back at the base camp?'

'Yes, Nkosi,' Samson said. He brightened. 'But we would have to go to Kariba to get the seeds!'

'Next month,' Mahoney said, and Samson grinned.

'I wish we had beer,' Samson said absently studying the coals.

'And fresh vegetables would be delicious,' he added. Mahoney grinned. 'How is the little one?'

Mahoney said: 'Gee, I'd forgotten about him.' He unbuttoned his pocket and looked down. The little monkey was pressed against him, his arms outstretched and with each hand he gripped a handful of the rough seam lining. He looked up and blinked at Mahoney.

'In the morning we'll get you some green stuff, boy,' he said. 'Go to sleep, you've had a big day.'

He transferred the monkey into the pouch of his haversack and buckled it down. The monkey sleepily transferred its grip to the rough canvas seams of the haversack pocket.

He picked up a hunting torch and played the beam over the river. No yellow eyes glared at him. He put the lamp down, the beam still on the river.

'We might attract a few right here.'

They ate the food in silence in the firelight. Then Samson scoured the pots and plates in the wet sand. They loaded the lamps and the rifles and four long gaffs into the boat, they heaped plenty of heavy wood on to the fire and put out into the river.

Each had a lamp. Samson sat in the bows and shone ahead, Mahoney sat at the motor, playing the beam in long slow sweeps up the banks. The boat was much lighter and Mahoney kept the throttle at quarter speed. They chugged up the black river.

It was half an hour before the lamps picked out the first pair of yellow eyes, far ahead. The crocodile was nosing across the river and it turned to face the light and marked time, then it began to swim slowly towards it. Mahoney took the boat twenty yards further upstream, then he saw a tree hanging over the water. He cut down the throttle and eased over to the tree and Samson loosely tied the boat to it.

They did not speak, Samson kept his beam on the crocodile's eyes, Mahoney swept his light around, looking for more. The crocodile drifted slowly down to them, mesmerised by the strong lamp. Mahoney's light swept up and down the riverbanks opposite to them. He saw no more eyes.

'He's a hermit.'

The crocodile was ten yards from them, squirming slowly through the water, its nostrils just poking above the water, its yellow cat's eyes gleaming in its high ugly forehead, its broad hard corrugated back twisting slowly in the water.

'All right, hold tight.'

Mahoney felt for the nearest .303 rifle, worked the bolt action and brought a bullet into the breach. Samson stood in the bows holding the branch with one hand and with his other he held the beam on the crocodile's eyes. Mahoney sighted down the barrel. The rifle rang out and the crocodile kicked and thrashed in the water.

'Right between the eyes! Die, you bastard!'

They lashed the beast to the gunnel. Mahoney made another sweep with his lamp and they pushed on up-river. Ten minutes later Samson said softly: 'Ah!'

They had come slowly round a bend in the river. There were masses of reeds casting long shadows, and some big rocks on the bank and there were mudbanks between the reeds. On a bank far ahead, half hidden in reeds, three pairs of yellow eyes glared at them. Then a fourth pair appeared through the reeds, then a fifth, and in mid-stream there was a swish of water and a sixth pair of yellow eyes turned to glare at them.

'This is more like it,' Mahoney said softly. 'Maybe you'll get your trip to Kariba sooner than a month. Hold the beam on them, I'll look for a mooring.'

He took the boat over to the starboard bank, searching the reeds for something substantial to hold on to.

'Nkosi, careful for rocks!' Mahoney jerked. In the diffused glare of the for'ard lamp he saw the rocks under the water. Then he heard a crashing through the reeds near him and he twisted around and saw a long dark form run down the bank into the water, a big crocodile running on its toes with its legs outstretched, like a dragon. It hit the water behind them and disappeared into the blackness.

'Jesus.'

Mahoney swung the boat hard into deeper water. 'Rocks?'

'Okay now, Nkosi.'

'Where can we stop?'

'I think there is a place right here, Nkosi.'

'Throw out the anchor, then, but don't get it wedged for ever.'

There were rocks below the water still. Samson threw out the small anchor and it caught behind a rock. It was shallow.

The boat lay downstream of the anchor, ten feet from the thick reeds of the starboard bank. It was not the best position. Mahoney had a horror of crocodiles and he preferred to have an open bank nearby when he was surrounded by them, as he suspected he was now, but it was as good as they would find at short notice. At least it was shallow.

They played their lamps back over the water. Mahoney whistled and Samson said 'Ah!'

There were eleven pairs of baleful eyes. The river was thirty yards wide at this point and the crocodiles were still upstream of them, perhaps sixty yards away. They came slithering down off the muddy banks, like filthy great maggots Mahoney thought, and slid treacherously into the dark water and began to swim slowly in a horrible armada downstream to the light.

Mahoney passed Samson one of the .303 rifles.

'I will start from the left and work in, you start from the right. Do not shoot until I do.'

They sat crouched in the boat, each holding a hunting lamp in his left hand under the barrel, the right holding the butt against his side. They kept the lamps played on the reptiles.

'Don't jump around,' Mahoney said, as he said to him every time this situation arose, 'unless you want a bullet through you. That would cure your thirst.' Samson grinned in the darkness. He was excitedly calculating his bonus on eleven crocodiles.

'We have fourteen bullets in our magazines,' Mahoney said, 'so there is no reason for not getting all the vile ones. It will not be as easy retrieving them,' he added.

He swung his lamp aside quickly and played it on the water downstream, looking for the crocodile that had run off the bank behind him, but he did not see any. Then he returned it upstream.

The crocodiles were drawing close.

'Right,' Mahoney whispered. Samson crouched lower in the prow and rested the elbow of his left arm on the prow. Mahoney shifted to get secure. He knelt up on the cross-seat in front of him, one knee resting. He did not think it was the best position but there was little choice. He brought the rifle up slowly and squinted in his lamplight down the barrel, the lamp trained on the left-most reptile. As he did so, he recognised the front sight of the rifle as Samson's. He felt a flash of irritation: Samson's rifle was an older and less accurate one than his own, but he shrugged mentally. It was too late to swap and the rifle was good enough. The crocodiles were twenty yards away now.

'Fire,' he breathed and he squeezed the trigger carefully.

A crash, a jolt that stunned, a kick, a spinning of the black night, the stars overhead reeling, a fall, a clutching, a stumble, the blinding smack of his face on the gunnel, the topple, the river coming sideways up to meet him, the splash, the cold water closing quickly over him, the roar of bubbles as he coughed, the water in his nose and mouth, the sudden blinding blackness of the water and the inward scream of terror. Mahoney was knocked over the side into the river before he knew what hit him.

He broke the surface, thrashing the water wildly, twenty feet from the boat and towards mid-stream. Dizzy, water-logged heaviness, a lamp flashing upstream, dreadful fear of the crocodiles. He struck out wildly for the boat. He could see the lamp trained on him through his splashing, then dully he heard the rifle cracking out over him, crack crack crack crack. He struck on frantically, dizzily, numbed by shock and exhausted by fear. He felt the current working against him, his clothes, his sandshoes weighting him. Crack, the rifle was going again, the lamp was momentarily off him. He was gaining on the water, the boat was only ten feet from him. It was rocking wildly. Then a wild shout, a scream of anger or terror or both, a large black shape plunging into the water next to him. Something grabbed him, wrenched at the tunic on his back, an arm silhouetted upraised against the stars, an axe coming down furiously. He was picked up out of the water by his waist and flung over the side of the boat. Then his legs were tipped after him and he fell into a heap. He scrambled up frantically, the boat was rocking violently, and the black man clambered over the side.

They sat in panting trembling silence, their heads hanging down, the water running off them, steadying up in the darkness. One hunting lamp lay in the bottom of the boat, its light stifled by a sack. From the bottom of the river twenty feet away the other lamp threw up a ghostly, twisting muddy glow. Mahoney lifted his throbbing breathless head and he thought he saw a long shadow flit under the water against the glow and he shuddered.

'Where are your cigarettes, Ndhlovu? I'll buy a thousand in Kariba.'

'In the front, Nkosi.'

Mahoney moved shakily up the boat and found Samson's packet of Star cigarettes. He lit two and passed Samson one. The black man lifted his head and Mahoney saw his hands were trembling too. He sat down opposite him.

'You are a brave man, Ndhlovu.'

Samson shook his head.

'But I wish you would clean your gun.'

Samson shook his head again. He talked to his feet. His chest was heaving. 'It is my fault, Nkosi. I saw the barrel was clogged with wet sand and I meant to clean it and then I forgot. If you had not given me your rifle by mistake it would have been me in the river.'

'Forget it, Ndhlovu.'

Mahoney shuddered again. He wondered whether he would have had the guts to go in after Samson. Adrenalin is a funny thing. Flooded with it suddenly, acting on impulse a man is capable of great bravery. Give him a moment to consider, and he may be a craven coward. But Samson Ndhlovu had stood in the boat sniping crocodiles, taking the whole scene in, having the time to consider, and yet he went in.

'What was happening? Why did you have to come in?'

Samson spoke with his shoulders hunched, talking to the ribs of the boat, still shaking.

'The Nkosi was about to become a crocodile's skoff.'

He pulled on his cigarette and in the glow Mahoney could see his heart still knocking against his black chest. 'There were two behind you, they came from over there,' he indicated with his hand the reeds behind them, i was shooting at them, but I was too excited and I was missing. I think I got some in the end. Then the Nkosi was a few yards from the boat and a crocodile came from mid-stream. My bullets were finished and I jumped in the water with the axe and hit him in the snout,' Samson snorted. 'I think he is dead, soon.'

Mahoney shook his head in the darkness.

'Do you wish to know something, Ndhlovu?'

'What, Nkosi?'

'I am declaring a holiday. We are going to Kariba. And I personally am going to see you get roaring drunk, then I'll bail you out of gaol and pay your fine myself. Come to think of it, I may get a little drunk myself.'

Samson laughed.

'When Nkosi?'

'As soon as we've skinned these crocodiles and any more we shoot tonight. Maybe even tomorrow.'

They finished their cigarettes and then Mahoney picked up the hunting lamp. It was nearing dawn before they returned to camp downstream with four crocodiles in tow.

The crocodile that got Samson Ndhlovu came up over a ledge in the riverbed as the black man stood up to his calves in water on the beach, washing the dirt off his hands. Mahoney was forty yards away in the bush, looking for firewood. The crocodile wriggled up from the depths in a flurry of mud-puffs. Samson saw the dark form darting up at him in the dawn light only as its yellow jaws snapped over his leg. There was a mighty thrash of the crocodile in the water as it jerked backwards, shaking its head. Samson was wrenched off his feet backwards, he gave one guttural scream. Then he was out in deep water and the crocodile pulled him under.

Mahoney heard the scream. He ran back to the campsite with the axe, crashing through the bush. He got to the beach and he searched the river in the half light but he could see nothing. He ran for the hunting lamp and his rifle. Panting, he shone the lamp over the water. He saw only the steady flow of the river. He saw a crocodile slither along the opposite bank and he fired quickly at it but he missed. Then he played the torch around the water's edge of the beach and he blanched. Of the lumps of crocodile flesh and monkeys they had dumped in the corner only one monkey remained. There were dragmarks leading into the water and the claw and slithermarks of crocodiles.

'You idiot! The place must be alive with crocs by now!'

He threw back his head.

'Samson!' he bellowed. 'Samson!'

He plunged out to the boat and he grabbed the twelve bore. He broke the breach frantically arid rammed two cartridges in. He looked around for a piece of cloth then he gripped the lapel of his shirt and ripped a strip off it. Whimpering, he wrapped the cloth round the two triggers and pulled back the hammers. Then, blindly, he rammed the barrels under the water and held the butt away from his side and he turned his face away and jerked the cloth round the triggers. There was a mighty bang and the shotgun leapt in the air, twisted and shattered, and the river shook and Mahoney was thrown on his back.

He scrambled up and ran back to the boat and started the engine.

Chapter Fourteen

A crocodile does not chew. It can only snap its giant jaws and break off and swallow. Accordingly, it does not eat big lumps of fresh meat. A crocodile catches you and it pulls you under the water and it holds you there while you struggle and it drowns you, then it drags you to its den and it leaves you there, waiting for you to rot. When you are good and rotten it breaks pieces off you and sucks and swallows the flesh and bone down.

A crocodile's den is a fearful place. It stinks and it is full of bones and it is dark. A crocodile makes a cave for himself in the river-bank, sometimes under a rocky ledge, sometimes a cavern hollowed out in the earth, with a tunnel leading to it. The den is above the water, but often the tunnel is not. Sometimes a crocodile makes a mistake: it does not completely drown you and it drags you to its den while there is still some life in you. You may come round, and find yourself in the dreadful place. The crocodile guards its den well against other crocodiles, and when it returns and discovers that you are not quite dead it drags you back through the tunnel into the water again and holds you at the bottom and makes a good job of it.

The impact of the double blast of the shotgun rattled the crocodile that caught Samson Ndhlovu. It wrestled with the struggling man at the bottom of the muddy water, gripping his foot fiercely and shaking its hideous head from side to side furiously, like a dog shakes a rabbit. The struggles of the man were growing weaker and the crocodile shook him once more and writhed backwards across the riverbed and it found its tunnel under the heap of rocks and dragged Samson Ndhlovu deep into its stinking den. It lay beside him, panting, its scaly ribcage and belly going in and out, its head lifted up and motionless, listening to the faraway bombardment of the water. Then it crawled slowly back out to the tunnel and lay in its mouth with its nostrils and nose poking through the reeds of the water beyond, watching.

Mahoney ended his bombardment when he ran out of ammunition in the boat. He sped back to his camp and got more for his .303 and the .22. He knew the habits of crocodiles with the loathing intimacy with which a man studies the habits of the arch enemy and he knew that Samson was lying in some hateful den somewhere nearby right now, waiting to rot. He thought he was dead but he knew that with the noise and percussion of his bombardment there was a chance that there was still life in him, provided he had not killed the man himself. The dawn had broken and Mahoney climbed back into the boat and he set out down the banks slowly, poking out into the reeds with his long grappling gaff. Just what he was going to do if he saw the signs of a den he did not know, but he was going to look. The crocodile retreated further back into its den when it observed the coming disturbance. Then it crawled out of the tunnel and swam under the water, away, until the disturbance passed. For over an hour Mahoney thrashed around amongst the reed banks, his gaff beating the reeds and his propeller churning the water. Then he returned to his camp and sat down in the morning sunshine at the fire and hung his head. He was shaking from tension and fatigue. He was flooded with relief that he was alive, he shuddered at the thought of Samson's fate. The temptation to fall back in the sand and quiver in the sun was almost overwhelming, but he forced himself to sit up and stay alert, though he did not know what purpose it would serve. He took his .303 and went to the top of the high rock where he commanded a view of the river, and he sat down.

Samson Ndhlovu had been a hunter. He had hunted buck and elephant and even crocodiles as a youth with spear and snare and axe. He knew the ways of the wild better than Mahoney. He knew how to smell out a crocodile's lair and he had more than once flushed a crocodile out of one. He had the African hunter's patience to sit dead still in the reeds for hours and watch and wait, which few Irishmen have, and which Mahoney certainly did not have. Samson Ndhlovu knew about crocodiles' lairs and he had been a miner and he knew what it was to be imprisoned in a hole in the ground with the rock just above his head. Samson knew where he was when he came round in the crocodile's lair and he was filled with the silent sickened scream of horror. The first thing Samson Ndhlovu knew was the blockage in his throat and nose as he coughed and dribbled. He coughed it up into his mouth and it ran over his lips, then he sucked in the fetid air of the den and he coughed again and sucked again, the thick stink of old rotting death and bones and mud and faeces in the darkness. The air was thick and black and wet and sharp and he coughed and sucked and coughed and sucked. He lay on his stomach in the black grotto, his body heaving, his lips in the mud coughing up the slime, and froth dribbling out his mouth. Then slowly he came round, blinking and coughing and heaving and at last he lifted his head. He saw only a patch of dirty grey light at first. Then his eyes cleared and he could make out the outline of the entrance to the tunnel and the watery crescent of light shining through the reeds. When he realised where he was, he made a stifled gargling noise in his throat. He jerked his body forward.

Then he felt the pain in his leg, his whole right leg up to his groin, the aching throb of lacerated muscles and bruised bone turning septic in the rotten mud, the heavy aching paralysis, and the further spasm of fear, of helplessness. He twisted over and pushed himself up on to his elbow slowly and ran his fingers down his leg. He winced as his fingers dipped into raw wet flesh. He tried to bend his leg and it hurt.

Samson looked up above, dizzily, and his heart leaped. He saw a chink of light shining in from the ceiling. He felt upwards excitedly but his hand touched nothing. He stretched his right hand out sideways and touched nothing. He dropped it in the mud beside him and he had a thrill of horror. He touched something wet and hard and there was hair on it. He jerked his hand away. He felt sideways and he touched rock.

He ran his hand up the rock then he got grunting on to his good knee and felt upwards. The rock sloped evenly at an angle over him. He leaned against it and got on to his good foot, and now his right leg throbbed very badly. He clenched his teeth in the blackness and he tried to straighten up and he banged his head on the rock. He knelt half bent and felt above him. He felt the other side of it and he touched sloping rock also. And Samson knew he was in a small cave made between the sides of two big rocks resting against each other.

'Nkosi!' he screamed but it was only a croak and the sound fell back into the chamber. 'Nkosi, Nkosi,' but the sound only filled the chamber and he began to cough and choke as he sucked in the stink. He coughed and coughed and he dropped to his knees, the nausea and the fear making him vomit. He retched and retched but nothing came tip but a little slime. And the more he retched the more he sucked in the air and retched more, until he was weak and dizzy. Then he lay down, shuddering, in the rotten mud and in his own slime, trying to filter the stink by cupping his hand over his mouth and nose.

The only way out was down the tunnel through the water, into the reeds and into the river. And what lurked there? And once in the water? How deep was the water and how strongly did it flow, and how accessible was the bank? He had only seen this part of the river in darkness by lamplight, he did not know where he was, not even what bank he was on, nor how long he had been there, nor whether the Nkosi was still around. He only knew it was daylight outside.

Samson put his hand to his hip and felt for his bushknife. It was there in its sheath, the stout steel tyre lever he had sharpened and to which he had added his handle of motorcar tyre. The tunnel was ten feet long and at the lowest part of it his whole body would have to go under water. He took the knife out of its sheath. He held it in his fist, the long blade pointing upwards. He made a move to crawl to the tunnel, then he stopped. He half turned in the darkness and gingerly stretched his hand out to the left again. He felt horrible wet and slimy things, and things that gave to his touch like dough. He felt bones, and he picked them up, but none of them were any good. Then his hand touched a stone, a smooth round river stone, he tugged at it and it came out of the mud with a suck. Samson whimpered as he dragged it over to him. He took a grip on it in his left hand. It was too big for him to hold with comfort. He held the knife up in his right hand and he began to wriggle forward to the slimy tunnel on his elbows and stomach.

The tunnel was low and small. The floor was wet and slimy and muddy. The air was better: Samson pulled great pants of it into his body, it smelt like glorious fresh air. Never, never again would he worry about beer if only he could have air like this, always. He wriggled his head and shoulders into the mouth of the tunnel, panting and wriggling and pushing with his good foot and knee. His bad leg worked too, and the gashes scraped over the floor of the grotto and his leg throbbed, but Samson hardly felt it.

He wriggled down the tunnel, grunting and panting, his teeth clenched and his face screwed up, the mud clinging to him. His shoulders, then his back, then his buttocks were in the tunnel. The tunnel was very long. He was getting there, he was almost within reach of the murky water that lay at the exit, his knife and his stone going before him. Then the water of the tunnel was suddenly ruffled, and the light was shaken up. Then the tunnel was full of a great rush of a splash then a loud sucking squelch. The crocodile stood poised in its tunnel. Head up, jaws slightly open, fat scaly belly panting, water dripping off it. It blocked the tunnel, cut off the light, leaving only enough to throw up its black horny silhouette. Poised, its monster's nerves tight at the life in its den. Black creature and black man lay poised in the tunnel, both poised, one terrified, one outraged. The monster hissed, he saw its dark shape at the mouth of the dreadful grotto. Scream, scream, scream in terror, faint, cringe up and die. He screamed the scream of a savage at bay, hating and terrified, terror turned to reckless wrath. He screamed at the dreadful black silhouette in the tunnel before him and the scream filled the tunnel, he screamed and the monster jerked, he screamed and he lashed out, knife in fist jabbing upwards into the blackness, eyes closed in scream, knife jabbing up, scream and the stone beating forward like a club, scream and the knife and the stone flailing and beating the black silhouette, grunting and screaming and splashing and flailing. He screamed and jabbed and lunged and beat. He screamed and beat and lunged long after the startled splash and the light came winking and dancing back into the tunnel. His own scream drowned out even the crack crack crack of the rifle.

Then he lay panting in the passage and the silhouette was no longer before him. Then he was whimpering and crying as he scrambled down to the water, his rock and his knife still in his aching arms. Then he was in the water with a gasp for breath like a crying child being ducked, then he was clawing at the mud and reeds with his knife under the water, his legs kicking rock and mud, he was crawling through the reeds, then the crack, crack, crack, crack of the rifle exploding all about him and the bullets smacking the water, then he was on his legs, slipping and sliding and gasping and grasping and scrambling and still the rifle was cracking out. Then he was crawling and scrambling and heaving himself up out of the water, pulling on the reeds and the reeds cutting his hands and spiking into his flesh and into his wounds and digging into his feet and still the rifle was going crack, crack, crack in his ears. Then he was on the mud bank and there was a firm soil under his feet and he scrambled up and up and he ran up the bank and over the top of it and he collapsed. He did not even hear the roar of the engine starting.

Chapter Fifteen

The water spread a lot in the next three months. It crept up the jungle slopes of the escarpment, it ran over the tops of the hills that had become islands, it pushed out and up and it ran around new hills and made more islands. North and south and west the great lake spread through the great valley like a fattening octopus.

It looked like a great blue octopus from the air, Suzanna de Villiers thought. She rested her chin on her thin knuckle and looked down through her window with steady heavy blue eyes. They looked like bedroom-eyes to the man sitting next to her, and he decided he was going to stick close to her during the day's tour over the dam workings and especially at the braaivleis the travel agents were putting on for them tonight, as part of their ten guineas worth. She *looked* a hot number. With a little grog inside her she would drop that aloof frigid air. And he would have two hours to work on her during the flight home to Bulawayo. And arriving at Bulawayo at two a.m. in the morning? Well, well, well, seven kinds of opportunities. And those titties heaving gently as she stared out of the window—

'Ladies and gentlemen,' the knowledgeable voice of the guide said, 'we are preparing to land at Kariba airstrip, where our bus is waiting for us. Fasten your seat belts please—'

Suzanna de Villiers did not move, she did not take her eyes from the window. She was thinking: somewhere down there Jake was once marooned in a tree. The man nudged her.

'I say,' he said jovially, 'we're coming in to land.'

'Oh!'

She busied herself with the belt. Then she looked at him and flashed a smile. She was glad to be friendly with anybody at that moment.

Blue, the water of the great lake was blue, like the sea. And it seemed as big as the sea. And from the real faraway sea, alerted by some sweet natural call, came the gulls and the sea birds, squawking and circling, and they landed and made a new home and they began to build nests and they laid eggs and sat on them. And flamingoes, never seen before, flamingoes came in from the faraway lakes to the north in their red-spread glory and they circled round the new blue water and they dropped into the shallow treed shores, and they made a home too, and they laid their eggs.

But the birds who had always been in the Zambezi Valley had laid their eggs already. They laid them in the tree tops where they had always laid them. And they sat on their nests in the tree tops and watched the strange water rising up out of the river, rising up to the base of the tree, then up its trunk and then into its branches and they twittered and squawked with anxiety. At first they had unprecedented supplies of food. Driven up from the river, flushed out of their cracks and holes in the ground came the hordes of insects that never before had seen the light of day. Millions of bewildered insects floated on logs and the insects and the caterpillars and the ants even crawled right up the trees, and the birds did not have to look far at all. But then the feast dwindled, and the birds still sat on the nest, and then they had to fly far afield to find their food, and the water climbed higher up the branches. And the eggs came out and the parents sat agitatedly on the naked young birds and watched the water lapping higher and higher up to them, and they twittered and squawked and clucked. Some of the fledgelings just learned to fly in time, and many were coaxed out of the nests and they were not doing too badly at all. But then they crash-landed into the water and try and flutter and circle as their parents might, they could not get them out of the water, and they drowned. But very many never did leave the nest, for the water seeped up through the bottom and first wet their feet and then their bellies and they could not scramble up out of the nest because they did not yet have the strength. And the parents sat on the rim of the nest and on the twigs above it and squawked and fluttered and flew around in circles but they could not stop the water lapping up through the nest and then over the top of it. The parent birds flew away, and they did not know what was happening. And it seemed as if God Himself had intervened, for they flew to new places and built new nests and tried all over again.

The animals ran before the rising water of Partnership. They ran in ones and twos and in their herds. Many ran across the great broad valley and then clambered up the sides of the distant escarpment and found new food and homes. But many ran up the jungled hills and kopjes and ridges and found sanctuary there. And they ate the grass and the roots and the leaves there and for a while there was enough for everybody. But then the trees and the ground were bare and the water ran around the hills and kopjes and the animals could not get off them to find more. They found themselves living with animals they had never lived with before, and they chomped and milled around uncertainly and set about looking for food in competition with other animals with whom they had never competed before, and they stripped the bark off the trees and they pawed and clawed up the roots. The water rose up, through the trees, up the hills and kopjes, and then there was no food left, and they starved. But still the water rose every day and they crowded closer together on the islands and then their feet were in the water, then their empty bellies. Some struck out off the islands heading for the escarpment and some swam to other islands. Some made it to the mainland, but many struck out in the wrong direction and they were exhausted by hunger and they drowned. And some, like the little impala buck, refused to leave their drowning islands because they were terrified of water, and the water lapped up over their emaciated backs and they drowned. And some, like the zebras, had no sense of direction and they swam to all the wrong places, to treetops they could see in the distance, and they swam around in circles until they were exhausted, and they drowned. And some, like the sable and the waterbuck, found their big horns too heavy for their thin necks in the water, and they drowned too.

But for all the rising water they did not like being rescued.

The sun came up over the escarpment in a fiery ball, a blinding flush of vermilion then gold that tinted the white froth of the wake of the boats, turned the naked treetops into golden sticks above the water, made the dark silent water flash silver. They were in the middle of the world and the rest of the world was a million miles away.

This was a big island, half a mile long, a hundred yards wide, and over a mile from the Southern mainland. It was covered with thick dry jungle and the jungle spread out into the water so thick you could scarcely see where the land began. The game ranger in the leading boat signalled to cut down engines and the other boats followed him slowly, gingerly over the submerged treetops and through the hanging trees to the deep side of the island. As they coursed through the trees the ranger in the middle boat called 'Snake!' and everybody ducked their heads to their knees and covered their eyes with their hands. The thick snake was coiled in a high fork. It lifted up its head and reared and glared down on to the black and white backs of the men passing under it.

'Stop,' the bronze young man ordered Mahoney. 'Get us round to the other side of that tree and stop underneath it.'

Mahoney pushed the machine into reverse and manoeuvred it round to the other side of the tree unhappily.

The man pulled on a pair of motor cyclist's gauntlets and pushed a pair of goggles over his eyes. He wore only a pair of swimming trunks. He picked up a short stick with a noose on the end. 'Want to help?' he grinned.

'Sure,' Mahoney said drily. 'I'll sit here and blow it to bits with a shotgun for you.'

The man grinned again. 'He's a beauty,' he said. He caught a branch and swung up into the tree.

'Hey, I haven't got any anti-snakebite kit in the boat.'

'That's okay.' The young man reached out for another branch and he climbed higher, watching the snake.

The snake coiled round the fork, watching him, and it slid its long scaly body tighter in sections and it lifted its head and flicked its tongue. Its glassy eyes watched and its forked tongue went in and out and in and out. The man climbed up higher carefully, his head bent up, watching the snake and in one hand he held the noosed stick and with the other he felt for his hold. He got to the bottom of the branch that held the snake and suddenly the snake uncoiled itself and slithered out of the fork and twirled around the branch and out on it and over the end of the branch to the branch next to it.

'Aw, come on now, Charlie,' the young man said.

He climbed back down the branch and began to climb the new one. The snake entwined itself high up in the branch and it lifted its head and turned its neck and its beady eyes watched and its tongue went in and out furiously. The young man climbed after it.

He edged up the branch, the stick held out before him. The snake slithered round and round the branch watching him, flicking its tongue. 'Come on fella,' the young man crooned and he edged higher and higher with the stick out. Then the snake found there was no further place to go but down the branch towards the young man.

'This way, this way, Charlie.'

'He's mad,' Emie, the New York newspaperman, whispered from the boat below, 'the guy's stark raving nuts—'

The snake made a dart down the branch. The stick darted too. Into the noose plunged the snake's head and the young man pulled it tight. A tug and a flick and the snake was off the branch and it wrapped itself convulsively round the stick and its tail whisked around the young man's brown thin arm.

'Well how d'ya like that!' Emie said, and his camera was going click click. The man started back down the branch. He clambered carefully, holding the stick out from him, holding on to branches. And the branch gave way. The young man stood in the fork bent sideways, his free arm out to regain his balance, the stick waving on the other side. In a twist he got his balance back. In a swift slither the snake was off the stick. It launched itself into the air and splashed down into the water.

'Damn it!' the young man said mildly.

In one movement he dropped into the water after the snake.

The snake slithered in a circle on top of the water getting its bearings. Now it was cutting across the front of the man in a lightning wriggle, its head a little up making for another tree and the young man struck across to intercept it. Splashing, arms snaking through the water, head up so he could see what he was doing, one, two, three, four, five, six, seven, eight strokes, and he was behind the snake, its flicking tail in front of his chin. Nine, and his hand came down on the back of the snake's neck and held it tight.

He lifted his arm high out of the water, his face screwed up and puffing, and the snake's head wriggled wildly between his forefinger and thumb and it entwined itself furiously round his arm. The young man dog-paddled back to the boat with his arm up high. He slung his free arm over the side and with a twist and a heave he was in the boat.

'Open the bag, please.' Mahoney held the bag open gingerly with the thumb and the forefinger of each hand.

'Well kiss me, daddy,' Emie said, 'how d'ya like this guy?'

The young man stuffed the snake into the mouth of the bag and his fingers slipped round the snake's neck. In a flash the snake turned and spiralled up his arm. It reached his shoulder in an instant. Its head flashed and its jaws opened and it sank its fangs into the young man's lower lip.

There were cries and a scramble in the boat. The snake clung, its body tightening on the arm, its jaws clamped shut working into the lip. In one movement the young man flicked off both gauntlets. He shot both hands up to his mouth. He thrust the forefingers of both hands into his mouth, with its long horrible appendage. He opened his mouth as wide as he could and he buried his forefingers into the reptile's jaws and he prized them open. He ducked his head and wriggled his jaw and manoeuvred his lip off the fangs. Quickly he slid his hand back to its neck and thrust it into the bag. The blood was welling in his mouth.

'Snakebite serum!' Mahoney gasped. He spun to the motor. But the young man made a noise in his throat and shook his head and waved his hand. He gave a big spit over the side into the water.

'Forget it,' he said, 'i'm okay. It's the back-fanged variety and they don't shoot their poison until they have got a real good grip. He only just got me.' He had another good spit.

'We still better get you a shot of serum.' Mahoney turned back to the motor.

'Forget it,' the young man said and he sucked on his lip and spat again, 'I'm allergic to it.'

'Wal, Jesus Christ,' Ernie said.

Mahoney looked at the young man, his mouth slightly open, full of awe. 'I take it,' he said slowly, 'that you're kind of head man in charge of the snake department round here?'

The young man dabbed his lip with the back of his hand, 'I hope I didn't damage his jaws,' he said. 'He's a beauty.'

There were elephant on the island and big waterbuck and little impala and razor-tusked bush pig and genet and porcupines and rock rabbit and antbears.

'The trick,' the chief ranger said, 'is going to be to clear the deck of the small stuff so that when we turn our diplomacy on the elephant we've got plenty of room to move about in. We're in luck, the jumbo are on a big kind of peninsula on the west side. We must keep them there, out of the way. Telephone and Pakitcheni'—he turned to two black men and broke into kitchen kaffir—'your job is to keep them on that peninsula. Thunderflashes.' He passed them a handful each: 'Let them off whenever they try to come back on to the main island. There is only a female and her calf so I think she'll be happy to stay there for a while away from the tumult.'

The two black men nodded.

'And if she really wants to get back and she charges, Nkosi?'

The boss pulled his earlobe and grinned. 'Jump,' he said, 'into the water and make like a fish.'

He turned to the others. 'Now here's what we do …' he said.

They climbed out of their boats, seventeen men, black and white, and waded ashore through the trees. On their shoulders they carried big bundles of rope nets and they followed the boss up on to dry land, then through the hot dry jungle. Buck scattered before them, big waterbuck and little impalas bounding high and gracefully, and bush pigs ran on their stubby legs grunting and snorting and kicking up the hot dry dust. They came to a narrower neck in the island and the boss called a halt. They unrolled the nets and they joined them together and they strung them across the neck, fifty yards wide and fifteen foot high. Emie found himself a hidey-hole behind a big tree near one end of the net and he carefully erected his camera and dug and barricaded himself in. Ferdie, the London newspaperman, very sensibly climbed a tree and tore a hole in his pants.

'Never mind, Ferdie, it's tax deductible,' Mahoney said.

Two rangers and four Africans concealed themselves at the edge of the high net. The remainder followed the boss in single file down the water line to the far end of the island. They reached the end and spread themselves out in a line across the island. Then they advanced through the bush shouting and beating on cans and they drove the animals helter skelter up the island towards the nets.

The buck and the pigs stampeded across the island leaping over bushes, sidestepping round trees, swiftly bounding and careening. Over the island they sped in leaps and bounds, the men running behind churning up the dust and snouting and beating on the cans. And into the nets stampeded the buck at full tilt leaping and charging in a rising cloud of dust and shouts and the pounding of hooves and crashing of bushes and bleats of terror and angry grunts and squeals. Charged into the net, head through the mesh, horns entangled, feet entangled, kicking and tossing and grunting. They skidded and swerved and turned around and stampeded back through the line of beaters and some jumped very high and clean over the high net, their legs and their bodies in one beautiful straight line. And from out of the bushes charged the gamesmen and pounced on the creatures fighting with the net, and grabbed their legs and held them down and tied them up. On ran the beaters coming up from the rear, each man for himself, throwing himself this way and that to catch a little beast, swerving to intercept, diving into the furious mass of pounding hooves and contorting kicking bodies. And the air was full of the grunts of men and animals and the swirling of dust and the crashing of bushes and bodies. For three minutes the pandemonium reigned, then the grunts and the kicking and the squeals and the dust settled down. And they counted their bag: five quivering impala, one doe waterbuck, one treacherous pig, fourteen deep scratches and one gored leg. Many animals had escaped.

'I vote Ferdie to catch the porcupines,' Mahoney said.

They picked up the frightened animals and draped them around their necks and they carried them to the boats. They tied their legs and they laid them exhausted from shock and malnutrition in the holds of the boat like cargo, then they went back to the nets and back to the foot of the island and they started all over again. They beat through the bush again and again. It took until noon to catch the fifteen impala and the three wild pigs. Of the bigger animals, only the waterbuck and the elephant were left.

They moved down the battered island in their line, spread out and beating the ground and beating their cans and shouting, and the tired waterbuck cantered wearily before them, head up and ears and tails flicking and the calves cantering bewilderedly next to their mothers in the dust and the old ram with his big horns keeping between the men and his does, snorting and kicking up the earth. But he was tired too. Through the bush they were driven relentlessly, not knowing what it was all about, and then again they came to the end of the island, to the water's edge. And they milled round the end of the island at the brink of the water, panting and their rumps trembling and sniffing the air and looking back and sniffing, their ears all cocked forward, looking from the bush behind them with its torments and the great stretch of water before them with its terrors. The men emerged out of the bush at a dusty trot, still shouting and beating their cans and they closed in and formed a semi-circle around the tired waterbuck, and the old ram snorted angrily and the does looked this way and that with their big eyes, trembling, and the calves milled and bleated in the inner circle of their tired hungry frightened mothers. And still the men came clattering closer and closer and there was no escape.

The old ram looked out across the water with his nostrils wide and his ears cocked forward, and he snorted and pawed the water uncertainly and he looked round at the men again. He went hesitantly into the water a few feet and sniffed and snorted and looked back again. Then he came out of the water with his knees lifting high and he trotted in a circle round his cluster of does and snorted and dropped his horns and pawed the earth and pretended that he was going to charge the line of men. Then he saw it was no good, he trotted back around his does, snorting the whole time, and he went back into the water a few yards with his legs lifting high. He went out farther than last time and he stood poised with his head and horns up and his nostrils flared and he looked out over the water again at the long dark line of the southern bank, a mile away, and he quivered. His does followed him a little way into the water and they stood milling around and watching him and then turning back to look over their shoulders at the dusty clanking chanting line of men. The ram took another two high steps forward into the water, and the water was touching the hairs of his belly and he shuddered. He looked back over his shoulder once more and now he saw the motor boats coming edging round each side of the end of the island too, cutting off his last avenues of retreat back on to the island. The old ram filled his lungs and gave a sort of whinnying snort of decision and announcement and he took one more look at his does, he took two more big steps into the water, then he lifted both his front legs and he plunged out into the lake. And his does took one last look too and trotted and then they jumped after him, and the little calves bounded beside their mothers with their noses stuck up in the air and their big little ears flapped back and they jumped in too. The line of dusty men on the banks cheered and the two laden motor boats beached and picked up some of the men, and then they sped after the buck to herd them across the treacherous water. The buck swam ahead in a cluster, head up, ears up, the does on the outside, the calves on the inside, nostrils flared, heading for the line of trees a mile away. The motor boats with their cargo came behind. The old ram swam ahead leading the way, but he looked over his shoulder at his does many times, and then he went to one side and slowed down and let them overtake him, then he swam beside them watching the hindmost doe and her calf. Twelve hundred, eleven, ten, nine hundred yards, and the trees still seemed a long way away.

The cluster of buck swam ahead with the ram, and the doe with the calf dropped farther and farther behind. She was tired and her calf was exhausted. They swam on, failing, their heads up but the water was smacking into their nostrils, the little calf was having a hard time keeping up with its mother and it began to drop behind. The mother took a deep snort of air and blew up her lungs and chest like a horse being saddled and trod water and waited. He caught up and they paddled on, but the little buck was very tired and it was still a long way to go and the others were far ahead. Then the little calf did something man had never seen before. His neck was very tired from holding his head aloft and the water was smacking into his nostrils and he could hold it up no longer. The little calf lifted his tired neck once more and he dropped his head down upon his mother's neck. And they swam on through the water, side by side, with the young leaning on the old.

The ram was glancing back over his shoulder at the two stragglers. Three hundred yards to go, the doe was very tired and her neck ached and the water was smacking into her nostrils too. The old ram was tired also and his neck was aching from keeping his head and his heavy horns aloft. But he kept looking round at his fifth doe, and then he turned round and swam back to her heavily. He got behind her and kicked her with his knees and snorted and chased her and encouraged her and she put her ears back and she blinked her big sloe eyes and kept swimming. But she was very tired and the shore was still a hundred yards away. She swam slower and slower and her head dropped lower and lower. She blew herself up with air to tread water and rest but then her head dropped lower and it was better to try to keep swimming. The ram nudged her from behind, but her nose kept dipping in the water and the nose of the calf resting on her neck was dipping under also. And the big old ram coughed and sneezed and blew his lungs up and lifted his horny head high. He struggled up alongside her, and then a little ahead of her, and she lifted up her head with one last effort and she dropped it on to the big broad wet tired neck of her mate.

So they swam on for the line of trees, side by side from biggest to smallest, on they swam, while the doe and the calf rested their heads. Fifty, forty, thirty yards to go and the big ram blew himself up again and again and went slower and slower. But his neck was aching very badly and he was very tired and his head sank lower. He gave a big snort and he jerked it up again and he paddled on with his nostrils wide open, heaving, but his head sank lower again. He jerked and sank and jerked and sank and he was going very slowly now. He was only twenty yards from the shore and the doe lifted up her head and took it off his neck and she swam beside him with the little calf still puffing and panting and resting on her.

But the ram was going very slowly now and his head was very low in the water. The doe and the calf swam ahead for the land and the big ram floundered after them. He snorted and puffed and blew water out of his nostrils and he shook his head and he kept paddling and he humped his back and he tried to blow himself up with air. His nose dipped under the water and he humped and shook it free and threw his straining neck up and his eyes rolled wide in his furry head, but his nose crashed under the water again.

There were only fifteen yards to go before his hooves touched bottom. He lifted his head and kicked again, but his head splashed back. He bellowed and the water frothed about his head and bubbles came out of his nostrils. Only fifteen yards to go. His horny head crashed back under the water and his hooves splayed the water underneath. They hit branches and for one wild moment the old ram thought he had touched bottom. But it was not the bottom, and his hooves caught in the branches and he kicked and pawed, but they were like a weed clawing him. He shook and he lifted his weary sodden head once more and he humped his big back and he gave out a bellow. He shook his head and snorted in air through his wide wet nostrils and then his head crashed down to the water again.

The old ram gave one last heave. He lifted his face out of the water and shook it weakly. The drops flew off his wet furry face and off his heavy horns. He gave one last try and snorted and he sucked in through his nostrils. His head dropped back with a loud splash and the old ram sucked in water and he sank. He sank like a stone and he did not come up again.

The does and the calves stood on the hot dry ground under the naked trees. They dripped and trembled and the calves fell down and lay panting and shivering. The does heaved and sucked their breath back and stamped their trembling legs and the water dripped off them on to the dry dust. The cocked their ears and they looked around and they sniffed the air. They looked around for their ram and they looked back at the water and they sneezed and coughed and snorted. They looked all around for him but he did not come out of the lake. They huddled and milled around for a long time, then the calves got back to their feet and shook themselves, and the does sniffed the new hinterland. Then one by one and then all together they began to shuffle off, and their calves trotted beside them, sniffing and snorting.

Chapter Sixteen

Now, a braaivleis dance was not an everyday affair at Kariba because you can't dance very enjoyably without women and there were very few women at or near Kariba. But this braaivleis had been widely advertised for months and every woman within a fifty-mile radius of the Wall was coming, and many from farther afield. Farmers drove a hundred miles to that braaivleis, from as far north as Lusaka and as far south as Karoi and as far east as Chirundu. The three white policemen at the new police post at the jungle township of Kariba had arranged the importation of every female telephone operator and postal clerk from Karoi, all two of them, and every off duty nurse from Sinoia Hospital, and anything else in a skirt they could scare up. They bounced and churned and wound over the rough dirt track that twisted down the side of the escarpment, hooting at elephant and scattering buck and monkeys and the shoreline near the dam wall was sprinkled with tents. And the police organised half-a-dozen convicts to clear a level patch of ground of its stubble grass and a tarpaulin was spread on it for dancing and there were two booze tents, and a fat ox and three sheep were slaughtered and in the late Sunday afternoon the two long trenches began to smoke and then leap in the sunset and the hurricane lamps in the tents were lit and the gramophone began to grind over the African sunset and the people began to roll up, engineers and Eyetie workers, farmers and policemen and the pressmen and tourists, a hundred and fifty men and thirty-three women. There was much jostling round the booze tents, and laughter and noise and every woman was dancing. It was dark and the braaivleis was in full swing by the time Mahoney and his boatload of Noahs arrived from over the black water, very high.

Mahoney and the boys had been drinking since late afternoon, ever since they had finally succeeded in getting the elephant and her calf off the island and across the lake to the mainland. It had been a hell of a job. The female would not take to the water because of her calf, despite the thunderflashes they tormented her with. After nearly being trampled to death a dozen times, they had succeeded in separating the calf from its mother, and fifteen sweating grunting shouting men had tugged and goaded the squealing struggling three-ton infant into the water and then they had towed and shoved it out into the lake. Then big mommy had discovered the abduction and she had charged the water like a tank after her offspring, flapping her great ears and trumpeting, and so they had induced the two beasts over the water.

Mahoney ran the boat aground on a treetop on the lakeshore near the braaivleis, and the boat keeled over and eight drunken white men and Samson Ndhlovu toppled into the water. Great shouts and splashes and thrashing from the discommoded Noahs and roars of laughter and boos and cheers from the braaivleis. The Africans gathered in the darkness whooped with delight, and their white teeth flashed in the firelight and they clapped heir hands. The eight white men waded ashore, slipping and tripping and Samson dragged the boat in. They made their way dripping and laughing up to the booze tent. Mahoney teetered a little as he lifted the cold bomber of beer to his mouth and grinned around at the jollity about him, taking stock. Women! God, he was hungry for women. He hadn't slept with one in six months, more. But not only the flesh of woman: the presence of woman, the soft female gentleness of woman, the womanness of woman – that's what he wanted. Someone to love.

A hand touched his shoulder.

'Yes, induna?'

'Nkosi,' Samson shuffled once 'I have need of money.'

Mahoney put his hand into his pocket and brought out two wet pound notes.

'Be back here by dawn.'

'Yebo, Nkosi! Thank you, Nkosi!'

Samson loped away delighted into the night, towards the native labour compounds.

Someone to love. Mahoney put the beer bottle to his lips and tilted back his head and looked down his cheeks at the dancing space.

Then he saw her. He pulled the bottle down sharply. He saw a tall willowy girl, with long straight golden hair, dancing. She was doing the rock and roll and her hips swung gracefully, and her breasts shook a little.

Those breasts. She had high cheekbones and heavy eyelids and a wide red mouth and her face was composed. Then her partner caught her eye and grinned at her and she smiled back brightly, politely, an unhappy woman trying to be gay. Her partner swung her away from him and her hair swept round her neck and her smile was gone.

Mahoney watched her intently. An unhappy lonely beautiful woman dancing in a crowd, a waif, a lonely lovely woman in need of loving. He could not take his eyes off her, a fascinating woman: Jake Jefferson's tart.

The music stopped, they moved to the edge of the canvas. The man talked jovially, intimately to her, she smiled and listened. He said something and turned and hurried away to the booze tent. Mahoney's heart knocked. Now was his chance. He was no good at making passes at strange women. He was drunk enough to try. What do I say? Supposing—but it was now or never. He took a breath and walked resolutely over the canvas to her. She had her head bent studying a fingernail.

'Excuse me—'

She started. She looked up into his lean bristly face with its eyes very blue against the brown skin and the hair matted from the water and the clothes still sticking to his body. Mahoney was smiling his most charming smile. It belied his nervousness.

'Will you dance with me?

'I'm afraid that—'

The music started. Mahoney heard it with relief. He grabbed her hand firmly and led her on to the canvas. Thank God it was a slow foxtrot. If it had been rock and roll he would have been sunk. He put his arm around her waist and pushed her out into the centre. She did not resist. She wanted to be led.

'Your name is Suzie. Suzanna something.'

She leant back in his arms.

'Suzanna de Villiers. How do you know? And yours?'

'Joseph Mahoney.' She leaned back in his arms and looked up at him.

'Joseph Mahoney!' She half-closed her eyes and studied him. 'The great Joseph Mahoney—'

Mahoney was surprised.

'You once rescued Jake Jefferson from a tree during the big flood.'

'Ah—'

'The story is all over Salisbury and Bulawayo. Everybody has heard of Joseph Mahoney.'

'Really?' Mahoney was pleased with his credentials. What a break. 'Actually,' he said, 'I didn't rescue him, he jumped into the river and I picked him up. He was really most courageous.'

'Oh,' she said. Mahoney detected the flatness.

What to say next?

'What happened to Jake Jefferson?'

'I was going to marry him.' She looked at him and then said, to stop him asking questions, 'But it didn't work out.'

'I see.'

He looked into her eyes. Blue and deep and hard. My God, he wanted to say, never mind, I'll love you, don't weep inside any more. I'll love you, I'll make you safe and whole and you'll make me safe and whole too. I love you already—

The record was an old Charlie Kunz. Suddenly the foxtrot changed to jive and Mahoney was sunk. He didn't even try.

'Look, I can't do this—'

He was not even momentarily embarrassed. It was a godsend. He took her hand and led her firmly off the canvas through the crowd and down towards the lakeshore.

'Where are you taking me?' she said, but she did not resist.

'Here.'

He pointed to a log at the edge of the water, and she sat down and he sat beside her. The braaivleis was a hundred yards away through the dark trees. She looked out over the silver water and he looked at her profile and he wanted to put his arms around her and kiss her, and tell her he loved her already, that everything would be all right now. He wanted this waif girl girl girl in his bed and beside him in the morning and walking about his bedroom in her nightie brushing her long hair and having breakfast with him. And never being lonely again.

She turned her head to him and rested her chin on her hand and said: 'Why do you stay here?'

Mahoney took a breath.

'Look.' He waved his hand over the water. The moon was up and the great stretch of water was silver black and silent and vast and the islands were bushy black and the trees poking up above the water were sad and bare. She nodded.

'It's beautiful.'

'Yes, and sad.'

She waited.

'Sad because it's dying. A great chunk of Africa is dying.' She looked at him.

'And you want to hold its hand,' she said.

Mahoney nodded. He looked at her, then he stood up slowly and he reached down and pulled her up to him. He slid his arms round her and pulled her hard against him. She looked at him steadily and then she yielded and she kissed him and she could feel his mouth quiver. And he felt a bubble of joy in his chest because he was no longer lonely.

'Suzie?'

'Yes?'

'I do believe I love you already.' She leaned back and looked at him, her eyes very serious. She nodded.

'Isn't it funny—' Then she sank back against him and she shook. 'Oh-oh-oh.'

Somebody trod heavily through the bush towards them.

'Suzie?'

'Scram,' Mahoney said loudly. 'Suzie, our transport is leaving for the airstrip right now.'

It was the plump young man. He sounded very injured.

At first light Mahoney was still awake. He lay on top of his sleeping bag, under his mosquito net and watched the first tinges of grey above the black line of the escarpment getting greyer. Dying, dying. Joseph Mahoney, twenty-six, nearly twenty-seven, unemployed, sentimentalist, kaffir-lover. Ditherer. Wanting to stop the clock, wasting time wanting. Lonely, hungry for love. Suzanna de Villiers lonely, lovely, hungry for love, sweet sad beautiful Suzanna four hundred miles away now.

You can't stop the clock. You can't stop the Batonka ceasing to be Batonka and wearing trousers instead of loin cloths, and listening to the voices of politicians on their saucepan radios, instead of the voices of their ancestral spirits, and drawing their water from steel pumps instead of praying with the Sikatongas.

And Joseph Mahoney knew he was not much longer for the valley.

Part Three

Chapter Seventeen

October is called Suicide Month.

In October the hot bush has not had rain for eight months. The bleak dry winter has gone and the flat bush is brown and the cattle are thin and the dams are dry. Spring has come and gone and the bush is hot again, but there are no new green things. By October the summer has come and the sun rises early into a merciless blue sky and it beats down on the shimmering brown flatland and the farmers' dams are hard and cracked and the earth is dry dust and the bush crackles and cries out, and the cattle stand with their heads down. Hot, fiercely hot, the sun a great dry merciless fire in a hot blue merciless sky. In Bulawayo the sun glares blinding white on the buildings, hot on the wide black roads so the tar melts and you screw up your eyes when you cross the street and your shirt sticks to your back and when you get home and peel off your socks your feet stink. When you get home you take off your suit which smells dank and you put on short trousers only, but the floors are warm underfoot and you daren't stand barefoot on the verandah where the sun has been shining. There is almost nothing to do but to go to the fridge and get out a cold beer and slump on to the couch and drink, or go out to the air-conditioned cocktail bars or to the Club and drink. If you live in the suburbs you can at least look out on to your garden while you drink your beer, but if you live in the flats you look out on to the hot dry streets and on to the hot shimmering red rooftops of the houses and their dusty backyards and on to the hot sanitary lanes where the garbage cans sit and the African servants forgather squatting in the sun and talking and picking their noses, and on the pavements the dust sticks to the dogs' urine patches. In the offices the men sweat in their suits and the office girls perspire between their legs, and the cars parked in the streets are too hot to touch. In the courts the lawyers and the magistrates and judges sweat under their gowns and sweat trickles down from under their wigs and the courtrooms are filled with the smell of Africans sweating. In October people in Matabeleland are irritable and they drink more and every day everybody looks up at the hot blue sky and says: Wish it would rain.

The High Court stood on top of a small hill in flat Bulawayo. It was an impressive building, looking rather like a fort with a big green copper dome. From its upper windows you could see the town spreading out flat to the east, the hot wide black streets of midtown, wide enough to turn a wagon drawn by sixteen oxen. To the west, far away to the west you saw the miles and miles of hot white square houses of the African townships laid out clinically in hot straight rows. And beyond the suburbs to the east and the township to the west were the hot brown shimmering horizons of flat bush, stretching away to infinity.

The Criminal Court was full. High up on the bench sat the judge in his hot red robes. At the foot of his bench, in a wig and with a black gown over his suit, sat the registrar. He was Joseph Mahoney. He had pushed his wig forward over his forehead, almost down to his eyebrows. He leant forward slightly in his chair, his elbow on the arm rest, his forehead resting on one hand. On the table in front of him stood the documents of the trial, the exhibits, the bloodstained shovel and in a sack at his feet was the skeleton of the deceased with chips hewn off the neck vertebrae, which showed that she had her head chopped off. In front of his table, a few paces away stood the bar where the two advocates sat in their wigs and gowns and butterfly collars. Behind them in a big wooden box stood a policeman and next to him stood the accused, a little wizened black man with frowning eyes and short hair turning white. He wore prison clothes and he was on trial for his life. And behind the dock were rows of public benches, crowded now with black sweaty faces, listening to the words of the red-robed judge sitting high up on the bench behind Mahoney.

From where the judge sat it looked as if Mahoney was resting his head on his hand listening to the judgment. Mahoney was not listening. He had listened to the trial and he knew what the judgment was going to be. He was asleep and he had been asleep since the judge had begun to speak. Mahoney had been the judge's registrar for nine months and he had perforce learned the art of sleeping sitting up. Mahoney slept in Court whenever he could safely do so, because he studied late into the night for the Bachelor of Laws degree.

His face was no longer lean and brown. It was fatter and it was white and he had shadows under his eyes. His hand frequently trembled and his fingers were stained with nicotine and every morning his tongue smarted and he coughed a great deal over his first cigarette.

The judge paused after each sentence so that it could be interpreted to the little black man in the dock.

'To sum up, then. I find as facts proven that you suspected your second wife of committing adultery. You suspected this for a long time, you spoke to a number of your tribesmen about it, asking them for advice and for confirmation of your suspicions. I find that you did go to consult Siamanga the witch-doctor to learn if your suspicions were well founded and that he threw the bones and purported to divine the answer and that he in fact did purport to confirm your suspicions. You decided to kill her and you thereafter in accordance with a preconceived plan lay in wait for her in the bush with the shovel, exhibit two. I find that as she came past you leapt out at her and belayed her with the shovel, and eventually chopped her head off with it. In short, I find that all the elements of the crime of murder are present in this case. Your counsel has argued on your behalf that extenuating circumstances exist in this case which would entitle me to pass a sentence other than death. He has urged on your behalf that you are a simple man, outraged by the adultery of your second wife and spurred on by your belief in the witch-doctor. I regret I cannot agree. You planned this murder, you were not consumed by a sudden passion. Nor do I consider your belief in witchcraft a mitigating factor. People in this colony must realise that crimes committed in the name of black magic are the more heinous because of it, not less so. We cannot have people being accused and punished on the mere words of witch-doctors. I find your reliance on the word of this so-called witch-doctor an aggravating feature. You had no other evidence of the deceased's adultery. I conclude that there are no extenuating circumstances in your case. Accordingly, in law, I have no option as to the sentence I must pass.'

The judge glanced down at Mahoney and waited for him to stand up and perform his duty. Mahoney did not move. The judge cleared his throat, but Mahoney did not move. The counsel began to cough at him.

'Mister Registrar,' the judge whispered down at him.

No response from Mr. Registrar.

'Mister Registrar!' The counsel coughed louder.

'Mister Registrar!' and the Court shorthand writer leant over and nudged Mahoney.

Mahoney was on his feet in a flurry. He blinked around guiltily and took a deep breath.

'Silence in Court!' he shouted.

He darted from his chair. He scrambled up the steps on to the judge's platform and darted for the judge's door. He flung it open and stood back quickly and blinked expectantly at his master.

The judge stared at him and sighed. He lifted his arm petulantly and motioned Mahoney over to him. 'The death sentence,' the judge hissed, 'I'm terribly sorry, milord.'

Mahoney turned from the throne and climbed quickly down to his seat at the foot of the bench. He stood up straight and cleared his throat and straightened his wig.

'Mister Interpreter,' he intoned. 'Tell the accused that he has been duly convicted of the crime of murder. Ask him if there is anything he has to say, or if he knows of any reason why the Sentence of Death should not be passed upon him according to Law.'

Mahoney sat down with relief.

The black man listened attentively, frowning very much. He

thought hard, then he shook his head at the interpreter.

'I have nothing to say milord,' the interpreter said. The judge leant forward.

'Mister Interpreter, explain to the accused that this is a very important moment. If there is anything at all he would like to say, now is his chance to say it.'

Mr. Interpreter said 'As your Lordship pleases' and he relayed the question to the little black man. The black man frowned and thought again. Then his frown lifted. He spoke earnestly to the interpreter. The interpreter listened solemnly and then translated literally:

'I wish to thank the Mambo for putting on his red clothes and going to all this trouble just to hear my case. I am very sorry for the trouble I have caused the Mambo.'

Mahoney closed his eyes and shook his head. Jesus. The judge nodded. 'Anything else?'

The black man nodded his head politely. 'Yes, I have something to say.'

'Yes?'

'I wish to ask the Mambo to hurry up and hang me because then I can hurry up to my wife. I think she is still doing the same thing in heaven.'

The judge looked at the little man. 'Anything else?'

The little man shook his head and the interpreter said: 'No thank you, milord.'

The judge looked down at Mahoney and Mahoney turned in his chair and looked up at the judge. The judge nodded. Mahoney stood up and addressed the Court.

'Hear ye, hear ye, hear ye, all persons are charged to stand and keep strict silence while the Sentence of Death is passed upon the prisoner at the bar.'

The interpreter sang out the translation. All the people in the courtroom stood, his Lordship, the registrar, the counsel and the public. The judge opened a volume of statutes on his bench and he read slowly.

'The sentence of the Court is that you be returned to custody and that the Sentence of Death be executed upon you according to Law. And may God have mercy upon your soul.'

The little black man stood looking at the judge while the interpreter translated the sentence to him. Then he lifted up his bony black arm and saluted in respect. The judge blinked and he sat down. The prisoner was led from the dock down the stairs into the holding cells below the courtroom.

The judge sighed.

'Court will adjourn until ten a.m. on Monday,' he said tiredly.

'Silence in Court!' Mahoney shouted and he moved out from behind his table. He mounted the platform and opened the judge's door for him. He closed the door and returned to his table. He selected a warrant from a drawer and began to fill in the details of the prisoner. The warrant had a black border round it and it is called a Death Warrant. He signed it.

Mahoney went upstairs to check in his judge's chambers and he found, not to his disappointment, that the old man had gone home. He took off his jacket and collar and he descended the stairs from the judge's chambers down to the big oak-panelled library below. It was a handsome library with shelves and shelves of books and there were red velvet curtains draped over the windows and on the walls there were portraits of old judges.

The library was hot. It faced west and the hot afternoon sun beat on the stone walls and windows. It made Mahoney's nerves prickle as he walked into it, his footsteps ringing lonely and hollow over the warm parquet flooring. The library was a hot dry tongue-smarting hungry place for Mahoney. It saved him a little bit of money but he hated the place. He always felt hungry and feverish when he entered it. He was hungry because he did not eat properly. Samson made his breakfast in the morning but Mahoney felt too rough to eat at seven. His head usually ached and he was still half asleep and his tongue smarted from too much smoking whilst he sat and burned the midnight oil of the night before. Breakfast at 7 a.m. nauseated Mahoney and in the end Samson simply put a fried egg between two slices of bread, put it in Mahoney's briefcase and he ate it later at the office. By noon Mahoney was famished and his tongue ached from his injudicious smoking. At lunch time he went out and bought two meat pies which filled him up and which he ate while he studied in his office for the hour. He did not go to a restaurant because he could not spare the time and because the restaurants he could afford did not give him enough to eat for his money. And he hated the hot walk to these cafés and the crowds that were always in them, he hated the Coca-Cola signs with their luscious rosy-cheeked girls the likes of which he had never seen in the flesh, the monstrous chromium Aggi Coffee machines spewing steam, the gay, badly painted murals of coconut palms and blue lagoons when he knew there wasn't a blue lagoon for a thousand miles; he hated the juke box that constantly proclaimed that life was a lot of fun, that we should rock rock rock around the clock to-ni-i-i-i-ght. He hated the sun burning down on his suited back as he walked back to the office still hungry, he hated the burn of the cigarette on his tongue after a quarter of a meal. So he ate two meat pies in his office, which filled him up, and he did some swotting. Sometimes he went to a bar and bloated himself on four shillings' worth of curried chicken giblets and rice, lots of rice, which made him feel full, good and full. But he still felt feverish when he entered the High Court library at the end of the day. His tongue still smarted and the palms of his hands were peeling and they were itchy and sweaty.

He saw his table in the far corner of the library littered with his books and his notes. And Mahoney wanted to cry out and charge the table, kick it and throw books at it and tear up his notes and scream. And he wanted to run out of the library down to the nearest bar and order himself a row of cold beers and flush his system with them, fray and soften up the hot dry-scabs on his soul and his smarting tongue, fill his belly with the balm of beer. Like every other sane person was doing at this moment in this desert.

Mahoney leant against the bookshelf and held his head.

'Oh Jesus, Jesus, Jesus.'

He sat down and he undid the buttons on his shirt and he kicked off his shoes, and he took out his pen and opened his notes. Automatically his hand reached out for his packet of cigarettes and he lit one. It burned his tongue. He put his hand inside his shirt and scratched the hot red nervous heat rash and then his hand went down to the back of his knee and he scratched the heat rash there through the dank material of his suit. He glanced up at the clock on the wall. Five o'clock. Three hours to supper, and another five hours' work thereafter and he would finish his night's quota.

Chapter Eighteen

Bulawayo is a pretty bloody name for a town to have, but then Bulawayo is a pretty bloody town. Bulawayo means Place of Slaughter, and Mahoney was wont to say: Man, it slays me. From the living-room window of his flat in Fort Street he looked across the dirt-red corrugated-iron roof-tops of the red brick houses in the brown dirt yards where fat unlovely housewives in slippers and curlers bawled out tattered native servants, where snotty-nosed children played with broken toys and swung on swings made of motorcar tyres: he looked down on to sanitary lanes where the dustbins stood and where servants gathered to squat on their haunches and chatter and pick their noses and gamble and play their portable radios, he looked on to the back doors of the servants' quarters where the windows were dirty and broken and the panes patched with cardboard: at nights there were candles burning behind the windows and from within there came the jumbled cadent monotonous rise and fall of cracked records played on old gramophones, the murmured jumble of singing broken by the coarse and uninhibited laughter of men and the shrill flabby laugh of their black women: he looked down on to the narrow strip of uneven tarred road flanked by dirty brown gravel where stunted jacaranda trees had grown and then given up, where the old cars of the people who lived in the red-roofed houses were parked. On the ground floor of the block of flats was an Indian merchant who sold everything from hairpins to guitars and bicycles and on the concrete pavement there were stains, and Africans gaped in the windows at the trinkets, and fat Indian children played in the gravel gutter. Beyond the red corrugated-iron roof-tops was downtown

Bulawayo where the shops and new office blocks towered up and beyond them lay the nicer blocks of flats, then the spreading lawns and hedges of surburbia and the Clubs. And beyond these, and on all sides of the town lay the vast flat bush horizons stretching to the end of the world.

On Sundays the unlovely Fort Street was still and listless under the hot sun and the chatter of the natives in the sanitary lanes was desultory and it seemed that there was nothing to do in the whole world but sit on the verandahs of Fort Street and drink beer until it was lunch time, then lie down on the slattern beds and copulate, waiting for Monday to bring something to do. If you lived on the other side of town in the nicer flats and in the lawns and between the hedges of the nicer suburbs, there was still nothing to be done with Sunday but sit on the lawns at the edge of the swimming pool and drink beer and gin-slings and play golf at the Club and then stand and sit around and drink beer and gin-slings and guffaw and then go home to sleep it off and copulate, and wait for Monday to bring something to do again. Sunday is a bad day in Bulawayo. During the week there are always the air-conditioned cocktail bars in all their different colours and subdued lighting and upholstery and get-ups where you can kid yourself it's a great life. But on Sunday even the cocktail bars are closed.

But that summer Mahoney did not care about Fort Street and the scores of arid streets like Fort Street, about the sun shimmering on the corrugated-iron roofs and the snotty-nosed children and the dogs' urine patches, the easy aimlessness of the pleasant lawns and hedges of surburbia, the vast shimmering horizons, for Mahoney was not only too busy, he was also in love.

At nine-thirty there was a short toot outside the back of the dark High Court library. Mahoney shoved his chair back quickly and ran his peeling hands through his hair and hurried through the empty bookbound hall to the back door and stepped out into the darkness. There she was, there was her car parked in the shadows. She flicked her lights once. Mahoney hurried over to the passenger side and climbed in.

'Hello, darling.'

'Hello, my love.'

She kissed him and then she pulled the lid off a cake tin. There were sandwiches and a Thermos of coffee. She watched him eat.

'You look starved. What did you have for supper?'

'Bully beef.'

'And?'

'Potatoes.'

'You can't live off that. In future I'm going to go around to your flat and supervise that boy of yours into lashing you up a decent meal.'

She watched him drink the coffee.

'How's it going?' she said.

'Bloody awful, thanks.'

'You'll pass,' she said.

'I'm not so cocksure.'

'You'll pass with flying colours.'

'I shouldn't have put so much time into that useless book. I should've started swotting earlier.'

'It's not a useless book. It's going to be a best-seller.'

'How do you know if you haven't read it?'

'Anything you do will be good. You'll pass with flying colours and the book's going to be a best-seller.'

'Suzie?'

'Yes, darling?'

'Thanks for staying in and coming round here bringing me skoff every night.'

'It's the Florence Nightingale in me. I'd do it for anybody.'

'Would you?'

'Would I, hell!'

Samson had it pretty good and he knew it. The Nkosi was, in Samson's book, an induna, a gentleman, a hunter, a good bloke. The Nkosi did not bother him, did not criticise him, all the Nkosi demanded was a moderately clean floor, no dirty dishes lying around, a bed that was made and clean clothes to put on. The Nkosi ate what was put before him and all he demanded was plenty of it. The Nkosi did not notice whether Samson was there or not. All

Samson had to say was, 'Nkosi, there is no sugar,' and the Nkosi said, 'Don't tell me, go buy it.'

Samson did not know what hit him. The Nkosi's new Nkosikazi with the long yellow hair burst into Samson's indolence like a summer thunderstorm.

'What does the boss eat for breakfast?'

'The Nkosi doesn't eat breakfast, Nkosikazi.'

'What? No breakfast!'

Samson blinked at her.

'You don't give him breakfast? How do you expect him to be strong?'

'The Nkosi say—'

'I don't care what he says. Now, every morning you cook him porridge and two fried eggs and tomato and bacon—'

The Nkosikazi had him shelling peas and scraping carrots and seasoning steak and roasting potatoes. She had him polishing floors and cleaning windows and every day he had to bring a grocery list round to her office to vet and he got minute instructions on what the Nkosi was going to eat tonight. She even had him sewing buttons and pressing suits. Samson dearly hoped that the Nkosi would not take it into his head to marry. He hoped that one day the Nkosi would say that they would go away to shoot crocodiles again.

At four o'clock the telephone rang in Mahoney's office.

'Joe, can you spare me a minute at half-past four? My car's in the garage and I need a lift. Can you fetch me at the surgery after work, please?'

After work Mahoney walked feverishly into the reception room of the surgery. There was only one man in the room, and it was Suzie's boss leaning on the desk talking to her. Suzie jumped up and closed the door behind Mahoney. The doctor came forward and took Mahoney's arm firmly.

'Suzie tells me you're trying to turn night into day and eating benzedrine like they were acid drops. Let's look at your hands.'

Mahoney left the surgery with Suzie half an hour later with his arm tingling from the intravenous injection. Suzie clutched the tonic prescription as if it were a prize she had won. Her car was parked outside, not at the garage.

And then at last, one stinking hot summer afternoon, it was all over. For five consecutive days, three hours in the morning, three hours in the afternoon, sitting alone in a big hall with a solitary invigilator, Mahoney regurgitated his learning. At five o'clock on the fifth day he walked out with ink on his face and hair and his lungs and tongue burning with nicotine, into the first bar and he flooded his jagged system with the balm of beer. Suzie came and joined him at the bar and asked him about the paper and how he thought he had done and he told her all about it and she thought he was very clever and she proposed a toast to Joseph Mahoney, b.a. ll.b., the greatest advocate and legal giant of them all, and she was so cocksure and so pleased it was all over that you would have thought she had written the examinations herself.

That afternoon the summer broke. The skies were black and there came a crack of thunder and the sky opened and down it came, hot and fat and straight and the dry brown bush was turned into a bog and the gutters of Bulawayo ran so full you could not cross them and at the intersection of Grey Street and Eighth Avenue a man took off his shirt and swam across the road.

'And now that the exams are over, what are you going to do?'

'First,' he said, 'i'm going to unwind. When in Rome do as the Romans do. We're going to go to a few of these parties, like good little Colonials are supposed to do. Bulawayo isn't such a bad little city if you just accept it and take it for what it is.'

'No,' she said, 'it's not.'

Chapter Nineteen

The year that followed was very successful and very beautiful and very happy and very gay and very passionate. Only in the end was it sad.

The success was in Rhodesia, the boom of rich young countries in Partnership, the rattle of pneumatic drills and the bangs and grunts and shouts of buildings going up and the rumble of the steam-rollers and the rattle of railway trucks carrying coal and steel and copper and chrome down to the sea, success was the thick rich ripe stench of tobacco in great golden bales and the singsong and hurly-burly of the auctioneer, success was optimism and energy in the air. 'Go north young man.' Success was Partnership between black and white, Equal Rights for All Civilised Men. Success was Joseph Mahoney, b.a., ix.b., Advocate of the High Court of Southern Rhodesia, Assistant Public Prosecutor, Magistrate's Court, Province of Matabeleland.

The Attorney General sent me on the High Court Circuit because I was unmarried. The circuit criminal sessions of the High Court were good fun in those days: there were no political crimes, no riots, no political murders, no petrol bombing of another man's huts because he didn't belong to the same political party, no burning of a man's crops or maiming of his cattle because he co-operated with the white man: it was all good clean crime, good wholesome murders and rapes and thefts. Circuit was a kind of busman's holiday in those days: I drove up in my black Government Rover into the Circuit town a couple of days before session started, and I settled myself into the local pub to get acclimatised and I read my briefs in comfort. The judge arrived the next day in his Government Humber with his police motorcycle escort and the town brass and I were there to meet him outside the hotel and we shook hands all round and went up to his suite for sundowners: the local magistrate was the guest of honour at that party, and etiquette required that we keep working on the sundowners until the magistrate left. Later in the week the magistrate threw his party and the judge was the guest of honour, then at the end of the week the judge threw his formal party and I was the guest of honour, and in between there were parties thrown by the Mayor and the local assistant Commissioner of police and the other brass, and in between, between ten and four, we tried the good wholesome murderers and rape artists and thieves. Then we drove on to the next town on the circuit.

Happiness was returning home to Bulawayo after a six-week circuit. Driving the Rover straight through town to Suzie's flat and laughing tense inside with excitement, loving every hot wide dry familiar street of Bulawayo, happy, laughing at the thought of her excitement when she saw me, her eyes going wide and her squeal of welcome and her jumping up and down as she hugged me. Running up the four flights of stairs to her flat. 'Joey!'

Her eyes opened and she dropped her hands to her knees and then she ran to me and flung her arms around me. We laughed and I twirled her round to look at her and she laughed and I reached out and squeezed her shoulders, pulled her against me and put my hand down behind her and squeezed her backside.

'Did you warn Samson I was coming home?'

'Yes, he's waiting and the flat's all ready and the fridge is full of beer and a big fat cold chicken and a bit fat cold bottle of wine—'

Wine and Suzie.

Samson beaming all over his wide black face.

'Welcome Nkosi!' as he flung open the door and we pumped hands.

God it was good to come home! The hot ugly flat, the view of the hot red roofs, and the stunted hedges and the brown horizons didn't matter.

'Fetch my bags from the black car, induna. And here's five shillings. Go to the beerhalls.'

'Thanks ver' mush, Nkosi!' beaming all over his wide black face.

'Now come here,' I said to Suzie.

'What are we going to do, oh master?' She came to me and put her arms round my neck and I kissed her. A long and succulent and sucking kiss and she worked her tongue into my mouth. I put both hands on her breasts and then I slid them over her belly and then over her soft shanks and she sucked on my tongue.

'We're going out on the town for a few drinks,' I said into her mouth, 'and then we're going to come back and unwrap that chicken and open that bottle of wine—'

'Mmmmmmmmm ...' she said into my mouth and she kissed long and sucking again.

Happiness was leaving the Courthouse at four o'clock in the hot afternoon, flushed with battle and the heat of the day and getting into the old Chev and picking Suzie up outside her office: Let's go for a drink. And we went to the roof garden on top of the new Carlton and drank cold beer as we watched the sun go down on Matebeleland, shining white and then florid on the new high white concrete buildings that were going up: or we went downstairs to the pink plush Flamingo, or across the road to the dark plush Zambezi or the red Carousel or to the high purple Vic or to the green Sheridan. Contentment was walking into the cool carpeted pinks and greens and inbetweens, the soft twinkle tinkle of the canned music and the cocktail glasses and the murmur of voices, Suzie walking cool and warm and straight and woman beside me after a hard day in Court. Contentment was taking two soft barstools under us, and snapping the fingers at the smiling black barman—

Two cold ones, Zebediah, it's been a long hot day.

Yassah!

Contentment was that first long cold sparkling swallow, the feeling Aaarrh and putting the glass down and looking sideways at Suzie, wide red lips on the glass and her eyes half-closed as she took the first cold bitter sip. Contentment was the cool of the air-conditioner beginning to soak through my suit on to my back and

Suzie putting her glass down and then putting her hand on to my knee and saying: 'How did it go today? Did you win?'

'I always win.'

She squeezed my knee and wrinkled up her nose. 'You jolly schmart, aren't you? Always win?'

'Well – almost always.' She laughed.

'Baby face. You've got such a young face, you know that. Sometimes, you don't look more than twenty not twenty-eight, you make me feel old.'

'You're only twenty-eight.'

She stroked my hair off my forehead.

'I sometimes feel old, and sometimes you look so young, like now, you always look young.'

'It's the good life I lead.'

'You,' I said. 'You don't look more than twenty-two. Twenty-two. Twenty-three, maybe twenty-five at the outside.'

True. She didn't look twenty-eight. My friends thought Suzie was twenty-two. She had that fresh blonde look.

'It's the Libra in you,' I said. 'Women bom under Libra always look good.'

Sometimes she insisted on speaking Afrikaans to me, to improve my Afrikaans; she delighted in being able to teach me something.

'You're so clever,' she said, 'I must show you that I'm better than you at something.'

'I'm not all that clever.'

'*Oh* yes you are.'

Happiness was a tall cold beer in an air-conditioned cocktail bar with a soft barstool under my bum and a b.a., ll.b. under my belt and getting known about town as a pretty hot prosecutor and people recognising me in the street. Happiness was dropping in at the Exchange Bar on the way home from Court, that old Exchange Bar with its high old Rhodesian ceiling and its high heavy old Victorian wooden counter with all the names carved on it and all the buffalo and eland and antelope heads on the walls, and shooting the bull with Max and the boys over a few cold Lions: the boys thought it was a pretty good joke on society having me as one of the custodians of the public conscience. 'The pot calling the kettle black,' they said down at the Exchange. Happiness was driving on to Suzie's flat; in Suzie's soft womanly flat, with all her little knick-knacks and things, her gramophone records, and her *Vogue* and *Harper's Bazaar* magazines and her *Reader's Digest* and her flower bowls which she filled every day, her sewing machine in the corner always with a new dress coming together. Contentment was: 'Hello, my love, go powder your nose, we're going for a drink.'

'Where?'

'Anywhere.'

'What shall I wear?'

'Anything, sexless. You look dreary in anything.'

Going into her little kitchen and opening the fridge, the fridge that always had something to eat in it, and getting out a cold beer and snapping off the cap and selecting one of her fancy glasses and wandering through with it into her bedroom and flopping down on to her bed with it and watching her get ready. Her bedroom always smelt warm and sweet and clean, of Suzie, and there were her bottles of lotions and perfumes and cosmetics and her hair-clips and her orange sticks and mascara, and when she opened the built-in cupboards there were all her dresses hanging and in the drawers were all her panties and suspender belts and bras that I knew, and it felt good.

'Aren't you going to shower?'

She had slipped off her dress and was sitting in front of the dressing-table in her filmy nylon negligée working on her face. She turned around and looked at me.

'Are we just going out for one or two drinks, or are we making a night of it? Because if we're going to be back early I'd rather bathe then—'

'I don't know what's going to happen,' I said.

'Joe, shouldn't we have an early night? We've been out late every night for ages—'

'Go and shower, darling.'

She looked at me and gave her knowing smile.

'You just want to watch,' she said cunningly.

'Go and shower,' I said.

When I heard the water splashing I climbed off the bed and went into the bathroom. There she was standing under the shower with her honey hair piled up high on her head and the water was running down her golden skin and her breasts and her belly were white against her gold. Soap on her face, and her eyes screwed up.

'God, Suzie you're lovely.'

She splashed the soap off her face and stood there to be admired and she smiled at me with the soap still running down her face and her slender neck. I lifted her chin and she leaned forward and kissed me, soft and gentle, water on her lips. I cupped her breast and it was cool and soft and wet.

I liked watching her dress. She was quite unashamed now, she liked me watching her, because she knew I liked it. She even flaunted herself a little, pretending she wasn't, because she knew I liked to watch her. She always put her bra on last, even after her suspenders and stockings because she knew her breasts were perfect, and whenever I said: 'Come here, Suzie,' she came and kissed me and petted me.

And she always put on her lipstick and mascara before her dress, so I could watch her leaning close to the mirror.

'Come here, Suzie.'

And she stopped her work and she sat poised leaning forward against the mirror with her chin stuck out and her golden hair hanging long down her golden back, one hand poised up in front of her eyelid holding the little mascara brush and she looked at me in the mirror with her good eye expressionless and then she opened the other eye and grinned at me.

'What for?'

'Come here, lover.'

And she always looked at me in the mirror for a moment more, dead serious again, still with the hand holding the brush up, then she lowered it and turned around on her little dressing-table bench on her pantied bottom and came stepping across the room on her high heels, her stockinged legs making that crisp shiny womanly brushing sound as they brushed each other and her breasts wobbled a little with each clip clip of her high heels and her eyes were loving and she stopped in front of me with her arms at her sides like a little girl waiting for inspection, playing the fool now. 'Come here—'

And she dropped the little girl foolery and she bent down over me and kissed me long and soft and sucking and her straight long hair brushed against my neck and her breasts in her lacy bra were full in front of me, cool and full and sweet in front of me, just the nipples under the lacy cups and I put my hand up whilst she kissed me, and I trailed the back of my fingers across the smooth fragrant bulges and she still kissed me and I put my hand down between her legs and trailed my hand up and down the soft secret place of her thighs between her stockings and panties, the soft olive smooth part. She kissed me while I did this, long and female, and then sometimes she pushed harder against me and I reached up and pulled her down beside me into a heap on the bed, her nose against mine and she said softly, into my mouth: 'Are we going for this drink or aren't we? This is for afters—'

Happiness was wine in the sun on Sundays.

So the summer passed and a winter, and a spring and then it was October again.

Chapter Twenty

Unhappiness came at the end of the second summer. The wetness had gone out of the earth and the bush and the grass were dull and there was dry whiteness in the blue of the sky.

I woke up and realised it was Sunday. My head ached and my eyes were scratchy and my nerves cringed for sleep but I was wide awake. I looked up out of the window and the sky sat on the earth like a big dull blue belljar. Suzie felt me move and she woke up. I swung my legs off the bed and sat up and looked at the floor. I could feel her looking at me.

'How do you feel?'

'Okay.'

She looked at me. 'You look all puffed up.'

'I feel it a bit.' 'Damn parties.'

I rubbed my tongue over my teeth and looked at the floor. I got up off the bed and pulled on a pair of shorts. I stood at the window and looked out. The street below was quiet and hot and the sun was glinting on the hoods of the cars. A little girl with dirty knees was sitting on the swing made out of an old motor tyre and a black man was pushing her back and forth. A white woman in a dressing-gown and haircurlers came out the back door and shouted 'Enoch!' and there was a shout from the servants' kia next to the sanitary lane and Enoch came out into the dusty backyard. Across the road a white man was sitting in a singlet on the verandah reading the newspaper and a black boy was polishing the Buick. And over the red roof-tops of Fort Street were the jacaranda trees of Sauerstown. Those new three-bedroomed houses on one-third-of-an-acre stands with the diapers hanging on the clothesline and the nannies pushing the prams; and beyond the long flat horizon of Matabeleland, brown now, stretching on to the end of the world.

What were we going to do today?

'It was a pretty boring party, wasn't it?'

I nodded.

'Same old crowd. Everybody the same.' She lay still and looked up at me standing at the window.

'Jane Philson has taken a great fancy to you.' I grunted. 'And her husband's got a great fancy for you,' I said.

'I'm not interested in somebody else's husband.'

I looked down at her. 'It's the same every party,' I said, 'everybody getting off with everybody else's spouse.'

She nodded.

'Listen, Suzie. I wasn't messing around with her. She just makes a bit of a fuss of me.'

'I know you weren't.'

'Are you jealous?'

'Of course I'm jealous.'

I bent down and stroked her head and then she smiled.

I went into the lounge and sat down in an armchair. Samson came through. 'Good morning, Nkosi.'

'Morning.'

'Coffee, Nkosi?' I considered.

'What the hell,' I decided, 'it's ten-thirty. Bring me a beer, make coffee for the Nkosikazi.'

Samson brought the beer and poured it carefully so as not to get too much head. He grinned at me.

'*Babbelaazi!*'

It was Zulu-Dutch slang he had learned on the mines. It meant 'hungover'.

'A little,' I said.

I took a long pull of the beer. It was cold and good and it felt as if it corroded all the muck out of my mouth. I lit a cigarette and started to cough, deep chesty spasms. Too much bloody smoking. Suzie came through in her shorts and blouse. She had good legs.

'So early?'

'It's Sunday,' I said.

She sat in an armchair and stared through the windows over the red roof-tops at the flat brown horizon.

'What are we going to do today?' I wondered too.

'We're supposed to be going to the Melks' for drinks before lunch,' she said.

'Yes.'

'Do you want to go?'

I shrugged. 'The same old faces, I'm easy.' She didn't say anything so I said: 'Do you?'

'Not really; the same old thing.'

'Yes. Good old Rhodesian custom.'

After a while she said dully: 'Let's go out into the country. We used to go a lot.'

'There's nowhere much to go in one day. You need a week-end to get to the good places.'

She sighed.

So we went to the Melks' house in the gracious Kumalo area, and we sat around the swimming pool in bathing costumes in the sun and drank beer and we talked and laughed a great deal about very little. There was very little to discuss, life was going very well. And the beer in the sun made me feel very good and sensuous and I looked happily at the women glistening in their bikinis under their suntan oil and Suzie was the best of them all.

We got back to the flat at two o'clock. I told Samson to put the chicken in the oven and to go home for the rest of the day. The bottle of wine was good and cold. Suzie had pulled her shorts and blouse on over her bikini and the wet showed through the seat of her shorts. My skin felt drugged and happy from the sun. Suzie went out on to the verandah into the sun and stood looking out over the roof-tops.

'I've got some new wine. Will you have some now?'

She looked out over the verandah.

'Might as well. That's all we do on Sundays, try a new wine.'

I looked at her profile. I decided to let it go. I uncorked the wine and put it in an ice-bucket and we sat in the sun on the verandah. I was feeling pretty good.

'Take off your blouse and shorts and sit in your bikini, Suzie.' She shook her head imperceptibly and took a sip of wine. I looked at her then I said: 'What's been eating you lately?'

She turned her head and looked at me a moment.

'Nothing.'

'Then say something!'

'What is there to say? We've talked about everything already.'

I began to get sore.

'Now what are you implying?'

'Well, what is there to talk about?' she said.

'There should be plenty for two lovers to talk about. We should stimulate each other.'

'What stimulation can you steam up in cocktail bars?'

'Cocktail bars? You speak as though that's all we ever do.'

'It is.'

Aw Christ.

'Aw Christ, Suzie. That's not true. Well, all right, we've been giving it a bit of a tonk lately. So what. I've only been in from the bush for two years and the first year I spent in hard labour over those exams.'

She nodded and the silence hung. She took a long sip of wine.

'Well, have you read any good books lately?' I said nastily.

'Not that you would consider good, no.'

'Well, why the hell don't you, then you wouldn't be complaining that we have nothing to talk about. Dickens, Shaw, Shakespeare, to name a few – what do you know about any of them?'

She didn't say anything.

'Well, when you do,' I said, 'and we still have nothing to talk about, then you can complain.'

I got up out of my chair and stumped through to the kitchen and got another beer out of the fridge. I snapped the cap off and stumped back to the verandah and sat down heavily. When I had nearly finished it the glow of the beer and the sun came back.

'I'm sorry,' I said.

She stretched out her hand and touched my knee, it's all right. Of course you're entitled to your fling. You've worked very hard.' I reached for the wine bottle and filled her glass. 'Like it?'

'It's good.'

I looked at her and she looked at me and then she grinned. She had begun to get along with the wine. She leaned over and kissed me and then slipped her hands behind her to her blouse buttons and began to undo them.

'Take everything off, Suzie.'

'You sensuous beast, you too, then.'

She sat in the chair naked, and leaned back with her eyes closed and took a long sip of wine. Her breasts lolled white on her red-gold skin.

'Suntan oil?'

'Only the olive oil for cooking,' I said. 'That'll do.'

I fetched it from the kitchen. 'You,' she said.

I poured some into my palm. I put it at the top of her chest just under her neck and then I smeared my hand slowly down over her belly and down her thighs. She lay back while I smeared her and her eyes followed mine and when I looked at her they were very deep.

'I love you, Joseph,' she said.

So we drank wine in the sun, glistening with the sun and the olive oil and the beer and the wine and we talked happily of nothing with long silences and we touched each other and we finished the bottle of wine and I said: 'There's another bottle, your turn to fetch it,' and she walked naked to the kitchen to fetch it and came back and I was lying flat on my back in the sun and I looked up at her standing there smiling glistening down at me, holding the wine, I looked at her glistening red-gold shanks and her pink belly and her pink breasts standing above me, and I said: 'Suzie, you are very beautiful.'

And she knelt down beside me and bent forward and her long straight honey hair tickled my neck and she kissed me and her nipples brushed my chest lightly and she slid them to and fro over me as she kissed me. And at three-thirty we went naked to the kitchen and she put the little frilly apron on and took the golden chicken out of the oven and the roast potatoes and I opened a can of peas and we carried it back to the sunny verandah and she arranged it on the cement floor with paper napkins and flowers and fresh wine glasses and I broke the chicken with my hands and we sat cross-legged opposite each other in the sun and we ate with our hands and pulled at the soft meat with our teeth and we drank the chill wine and we grinned at each other. And when we had finished the chicken I looked her in the eye and I lifted my hand slowly and aimed it at her nose and crooked my finger and said: 'Come.'

And she made to bite my finger and then she took my hand, we got to our feet and I picked up the rest of the bottle of wine and we left the chicken bones and the plates and the crumpled napkins and walked through the lounge into the hot bedroom and I sat down on the bed and lifted the bottle of wine to my lips and she stood with her belly next to me and then I passed her the bottle and she took a swig and then she moved on to the bed joyously and I pulled her on top of me and she flanked herself on top of me, and under me, and to the side of me and I held her pink and gold oily body: but best of all she liked it under me, flat on her back.

Afterwards I lay still and sweating on top of her, drugged with her and the wine and the sun but my mind was very clear. Then I slid off her and lay beside her with my eyes closed.

She lay still beside me for a long time and she thought I was asleep. Then she kissed my face very gently.

'A baby,' she whispered, 'I want your baby. Your baby in my belly.'

That was the first time it came into focus. Life was not wine in the sun on Sundays. It was the lawns and hedges of suburbia there outside my window, and the parties every week-end, Jane Philson making passes at me and George Philson making passes at Suzie, and the new mortgaged three bedroomed houses of Sauerstown and the Club and the pub, and the flat brown horizons.

I lay there with my mind very clear and I pretended to be asleep.

That was the second summer.

Unhappiness came in the winter.

All the warmth had gone out of the earth and the earth was dusty brown and the trees were bare and out there the horizon was very brown. We stayed mostly at Suzie's flat that winter because it was warm and she had carpets on the floor. In the mornings the sun rose joyless bright in a blue sky but there was no warmth in it and in the evenings we had our sundowners inside with the curtain drawn and the heater on. And in the evenings, the long silences between the two armchairs. Sometimes I tried to write my book but it didn't work. And there was no wine in the sun on Sundays. And another year gone.

'What do you want, Joseph?'

'I don't know. I wish I did.'

'Do you want to go into private practice?'

Private practice. Work like a nigger, decent money if you succeed. Almost bound to succeed, the attorneys know me and I'm nobody's fool in a trial and the country's booming. But work like a nigger. And for what?

For three acres out in Hillside and a swimming pool and a Rover, driving to Chambers every day, those hot-in-summer cold-in-winter Advocates' Chambers in Eighth Avenue and getting all steamed up about Potts versus Potts and Regina versus Tickey. And drive home to the three acres at the end of the day. And always those flat brown horizons. Not out there in those horizons working in the African jungle with the African people, working towards something or conserving something, not working with your hands and your sweat and your compassion and your ideals, where lions roar and buffalo snort and jumbo steamroller through the bush and black men trust you and call you Elder Father: but here, here in this little city in your hot and cold dry chambers and going home every night to your three acres in Hillside and your skin white under your white-collared shirt because there is no more wine in the sun on Sundays now you've got kids: neither fish nor fowl, neither a high-powered counsel nor a man who works with his heart and his hands: just a small-town lawyer making five, six thousand a year.

'No, not private practice,' I said.

'Do you want to stay in Government Service in the Attorney General's office?'

'God no, that's worse.'

'It's secure,' she said.

'Yes, Suzie,' I said, 'it's secure.'

She looked at me studiously with those steady blue sphinx eyes.

'Do you want to write?'

'I'm no writer,' I said.

'How do you know?'

'I know,' I said. 'I've read what I've written, you haven't.'

'I've read some.'

'Maybe fifty pages. Then you get bored.'

'Oh Joe, what do you want to do!'

I got up and went to the window and opened the curtains a little. I looked down on to the lights of the cold flat town.

'I want,' I said, 'to be in the Zambezi Valley.'

'That's impossible,' she said softly.

'Yes, that's impossible.'

She was silent. Then: 'What are you afraid of, Joe?'

I could see the lights of Hillside twinkling. I was afraid of a lot of things. I was afraid of Hillside. 'Nothing,' I said.

Rhodesia was booming. To get any kind of flat you had to sign a lease for a year. Suzie's lease had expired and there was a clause which provided that renewals had to be for a minimum period of six months.

'Joe, I don't want to renew the lease for another six months.'

'Why not?'

She didn't answer for a moment.

'I'm tired of that flat.' She looked at her fingernails, 'I don't want to commit myself to it for another six months.'

'But what are you going to do?'

She looked at her fingernails, 'I don't know. I may decide to go away for a while.'

That was the first time I was afraid. 'Go away! But – where to?'

She looked at me, her long hair hanging straight, her eyes sad.

'I don't know. Oh, I don't know anything. I haven't—haven't decided anything except that I'm not renewing the lease.'

I was relieved. 'When must you quit the flat?'

'End of the month.'

'But that's the end of this *week*!'

She nodded.

'But … when did you give notice that you weren't going to renew the lease?'

'End of last month.' She said it guiltily and looked away.

'Three weeks ago! Why didn't you discuss it with me?'

She looked guiltily at her fingernails. 'What's there to discuss?'

'What's there to discuss? Don't be a damn fool. Where'll you stay?' She shrugged.

'Private hotel, I suppose,' a little defiantly.

'For how long?' She shrugged again.

'Until I decide what I'm going to do with myself.'

I leaned out and put my fingers on her chin and pulled her face round to me. 'Suzie have you given notice at your job too?'

She stared at me a moment, and then shook her head once. I breathed out.

'Now listen,' I said. 'Okay, so you've given up this flat. You're not going to any crummy boarding-house. You're coming to stay at my place. Nobody need know and so what if they do.'

She looked at me then she turned her head away.

'Until?' she said.

I didn't know what to say.

'Well,' I said, 'until we decide what to do—'

But I never did decide.

Suzie's gear in my flat. Her flower bowls on my window-sills and her rugs on my floors and her reading lamps and her sewing machine and occasional tables and her ashtrays, all the things women collect to make their nests. It was very comfortable. And in our bedroom there were her perfumes and powders and eye shadow and her hair-clips and ribbons, all smelling of Suzie, and in the cupboard were her dresses and her panties and her bras and her stockings and her shoes and her hats. And in the bathroom her face cream and her cap so she wouldn't get her hair wet in the shower and her pink sponges and her back brush and her negligée hanging behind the door. And it was all very warm and it felt good. And in the morning Suzie getting up and sitting in front of the dressing-table in her negligée and brushing her long gold hair and sitting beside me on the bed sipping the tea and then stepping around the room in her panties and bra as she got ready for work. And coming home with Suzie in the evening and having a drink and sitting in front of the heater, or maybe going out for a drink to the Club or a pub and coming home, and then the ritual of preparing for bed. It was very good and it seemed it could go on forever. And so the winter nearly all passed and then it began to breathe of spring.

Spring is a funny time in Matabeleland. The bush is brown and the dust is dry, and the dogs' urine patches are just as black. There are no new buds in the spring, no blushing of the earth, there is no change in the red roof-tops and the lawns and hedges are as lack-lustre as before. Spring is in the bowels and you begin to think: soon it will be warm and we will have wine in the sun again.

She said: 'I gave my notice in today.'

I put my glass down. 'You *what?*'

'I said I gave my notice at my job today.'

I stared at her. She looked guiltily at her glass.

'Where're you going to work?'

She shrugged. 'England. Or Europe maybe. Or maybe the States.'

I sat back. 'Jesus,' I said.

She didn't look at me. 'What?'

'Why the hell didn't you discuss it with me first?'

'What's there to discuss?'

'What's there to discuss? Jesus, Suzie you're only living with me. You're my lover, my ...'

'Your mistress,' she said quietly.

I looked at her.

She nodded and looked at me.

'I don't want to be your mistress, Joey.'

I nibbled the skin inside my lip. I was afraid.

'What do you want to be?' I said slowly.

She looked away. I had done it. She shrugged.

'My wife?'

She shook her head. 'No, not if you don't want me.'

'How do you know I don't want you?'

She shrugged again. She said sadly: 'You'd have asked me if you had.'

'Well, I do want you,' I said.

She just looked at her glass and ran her fingers up and down the stem. Then she shook her head again.

'No, you don't, not really and truly. Maybe some time, you'll want me one day, but not now. You showed it a moment ago. You asked me what I wanted to be, you didn't ask me to marry you.'

I said nothing. She was right.

'I don't know what you want,' she said. 'I've shown you what I want, I've slept with you, I've shown that all I want in the whole world is to love you for ever. But I saw you wanted something else. So I gave you the chance. I began to go away, and you stopped me and told me to come and live with you. And I came, but you still don't know what you want.'

I said nothing.

'You dream,' she said sadly. 'You're a dreamer. You're restless. You want out. You're afraid of those flat brown horizons you're always talking about and the three acres in Hillside. I don't know.'

I kept quiet.

'But I know what I want,' she said, 'I'm almost thirty and I'm good and ready but you're not.' I could not deny it.

She said to her glass: 'I've seen you, Joey. Trying to write your book. Trying to find something good and useful to do, and you're frustrated so you drink too much. And getting irritable with me because all I want is you. You somehow feel I'm not with you, not up to you. So we make it up by drinking.'

'Balls.'

'It's true. And I don't want to marry you if you feel like that. If the only time you feel companionable towards me is when we're drinking. Or in bed. I don't want you to feel trapped and restless.'

I got angry. Even then I could have made her marry me if I had asked her. But I said: 'Well, that's fine. You have me all figured out. So we can part without regrets.'

'Don't be bitter, Joe.'

'Bitter? Me? Oh no! Me, I'm bursting out all over with bonhomie and godspeeds.'

'We've had a good trial together, Joe. And a good time. Let's remember each other like that.'

I got up. I said, 'Is this the kind of corn you read in your women's magazines? If you read anything better you wouldn't be going away.'

And I left the room and got myself a beer.

We didn't talk about it any more that night. I figured, anyway, that I still had a month to think about it.

The next evening she came home with her sea ticket.

'Train to Beira, catch the boat. Then Dar-es-Salaam, Pemba, Zanzibar, Mombasa. Mombasa – Port Suez, then Port Said. Genoa. London.'

I was staring out the window. 'Sounds okay.'

'It'll be fun,' she said. 'Then,' she said, 'I've also got a ticket Liverpool to New York.'

I turned round. 'New York?'

She nodded. I stared at her.

'Now listen Suzie. How long are you going away for?'

She looked at me steadily. She said slowly, 'I don't know, Joe. Until you've grown—' She changed it. 'Until you're good and ready.'

'I'm good and ready now,' I shouted.

She looked at me, then she kissed my chin.

'No, you're not, Joey.'

She was right. I still had a month to think. Out with two beers. We sat in front of the heater.

'You can have my rugs and lamps and things. I only want the little horses.'

'I'll pay for your things.'

'You can't.'

'I can and I will.'

'I'll sell the record player and records. You won't want them.'

'I'll buy them too.'

'Joe, I don't want to take your money.'

'You will,' I said.

She twiddled her glass and looked at the heater. 'This is awful, isn't it. Dividing the household goods.'

'Yes, it is,' I said.

'I'll buy your fishing rod and gear too,' I said.

She shook her head. 'I'll take my rod and reel. It'll be my souvenir of our happy days. It won't take much room.'

'No. The rod collapses.'

'Yes.'

'You can lay it at the bottom of your trunk.'

'Yes.'

After a while I said: 'Suzie, you'll write to me, won't you, and tell me where you are?'

'Yes.'

My nose tingled and my eyes burned.

I had a month to get used to the idea. Or to try to get used to it. Or to decide. Or something. In the evenings I waited for her to come home and I walked around the flat restlessly. As soon as she came home, we went out for a drink to avoid the silent feeling of the flat. It was better in the bar. Mostly we were kind to each other. We went to shows and I took her out to dinner. We took a week's holiday and we drove the five hundred miles to Inyanga and we took the thatched fishing cottage on the Pungwe River. The river ran clear and clean and ice cold over the rocks right outside our cottage door, and the sky was ice blue and in the early mornings there was mist like smoke on the water and in the gorge and there was frost like snow on the grass in the mornings, and on the window panes. We lay in bed in the early mornings, feeling each other warm and safe under the blankets watching the sun seep down into the gorge and melt the frost, and listened to the safe cheerful sounds of Samson building the fire in the lounge and then making tea and then the sizzling of the bacon over the wood fire stove, and we wondered why Suzie was going away.

'It's a holiday!' Suzie said, and swept her long gold hair off her face as she sat up in bed all huddled up with her breasts pressed against her knees. 'Don't let's even think about it—'

The sun came down into the gorge and melted the frost and

chased away the mist and left the little valley brisk and clean and clear and the water bubbling and we put on our warm gear and we put some beers in my knapsack and a bottle of wine and some chops and we explored the rolling Inyanga downs, tramped over the cold pink heather and through the pine and wattle forests, over the hills and we found trout streams and followed them and at midday we built a fire beside a stream in the clear cold sun and cooked our chops and drank our beer and drank our wine round the fire on the rocks beside the streams. And in the afternoons, when we were good and tired from the tramping and our cheeks were red and burned from the cold, we tramped back over the hills and through the forests to the thatched cottage at the Pungwe: sometimes I ran down the heather downs, loping over the little pink bushes and I looked back and there was Suzie skipping down the slope, skipping skippity-skippity with her hair flying and her breasts bouncing and her wide smile all over her face, as the evening mist came rolling over the hills, and there were fine cold stinging water drops in the mist and they stung our cheeks and wet our hair and we laughed, good and brisk and warm and cold and tired. And when we got down into the gorge, there was our thatched cottage beside the darkening river and the smoke was coming out of the chimney stack, and we flung open the wooden door and there was the fire roaring in the grate, big red glowing logs and the two armchairs pulled up in front of the fire and the table laid, and the smell of cooking, and Samson beaming all over his big fat black face.

'Welcome, Nkosi!'

And a hot steamy bath, the water gushing out of the woodfire cistern with Suzie's soft womany soaps and smells all around, and then sitting stretched out in the armchairs with our feet on the grate and the thatch above our heads and the fire flickering deep and warm. And the warm knowledge of the deep double bed next door.

On the last night we came home from the hills and we had our hot baths and we climbed into the old box Chev.

'Samson!'

'Nkosi?'

'Here is ten shillings. Go to the village over the hills and drink beer.'

'Yebo Nkosi!'

Samson grinning all over his face.

'But do not try to steal the Manyika women. Remember you are a Matabele and a horse does not mate with a donkey.'

Samson's belly laugh ringing out over the Pungwe Gorge.

'The Nkosikazi and I are going to eat at the hotel tonight. Do not wake us too early.' And we drove the fifteen twisty turning miles over the dirt roads through the heather downs and the forests and the mists to the old Rhodes-Inyanga Hotel, stuck up there in the forests, the grand old house that Rhodes himself once lived in, and we drank brandy in front of the great fire at the old wooden bar counter with the stuffed trout on the walls and then we went through to the big old dining-room, and as Suzie walked ahead of me in her swinging tweed skirt I looked at her and I thought: 'What a lovely girl. What lovely legs.

And we sat near the big log grate with logs as big as a man, glowing and leaping and crackling and sparkling and flickering gold on Suzie's hair and the shiny black waiter in his white starched uniform poured the wine very correctly for me to taste and then I said: 'Well, here's to us, Suzie,' and she said: 'Yes.'

And we both realised it was the last night of the holiday. We drove back to our cottage through the hills and when we passed the African village we heard drums and singing. I ran the old Chev down the steep hill to the cottage and rolled to a stop on the grass and I switched off the lights. The moon shone on the smoky swirly mist and we could see the glow of the dying fire through the cottage windows.

'It's beautiful, isn't it?' She sat still and looked at the river.

'Yes.'

'And sad.'

My heart was breaking and I turned to her. 'Suzie!'

She turned slowly and looked at me with her big heavy eyes. 'Suzie, don't go away!'

She looked deep into my eyes looking for something. But I could not say it. Then she patted my knee.

'But I must, darling dreamer.' Then she patted my knee again.

'And now to bed, my love.'

In the morning we packed up quietly. The mist was still on the Pungwe but the sun was up. The cottage was empty and closed and it looked very lonely. Suzie stood at the car door and looked back at it for a moment, then she climbed in and her eyes were wet. I put the Chev into gear and we began the lonely climb out of the gorge into the morning sun. When we got to the top of the gorge we stopped and looked down. Far below was the twisting tumbling river and the cottage in the mist.

'Oh,' Suzie said.

Then we got back into the car and we drove through the downs and the forests, past the Rhodes Hotel, and then we were on the road to Rusape, through the craggy rock country, and we didn't talk. We were both thinking: only another ten days.

We got to Rusape Village at ten o'clock. I gave Samson sixpence for a Coca-Cola, and Suzie and I went and sat on the verandah of the old hotel and had tea, very quietly. I thought of the mornings ahead, getting up in the mornings with the warm Suzie smell in the room, Suzie brushing her long honey hair in front of the mirror. And each morning would leave one less, and then it would be the last morning, and we would carry her bags from the flat to the station, and the next morning I would wake up alone and the flat would be empty.

'Suzie,' I said.

She put down her cup and looked at me steadily. 'Suzie – don't go away!'

She looked at me sadly. And then she shook her head.

'Suzie?'

'Yes, darling?'

'Let's get married then.'

She blinked. 'What?'

I was excited. 'Let's get married.'

She blinked again. 'When?' she said faintly.

'Right now! Here in Rusape.'

She looked bewildered.

'At the Magistrate's Court. Special Licence,' I said.

'But—' she stopped.

'But?'

'But – what about my hair?' she giggled faintly.

'To hell with your hair,' I said.

She looked shocked and laughed again.

'To hell with my hair. I mean: do you really want to?'

'Yes.' I felt weak and was shaking a little.

'All right, then.'

We stood up and walked off the verandah into the dirt road. The waiter came running after us with the bill and I gave him five shillings dazedly. Samson saw us and put down his bottle. I waved to him to wait. We walked down the gravel sidewalk, through the natives, towards the old Magistrate's Court. I looked straight ahead of me and I felt dazed and excited and frightened. I looked sideways at Suzie and she was looking straight ahead too. She stretched her hand sideways without looking, and took my hand and I felt it was damp.

We stopped outside the old Courthouse.

'Well—' I said 'here we are.'

She put her hand to her hair mechanically, and her hand was shaking.

I wanted to run. 'In we go,' I said soberly.

She hesitated, then she walked beside me up the steps, holding herself very straight. We walked into the Clerk of Court's office and it seemed unreal.

'Yes sir?' His voice seemed to ring.

'We want to get married,' I said.

'Yes sir. Special licence?'

'Yes. Now, please.'

'Yes sir.'

He pulled out a form and pushed it across the counter. I completed it and my hand was shaking too. 'Five pounds, sir.' I handed him a crumpled fiver.

'I'll see if the Magistrate can do this right away, sir. Five minutes please.'

He disappeared with the form.

We stood at the counter. I looked at Suzie and she was staring straight ahead.

'A flower,' she said blankly, 'I want a flower to hold.'

I looked around stupidly. 'No flowers,' I said.

'Can't I have a flower?'

'A flower—' I said.

I walked to the doorway. There was Samson standing by the car, a hundred yards away. I beckoned to him and he came running.

'Flower,' I said, 'go and get some flowers.'

'Flowers, Nkosi?'

'Steal one. Quick. Any kind.'

He looked at me strangely and then set off down the road at a run. I went back inside.

Samson came back a minute later. He had one yellow winter daisy plucked from the roadside. I gave it to Suzie. She took it and looked at it dazedly.

The clerk came back. 'This way, sir.' He beckoned through the door.

I looked at Suzie. She was white. I motioned her forward. She looked at me shakily.

'No.'

'What?' I said.

'No.'

I was in a daze. 'Why not?'

'No, Joe.' She was shaking.

'All right. But why?'

'Because. Because of the look in your eyes.'

I looked at her.

'Because we quarrel. Because you're clever and I'm not.'

The daze was turning to laughter.

'Oh.'

She looked at me and then she laughed too.

'No, Joe. It'll keep. Not now, like this.'

'Okay.'

I laughed nervously. She laughed. We both laughed in the Clerk of Court's office. The clerk looked at us. Samson was a blur. We laughed into each other's faces.

'Look at my hands,' she laughed. 'Look how they're trembling.'

'Mine too.'

'Let's go and have a drink.'

'Two drinks.'

'Six drinks.'

We turned and left the clerk. We didn't even thank him. We stepped out into the cold bright sunshine. We walked diagonally across the street towards the hotel. Suzie held out her hands again. She burst out laughing afresh.

'*Weet jy wat!*' she laughed in Afrikaans.

'What?'

'We didn't even have a ring!'

I threw back my head in the middle of the road and laughed.

Samson thought we were nuts.

The ten days went heavily. We met after work and had a few drinks quietly in the bar. We did not talk much.

'I've asked some people around for a farewell drink on Saturday.'

'Who?'

'The usual crowd.'

'Okay.'

When we went home we wondered what to do until she came to my bed.

In the last week she took out all my clothes and sewed on buttons and mended tears and darned my socks and she made a list of all the clothes I owned and pinned it up inside the cupboard door. She took my two suits to the cleaners, one at a time.

'You'll need another suit.'

'Why?'

'You've only got two. A man in your position should have several.'

'Two are enough.'

'No, they're not. I'll go down to Meikle's tomorrow and bring some home on approval, so I can help you choose one. Otherwise you'll buy something awful.'

'What's it to you how I look from now on?'

'I like you to look nice. You're handsome when you're well turned out,' she said.

She laid in a large stock of canned vegetables and fruit.

'The best place to buy meat and so forth is that little butcher on Fourth Avenue.'

'Okay. Tell Samson.'

'You can buy good cheap vegetables at that Greek next door, but I know you won't so I've laid in some tinned stuff.'

'Okay.'

When she had jacked me up, she set about her packing. We dragged out her trunk and pulled her suitcases out from under the bed. Drawer by drawer, hanger by hanger, she laid her clothes out on the bed, and then dispatched them to the suitcases and the trunk.

'This I won't need till I get to England, so into the trunk. This I won't need. I'll wear this on the boat. I'll need that—'

Into the trunk and suitcases they went, laid neatly, flat, sensibly, economically, things tucked in here and squeezed in there, a proper place for everything as only a woman can pack, even though it's impossible, because I've tried it. I sat on a chair and watched her, her long body bending and stooping gracefully. A lock of hair fell across her face and she blew it aside. It fell back and she scooped it behind her ear, and after a little while it fell back across her face again. In the centre of the floor grew a pile of things she was discarding.

'Samson can have those for his girlfriends.'

Outside it was still cold and it still got dark early, but the dry bite was going out of the night. I thought of the summer coming, the long hot summer, the Sundays and the big trout in the Inyanga streams, and the sun setting over the Zambezi, but no Suzie, and I wanted to sob out loud.

She picked up her fishing rod and pulled it apart at the connection. She looked at the pieces sadly.

'Oh well, into the trunk.'

'Suzie.'

She turned and looked at me, holding the two pieces of fishing rod. 'Yes?'

I looked at the rod and I looked at her.

'It was good, wasn't it? Fishing at Inyanga?'

She nodded. 'And the pools,' she said, 'that deep pool where we swam.'

'And the wine.'

'Yes. And the wine.'

I nodded. 'And the Zambezi,' I said.

'And the Victoria Falls,' she said, 'and that place we saw the elephant crossing the river with her baby hanging on to her tail.'

'Yes, the baby.'

I looked at her standing there, tall and shapely and sad.

'And Sundays,' I said, 'in the sun.'

She nodded.

'Yes. It was all wonderful. It's been a very good two years, Joe.'

And she turned and laid the rod in the trunk. And I thought of the summer coming, the long hot summer and the tall green grass and the wetness in the earth and the sun shining on the trout streams and the sun setting on the Zambezi and fire flickering outside the tent. And I thought of the next winter, the warm woman smell of Suzie in the room and sitting up in bed having tea and the brisk sound of her nyloned thighs as she walked around the room getting dressed and I thought: Nothing will be the same. Summer and winter will never be the same without Suzie. And no wine in the sun on Sundays.

Then she started on her little things. Off the walls came her pictures and her knick-knacks, her poster of the bullfight in Villa de Manica and her bottle opener from Inyanga and her wooden masks and carvings from Wankie and the Victoria Falls, her chunk of twisted wood from the valley, her postcards of the places we had been to, her this and her that. Off the mantelpiece and the window-sills came her collection of swizzle sticks she had hijacked from every bar we had patronised, her collection of matches, her champagne corks from memorable occasions, her collection of hotel menus, off the dressing-table came her tins of hair-clips and her bottles of lotions and her perfumes and creams, her ribbons and her nail polishes, and all the things women collect. Before my eyes she stripped the flat of everything that was hers, and the walls and the mantelpiece and the window-sills and the dressing-table stood bare and the flat and I became desolate and heartbroken.

On Saturday some of the crowd came to the flat for midday drinks to say good-bye to Suzie. The flat was rather bare and we just put two cases of beer in the middle of the floor and we helped ourselves. Two o'clock came and nobody showed signs of moving, so I sent Samson downtown to the Greek for six barbecued chickens and I went down to the Cecil Hotel and got four more crates of beer and I broke out the last demijohn of wine. Suzie was the centre of conversation and she moved about from clump to clump, passing beers and directing Samson to fill wine glasses and joking and laughing at reminiscences and promising to send postcards. She was beautiful in her going away gear. I looked at her legs moving inside her skirt and pressing against the cloth. I saw the soft fold of her legs as she sat and crossed them, the nylons making a brisk soft woman sound, I looked at her slim ankles, I thought of the soft part of her legs where the stockings ended and the garters clipped on, that smooth soft secret olive skin of that part of her thighs. I thought of her small belly, firm and soft, just a little bulge, just the right amount, with a dull line where the remnants of her summer tan began. And despair clutched at my guts. I thought: you may never make love to this woman again, last night was probably the last time you will make love to her. She will meet someone else in England or Europe or the States and she will make love to him in some strange bed in some strange town, take off her clothes and lie down with some man who has the courage to marry. And you will be stuck here in Matabeleland, going to Court every day and coming home to an empty flat, hot in summer, and cold in winter, no wine in the sun on Sundays, everything will be as dull but without Suzie and you will cry out: Why—oh why didn't I do it? And I didn't know what to do I was so unhappy. She looked at me from time to time through the hubbub and the smoke and she smiled her bright sad secret smile to say: Cheer up, darling. Twice she left the people she was talking to and went to the crate and opened a bottle of beer and gave it to me. 'Here you are, darling.'

Someone went out and got more beer and another demijohn of

wine and later in the afternoon singing broke out, like – My name is Cecil, The West Virginia Skies, Die Alabama and Bokkie Jy Moet Nou Huis-toe Gaan, which was cheerful enough. Some bright soul started a very beery solo of Red Sails in the Sunset, but when Suzie's lip trembled somebody shut him up. She came up to me through the chatter and whispered: 'Wish they'd go. I want to be alone with you.'

'Yes.'

She looked at me and her lip trembled once. 'The wine and the chicken,' she said.

I nodded. 'Suzie – I love you.'

'Yes,' she said, 'I love you too.'

And squeezed my arm and went to answer some call from the crowd.

At six-thirty we left the flat for the station. They were all pretty tight, except Suzie and me. Suzie wasn't drinking much. I had drunk a lot of beer but the glow of it had worn off, and now I was just sad.

We had taken her trunk to the station the previous night, and all I now carried was her small suitcase. She held my hands as we jostled tipsily down the stairs with a lot of noise. She looked straight ahead of her and her eyes were wet and her face was set. When we got to the entrance of the flats, she stopped suddenly and held out her hand and said: 'Feel how warm it's getting.'

There was a new warmth in the air. We looked at each other and we were both thinking of the same thing, the long hot summer that was breaking, the bush and the rivers and the camps and the Sundays in the sun, but without each other.

'Yes,' I said. I looked at her and there was a catch in my throat, and I took her arm and hurried her on to the car. The others were scattering noisily across the road to their cars. As I held the door open for her she turned back and looked up at our flat windows and the balcony, empty windows and balcony, and her mouth trembled.

'Come on,' I said gruffly and I turned her round. I started the car quickly.

I turned down Fourth Avenue, then right into the wide Main Street. The neon lights in Main Street were patchy and the road was almost empty. The Victorian shopfronts squatting amongst the new skyscrapers. We didn't say anything and as we waited at the traffic lights I looked at her and our eyes were burning. Max hooted cheerfully at us from behind when the lights turned green. As we passed one of our favourite pubs Suzie said:

'There's the Zambezi Bar,' and I said, 'Yes, good joint,' and we both thought of the nights we had spent in the Zambezi Bar, the good nights and the wasted nights we had spent in the Zambezi.

It was dark by the time we got to the station. It was crowded mostly with natives. They milled around in shabby clothes, umfazis with their piccanins, squatting on the platform eating a chunk of bread and drinking a bottle of Coca-Cola, suckling babies, carrying big old suitcases, bundles of property on their heads, jabbering. The train to Salisbury, Umtali and Beira was already in. The train smelt and looked exciting, of pastures new. We found Suzie's compartment. She was sharing it with three white women. There were photographs of the Victoria Falls and the Wankie Game Reserve and Salibury's new skyscraper skyline on the walls. I pulled open a top bunk and put her suitcase on to it. Our friends were waiting on the platform. I took Suzie's hand and led her outside into the corridor. We were alone for the first time since noon. I held her waist and looked at her, and then her eyes began to fill with tears and her lower lip curled up and she put her knuckles to them.

'Oh, Suzie—'

She wouldn't lean her head against me. She stood rigid with her knuckles to her eyes.

'Suzie,' I took her head and pulled it against my shoulder, 'I hate to see you cry.'

She sobbed against my shoulder.

'Suzie,' I squeezed her. 'You're coming back, aren't you?'

She just sobbed. I pushed her back from me and shook her hips. 'Suzie! You'll come back soon.' She shrugged tearfully.

'Suzie!'

'Excuse us please.' The corridor was suddenly full of people climbing aboard, carrying suitcases, stepping awkwardly past. We separated to let them through. The second bell rang on the station.

Suzie sniffed loudly and dabbed her eyes with a Kleenex. She let a man pass and then stretched out her hand and took mine.

'Darling. I must say good-bye to the others on the platform.'

We jostled down the corridor. The crowd was gathered at the door, and cheered. I stopped and turned to her.

'Suzie, you'll come back.'

'Yes,' she said, but we both knew it wasn't a promise.

Everybody was talking and laughing and full of beer, and giving Suzie last minute advice. She laughed and smiled brightly, and promised to write. I held my arm round her and we had to join in the banter. The third bell rang and people were milling all down the long platform and waving and kissing good-bye, and shouting. Suzie grabbed hands and gave fleeting kisses all round. I lifted her up on to the train. It gave a jolt and then a long creak.

'Good-bye, darling,' I said.

Good-bye, Good-bye Suzie, Good-bye, Happy Landings kid, Cheerio Suzie, Remember to write, See you next year in England Suzie, called the crowd.

Good-bye, yes, yes, Suzie called.

She smiled brightly with her wide mouth, but her eyes were wet.

'Good-bye darling.' I stood on the steps as the train began to ease forward.

'Good-bye Joseph, darling.'

She bent down to me and her hair fell across her cheeks and on to my face, the smell I knew so well, and she kissed me once, quickly and very warm.

The train began to roll. 'Good-bye,' and I stepped off on to the platform.

She looked at me, her eyes full of tears, and the corners of her mouth curled up for a weep, then she lifted her eyes to the crowd behind me, and waved and smiled as brightly as she could.

And she was gone.

The others went back to the flat to finish off the beer. I said I would join them but I did not want to see the naked flat and I didn't want their cheerful party talk. And I didn't want to drink beer. I had been drinking beer for over seven hours. Seven o'clock is a hell of a time to say good-bye to your love when you've been drinking beer since noon. You feel sluggish, and dyspeptic and only a little drunk, and you feel that more beer won't make you any drunker. And there was a big lump in my throat and my eyes burned and I could not face the naked flat.

I drove downtown to the old Exchange Bar. I sat up at the big old wooden bar under the buffalo and sable heads, where Suzie and I had often sat, and I drank a row of whiskies. I thought of Suzie in her green compartment with the photographs of Victoria Falls and the Wankie Game Reserve, rumbling through Africa in the night down to the faraway sea and the ship and the lovers she would meet, and then I thought of the flat I would go back to, empty and denuded and no Suzie, a lot of empty beer bottles and cigarette stubs, and old smoke, and I cried.

Part Four

Chapter Twenty-One

Beer, cigarettes and sex.

I woke up with the taste of all three very strong in my mouth. I was pretty used to that taste and that feeling these days, but this morning it was very bad. There was the dry ache behind my forehead, and when I opened my eyes my nerves cringed for sleep. I was in a strange room. Then I felt the girl against my back and I began to remember. The drinking and the strip poker and the girls. But I couldn't remember which one had her backside against me now.

It was Monday and I was in Court today, and my nerves cringed again. I got out of bed and looked at her. She looked puffed up too, and her mouth was open a little, and she didn't look very sexy now. I remembered her, but I still couldn't remember her name. I looked down at the floor but there were no dead French letters and I cursed.

I remembered it all pretty clearly now. The usual noon-time drinking at the Club, the hair of the dog that bit you on Saturday night. Beginning to feel human again on your third beer. Then Max arriving with his current doll and her friend who had just been transferred from Salisbury. And then Eddie and his doll. And we drank beer at the Club until the bar closed at two-thirty in the afternoon, by which time we were beginning to get along with the beer. The usual Sunday afternoon in Rhodesia, especially in winter. Going back to Max's cottage for more beer. Sitting round and drinking and getting bored. Then Max very sensibly suggesting strip poker. Eddie's girl a bit coy at first, getting the funks when she had to take off her bra, but we bullied her into it. Then we were all in the nude, sitting round the table and we began to play for forfeits, because there was nothing else to play for. Forfeits like doing a belly dance and pretending you're having a shower. Then we were all playing charades, then we were all dancing together and swapping partners, then we were all doing the limbo in the nude to Harry Belafonte, everybody clapping to the beat of Belafonte, and the broomstick getting lower and lower, and the girls falling on their bums, legs up in the air, and everybody laughing hilariously. Then we were all doing the Conga through the cottage. Max slipped in the kitchen and we all fell in a tangled heap of arms and legs and squeals and guffaws. Then somebody was shaking a beer bottle to make it fizz and then holding his thumb over the top and squirting everybody else with beer, then we were all shaking beer bottles and squirting each other, chasing each other round the lounge, squirting beer over each other, dripping with beer, beer running down our laughing faces. God knows what Max's furniture must look like now, then Eddie's girl collapsed, spreadeagled over the table, and Eddie pouring beer over her and lapping it up off her belly and Max jumping up and down on the settee and announcing that he and his doll Ruby were going to show us what really can be done and trying to do it standing on their heads on the settee, their legs waving in the air. Then memory sort of faded out: I remembered it was dark and cold when we got outside, and I remembered stopping at the traffic lights at Selbome and Grey.

I looked at the girl in the bed. I still couldn't remember her name. It didn't seem very funny now, with my head thumping and my hands shaking and the prospect of Court. I couldn't even remember what cases I was doing. The sun was just coming up and it was cold. I was in a flat somewhere in town. I got up off the bed and looked for my shirt. The room stank of beer and cigarettes. My skin and my hair were sticky with beer. She woke up.

'Where're you going?'

'I must go home. I'm in Court and I haven't read my cases.'

She looked at me. 'What's the time?'

'About six-thirty.' I said. 'The sun's coming up.' I put on my shirt, it smelt of tobacco smoke.

'Don't you want some coffee?'

'No time,' I said.

There was a noise of the kitchen door being opened and somebody moving around.

'That's the cookboy,' she said. She got out of bed and walked naked across the room to the door holding her head. She opened the door and poked her head round.

'Kefasi!' she called. 'Bring some black coffee, quickly, please.'

'I haven't got time,' I said. 'Have you got any Alka-Seltzer?'

'Aspirin and Alka-Seltzer.'

'Both.'

'Will you have a beer, a regmaker? It's the only thing.'

I shook my head, she was right but it was a treacherous remedy.

She brought me a glass and three aspirins. I chewed the aspirins and drank the fizzing Alka-Seltzer, swallowing the pieces.

'That was quite a party,' she said.

'Um.'

She counted on her fingers. 'Six and a half hours.'

'What is?'

'My cap. I have got to wait eight hours before I take it out.' Thank God for that.

'Keep it in till lunchtime,' I said. 'Wear it to the office.'

There was a knock at the door. 'Leave it outside, Kefasi,' she called. There was the sound of a tray being set down. Another girl's voice called from the other end of the flat: 'Kefasi, tea please.'

'I must go,' I said.

She shuffled across and put her arms around my neck and nuzzled me. It was the last thing I wanted. She smelt of beer and cigarettes. Her back was plump and her breasts were too big. Then she asked the usual: 'When am I going to see you again?'

'I'll call you tomorrow, just give me your number.'

She wrote it down on my cigarette box, but she didn't give me her name.

'How did you say your name is spelt?'

'Lilly,' she said. 'L-i-l-l-y.'

'Okay, Lilly,' I said.

'*Mary*,' she said. 'And you spell that M-a-r-y, in case you have trouble with it.'

'*Miss* Lilly,' I said. 'I was trying to be funny.'

'*Mrs.* Lilly,' she said, 'I told you that too.'

I don't like it when they announce afterwards that they've got husbands. I wanted to find out whether he was alive or dead, divorced or what, whether I was likely to find myself cited as co-respondent, but I couldn't let on I didn't remember anything, could I?

'I know,' I said, 'I must be going.'

'All right, Joe.' She smiled a little thickly.

I had to kiss her good-bye. I tried to make it one on the cheek, but she wriggled it round to the lips. Her breath wasn't very good and her lipstick was caked and dry and her mouth felt a bit rubbery.

I got outside into the cold dry sunrise. I was in Borrow Street, a pleasant avenue in summer but now it was dead and dry. We had had very little rain the summer after Suzie left. The cattle were thin and the dams were drying. I found my car and noted with relief that there were no new dents. I drove up Borrow Street into Selborne Avenue. There were lots of blacks coming into town from the locations on bicycles to work, but otherwise the streets were still quiet. A piccanin in tatters was selling newspapers. I stopped and bought one.

I looked at the headlines dazedly while I waited for the lights to change. More trouble in the townships yesterday, more gangs of black thugs of the African National Congress beating up people who didn't belong to the party, but the news glanced off me. We were getting used to the political thugs, and I felt too bad because of my hangover.

I got home and had a hot bath to get the beer and smoke off me, and I held my head under the cold tap. I still felt very bad.

My hand trembled as I opened the first brief on the table. I held my head as I read it. Halfway through I grinned, hangover and all. This would be a walkover. A rape. The facts were that Tickey, villain of the piece, had broken out of jail, and having been inside for a cool eighteen months was feeling pretty sharp. At dawn he was creeping through the undergrowth on the outskirts of town, when he came upon a footpath and who should be walking down said footpath but our Annie, the complainant. Annie was a heavyweight and Tickey got a romantic seizure. He leapt out in front of her brandishing a stone and announced that this day he was going to lay her. But – a smart cookie, our Annie. Instead of crying, 'Maiwe – Maiwe – Maiwe – today I am being killed at this place by a bad man,' and putting up a perfunctory struggle, *she* went all coy and girlish. Tickey thought he had never had it so good. Annie promptly lay down on the side of the path and hitched up her skirts. Tickey beamed all over and dropped the stone. Annie beckoned him down between her legs. Tickey got down on top of her happily. Annie slipped her hand round the side of her buttocks and gently fondled his genitals.

'What are you doing?' Tickey demanded, suddenly very nervous.

'I'm only helping you.' Annie cooed.

Show me the man who objects to that.

Then, as Tickey was getting all steamed up, Annie slipped her hand down to his testicles and grabbed them and crunched them very hard.

Tickey howled and leapt off her, but Annie hung on doggedly and gave them a good twist. Tickey hopped around the path clutching his family jewels. Annie let go and picked up the stone and carefully smote him on the brow. Then she tied him up and sat on his chest while she waited for someone to pass by and fetch the police.

Now – there's a tip.

Then I opened the next brief and I stopped grinning. Political arson. I groaned. Some case. Senseless destruction. Politically inspired crimes of violence had become common in the last six months. Black gentlemen in city clothes were taking to the bush, rounding up the tribesmen, and telling them they had to join the Congress and form committees and take action. Burn the dip tanks the Government supplied for keeping their cattle healthy, burn the old school, burn the crops of the tribesmen who wouldn't join the Congress. Somehow the action was going to bring freedom. Freedom from what? Some case. I groaned. Not because I was thinking of the destruction: the police always caught the boys who did it because they always operated in press-gangs and they bragged about their action before and after. I groaned because I didn't feel like trying three dumb cocky peasant boys who would drag the trial out and make garbled long-winded political speeches.

Samson came in.

'Coffee, Nkosi?'

'Bring me a beer.'

He brought it and waited while I took the first long swallow. It went down like a mountain brook.

'Breakfast, Nkosi?'

When last had I eaten a meal? Christ, Saturday night.

'I better,' I said. 'And bring me another beer.' My intentions were very good. Monday and Thursday afternoons were usually my afternoons for Sylvia. Sylvia was a big strong girl. She was a filing clerk in one of the Government offices. Sylvia had come up to Rhodesia from Johannesburg to seek her fortune. She wasn't quite Country Club material, Sylvia, but she had these good strong legs, and thick brown hair and blue eyes and rosy cheeks and full red lips and her skirts were always tight, so she had to take very short steps, and her bottom had a way of jerking inside them, like two pigs struggling in a sack. You sort of wanted to charge Sylvia, and when you feel like that you don't mind her accent and her chewing gum and her conversation. She bothered the public prosecutors very much when she came up to our offices. Like the rest of the boys, I had had my eye on Sylvia even when Suzie was in town, but, of course, I had kept my hands off.

Sylvia had not made her fortune in Rhodesia, on account of being so dumb that she had to be a filing clerk, she had not made the Country Club, where all us eligible types hung out. But she had scooped up this young Cockney immigrant who was an apprentice panelbeater. They were going to settle down together and carve a future in this bright big country of Rhodesia, as soon as he had finished his apprenticeship. Meanwhile, every Monday and Thursday he went to his apprenticeship classes at the Technical College, from five to eight o'clock. It had not been very hard to talk her into it.

Mondays and Thursdays, five-thirty to seven-thirty, suited me very well. On Monday you were tired after a heavy week-end, and a quiet lie-in and a few beers and then a moderately early night set you up for the week. Thursday was good too, because you want a quiet sensible night before the week-end. Our arrangement was very straightforward and restful. We had a couple of cold beers and then she stretched up above to her cupboard and brought down her hatbox. She unlocked it and there was a collection of all the contraceptives science had thought up. I think she liked having her secret cache of contraceptives, she felt sophisticated. She swore her apprentice panelbeater didn't sleep with her, being a very earnest apprentice panelbeater.

However, my intentions to have an early night were so strong that I had phoned Sylvia and cancelled our appointment. I had phoned Isabel Weston and asked if I could take up her long-standing offer to use her sauna bath. Isabel Weston was a gushing middle-aged, middleweight who fancied me as a son-in-law. She owned a big house with a swimming pool and tennis court and she owned a domestic services and employment agency. And in the apartment above her office, which Isabel used as a sewing room, she had a sauna bath. '*Awfully* good for one,' Isabel Weston had said, '*cleanses* the whole system. *Do* try it.' So this Monday afternoon after Court I was going to cleanse my whole system, which sure as hell needed cleansing.

As I waited at the traffic lights of Selbome and Main Jacqueline crossed the road and my chest gave a little flutter. Somehow she reminded me of Suzie. It was the eyes, the slanty eyes, and the long hair. But Jackie had thick rich dark red-brown hair. She wore it up on top of her head to her office, but other times down, long and straight. And the breasts, jutting. Her skin was that rarity with redheads, creamy-pale and smooth, which turns golden in the sun. She did some part-time modelling for dress shops. I hooted and she turned and smiled and waved and walked on, very elegant. She was blushing. My chest fluttered again. I thought: Now, *that's* the girl you should cultivate, Mahoney, instead of these empty booze-sodden sex-sodden relationships – Jackie is soft and good and clean.

There was a rapport between us, Jackie and I, we both knew it and we both chose to do nothing about it. I had taken her out a number of times since Suzie had left me, and we had only kissed, then we had tacitly agreed to go out no more. It was too intense, too fraught with the danger of pain. I guess we both thought: We are so attracted because we both have soft hearts and they are both broken. She had just come through a very unhappy love, we were both very lonely. She was in no fit state to make decisions and I was in no fit state to undertake her affection. It would have been irresponsible. And deceitful. I watched her cross the intersection and I thought: Leaving that girl alone is the only honourable thing you've done for a hell of a long time, Mahoney.

Then the traffic lights changed to green.

I parked outside Isabel's office at four-thirty. The stunned feeling had gone, as it usually does about that time, but I still felt very bad.

'Come in, dear boy—'

She was plumpishly attractive, Isabel, greying hair dyed very blonde and cut very sleek and stylishly. She must have been very good when she was twenty-five, even thirty-five, but at forty-five she had to be strongly corseted.

'This is Joseph Mahoney,' she said to one of her customers, 'Advocate Mahoney, you must have read his name in the paper, a great friend of the family.'

'A great friend of the family.' The family consisted of old Herbert Weston, a nice fat old boy who was obviously past it, and Lai, very sweet and young and shy, fresh out of secretarial college, whom Isabel fancied as my mate. Old Herb had made his money out of livestock, starting with nothing, and Isabel's father had been a fishplate checker on South Africa Railways, though her accent conscientiously covered all that, and she would have liked a real live lawyer in the family.

She led me out the back door with a brisk no-nonsense smile, up the fire escape to the apartment above the shop. The door had 'Isabel's Agencies' printed on it in small sedate black letters. She opened the door. It was a bachelor apartment, lounge and bedroom combined, with a kitchenette and a bathroom, and a verandah overlooking Rhodes Street. There were two Singer sewing-machines and a tailor's dummy and there were piles of files lying in the corner, and there was a refrigerator and a table and a bare bed and some armchairs.

'It's very kind of you to let me use your sauna bath, Mrs. Weston.'

She led me into the bathroom: there was an asbestos barrel beside the tub. She bent and switched on a wallplug.

'There, give it five minutes to warm up then get undressed and get in. You zip this cover up to your neck – so. Hang your suit over a chair next door. I'll come up again in about half an hour, and tell you to get out – you mustn't overdo it the first time.'

She twiddled her fingers at me and was gone.

I got undressed and climbed into the barrel and zipped the cover up to my neck. I felt shagged out. In two minutes I was wet. The sweat was running off me. I rubbed my arms across my chest and it was slippery. It felt as if all the beer and the cigarettes and the bar air of the last week, the last six months, was running out of. me. It was very hot and I wanted to get out, but I stuck to it, and the sweat poured off my face and matted my hair to my forehead.

Isabel Weston came clicking briskly in the flat twenty-five minutes later.

'My you *are* perspiring!'

She dabbed my face with a wet cloth and switched the machine off. She was holding a big white towel.

'Now get into that cold shower, my boy, and then rub yourself down, and you'll feel a new man! You must lie down for fifteen minutes afterwards. And, by the way, I've put an ice-cold beer on the table in there for you!' She twiddled her fingers at me again and was gone.

The cold water stung. I rubbed myself down with the towel and my body glowed red. I looked at myself in the mirror and decided I was putting on too much weight. It's the beer that does it. I felt good, good and clean and limp and tired. I decided I was going to taper off the beer. I draped the towel round my waist and opened the bathroom door and stopped. Isabel Weston was sitting in the armchair looking at accounts and she was wearing cats-eye spectacles and a seamstress smock with an T embroidered on the pocket.

'Well!' she said, very bright and businesslike. 'How do you feel now?'

'Marvellous.'

'Do call me Isabel, dear boy. Now,' she got up, 'you must have a fifteen-minute rest, most important. Here's your beer.' She had it standing ready on a little tray. I was very thirsty. I swallowed deeply and it seemed to spread itself out into my arms and legs.

'Now lie down on yonder bed.'

'Thanks, Isabel.'

'And I'll give you a little rub down, and a little astringent lotion to tighten you up again. I did a bit of Phys. Ed. at college.

'On your stomach and relax completely.'

I lay down with my eyes closed. I heard her push her sleeves up, puff on her cigarette and blow the smoke to the ceiling, then put the cigarette down on the ashtray. She began to knead my shoulders. It was very relaxing, and I was exhausted: I began to float, only half awake.

She squeezed my shoulder.

'Now turn over.'

I turned over and she draped a damp Kleenex over my eyes. 'Joseph.'

She lifted the Kleenex. I looked into the shadowed face of Isabel Weston and her naked aging breasts and belly, poised astride me. Her smock lay on the floor.

Well, my intentions had been good. And I made a habit of avoiding involvements with married women.

Whenever possible. But it wasn't possible now. Quite apart from the fact that Isabel Weston tipped the scales at a hundred and forty-five and had me pinned to the mattress, it would have been impolite. And it was very pleasant, Isabel doing all the work. Then just as she was getting down to the short strokes – it hadn't taken her more than three minutes – there came this knock on the door. Isabel crouched poised on top of me like a sprinter at marks. Who is it?'

'It's me,' the old fat voice said, 'Herbert.'

'Oh my God,' she breathed.

She jumped off me and tugged me off the bed. She tugged me across the room to the built-in cupboard. 'Half a moment, Herbert,' she called, very cool. She pushed me into the cupboard, and flung my jacket in after me. She kicked my shirt and socks and tie under the bed and slammed the door and locked it. 'Hey,' I wanted to shout, 'what about my pants?' But it was too late. I stood panting in the darkness amongst dresses and smocks.

It takes a few moments to adjust to these circumstances. At first there is only the panic, the self-preservation instinct and you can't think of anything except the scramble for escape. Then, in hiding, the solid fear sets in. Indignity, acute embarrassment, divorce, civil action. Oh Christ. Then you start scratching desperately for excuses: Who could blame me, I hadn't looked for it? Then hope: Herbert was a silly old bugger. Rumour had it that he had been cuckolded for years. Perhaps he wouldn't even mind. And the desperate hope that he wouldn't find out, wouldn't even suspect, faith in the cool businesslike Isabel Weston, it was her trouble not mine, she would get me out of it. But: Oh Christ.

I decided to put on my suit jacket, for all the good it would do. I heard Isabel open the door. Oh Jesus.

I crouched down and looked through the keyhole. I could see the front door and the end of the bed. Isabel was dressed in her smock and high heels. Herbert was big and fat and he was looking bulbously over her head into the flat.

'Herbert,' she was saying briskly, 'what brings you here?'

'Passing on the way home,' he said in his soft fat voice, 'and saw your lights on. What're you doing working at this hour?'

'Oh,' she said carelessly, a little shrilly, 'you know how things pile up.' She suddenly had a brain wave. She waved her hand at her own dress lying on the chair: 'Altering my own dress, actually.'

My legal ear picked up the contradiction but fat Herbert didn't seem to catch it.

'I had a sauna bath and I was altering my dress while I cooled off—'

Christ, three different stories, Isabel – but if he hadn't picked up the first contradiction, it was a good embellishment, it accounted for her being naked under that smock – 'I'm ready to go now actually, how about driving on to the Club, I'll meet you there. I'm dying for a drink after that sweat—'

She was still standing in the doorway, busily, coolly, barring his way. Christ, she had done so well, shouldn't she let him in before he got suspicious – I was glad she was barring his way – get him away Isabel, tell him the house is on fire—

'I see you've already had a drink—' he quavered.

Oh God, my glass of beer half finished—

Herbert was looking bulbously over her head into the room, his rosebud mouth pursed. His big fat chest looked as if it was beginning to heave.

'Oh,' Isabel flicked her head and waved her hand, 'that's an old one I had lying in the fridge since the office Christmas party!' She giggled as if it was funny. She was beginning to crack.

'Since when do you drink beer?' He didn't look at her, his eyes were roving round the flat over her head. My chest felt hollow.

'I had to drink something after that sweat—' she insisted, a touch of indignation in her voice, getting back in control. Then she had another flash of brilliance – 'That's why I said I was dying for a drink, because I don't like beer—' It was good, but she said it too quickly. For God's sake stop blocking his path. She decided attack was the best defence: 'What's the meaning of all this cross-examination anyway—' She was brittle, she was used to using this on Herbert.

But Herbert looked as if for once in his life he didn't care.

'Working, you said,' he said in a high voice, 'working on things that had piled up—'

My heart was knocking in my ears. The silly old bugger wasn't such a silly old bugger. That's how he made all his money out of livestock, I thought irrelevantly, by not being a silly old bugger—

'I'll get dressed—' Isabel began.

Herbert's fat chest was heaving. He had a flushed excitement on his fat face, a twitch to his rosebud mouth.

'Working?'

He lumbered past her, into the room, puffing, towards the bed.

He looked very big, through the keyhole. Isabel hurried beside him. He bent down at the bed and pulled out my trousers and held them up. They looked a very guilty pair of trousers, dangling there.

'What's this?'

Isabel snatched them from him. She was cracking again. Her voice was tight and giggly, not querulous.

'Oh. There they are! I've been looking for them! They're a customer's. You know I run a bachelors' service. They need repairing ...' She made to toss them aside. Herbert snatched them from her and she tried to snatch them back. He held them up high.

'Repairing? They look perfectly good to me.'

Isabel laughed.

'Repairing, altering, it's all the same to me. They need letting out, he's put on a bit of weight – like all of us, aha ha ha,' – she snatched my pants back. She sat down on the bed, and took up a pair of scissors. 'I've just got to let them out down the seam at the back here, you see—' She started snipping feverishly at my trousers. They were a good pair of trousers before she started on them.

Herbert bent down under the bed again, and produced my sock. He dangled it up in front of him, wheezing. It looked a very undistinguished sock.

'Does he want his stretch-nylon socks let out too, Isabel?' He sniffed it angrily. 'There's nothing wrong with this except it needs washing'—Oh, the indignity of it all—'or do you take in laundry nowadays?'

Isabel was staring paralysed at the sock. She had cracked up, she had no answer. I closed my eyes.

Herbert turned and lumbered out of view. I heard him wheezing in the kitchen, into the bathroom. My heart was pounding, my mind was stuttering. He came lumbering back into view, heading straight for my cupboard, belly first. Then he was up against the cupboard and I could see nothing. The cupboard door shook as he wrenched at the handle.

'The key, give me the key!' he shrilled.

'Get out of my flat, you brute, I'll call the police!' The sound of Isabel flying at Herbert, beating him with her fists on his barrel chest. Still the door shook. Then the thud of a swipe and a cry from Isabel and the sound of her reeling across on to the bed and I got the impression Herbert felt a brute for the first time in his life and loved it.

'The key!' he shrilled. 'Give me the key, or I'll tear it open with my bare hands!!!'

I winced.

Still the door shook. I stood among the dresses and smocks in the dark and watched it shake, quaking. I longed for my pants. I lowered myself to keyhole level.

There he was, looking like the back of an elephant, scratching in the tool-box of the sewing machine. 'All right, all right!' he was shrilling. Isabel was climbing off the bed and flying at him, her smock burst open, Herbert turned and lumbered back towards the cupboard holding a screwdriver. Another swipe and Isabel was on the floor. I straightened up and closed my eyes. Then he was attacking the lock with the screwdriver.

I admit I was shaking, but I was now calmer. I was resigned. All was lost, it was a fair cop. I had been caught. I had to take the consequences, I had to take my medicine. I would not even resist assault, he was entitled to assault me. I straightened myself amongst the smocks with as much dignity as I could muster without pants.

I heard the screwdriver drop and the door crack as he kicked it. It sounded a very satisfying kick. He kicked again and it cracked through. His podgy fingers appeared and Herbert Weston pulled with his two hundred and fifty pounds and the door burst open. And there I was.

Then Isabel switched the lights out.

Not before Herbert spotted the location of the Mahoney genitalia, however. I hadn't bargained for that. I don't know why, because come to think of it it's a fitting part of the anatomy upon which to wreak revenge, in the circumstances. Before I could muster any defence action, I was heaved out into the black room by same and following Herbert Weston very closely.

'Lights!' he was screaming. 'Put the lights on, you bitch—'

Isabel attacked Herbert again. I could make out her arms flailing.

Then Herbert grabbed her hair and held her at arm's length and towed us both very effectively out on to the verandah. Now, to submit to justifiable assault is one thing, but to have the family jewels mauled about is another. And to be dragged out on to a public verandah by same is rubbing it in. I did not want to hit the old man but I had to. I mean—the family jewels! Then as I drew back my hand to swipe, Herbert Weston slipped. He let go of me and dragged Isabel down with him. They rolled through the French door on to the verandah. I stood gasping. Herbert was rolling on his back still holding Isabel's hair, and tugging, and Isabel's smock was up over her stomach and her backside was struggling in the moonlight. Isabel was screaming and Herbert was bellowing, and windows were opening and people were watching and shouting.

I turned and grabbed my trousers and pulled them on and I grabbed my clothes and I ran out of the flat into the night.

Tuesday and Wednesday I lay low. Every time I came out of Court I expected to see Herbert Weston waiting, or the sheriff with a summons citing me as corespondent in the divorce action. Every time the telephone rang my chest tingled. I went back to my flat in Fort Street after work and had tea for the first time in six months, which astonished Samson, then supper, then bed. Samson asked me if I was sick. Actually I had been to a doctor because you don't take chances with the family jewels. I had to be careful how I walked and how I sat down on Tuesday. The doctor had told me to lie low, and alone, and early, and to lay off the beer for a couple of days. But there was a genuine element of remorse as well, so real that on Thursday morning I telephoned Sylvia and cancelled our appointment again. I said I had to work on a big case. My reason was genuine remorse. I felt it was dishonourable to take other men's women. Quite apart from the hazards. And during the last two nights I had been thinking of Suzie, the cleanness of Suzie, the goodness of Suzie, and I felt lonely and unhappy.

On Wednesday night, I pulled the big cardboard carton out from under my bed. I heaved the fat scrawled manuscript open at random and read with a cup of tea in my hand and nothing in my heart. I read a page and then I flicked ten pages and read some more. God, what corn! What crap. Nothing. The only pieces that glowed were the pieces I had written drunk, drugged from wine and the flesh of Suzie, the sweet, salty, sweaty oily sunshot flesh of Suzie on a Sunday, when I wrote about Suzie. It was hopeless. I was blunted, blunted by thoughtlessness, by feelinglessness, by a year of nothing. On Thursday I opened the manuscript and read over the last chapter, and I held my pen and I smoked cigarettes one after another, and stared at the blank new page and the page stared up at me, and in the end I called Samson to bring me a beer. I drank four beers while I stared at the page, and then I chucked down my pen and I went downstairs to my car and drove to the Sheridan.

The Sheridan was a good cocktail bar. It was crowded, well fed, well dressed, well heeled people going home from the office to the Club or to their lawns and hedges. I sat down on a barstool in the corner. I wanted to drink alone, I wanted to try to start thinking and feeling again. I stared into my beer and let the noise of the bar wash over me. And slowly I began to feel again.

A hand fell on my shoulder and I turned around. Max, grinning.

'Joe-baby, where you bin these last couple of days?'

'What'll you have, Max?'

'Lion,' Max said. 'Why so glum?'

We had few beers. My mood was broken. I bound him to secrecy and told him about Herbert Weston catching me on the job with Isabel and Max laughed so the tears were running down his face, and when I came to the bit about Herbert grabbing the family jewels he screamed and his face was wet with laughing, and I was laughing too, now. I wasn't remorseful any more.

This guy Max. Swarthy, stocky Greek with a fat happy handsome face and the women loved him. Always happy, always thinking of somebody to screw and something to drink. Last year we went down to Cape Town together on holiday. We booked a suite in one of the best seafront hotels. When we checked in the manager handed me a bundle of letters. They were all from Cape Town girls, over two hundred of them, setting out their vital statistics, and saying how they would just love to work for our new airline as hostesses, and begging for interviews. Max had only preceded our arrival by advertising in the Cape Town papers that two young directors of a new international airline would be arriving in Cape Town to recruit air-hostesses and that all interested persons should apply, in own writing, care of our hotel. The advertisement stressed that the successful applicants would be mature, attractive, unattached women of specified vital statistics.

We started off our holiday by solemnly interviewing the most promising fifty or so, and wining and dining them in rapid succession. They nearly bludgeoned each other to death over us, and for the whole month we never slept alone. We told them they would be advised of the result of their applications in due course.

We had another beer. Max wanted to go on to the Club to pick up some birds but I didn't. He tried to bully me but I was determined.

'Remember Mona's toga party Saturday night,' he said irritably.

'Okay.'

I had another beer alone, but I did not start feeling again. I went home. There was a note under my door from Sylvia saying her panelbeater had the flu, so I could come round any time. I screwed the note up. I went to my table and sat down and stared at my manuscript. It didn't look any better and I chain-smoked five cigarettes without writing a word. I felt dead, blunted, dull. I had forgotten how to feel and think and write. I had been blunting myself for nearly a year, since Suzie left.

I had another beer while I sat at the table looking at the manuscript. It was hopeless. I thought of Sylvia, lying in bed all plump and luscious and dumb and pink in the glow of her pink lampshade, with her hatbox of contraceptives and her little wooden crucifix facing the wall for the occasion. No, I thought. I tried to think about the manuscript, but I was thinking about Suzie again. Oh, Suzie, where are you? Maybe there would be a letter tomorrow telling me she was coming back. Even telling me where she was, anything. Then I could—but I knew there would not be a letter. I thought hard about Sylvia, her plump thighs, and her legs wrapped round me, banging her hips up against me, and her nails clawing my back, and mouthing dirty words in my ear, to stop me thinking about Suzie. Then came the thought that made me so furious I wanted to shout and I felt strong enough to shake the whole flat apart, the thought that some other bastard might be doing just that to my Suzie.

I shoved back the chair and walked out of the flat. I drove my car hard round to Sylvia's.

Chapter Twenty-Two

I woke up late on Saturday with a wine headache which made everything a little mad and very hard to grip, and I was determined about only one thing: I was not going to Mona's toga party tonight. All I wanted to do was steady up, I felt too bad to feel anything else. Then, when I got to the office at noon there was a telegram from Dar-es-Salaam: 'Arriving today flight EAA 742 for Monas shindig can you put me up if not go to hades I'm staying anyway luv Lola.' I put my hand to my head. Lola. I telephoned EAA and checked the flight arrival time. Then I drove out to the airport.

It was brown and bare but the sun shone brightly. I waited on the small balcony feeling very shaky and thought about Lola. Some Lola. A Yank. A goddam Eyetalian Yank. 'And they're the worst kind!' Lola said. Spent half her life in Chicago and the other half in East Africa miming hairbrain businesses and doing good deeds. Lola once wrote to our newspaper editor:

'An advertisement appears daily in your paper:

"If it's safe in water
it's safe in Lux."

Now, sir, about my goldfish ...'

The plane came in and the gangway was put up and out steps Lola on to the tarmac all bounce and smiles and waves, ravishing as ever, in the lowest-necked bare-back thigh-split evening gown.

She thew her arms around me and jumped up and down and demanded breakfast and where's her luggage and stop ogling my titties haven't you seen a girl in a v-neck before and how's Honeytalk and how the hell do you propose entertaining me and God what a sour bunch they were on the plane and where's the bar – the passengers and the officials and the native porters were ogling her. Seems she was having this all-night bender on a high-powered Italian tycoon's yacht in the Indian Ocean when she suddenly remembered Mona's party and didn't have time to change or couldn't give a hell about changing. Some Lola. I bundled her into the car as quickly as I could and we drove back to town. She never stopped talking except to laugh and to dig into the biggest handbag and pull out one of the magnums of champagne she had hijacked from the tycoon's floating cellar and she opened it with her teeth. Champagne fizzed all over the car. I drove her straight to my flat and made her put on my jacket and I hustled her upstairs before some cop ran her in for indecent exposure. I never saw a sexier outfit. Then she starts unpacking her suitcases all over my bedroom.

Three wigs, four pairs of false eyelashes, a hatbox of cosmetic gear, seven model linen suits, four pairs of Charles Jourdan shoes – at twenty guineas a pair – 'Met this old geezer at the Casino in Reno, gave me five hundred bucks to gamble, it wasn't stealing was it, Honeytalk, I just decided I didn't like him' – a Christian Dior nightgown, a toothbrush, and no bras, no girdles and no pants. The whole time she is talking and taking swigs out of the magnum – 'I've started this Secretarial School in Dar for lady wogs, fantastic success, they love trying to eat with knives and forks, trouble is all this generation of blacks have got flat feet, I throw in a course on birth control as well, so I am doingthe country some good, aren't I, Honeytalk?'

She festooned my bedroom with her gear, then she threw herself down at Suzie's dressing-table and began to take off her face. She tugged at her glorious black beehive and tore out the artificial wiglet, she plucked off her thick false eyelashes, out with a bottle of blue methylated spirits – 'same stuff as you use in stoves and I need to buy it in bulk' – and starts wiping the colour off her lovely face. She wiped off ten years in ten minutes and she looked fifteen years old.

'Run my bath, Honeytalk, while I book a call to Jo'burg. I wanna screw a new dining-room suite for my Secretarial School out of Monty.'

Monty was Lola's sugar daddy, a frightfully English old bwana with oodles of boodle who lived in South Africa – 'He's my sleeping partner which don't mean what you think, it means he puts up the dough and I put up the know-how, people think I screw for him but he's just my dear old sugar daddy and I love him to its—' I ran her bath while she booked the call, reversing the charges. Then she bounced into the bathroom clutching the magnum and a bottle of bathsalts.

She thew the salts into the water and the bubbles climbed up to the rim. She whipped off her dress, leaped in and began scrubbing herself vigorously. She was a lot of girl, Lola. It was exhausting just to watch her. The champagne was not doing my hangover any harm. I suppose I could have loved Lola, if I let myself. 'Well then if you don't want to marry a hard-arsed little bitch like me you must marry my sister, I refuse to let a gorgeous beast like you out of my family. She's the pretty one and she's saving up the pie bit for the nuptials, when're you coming to Chicago? Are you still in love with Suzie?'

'Yes.'

She took a swig of champagne and passed the bottle back to me and got to her feet and began soaping her crotch energetically.

'Forget her, Honeytalk, you two didn't get on intellectually, otherwise you'd have married her. You know what you want?'

'What?'

'A soulmate. Somebody who moons around in a daze like you and ponders the imagery in Macbeth over the ham and eggs.'

The telephone rang in the passage.

'That's my Jo'burg call, answer it, Honeytalk. If a woman answers it's his wife, the old bitch is ganging up on me to get Monty to disinherit me. Say you're Harold Macmillan or somebody, and you want to speak to his nibs. If Monty answers, gimme the receiver.'

I went out into the passage, a woman answered.

'May I speak to Sir Monty, please?'

'Who's speaking?'

'Mr. Macmillan.'

'I'm afraid Sir Monteray is at the museum this afternoon.'

I put my hand over the mouthpiece, and leaned into the bathroom. Lola was still soaping her fanny happily. 'He's at the museum,' I said.

'That's where he belongs, antiquated old basket.'

'Any message?' the old dear said.

'Ask him to call me at No. 10,' I said. 'It's about a new dining-room suite for my new black Commonwealth Finishing School.'

Lola was reeling in the bubble bath with delight.

I had to scrub her back while she told me a long story about an Englishman an Irishman and a Jew, then she rubbed herself dry with a towel till she glowed. She insisted that I give her a piggyback to the bedroom then she flung herself down in front of Suzie's dressing-table again, drew a pencil line down her nose and a pencil line across her cheeks, put in two dimples, two high cheek bones, put on her blue eyelashes, put on ten years in ten minutes, stuck on a wig, stepped into a Susan Small model at fifty guineas a throw, put on a pair of Charles Jourdan shoes. And no pants. She swallowed her birth control pill with a swig of champagne. And off we went to case the town before Mona's party.

The cars were parked deep outside Mona's flat. The grass was brown and the gutters were full of dust. Mona had the penthouse on top of the twelve-storey block, but we could hear the music and gabble of voices down in the street. I had to stop Lola from trying to direct the traffic at the intersection. Some Lola. Max was sitting in the gutter, egging her on. I pulled them both inside and shoved them into the elevator, and we where whisked up to the penthouse. Mona appeared at the door, music and guffaws and voices flooded out. She was swathed in blue muslin, gathered at the waist, and draped over one shoulder, and her hair was piled on top of her head and she wore green laced sandals and she held a long glass in her hand. You could see her breasts were swinging free under the muslin.

'Lola! You Made It!' Mona's words always began in capitals.

Lola flung her arms round Mona. The two were great chums. They kissed and gabbled and Lola was gone through the mob with squeals and oohs and ahs and hullo-theres and kisses all round and much laughter.

'Max and Honeytalk, you can't go in until you're togged up, no underpants allowed.' She led us through to the main bedroom to change into our sheets.

The big living-room opened on to the roof garden. There were cushions and mattresses sprinkled along the walls and the only lights were from candles stuck into bottles and from the portable charcoal barbecue burners flickering outside on the roof garden. There must have been eighty people in the flat, the men draped in sheets like Roman togas and the women swathed in muslin and nightgowns. I knew most of the people, they were at most of the parties most of the time talking vivaciously about nothing mostly. They were standing around with drinks in their hands and laughing and making jokes. There were half chickens and mutton chops and boerewors roasting on the barbecues and there were bowls of punch doing the rounds and there were seventy-seven kinds of savouries, and enough booze to float a Queen. And beyond the roof garden lay the red roof-tops of Bulawayo, among dusty avenues, wide enough to turn a wagon drawn by sixteen oxen. And beyond the avenues the flat bare lights of Mzilikazi and Tshabalaba and Mpopoma and Iminyela, and beyond the flat black dry silence of Matabeleland, all the way to the horizon.

People were smooching to the record player, arms entwined. As the girls slunk past the candles you could see their contours. I saw Lola laughing near the barbecue burners with three men as she was telling them a story with much gesticulation. A girl passed with a tray and handed me a glass of punch. Her fingernails were purple and perfect and an inch long. 'Have an aphrodisiac,' she said and wandered on, the candlelight shining through between her legs. I took a big swallow of the punch to get rid of the heavy feeling in my head from drinking too much of Lola's Eyetalian tycoon's champagne. Another girl passed and popped a savoury into my mouth. 'Excellent caviar,' she said. I saw Lilly – *Mary*, I said to myself, remember her name is *Mary* – Mary Lilly – standing in the corner in a group of Romans of both sexes. She twiddled her fingers at me coolly, and I shuffled over. 'Why didn't you phone me?' she accused. Her nightie was slung low and her breasts were definitely too big.

'I lost your number,' I said.

'Liar,' she said. 'Anyway my husband's in town for five days, call me on Wednesday.'

'Definitely,' I said and I took a powder, gratefully.

The girl with the inch long nails and the punch tray passed. 'Have another aphrodisiac,' she said. I must lay off the booze, I thought. I am sodden through with it. I caught a glimpse of myself in a mirror. Heavy, I thought, and white and fleshy. Twenty-eight, nearly twenty-nine, and what happened to all your stout-hearted intentions? I took another punch and took a big swallow. Max passed happily. 'Like shooting sitting ducks,' he said. I knew most of the people, but I felt that I wouldn't be able to laugh with them because they didn't seem funny to me any more. I felt heavy and sober and sour and it didn't feel as if any more booze could make me feel any different. I swallowed the punch in one go, and looked around for the girl with the tray. Automatically. Time enough tomorrow to steady up. I must get out of this way of life. I must get back close to the earth. I wish I could get back into the bush, to the Valley, to Nyamanpofu even. Lola waved to me and beckoned me over. She was standing with Mona and Max and two men. Lola was telling a yam about her Secretarial School. She said she had a magic mirror on the wall and she overheard two of her students saying to it: 'Mirror, Mirror on the wall-i, who is-i the most-i beautiful-i of all-i?' And the mirror replied: 'Snow White you black bitches and don't you forget it.' And that's how that story started. We were all laughing.

The punch was beginning to work. I looked around the roof garden and the lounge. There were many women I had slept with. I began to feel good again. I went to the bar and got myself another big punch. I thought: Life is pretty good. Henry Potterton was saying to a young sunburnt man:

'Let Nyasaland go, if she wants to, I say. What do we want her for, her with her two million screaming blacks making trouble. Northern Rhodesia, yes, we want Northern Rhodesia, because of her Copperbelt and she's got seventy thousand whites, but Nyasaland?'

The sunburnt young man said: 'But if we let Nyasaland go, it means Federation is a failure, Partnership is a failure, it'll create a precedent and then Northern Rhodesia will want to leave us too—'

Potterton said: 'Partnership, my poor aching ass. Partnership is a failure, Partnership is a myth, always was. How can we have Partnership with two countries full of savages screaming for independence. The only solution is to let Nyasaland go and to hang on to Northern Rhodesia with force and arms. We got a Federal Army haven't we?'

'I was thinking of partnership on a wider basis than just economics,' the young man said, 'I mean partnership between all the races, in all three partner territories, that's what Federation stands for, not just economic partnership. The races have got to learn to live together, we've got to give the blacks a chance to evolve to our standard, that's the purpose of Federation, so that on both the personal and the economic level we build a partnership ...'

Potterton snorted. 'How can you expect to have a Partnership between a few hundred thousand civilised whites and seven million savages, except on a master and servant basis? I tell you, it's a myth. I tell you, the South Africans have got the right idea. What do you say, Mahoney?' He turned to me thickly.

'I say let's get among the punch.' I didn't want to talk about politics.

'Are you Joseph Mahoney?' the sunburned kid said. I looked at him.

'Yes.'

'I've heard about you,' the sunburned kid said. 'You used to run the Nyamanpofu post back in fifty-seven, didn't you? I've just taken it over. My name's John Swinton,' he said.

His eyes were blue and clear and his hair was bleached from the sun, and his smile was keen. I looked at him carefully. He was young and fresh and strong and dedicated. I used to be like that, I used to be sharp and full of determination and love for the bush and the munts once, like young Swinton.

'The munts still talk about you out there,' he said.

'Do they?' It felt good but it also made me feel bad. What had I done since I left? God, I wanted to go back.

'How do you like Nyamanpofu?' I said.

'Very much, I like the work. There's a big land development scheme I've just started—'

'Where were you before?' I didn't want to hear about his challenging land development scheme.

'I was number two at Sable. Nyamanpofu is my first sole command. I was sorry to leave Sable.'

'Why?'

'I had just begun to make headway with the munts.' He smiled openly, shyly, proud. 'They were a good bunch. When I got news of my transfer I called an indaba of the headmen and told them I was going. Then the oldest stood up and said: '—Swinton broke into Sindebele—'"Why does the Government send you away from us?" I said: "Old man, because I have no wife, the Government finds it cheaper to move me rather than a man who has a wife." He said: "Why then do you not buy a white woman for a new wife, then the Government will not move you away from here." I said: "Alas, I have not enough cattle to buy a wife."' Swinton reverted to English: 'The next day I was sitting in my office and the headmen arrived driving twelve head of cattle. It was a present so that I could buy a wife.'

Damn you, Swinton. Damn your dedication and your keen eager-beaver doing and achieving. What bloody good are you doing stuck in the bush, Swinton, playing big white chief over a few thousand munts who think the world is flat? But, Christ, I envied him. I looked at him.

'I envy you,' I admitted.

He grinned.

'I envy you having all this crumpet around seven days a week.' He nodded across the crowded, diaphanous room. A tall blonde called Monica was smooching in a short lacy toga with Mike Sheffield, her long smooth legs looking hairless and waxen, her thighs stroking each other softly and hairlessly under her short transparent toga.

Swinton grinned happily. His eyes were sparkling. He was very handsome. Something stung the side of my face and dropped to the floor. It was a French letter. I looked across the room and there were Judy and the girl with the long purple fingernails leaning against the wall laughing. Judy held up her finger and there was another French letter hooked over her fingertip and she pulled it back with her other hand by the teat and let it fly and it hit Swinton on the forehead and he laughed. Max came to the table to get another punch. Mona came up.

'When does the orgy begin, kid?'

'Right now, you greasy Greek. Come on—'

She took Max's hand and pulled him on to the dance space. She started to smooch round the floor with him. She locked both arms round his neck and smooched with her crotch pressed right up against him. Her spine was arched in towards him and her breasts pressed against him. The candlelight shone through the muslin and the curves and mounds of her back and buttocks showed through, the length of her legs and the candle threw fleeting shadows between the back of her thighs. She loosened one of her arms and ferreted it under the folds of sheet across his back. She began to drag her fingertips across his shoulder blades, and down his spine. 'Undo, me,' she said.

There are some women who are born to copulate. Their skin has a plump rubbery texture, and it is very smooth and often olive in colouration and creamy to the touch, and the flesh indents when touched only lightly, with resilience. They bruise very easily, though they are strong women. Every part of her, the flesh on her strong shoulders, the flesh on her face, her cheeks, the length of her arms and legs, her fingertips and toes, her slightly translucent fingers, her mauve fingernails, the way her toes sit snuggled together yet can stretch and spread into grass and sand and carpets, every dimple and crease of her is a sexual thing. There is a faint smell of body about her, like a sweaty musk. Her breasts are usually heavy and buoyant, and her nipples are brown and big and they become erect very easily. Her thighs touch on the inside, and curve outwards then inwards to her knee and her buttocks are large and soft and dimpled and enveloping, like the flesh of fruit secretes the pip. And when you kiss her she sucks, and her mouth inside is slimy.

Such a woman was Mona.

Max undid her. As he undid her she took a long slug of wine. She grabbed a handful of Max's hair and tugged it as he undid her. Then she danced off with him against her, with only her sandals on, her big mouth smiling red and creamy into his neck. The olive of her body was broken only in the line across her back and a triangle across her buttocks where her bikini covered her at the swimming pool. The backs of her thighs were luscious below the cleft of her silken buttocks and her buttocks had two dimples at the base of her back.

The rest was very confused. I don't remember whether I made a date with the girl with the long purple fingernails or with Monica. I remember arms and legs and bodies and togas whirling and swaying and shaking and laughing. I remember going to the bedroom to lie down and finding it all infested with bodies. I remember Lola passing out stone cold on top of the piano. I remember leaning over the top of the roof garden wall with Adeline, looking down into the street and telling her I loved her and seeing the convoy of police trucks screaming along Main Street and turning up Seventh Avenue towards Mzilikazi. I remember the telephone ringing above the thump of the music and the clatter of voices and the swing and sway of the bodies and Mona shouting into the receiver: 'I'm not going to let a bunch of bloody kaffirs break up my party, what else do we pay you policemen for?' The girl with the long fingernails said: 'What's happening?' and Mona said: 'The natives are revolting,' and Potterton said: 'Oh, my dear, they don't smell that bad,' and everyone laughed.

Swinton grabbing the phone and shouting into the receiver with a hand over his ear and then shouting: 'Trouble in Mzilikazi, all Police Reservists to report to their Stations immediately—' Boos and cheers. Plummeting down in the elevator, grinding at the starter button of the Chev. Then blank.

I woke up on the settee in my lounge at dawn, with a hangover like a Boeing wing. I was stiff and aching. I tottered through to my bedroom. Lola was lying across the bed in her Christian Dior nightgown with a pair of handcuffs dangling from one wrist. I couldn't even bear to think how she came by those or how she got home, and I didn't try. I pulled on my blue denim Police Reserve overalls and left the flat.

When I got down the street I couldn't find the car. I walked the six blocks to the Central Police Station, and I walked into the Charge Office, up to the counter. The sergeant looked tired.

'Reservist Mahoney reporting for duty,' I said thickly.

The sergeant looked at me. 'You sober now? How's your girlfriend?' He rubbed purple teeth marks on his wrist.

I blinked at him. 'Don't you remember?'

I shook my head.

The sergeant glared at me, then he decided not to say it. 'It's all right, sir. We cleaned the trouble up. You can go home again and sleep the rest of it off.' He peered at me closely and then he said: 'Your car's parked in the yard at the back.'

I drove back to Fort Street slowly. The natives were just beginning to come into town on their bicycles from the townships, a black, straggling river. I let myself into the flat and went to the window. I saw the morning, the sun already shining brightly on to the red rooftops, and the sanitary lanes with their garbage cans and Africans and the brown horizon, and I smelt my own body, tobacco smoke and beer and gin-punch upon me like a fuzz and my tongue smarting and my strong breath, and the thud in my head and the prickling, and I knew that a lot of days had been like this for a long time, ever since Suzie had left. And every day would be like this, unless I took hold. And I carried my garbage can of remorse and I hankered for the cleanness of Suzie.

Useless!

Useless useless useless.

It had to be Swinton who grabbed the phone and took the police message, while the rest stood grogged like Roman fools. Swinton who took command, Swinton with the brown sunburnt face and the keen blue eyes, the boy from the bush, the boy doing a good keen day's work amongst people who needed him, helping and organising people who needed his help if there was to be Partnership, Swinton who was concerned about the drought and the crops and the cattle, Swinton using the patience of Job and delivering the judgments of Solomon, Swinton whom black people respected so much that they gave him lobola for a wife. Emergency, therefore take command. I was like that once. But I stood grogged with the other Romans. Decadent Romans while the townships were afire. And too drunk to go on Police Reserve duties when needed. And the cops had to drive me home and fight with Lola, drunk and biting. Take hold.

Do something. What happened to the undergraduate zeal that made you quit the bush to come to the reality of the City to do your goodness? Undergraduate, yes, but at least it was zeal, not this flesh-potted bluntness' Do something. Take stock. Stop drinking.

I went to the bathroom and soaked my head in iced water for ten minutes. Then I went to my cupboard and hauled out the big cardboard box containing my manuscript and thumped it down on the table.

Part Five

Chapter Twenty-Three

For Samson it was like the old days: the Nkosi did not bother him provided he produced enough food to keep him full and provided he found clean clothes in his cupboard and his bed made when he came home. At five o'clock the Nkosi came home from the office, and he threw off his clothes and shouted: 'Samson, fill the bath.' For the next three-quarters of an hour the Nkosi was silent as he lay in the bath and the only thing Samson had to do was to hang up the Nkosi's suit. He wondered what the Nkosi lay there thinking about. He was a strange one, the Nkosi. He came out from the bathroom naked and he went to his bedroom and pulled on a pair of short trousers. When Samson heard the bathroom door open he made coffee. The Nkosi sat down at the dining-room table and pulled his pile of papers in front of him and he rolled a cigarette and started reading his pile of papers with a frown. Sometimes the Nkosi spent a long time staring in front of him thinking his strange thoughts. Then the Nkosi would start writing on his papers again, slowly at first, then more and more quickly. At half-past seven or eight o'clock Samson would go to the Nkosi's side and stand there until he looked up and said 'Yes?' and Samson said: 'Your skoff is ready, Nkosi,' and usually the Nkosi said: 'Put it in the oven and you can go.' And in the morning at seven o'clock or thereabouts when Samson went back to the flat in Fort Street the ashtray on the Nkosi's table was full of stubs, and the floor too, where the Nkosi had flicked them. He had to shake and keep at the Nkosi to make him wake up and get up so that he would not be too late for the Court. Sometimes, but not very often, he came into the flat and found the Nkosi still sitting at the table and writing.

But the Nkosi, although he spent much of his time writing on his paper, was also a sensible man: the Nkosi had some girlfriends. Sometimes there was a girl in the Nkosi's bed when Samson came into the flat, and sometimes the Nkosi was not in the flat when Samson came to work in the mornings. Sometimes there was a stranger in the Nkosi's bed, but usually it was one of the three.

Another umfazi who came to the Nkosi's house often nowadays while he was writing on his papers was the woman Jek-i, the tall umfazi with the long red hair and the big slanted eyes, the one with the very good bosoms. But she only came in the daytime, and she was never in the Nkosi's bed. He could not understand this because he could tell that the woman Jek-i was much bothered by the Nkosi and the Nkosi was much bothered by the woman, yet they did not make love. In Samson's view she was the best umfazi. Samson quite liked all the Nkosi's umfazis, and he approved of his having three or four women, for then he was less likely to take it into his head to marry one of them. So it was a good thing that the Nkosi did not sleep with the woman Jek-i.

So Joseph Mahoney wrote his book. He went at it like a bull at a gate. It was all steaming round in his head now. It was not easy, for Mahoney was not writing a story. He was writing a philosophy, a poetry, a jumbled collection of thoughts and feelings. It was hell. It threatened to contain everything he had ever thought, felt and imagined, and it was hell being imprisoned in that turbulent ocean without the lifeline of a story to hang his thoughts upon. He knew what he wanted to say, but the agony was finding a place for it. The pages ranged in huge strides from fantasy to God to atheism to politics to the seasons to the myths to the glories of life and love, to the futilities of life and love, the horrors of suburbia. Suburbia, the crest and the trough of being alive, of being a taxpayer, a parent, a neighbour, a car-owner, a school-fee payer, the stultification of the lawns and hedges and the nice little house, the Club and the holiday once a year at Margate, clubs, pubs and adulteries and the Loyal Women's Guild, beer, cigarettes and sex under the hot dry sun.

'What's your book actually about?' and Mahoney sighed and said:

'Oh, it's a collection of thoughts' and when pressed he said: 'I don't know. It's a garbage can.'

'What's it called?' and Mahoney said 'The Birth of a Bum' and people thought that was pretty good, is it full of sex?' and Mahoney had to admit it was pretty full of sex. In fact, when Mahoney considered it, it was in parts the dirtiest book going because life is dirty. Then for a hundred pages the reader was transported through a jungle of aesthetic musings and scenes as sexless and turbulent as thunderclouds. In parts it was unintelligible to anybody but Mahoney, and sometimes when he went back five hundred pages it was unintelligible even to him. At times Mahoney thought it was good, good, brilliant. And at times he wanted to burn the whole bloody thing in shame.

Jackie understood when he showed parts of it to her. She pored over the pages with her executive-secretary concentration, her hand buried in her long red straight hair, her heavy-lidded green-brown eyes devouring the words he had written. 'Oh yes, Joe! Oh yes! I understand exactly what you're driving at. Thank God somebody else feels about things the same as I do!' Sometimes she laughed out loud and sometimes she almost cried. 'Do keep at it, Joe. It'll knock Ulysses into a cocked hat. Palinurus too. Oh, I wish I could write!'

Solly Berger was allowed to read bits when he came to town and visited him. He sat with his lower lip jutting out and he pulled on his long Jew nose while Mahoney fidgeted.

'It's a load of crap, isn't it?' he said, and Solly looked up with his shrewd creased eyes half-closed.

'No,' he said, it's good. Parts of it are bloody good. But I'll tell you something: it won't be published. You've got to be James Joyce or Dylan Thomas or Albert Schweitzer or somebody before you'll get any airy-fairy mess like this published.'

'I couldn't care if it's never published. I just want to get the damn thing finished and off my back.'

Then Cynthia wheedled a few chapters out of him. She sat on the floor in her shorts with her strong shapely legs tucked under her and her pretty pug face screwed up in a frown, her jaws working on the gum. She was not an intellectual like Jackie and Solly, she was only an office typist, but she was intelligent. Mahoney watched her out of the corner of his eye nervously. Why should he worry what she thought, she was only an office typist. At first she plodded carefully through the scrawled pages, then she began to skim over the pages and then flick one or two. Then she said: 'I'll make some tea' and later: 'Look – who'm I to judge, I'm not a highbrow. To be quite honest I don't understand it, so who am I to judge? I like a story, that's what I read a book for—'

Just as Suzie had said.

'Don't spoil it by trying to put more story into it,' Jackie said. 'What does it matter if it's not published? It's for you.'

'It's not, you know,' Mahoney said.

He went back to the beginning and began to thread a story through the morass.

Chapter Twenty-Four

October in Matabeleland is called Suicide Month, and September is just as bad.

From the flats you look out on to the hot dry streets and the hot shimmering red roof-tops of the little houses and their dusty broken back yards and on to the hot rough sanitary lanes where the garbage cans sit and the African servants squat in the sun talking and picking their noses. In the offices the men sweat in their suits and the typists perspire between their legs and when you touch the cars in the streets you get burned. In the courtroom there is a stink of African sweat and the lawyers and the magistrates and the judges sweat under their gowns. You drink more in October and every day you look up at the hot blue-white sky and say: Wish it would rain. But still the rain does not come. It does not come until the earth is dead, in November.

It was the first day of October when Suzanna de Villiers came back. She knew as the plane bent down over the flashing brown bush that she was doing the wrong thing. Not because she didn't like Bulawayo – it was home now. She was making a mistake because she was coming back to see Joseph Mahoney.

Bored, the town bored her. Why? That was Joseph. Joseph and his brooding. Joseph and his explosions. Joseph and his frustrations and his theories. Suburbia, his pet horror. Suburbia, she had never thought of it before as anything but the normal place you go to, like heaven or hell when you die. Joseph and his musings and his desire to talk about things.

He was not good for her. She was not good for him. She irritated him because she was not a high-powered intellectual. She made the town emptier and flatter for him. He was not good for her because she was afraid of him.

Suzanna de Villiers walked through the quiet concourse of Bulawayo airport. Nine o'clock on a Sunday morning. There were a few people standing at the glass doors to meet the dozen passengers. The plane had been two-thirds empty, more than. She recognised a few of the waiting faces but she walked past. Quiet and hot. She waited to get her baggage and the black porter put it in the back of the blue and white Central African Airways bus. She climbed into the bus and sat down in the first seat in the front. She was the only passenger into town. The black driver waited until all the people were out of the concourse and then he came to her for the fare. Suzanna opened her bag. She had six pounds and some silver and a few hundred Congolese francs and in the bank she must have about twenty pounds. She paid her half-crown and the bus driver took a last look round then ground the engine into life. She sat back as she was vibrated into town. She looked at the hot dry gardens of suburbia.

Well, I'm not afraid of him now. I've got Frank. Frank is clever too and he finds me good enough. But then she realised that Frank was the very reason she was coming back to Mahoney, even though Mahoney had never really asked her to marry him, not of his own accord. He had only asked her in panic. Frank had asked her properly. And when his contract was up they would go back to Hartford, Connecticut, and have a nice house in Chestnut Street and Frank would go into private practice and they would have a fine life together. Frank's people had money, too, and they would get a week-end log cabin up in the lakes. It was a fine country for kids to grow up in. And Suzanna was going to say Yes.

And then the Belgian girl had come in to have her baby, the only white baby ever bom at the hospital. And as it slid out into the African midnight with the sound of crickets and the warm night noises of the jungle, Suzanna picked it up and smacked it and it cried and she wrapped it up and held it. And then Suzanna de Villiers knew that she first had to go home to see Mahoney.

The bus took her to the city air terminal and stood vibrating outside waiting for her to get off. She climbed out into the white sun. All was dead quiet in Abercorn Street. There was her old flat, up in Tregar House. There were different curtains in the windows. There was one tired ground hostess behind the quiet polished counter, amongst the beautiful photo-posters of the Greek Isles and Naples and the Riviera and the green English countryside.

'Can I leave my bags here for a while, please?'

The girl had slightly red eyes and she was pale under the chic make-up. She had had one hell of a party last night. She smiled professionally.

'I'm afraid we're closing now that the morning flight's in. We won't open again until six tonight.'

So that was it, that was another step in the wrong direction. She did not want to arrive at Joseph's flat with her luggage, because then it was so easy to stay. She had wanted to leave her baggage at the terminal and find a room in a boarding-house and then collect her baggage and then find Joseph. Then he could not insist on her staying in his flat.

'May I use your phone if I pay for it?'

She phoned the Russel. Sorry madam, no accommodation, fully booked with regulars. She telephoned the Gables, that mausoleum. It rang a long time. She could imagine it echoing down the long green desolate Sunday passages. At last a tired old lady answered it. Sorry, the Gables had a waiting list.

The ground hostess was standing behind the counter, patting papers straight and looking politely impatient to close up.

'Can I get you a taxi, madam, to one of the licensed hotels?'

'Yes, please.'

But that was silly, to pay two pounds ten a day, when she only had twenty-six pounds in the wide world, when all she needed was a place to dump her bags for a few hours while she found something reasonable. She would handle Joe.

'Fortwell Court, Fort Street,' she said to the taxi driver. But as she climbed the familiar red steps of Fortwell Court up to the fourth floor with the taxi driver carrying her two cases behind her, she felt her heart pounding with delicious excitement and she knew she could not handle Joe.

She pulled her hand mirror out and glanced quickly at herself. She patted her hair and ran the tip of her tongue over her lips and she smoothed the blouse over her bosom. She knocked.

Mahoney came to the door barefoot and in only a pair of shorts. His hair stuck up and he had ink on his face and chest.

'Suzie!'

She smiled, 'I haven't come to stay and I haven't come to make you marry me—'

'Suzie!'

In one movement he was over the threshold and he had picked her up. He carried her into the flat. Her only words of protest as he laid her on his unmade bed were: 'What about Samson?' and Mahoney said: 'It's all right, he's got the day off,' and she held out her arms to him.

'Don't give me a baby, don't, don't give me a baby, not now, don't kill us forever—'

But Mahoney closed her mouth with his and then they were soaring up up up and higher than the sky and higher and then there was nowhere and everything and completeness and floating and then an explosion and then a tumbling.

She lay half underneath him in the sweaty October Sunday morning and held him to her and stroked his head and his back.

'But,' she said, 'you will leave me.'

Mahoney shook his big head into the pillow. 'Marry me.'

Go away, Suzanna de Villiers. Go away, get up and get out while there is still a moment. Go far away so that you do not kill him and so that he does not kill you. Go anywhere, to England or South Africa or Hartford. Connecticut with Frank even, but go away before you kill the both of you—

She stroked his back. She lay still half underneath him, thinking and looking up at the ceiling. She turned her head sideways and looked at the white-blue sky through the window, the sky he hated. She frowned and then she sighed and gently lifted her hand to her breast. She ran her hand down over her breast and her flat stomach and her hip and her thigh and she felt tears of reckless happiness in her eyes. She sobbed.

'Shut up, you,' she said to herself softly.

Chapter Twenty-Five

I don't care. I don't care any more. I'm happy I've come back, I feel whole again now. I'll stay, I'll even live with him until he's good and ready to marry me. It used to worry me but it won't now. And if I go to hell, well that's just too bad. Anyway, if I go to hell, Joe'll be there too, so that's okay. I don't care as long as old Joe's there. Old Joe, I bet he'll talk the Devil into a cocked hat too. He and the Devil'll get on well, probably. That's funny. That's quite funny. You shouldn't joke about things like that but it is quite funny. And if the old Dominee comes around telling me I'll burn in hell I'll just set Joe on to him. I'd like to see that. He's a bully, Joe. I should know. But I don't care. So what if he's a bully. It's not so much that he's a bully it's just that he doesn't suffer fools gladly. An intellectual. Always reading and writing and pondering. The things he knows. Well so what if I'm not an intellectual. Most men are cleverer than their wives. How many girls are intellectual? And the ones that are look like the back of a bus. How would he like that? A man likes to be always right. How would he like it if I could talk him into a cocked hat? Like that Jackie friend of his. She's an intellectual, I suppose. Joe wants somebody who gives him peace. So I'm not an intellectual and I'll never be but it doesn't matter so long as you're happy together. I'll look after him well and keep him happy. I won't nag him and always be wanting attention and a good time and he'll be able to get on with his writing. That's the most important thing for a wife to be. That book. I wish I could help him with it. I'm no writer, I don't know much about literature and so forth so how can I judge? But it bores me. But it's his book and it's all important to him so I'll give him peace and encourage him and tell him it's good. Maybe it is good. I don't know, but I don't care either – it's him I care about.

Suzanna de Villiers had a spring in her step although it was as hot as hell in Eighth Avenue with the sun melting the tar and beating white off the Victorian façades of the shops and vibrating thick through the tin roofs of the shop verandah fronts. Her legs were fatter than before, and brown and smooth and she did not wear stockings and her sandals had highish heels and her hips swung a little as she walked and her cotton frock was fresh and crisp and her long straight hair jounced and you could tell her bosom was all her own from the way it vibrated a little with each step. Samson walked behind her in his white uniform, which he did not like wearing, particularly in public, and which the Nkosi had never suggested that he wear but which she had insisted on buying that very morning at the Indian store below Fortwell Mansions, as a surprise for Joseph. It would be nice for Joseph to come home from Court and find Samson all smart and the flat all jacked up with those bits and pieces that men never get round to and couldn't manage even if they thought about it, which they don't. Everybody has their boy in a nice white uniform. Joe isn't rich but that's no reason for him to live like a pig like he does. No curtains, no carpets, no ironing board, that sort of thing, Joe. Joe's not hard-up, I don't know how much he's got, but he's not all that hard-up. He probably doesn't know himself how much he's got. I bet he doesn't. I bet he doesn't know what it costs him to run that flat and how much he spends on beer and poker and the horses and on his girls. I don't care how much he spends, it's not my business but I want the flat to look nice and he'll like it okay and it won't cost more than a few quid. A few flowers and a couple of cheap vases from the O.K. and a few bits of crockery, and an ironing board, that sort of thing. He needs another suit but I won't mention that until he's got over the shock of the ironing board. He's got a thing about clothes, a suit is a good suit until he's coming through the pants. And shirts – why have more than three white shirts, he says, when you've got a boy to wash every day? Those shirts are terrible, only one is not shabby. But oh no, they're all good shirts still, he says. Maybe I'll sneak in a shirt, a drip-dry. Socks, he's all right for socks. Shoes, he needs another pair of shoes. I could get Cuthberts or Bata to send some up on approval. He'll squeal like a stuck pig but it's worth a try. He can only send them back. Why do men hate so to spend money on clothes? Or is it just Joe? I think it's just Joe. All the other chaps are smartly turned out. You've got to take a chap like Joe in hand, otherwise he'll walk around quite happily like a munt and think there's nothing wrong. Joe doesn't realise that people notice these things and they talk. He thinks everybody's as dozy as he is. That's my job, to see he's well turned out and well fed and so on. That's where I help him, where I can put my foot down and be right. And he'll take it. He'll accept it. He likes things the way they always were before but he'll get used to it. He doesn't think about things like that long enough to keep up a resistance for long. I'll get that flat nice and cheerful. And some planks and some bricks for bookshelves. All his thousands of books on window-sills and heaped all over the floor! He says that he knows where everything is now and it'll get his filing system all out of order if I start packing them in shelves. How he can find a thing now I don't know, but he can always put his hand on the book he wants. Anybody would think he's as mean as hell the way he refuses to make himself comfortable. Well that's my job, I'll make him comfortable. He'll like it sure enough. I suppose I'll have to take a room in a boarding-house until we can get married but I'm going to jack up that flat. And then when we get married everything will be in apple-pie order. He'll like it when he sees it all ready. That's half his trouble, that's why he thinks Bulawayo is such an awful dump – because he lives like a pig and he's got no comforts and he works like a slave and he doesn't eat properly and so he's a bag of nerves and irritations. I'll stand between him and all those irritations and his life will work smoothly like clockwork. Of course Bulawayo is a dreadful dump when you live like he does. What can you expect? He'll be fine when we're married and he's properly looked after. Sure, it'll work out.

Samson followed behind her carrying the big basket half-full of groceries. He walked with a spring too, head up, waving to friends and winking at the black girls more cavalierly to cover his embarrassment at wearing the white uniform. What did it really matter this once? The Nkosi would say he needn't wear the white uniform in town. In the flat, all right, but not in town. The Nkosi would understand, he was a man, he was his friend. They had hunted crocodiles together which is a man's work. A Matabele's work.

Suzanna walked into the supermarket with Samson behind carrying the basket. He followed her from stand to stand as she ruminated and plucked off tins.

'How much beer has the Nkosi got?'

'Four bottles only, Nkosikazi,' Samson said promptly.

'Well we better lay some in. Give me a dozen pints of Lion, please.'

Samson plucked at her short sleeve.

'Nkosikazi?'

'Yes?'

'The Nkosi never buy pint bottle. Cheaper if Nkosikazi buy big bottle.'

Suzanna smiled. 'All right. Six quarts of Lion, please,' she said to the man.

Samson plucked her sleeve again. 'How much, Nkosikazi?'

'I don't know. All the same price. How much for a quart?' She turned to the man again.

The little man beamed sourly. 'Three and a penny, madam.'

Samson shook his head. 'Only three bob,' he said. 'Where I always get beer for the Nkosi, only cost three bob.'

The little man looked peeved, and tapped his fingers. 'Save sixpence,' Samson said.

Suzanna grinned. 'All right. Will you get it?'

Samson beamed. 'Always.'

'So how much must I give you. Six threes are eighteen.'

Samson shook his head. 'The Nkosi got account for that shop.'

'Ah,' Suzanna said wisely. 'All right, off you go and then take the skoff home.'

'Okay, Nkosikazi,' and Samson left with the basket, looking relieved.

She went to the Men's Department. She went along the counters studying the shirts. Drip-dries, that's what he needs, cotton, not nylon, nylon's too hot. Might as well get two. Might as well get three, might as well be hung for a sheep as a lamb. She picked up three shirts.

'Yes madam?'

'I want—' she turned around to the voice and stopped. Jake Jefferson was looking down at her. 'Hullo, Suzie.'

Her eyes widened.

'Good God, Jake! What are you doing in Bulawayo?'

'I'm just down for a few days for a conference.'

He was fatter. And whiter and older, more lined. His good looks were sort of blurred. Suzanna looked at him. She felt nothing, only compassion. He was beginning to get old and he was still unhappy.

'You're looking lovely,' he said. 'You've put on some weight again.'

'You're looking fine too, Jake.'

'When did you get back?'

'Two days ago.' She spoke measuredly, carefully.

'Did you get my letters?'

'Yes. Thank you.'

'You didn't answer them.'

'No, I didn't.'

They looked at each other. 'Did you get your promotion?'

He shook his head. 'I'm sorry, Jake, I really am.'

He nodded.

He looked at her steadily.

'What are you doing in the O.K. Bargain Basement?'

'This is the only place I can afford to shop,' he said.

'Oh.'

'And you?'

'I'm buying some shirts.'

'For Joseph Mahoney?'

'Yes.'

He nodded. 'Where are you staying?'

'With him for the time being.'

He closed his eyes a moment and nodded. 'Are you going to marry him?'

'Yes.'

'When?'

'Just as soon as we've got used to being back together.'

'Are you sure you're going to marry him?'

'Yes.'

He looked at her and shook his head, 'I'm not,' he said slowly. 'And if you do it won't work.'

Chapter Twenty-Six

The Great Mahoney's bitten the dust – Another good man goes west – Two minutes silence, chaps, to mourn the passing of one of the boys – What'll the pubs do now – Well what do you know, what do you know! – Can you see old Joe pushing a pram – Well for Chrissake. Imagine him pushing a pram.

The usual. The usual crap and banter, the usual bull-shooting and buying of beers. It was supposed to be a secret, they would sneak off to Balla Balla or Essexvale or Gwanda or somewhere and get the District Commissioner to jack them up with a Special Licence. But as Max put it, if you're anybody who's anybody in Bulawayo you can't fart without everybody from North End to Kumalo sniffing the breeze and laying odds who done it.

Mahoney walked out of the Courthouse in the afternoon sun, on to the hot dry pavement and tarmac of Seventh. Out of the Courthouse behind him, alongside him, ahead of him, hurried the other civil servants, disgorging on to the pavements, hurrying over to their cars: out of the Post Office block across the road emerged the civil servants, hurrying to their cars: out of Charter House came the business men, the bright young execs and the trainee execs and the typists and the private secs and the buyers and the salesmen, into their cars going home to the clubs and the pubs. Thank God it's Friday. Cars going home, north up Fife to the nicer blocks of flats between the little old red-roofed houses with their red concrete stoeps and their red dust backyards, and beyond to the new flat third-acre modern houses of Sauerstown and North End, where the lawns struggle and the neat hedges are still trying to grow up.

Where you can see the nappies hanging on the washing lines strung across the backyards between the kitchen door and the servants' kia, where the black nannies push their masters' babies in the hire-purchase prams down the flat gravel roads so that the Nkosikazis can also go to work to pay for the nice new furniture and the new car and the new house and all the other nice trinkets, cars going south and east to the old flats in Thirteenth and Fourteenth and Fifteenth, the pre-war jobs built among the red-roofed red-bricked houses with the red stoeps and maybe a row of ferns on the verandah in paraffin tins painted green and the rickety chicken coops and the battered kid's tricycle and the packing cases and the motorcar shell and the broom with no bristles left and the servants' kia with its cracked window patched with cardboard, and beyond to the new modern little houses back to back and cheek to cheek on the quarter-acre stands of Sunnyside, and beyond to the old mature three-acre gardens of Hillside and the modern mansions of Kumalo with the swimming pools and billiard tables and sundowners on the lawn, to the parties at the Club and golf in the mornings and gin-slings at noon and a drive to the Matopos on Sunday and four weeks at Margate every year. Mahoney looked at them queuing at the intersection in their hire-purchase motorcars to go home to their hire-purchase houses and he realised he was almost one of them. Almost a suburbanite, a Bulawayo suburbanite at that, the flat horizon brigade, a Club man. He felt a moment's twinge of fear, of horror almost, then it was gone. He looked at the feeling in his breast and turned it over. It was relief. Relief that the straggle was all over, relief that there would be no more struggle, that now he was going to let life wash over him instead of trying to divert the flood into other channels.

He turned into Fort. It was thick with bicycles, blacks riding home to the locations, to the flat straight-laned dirty brick and dust oceans of Mzilikazi and Mpopoma and Iminyela and Tshabalala. A girl was walking ahead of Mahoney, an office typist, maybe, or a shop girl going home to one of the flats. She had good legs, a little plump maybe but good in high heels, and her skirt fitted tight across her buttocks. She took short steps because her skirt was tight and with each step her buttocks jerked from side to side against the material, the skirt curved inwards over the mound of her buttocks and clung down the back of her legs so you could make out the line of her panties and the clip of her garter tight and slack tight and slack went the skirt over her buttocks and the back of her legs, with each short step there was a faint dent where the cheeks of her bottom moved. She glanced backwards at Mahoney and met his eye and she tossed her seventeen-year-old head and walked on. And Mahoney looked at her legs again and he looked away and tried to think of something else. He thought of something else but he knew there was a feeling inside him that squirmed. All that was over too, along with the struggle. And he wanted to hurry back to the flat to Suzie to reassure himself that it did not matter about the girl.

Suzie was there, in shorts, a lock of hair hanging limp over her face. In her hand was a saw, on the floor bricks and planks. There were curtains in the window. His books were off the sill, no longer heaped in the corners. There was a book case made of bricks and planks. There were two big grass mats. There were flowers in two vases.

'What do you think?'

Mahoney smiled. He forced a smile. Why should he not be pleased? God knew it was an improvement. 'Very very good.'

Suzie breathed with relief. It was good. The room looked comfortable. It was transformed.

'I've only just started,' she said excitedly.

He nodded. But there was that feeling inside again. The room was gone. Life was changing suddenly. It was merging with the rest of Bulawayo.

'Let's have a drink,' he said, and he felt better, and she said, 'All right.'

'Come here,' he said. She came to him and he put his arm round her and down over her buttocks and squeezed the back of her long smooth legs.

'Everything's going to be fine,' he said and he kissed her: '*Now* bring me a beer and then we'll go out somewhere.'

They went to the green Sheridan and then to the pink Flamingo and then to the red Carousel and then to the purple Vic. And in the pinks and greens and air-conditioned inbetweens the claustrophobia of the redecorated flat and the brown horizons and the office girl with the legs were flushed out and as he looked at her long tanned legs as she walked to the Ladies' he felt only unqualified relief, relief that those legs were his for ever, relief that never again would he have a choice. And they talked about what they were going to do and what it was going to be like and they laughed and joked and afterwards they went on to the Wamborough and danced to Antonio and they met Max and the boys and their girls and they had a wonderful party like everybody else was having all over Bulawayo and everybody made jokes and wished them luck and Antonio got to hear about it and he made a little announcement – that well-known public prosecutor and hees beyoutifool bride-to-be – and he played For They Are Jolly Good Feh-hel-lows and they went home very late and very happy.

The next day was Saturday, and when they woke up the bedroom was already hot and the sky sat upon the dry red-roofed town like a hot blue belljar.

Chapter Twenty-Seven

October was bad. The whole of the earth was hot and dry and the bush crackled brown and hard and brittle and hot and the cattle were dusty and thin and the river-beds were hot and sandy and dry and the fish died in the dams. The Government officers rode out into the Native Reserves in their Landrovers and the District Commissioners called all the headmen of the kraals together for indabas and the Government Land Officers warned the headmen that it was going to be a bad year for rain in Matebeleland, that the rains would come late and they would not last a long time. The earth was dry, they said, and the grass was gone and the cattle were chewing the dust. The people must thin out their herds, the District Commissioner and the Government Land Officers said, each man must examine his herd and see which beasts he favoured the least and he must sell them to the Government for money so that the Government could slaughter them while there was still flesh on them for men to eat. And the people must sell their goats which trample the land and strip the earth of the little which the cattle could eat, for goats are useless creatures. And the people should take the money which the Government was offering for the beasts and buy food for their families for the crops would be bad and the people would be hungry this year. And when the rains did come and the grass grew again it would be better for the men who had sold some of their cattle and their goats for there would be more for those they kept to eat and next year they would be fatter and they would be better able to survive the winter. The headman sat in their circles on the hot dry ground and listened politely to the Government officers and they agreed that it would be a good thing to sell some of their cattle for money while there was still flesh upon them and they promised to drive the beasts they favoured least to the meeting place next week when the Government would come and buy them. But the headmen did not like to sell their cattle because a man counted his wealth in the number of cattle and goats that he owned and in the number of daughters he had which he sold for cattle as brides. And the tribesmen consulted the witch-doctors who make the rain to come and the witch-doctors told them that the white men did not know what they were talking about because the white men did not understand how to make rain, and they told them that they should not sell any cattle or goats. And then there came some black men to the Native Reserves, strange black men in city clothes who drove up in motorcars and they held indabas too and they told the tribesmen about the Freedom that they were going to bring to the country, how all men would own many cattle and goats and motorcars too, like the white men did, and that they should not sell any cattle or goats to the Government because it was all the white man's trick to cheat the people out of their wealth so that they could keep them poor and powerless for ever. And the men in the city clothes told them about the Party, which was a new thing never heard of before, and they told the people to form committees and they said that each man should pay one shilling towards the Party to show that he belonged to the Party, and when the Party brought Freedom to the country those who had cards would be the first to get many fat cattle and motorcars like the white men had. And on the appointed day when the Government man came to the appointed place to buy, no man came with any cattle. And October grew longer and hotter and the earth became harder and drier and many of the old water holes began to dry up and many of the cattle and the goats died. The tribesmen hoed the hot dry soil and watched the skies but no clouds came, and many men put their clothes and their trinkets in an old sack or in a bag and they walked the long hot roads to Bulawayo to look for work to make some money to buy some food for their families because the rain did not come and the mealies did not grow.

The tarmac streets were hot in Bulawayo and the tar melted and when you climbed into your car you put a newspaper on the seat so that you did not burn yourself and even the steering wheel was hot. And you opened all the windows and started the engine and loosened your tie and took off your jacket and you drove down the street in the queue and the sun shimmered off the hood of the car in front of you and it beat up off the tarmac and it shone white off the white walls of the new office blocks and red off the low Victorian shop fronts of Main Street. And you looked at the typists and the telephone girls and the shop girls and the secretaries skipping across the road to the shelter of the shade of the shop verandahs and to their hot cars and you knew that they were wet under their armpits and they smelt of sweat there despite the Mum and Odo-ro-no, and that their thighs were moist and salty no matter what they put on there to kid themselves and their men that they were all sweet and fresh and fragrant there all the time like the magazines say that women are or at least can be, if only. And you look down Seventh, down the wide brown yellow avenue of jacarandas separated by the hot black shimmering tar and its crocodile of metal hoods of motorcars heading out to the suburbs and to the flats and you see the sun beating down on the red tiled and corrugated-iron roof-tops and the red dirt of the backyards and the diapers which dry in half an hour, and you come home to the hot house with its browning lawns and its hot red stoeps, home to the flat with its all-glass main wall of the sitting-room overlooking a hot quiet strip of tar and gravel and dry jacarandas and the hot metal hoods of the cars parked outside and the hot red roofs of the houses and you say to yourself: A drink, what I want is a drink, ice cold. Or you go to the soft plush air-conditioned Sheridan or the Vic or the Carousel or the Wamborough where Matabeleland and its hot white red-brown town is shut off by the pinks and greens and inbetweens and the cool canned music, or the Club. And there is only one thing to do in the hot wide flat world and that is to go home to sleep off the cold beer and the gin-slings and to screw your gin-slung sweaty-thighed woman. And in the end, in fact pretty soon, that is all you think about, that and your salary and the hire-purchase instalments and tonight's party and next week's party and that is all there is to think about anyway, because not even the kaffirs were really a problem in those days.

That October was more like that than other Octobers. It was the beginning of bad times.

That last Friday of that bad October Mahoney drove to the Courthouse early. He had been awake since dawn, even though he had been to bed late. He had been wide awake with the first light, staring at the ceiling and at the blue belljar sky and he knew that it would always be like this, waking in the morning and seeing the sky and going to the Courthouse and coming home and drinking beer and going to the Club and coming home and copulating: And you can never get away from it, never except maybe down to Margate for four weeks a year and it takes you three days to drive there and three days to drive back because you've got to consider your wife and kids and when you get to Margate you sit on the beach in the sun just like you do here and you go back to the hotel early so the kids can go to the Kiddies Lunch and you sit on the hotel verandah and have a few beers and then you and your wife go into lunch at one-fifteen at the latest because otherwise the management and the waiters get cheesed off because after all the hotel is only costing forty bob a day per adult and quarter price for the kids and what can you expect for forty bob, but that is all you can afford. And then after lunch you go to your hotel bedroom and have a snooze and maybe you screw your wife if the kids are away with the nanny, if you can afford to bring your nanny with you, and then you go down to the beach again or maybe for a drive and have some tea at one of those beach-side cafes with Coca-Cola signs and the chromium Gaggia Espresso coffee and milk-shake mixer jobs with a juke box in the corner and the teenagers sitting on the Formica chairs at the Formica tables drinking Coke, man, and Choco shakes and chewing gum and saying 'Jeez-like las' night woz a ball, hey?' and 'Jeez-like man but ou' Cynthia's a doll hey, I jus' somma' wanna screw her, man.' Or maybe you go and have your tea on the verandah of one of the other nice hotels along the beach front and you see the dear old souls down from Rhodesia or Jo'burg having their annual holiday, also drinking tea, and the youngsters with their strong tanned bodies and the girls from up country having their holiday and you think, I suppose you think: Jeez, I'd love to screw that one. But of course it's out of the question and anyway you wouldn't because after all you've got kids and responsibilities and so forth. Or maybe you take your wife and kid for a drive in the country and you stop for tea, and you think how nice it would be to live down here with the seaside only a few miles away and you could go and spend your Sundays down on the beach with a picnic lunch in the picnic basket you bought at the O.K. Sale, that's the only reason why you could afford it: but of course living down here is out of the question, too, because you're all settled in Matabeleland which after all has the highest standard of living of them all and you've got your house there and your servants and your job and you're doing okay up in Rhodesia and your kids are at school and anyway how could you afford to chuck up everything and move and start at the bottom again, you wouldn't get another good job like you've got in Rhodesia. How can you take a chance now you've got the kids? And after your four weeks you drive back across the Limpopo back to Matabeleland and for another year you wake up under the blue belljar sky and you go for sundowners at the Club and the Sheridan and the Flamingo and the Carousel and the Vic and you talk about the same things you talked about last year and you look at your best friend's wife and you think: I'd love to shag Connie; and you know that Connie's thinking the same thing. And after a few years you even think this life is just fine and you cease to notice the brown horizons and you forget you're only a big fish because it's a bloody small pond. You don't even think it's a small pond.

Mahoney left the Courthouse at four o'clock that Friday afternoon and got into his hot old box Chev and ground into the queue of hot cars driving down the hot tarmac road. He drove slowly down to Suzie's surgery. There were the office girls going home, pretty pink girls with panties wet with sweat round the crotch and wedged up wet and sticky in the cleft of their buttocks, smelling at least of meat round there, not sweet and fragrant like the women's magazines pretend. And he thought: and after the passion has been spent inside them, when you're lying hot and sticky and enervated and sexless beside them in the awful emptiness of passion spent, what then? Reality. Reality of the sun in the sky shining down on you and there is nothing left, but kidding yourself all over again, till you want it again. Go out to the Club or down to the pub and after a couple of beers you begin to feel better and there is something to talk about again, something. It can even become good fun, even interesting on your fifth beer, and you can look forward to it again. But then there is tomorrow again and the sky and the sun and the horizons and eff-all else but the reality of passion spent. And he saw the office men and women emerging from their offices and driving back to their flats and homes in the suburbs, this side of the horizons, and to their clubs and pubs *en route*, and he thought: they will do this every day until they are sixty years old, and so will I. And he waited suspendedly for Suzie to emerge from her office so that he could forget the thought in the proximity of her, in the comfort of the relief of having her, so that he thought only of tonight.

'Where are you going?'

'For a drink,' Mahoney said.

'But it's a bit early to start drinking. It's only five past four.'

'What else is there to do?'

'Go to your place and have tea.'

'And?'

'And talk.'

'About?'

'What do you mean, what'll we talk about?'

'Well, what is there to talk about?'

'Same as what other people talk about. Why should we be so different!'

'Maybe I am different.'

'Oh Joe! What's the matter?'

'I'm sick of spending my time going for drinks, that's the matter.'

'But you suggested going for a drink.'

'I know.'

'Then why did you suggest it?'

'Because what else is there to do?'

She sat back silent. 'Well, let's go and look at a flat. Mrs. Smythe in my office, her sister-in-law is having a baby and they're giving up their flat and she says she's sure we could get first option.'

Mahoney drove on.

'Well,' she said, 'are we going to look at this flat?'

'We're going to have a drink.'

'I thought you were sick of doing nothing but drinking.'

'That's right. But when in Rome, you've got to do as Romans do, or else you go up the wall.' He pulled up outside a hotel.

'Aren't we going to look at the flat?' she pleaded, '—something constructive.'

'After we've had a drink.'

After the first drink she put her hand on his knee.

'I've read about how you feel. People often panic when they're about to get married.'

He did not say anything, he did not really know how he felt himself, so how the hell could she know? After the second drink he began to feel better again. She was. beautiful with long smooth tanned legs. He thought of her white breasts, of her soft flat belly and her long naked back. He thought of having her there safe and loyal beside him in the mornings when he woke up, of having her clicking round the flat in the evening in a diaphanous nightie as she brushed her teeth and brushed her hair before bed, he thought of Sunday mornings when they lounged around all morning reading the papers together. When he thought of those things he felt the relief of surrender to security again. Oh what the hell, he thought, why worry and struggle against whatever it is? And he began to be happy with her again.

'One more drink then we'll go and look at the flat,' he said kindly.

And she picked up his vibrations and she was relieved and happy again.

It was a nice flat. Two bedrooms and a lounge cum dining-room. Anywhere in the world it would be a good flat for a young couple. Suzie was delighted.

'We must go and fix it up with the agent tomorrow,' she said excitedly.

'Flats aren't easy to get,' Mrs. Smythe's sister-in-law said, 'as fast as they put them up they're full.'

'You can work on your book in the spare room and I won't disturb you,' Suzie said.

As the woman moved away she leaned closer to him: 'And I'll be just through the wall waiting for you when you come to bed.'

'It's got a lovely view,' said the woman.

She pulled back the lounge curtains. The flat was on the eighth floor of the block. The lights were coming on in the city, far below.

'And a balcony!'

'Yes, a balcony. And you get the sun most of the day.'

'Isn't it a nice flat?'

'Yes, it is,' he said.

'And it's only a few minutes' walk from the Courthouse. And only a few more minutes to my office.'

'Yes,'

'My fiancé is an advocate,' Suzie said proudly.

'Oh,' said the woman, impressed.

As the woman turned away Suzie said: 'While you're writing I can lie out here in my bikini.'

When the woman was out of earshot, Suzie said: 'And we can have our wine and chicken on Sundays out here and not a soul can see us.'

He felt the sweaty security of Suzie and the sun and the wine and he felt happy.

'We've got to give two months' notice,' said the woman, 'and we're giving it at the end of the month. When are you getting married?'

Suzie said: 'We'll probably arrange it to fit in with the flat.'

When they got back below to his car she said: 'What d'you think?'

'It's a nice flat.'

'Shall we take it?'

'I think so. But we've got a week yet before they give their notice, let's look around.'

'But I don't think we'll find a better one.'

'Let's go and have a drink and some skoff somewhere and we can talk about it.'

When they were having their drink she said: 'Joe. You do want to marry me, don't you?'

'Of course I do.' And he meant it.

'I'm good for you,' she said, 'I keep you reasonably on the straight and narrow, I look after your food, I don't interfere with your writing as long as you don't take out too much of your irritability on me and furthermore I love you and you know I would never be disloyal to you.'

'I know, Suzie. Your third gin is going to your head.'

'*In vino Veritas,*' she said. 'Oh! – it's a lovely flat. Well,' she said, 'I'm going to see the agent tomorrow. You shouldn't be worried by such things.'

And he felt Suzie close to him, beautiful loyal Suzie of the long legs, and he saw, felt Suzie in that flat, Suzie in the morning doing her long gold hair, Suzie organising Samson, Suzie telephoning the grocer and ordering food and plenty of wine and beer, Suzie lying naked in the sun on the balcony warm and slippery and glistening in olive oil, Suzie's wide red moist mouth smiling happily and lasciviously in the sun, Suzie tiptoeing into his study while he was writing and pressing her breasts against his shoulder and her face against his cheek. Suzie jacking up the movie tickets, Suzie arranging the parties and accepting invitations, Suzie being very proud of him, Suzie standing between him and all outside irritations, Suzie sliding into his bed at night and twisting herself around him. Forever, it will be Suzie, Suzie giving him everything, beautiful Suzie. And he would never have to fret and struggle and resist again. He would never wake up on Sunday mornings feeling worthless and empty and besotted again. And she would give him a family and he would become immersed in happy stable respectability and go from strength to strength, he would in due course become Attorney General thanks to her for being a good wife and stable influence, and they would mature in prosperity together and look back upon successful lives together.

They thought and talked about these things together over their drinks in the pinks and greens and inbetweens of the cocktail bars and they got very warm and loving and grateful towards each other and the world was very safe at last. And they went on to another cocktail bar and they laughed and made jokes and they drank more and danced and they had dinner and champagne and got rather drunk and very happy and then they went to his flat. And without bidding she bent her arms up behind her back and unzipped her dress and slid it off over her shoulders and let it drop to the floor. She unhitched her stockings, fiddle fiddle front and back and she peeled them off and she looked steadily into his eyes the whole time she did it. Then she put her hands up behind her back again and unhitched her bra and slipped it forward off her shoulders. She stood still looking at him for a moment then she took a step towards him and stretched out her arms and brought his head down on her.

'Come, my love. My love, my love, my brooding love.'

She kissed him long on the mouth and then while she kissed him her fingers went to his shirt and undid the buttons, and then his tie and she pulled it off him and then she stood on tiptoe and pressed her breasts against his chest while she kissed him. Then she took his hands and pulled him to the bed and she leaned over him and brushed her breasts over his face and pushed her nipples into his mouth and then her fingers felt for his belt and they made love.

Chapter Twenty-Eight

The next day was Saturday, the last week-end of October. Saturday, oh Saturday, the best day of the week, the end of a week of heat and work, jolly good show. Hangover tomorrow, but no bloody office, chaps. Nooners at Club and pub, a few beers and gin-slings until closing time at two-thirty – then go home and, well, you know what. A bit of Rhodesian P.T. See you later at the Club, see you later at the Jonas' party, good show, it's going to be a whirl, I hear. Too bloody hot to play golf but maybe meet you at the Clubhouse.

Saturday. Leave the office at eleven-thirty, down to the Sheridan for a few cold ones waiting for Suzie to come by from her shopping. 'The town's like the madhouse, I couldn't get parking within four blocks – Phew! Ah Suzie! – The most beautiful thing in town, have a drink my love, what the hell. You know Pete and Mike and Sarah, sure you do, what'll you have, a cold one? What've you got us for lunch?

Lunch. The desultory sounds of Suzie padding round the kitchen in her shorts and bare feet fixing lunch, the bottle of Lieberstein in the fridge getting good and cold, the paper napkins and cutlery ready and waiting on the two occasional tables, sitting in swimming trunks on the verandah overlooking Fort Street and thinking beautiful thoughts on your sixth cold beer while Suzie pops in and out reporting on lunch. Don't hurry lunch, Suzie, come and relax and have a beer. Switch off the oven and get into your bikini and sit down out here and relax. That's right. Bring two more cold ones while you're up. Good girl, darling. I've had some red hot sure winner ideas for my book sitting out here. This book's going to be a best bloody seller, you know that? It's bloody brilliant, that's the only way to describe it. Brilliant. I think bloody well on Saturdays. You're a beautiful girl, Suzie. You've got the best pair of titties in the whole flat world. And the best pair of legs. Take off your bikini top, darling.

Saturday morning, the last Saturday of Suicide Month. Mahoney woke at seven o'clock – the sounds of Samson in the kitchen making coffee. Saturday. Every Saturday from now on, for ever. The sun was pressing down on to his bed out of the mercilessly blue sky, not one wisp of cloud. The sky was hot and empty and it went all the way to infinity. Seven o'clock in the morning and he was sweating under the single sheet. The room was white and dry and he knew the parquet floor was warm. He remembered the flat they had seen the night before. It was a lovely flat with a wonderful view. A view of the hot flat town and the flat brown horizons. And after a while your own horizons became circumscribed, flat and brown too, only you don't realise it because you have nothing to measure horizons by except the long flat brown one though the window and the cushy aristocracy of the Club and the cocktail bars. A big fish in a small pond, big fishes all of us, the pigmentocracy. And Suzie will have a baby and then another and another and for ever after you will be a big fish in this pond and you will never know any other pond except once a year when you drive down to Margate for your holidays. And every Saturday will be like this, nooners at the Club and pub and wine in the sun. And Mahoney wanted to start running down to the sea.

At eight o'clock Suzie drove him to his office. She said: 'Shall I go and see the agent about that flat?'

'We had better wait,' he said.

Later they lay naked and panting on Suzie's bed in her boarding-house, thick with the sun and the wine, but his mind was very clear in the calm of passion spent. She stared at the ceiling, numbed from the words she had heard, believing but not daring to believe, and her heart breaking and crying out.

'*Et tu, Brute,*' she said dully. 'That's the only bit of Latin I know. That and *in vino veritas.*'

He said nothing.

She sat up quickly. She pulled on her shorts and blouse. She sat down on the armchair and rested her chin on her hand and stared out of the window.

'For God's sake go, then. Give up your bright job. Give up being a big fish in a small pond. Go and widen your horizons. Escape the quagmire of suburbia as you call it. Escape me.'

'Suzie, it's not you. It's marriage.'

She shrugged and didn't look at him.

'Oh yes, it's me all right. It's me. I'm not big enough to contain you. I just think you're wonderful, I just admire and applaud you, but I don't keep up with you. I can't. I'm just an ordinary simple girl who wants a home and babies and who's quite happy to let you get on with running the world. I'm just a nice little suburbanite at heart and you're not. I've been kidding myself I'm all right for you, that we can be companions like you want a woman to be. But the only way I give you anything is by getting drunk with you and having these orgies.'

'That's not true.'

'It is. Half your dissatisfaction with the way of life here is because that's the only way of life a dreary suburbanite like me can offer you.'

She sat perfectly still, her tanned legs crossed, resting her forehead on her hand and she looked at him with blue sphinx eyes.

'What if you're pregnant?'

'I don't think I am. But even if I am it would be folly to marry you. I'll go away and have it and keep it and call myself Mrs. Joe Soap.'

She sat still, waiting for him to go.

'Please go now. Where is your courage? You've always wanted to escape this quagmire of suburbia, so have the courage to do it. Go but don't come back unless and until you've found out what it is you want, or whether you are in fact a real bum.'

'Suzie.'

'Yes?'

'I love you.'

'Yes,' she said.

He stood, not knowing what to do, not believing that it could all be as simple and devastating as that. He wanted to cry out in loneliness and fear and in pain for hurting Suzie and also himself.

'Please go.'

'All right. Good-bye Suzie.'

She continued to sit still, her head supporting her chin, looking past him across the room. 'Good-bye, Joe.'

So there was nothing more to do, just walk out of her room and go.

He closed the front door and started walking down the steps. He heard one loud stifled sob from behind the door. He stopped and listened but there were no more and he walked on down the stairs. The street was empty and hot and bright and dull and dusty under the sunshine. He climbed into his car and it was hot and the seat burned his bum. He drove down to the Victoria and he drank a row of cold Lions and there were tears in his eyes. At eight o'clock a hand tapped his shoulder and he turned and there were Max and the boys and he did not get back to his flat until two o'clock in the morning. There was a girl in his bed when he woke up and he had a hangover which only another row of cold Lions at the Club would cure.

Chapter Twenty-Nine

November was very bad. It was the month of waiting, waiting for the rain to come, waiting for the cattle to die, waiting to leave. In the hot flat city of Bulawayo it was very dry, but there was beer. Out there in the brown horizons there was no beer, and the earth was hot and hard and bare, bare-arsed hard-arsed baked dusty gritty bare and as hot as all hell and no grain left in the grain huts and the cattle and the goats which the wise men and the strange black gentlemen from the city had said should not be sold stood thin and weak with their heads hanging down and then many lay down under a naked thom tree and they never got up and their bones pressed up against their hides. And the men whom the wise men and the strange black gentlemen from the city had advised found that there was not enough to eat and they packed their little goods in bundles and they set off on the long hot roads to Bulawayo to look for work, and they came to Mzilikazi and Mpopoma and Tshabalala townships there on the fringe of the brown horizons outside the white man's town and they sought out their tribesmen and their relatives and friends who already were accustomed to the ways of the city. They shared the blankets of their tribesmen and their porridge and every day they went out into the city and they looked for work. They walked the hot wide streets of Bulawayo and they went to the back of the shops and the offices and they climbed the blocks of flats and they waited outside the factories, but there was not enough work, not nearly enough.

Mahoney's flat in Fort Street grew emptier. It was easy to sell things in those days, even in the drought, and anyway Mahoney did not have much to sell. The only thing he kept was the table and a chair. Every night of November he sat at the table with a bottle of beer and an office ball point pen and his manuscript and wrote feverishly, trying to finish the book that would just never be finished, trying to forget the burning behind his eyes in a fog of creation and alcohol and smoke. His words sprawled across the pages, his writing getting bigger and rougher and his sentences longer and his language more obtuse and his imagery more intense and more elusive, but he did not still the pain in his breast and the book only got longer, no closer to the end. He did not visit Suzanna de Villiers and she did not call him.

On the twenty-second day of November he saw her in the street. She was looking into a bookshop window. She did not see him at first and he stood still and looked at her. She stood with her fingertips of one hand touching her chin, looking into the window. She was thin, her face was thin and sad but it was composed. He wanted to ran to her and throw his arms around her and tell her that it was all all right now, everything was all right, they would get married and live happily ever after and never be lonely or apart again, they would stay right here and get married or go off around the world together, or anything, just so long as they were together and the pain in her thin body and his was stilled forever. He hesitated, then he was about to crunch his heart and turn away. Then she turned and she was looking at him.

She stood quite still next to the window under the hot corrugated-iron roof, her fingers still lightly at her chin, her long straight hair hanging down the sides of her face, looking at him. It seemed a long time that they stood there. Then Mahoney said quietly: 'Hello.'

She blinked. 'Hello, Joe.' They stood five paces apart.

'How're you?' he said.

'Okay, thanks.' It was an empty question and an empty answer. 'How're you?'

'Okay.'

They looked at each other, knowing what they wanted to say, not knowing what to say.

'You're pale,' she said after a moment, 'you look pale and

exhausted.'

'I'm okay.'

She nodded, without taking her eyes away. 'How're your hands? Swollen and itchy?'

'Yes.'

She nodded.

'You need a rest,' she said. 'This break will fix you up.'

Mahoney nodded. 'You're thin.'

'Yes,' she said. 'I am a bit.'

'Are you eating.'

She nodded. 'Yes.'

'Properly.'

'I'm not hungry.'

Mahoney got impatient. 'You must eat, Suzie.'

She closed her eyes briefly and nodded. 'I will again soon. When I'm over you,' and the words struck terror in him.

'How's the book?'she said.

Mahoney blinked impatiently. 'Okay.'

'Is it nearly finished?'

'Yes.'

For the first time she looked away. 'That's good,' she said.

Mahoney breathed out sharply through his nostrils. 'Oh for Chrissake,' he said.

She looked up. 'What?'

He shook his head. 'Nothing ... I love you, that's all.'

'Yes,' she said.

He waited.

'Well, do you love me?' he demanded.

She did not look up.

She nodded. 'You know I do.'

'Suzie.'

She did not look up.

'*Suzie*,' he said angrily and she looked up at him and her eyes were very deep.

'Yes.'

'Suzie. Well, then ...'

She shook her head. 'No,' she said. She shook her head again. 'I guess I must be going,' she said steadily, 'it's nearly time to get back.'

'Suzie.'

'Yes.'

'Let's have a drink this afternoon, after work I'll pick you up.'

She looked at him and then she said: 'Good-bye, Joseph.' And she turned and she walked away down the pavement.

'Suzie!' he said angrily, but she did not look back.

He stood looking after her, the movement of her legs. He wanted to bound after her and grab her arm so the pain made her come to heel while he told her that she was bloody well going to listen to him and she was going to be there outside her surgery at four and they were going to bloody well talk it out or else. Then he thought: She's right and there're still eight days left and for Chrissake I don't know my backside from my elbow any more either. I don't know anything any more. I'm a bloody wreck, menace, I'm good for nothing. I'm getting nowhere, my book's a bloody failure and I'm losing cases in Court like a bloody beginner.

Chapter Thirty

The party started at about half-past three in Mahoney's office, when the boys started coming out of their courts. On the floor were three crates of Lion bombers. There was the usual crap, the wise cracks, the little speeches. Then the typists went home and the boys got down to it. At five o'clock someone was sent down to the Exhibit Room and came back with a sack of assorted beers and some Scotch, stuff that had been confiscated by courts to the Crown over the year but which nobody had had the heart to destroy. Then, the women out of the way, the Chief made the presentation. He made a beery speech which was punctuated with gaffaws and heckling and hear hears with many references to Mahoney's lechery. Then he presented the office present, a small square parcel. It was a cardboard carton containing one gross of French letters. Ha ha ha, estimates as to how long they would last him, this is just an emergency kit, etcetera etcetera. At seven o'clock they adjourned down to the Exchange where Mahoney had arranged to meet Max and the boys. Solly was in town and he took Mahoney aside and gave him some fatherly advice on how to be a successful bum without staying one. At nine o'clock the party broke up and Mahoney walked back to his empty flat in Fort Street to pack, with ten beers sloshing round inside him, completely sober.

Samson was sitting on the floor in the kitchen.

'I told you this morning not to wait,' Mahoney said in Sindebele.

'I wanted to wait for the Nkosi.'

'Go home now, induna. I will still be here in the morning. But come early, I want to be on the road with the dawn.'

'Can I not wait, Nkosi?'

Mahoney smiled sadly. 'All right, induna.'

He went to the fridge. There was half a pint of milk and some butter and three eggs and six beers.

'You can have this food.'

'Thank you, Nkosi.'

Mahoney took two beers from the fridge. He held his hot swollen peeling palms against the ice box. Then he opened the beers and held one out to Samson.

'Good luck, induna.'

'Thanks seh.'

They sucked out of the neck of the bottles.

'Come to the room and help me pack my belongings.'

'Has the Nkosi eaten?'

'No. Is there anything to eat?'

'Only the eggs.'

'Come, let us pack.'

They went into the bare bedroom. 'Bring out the suitcases and the rucksack and sit down there.'

Mahoney opened the built-in cupboard. He started on the shirts. He took three. The rest he threw on the floor.

'You can have those.'

'Thank you, Nkosi.'

'Socks. I'll only need a few. These. Take those. Ties. I better take two. The rest are very bad anyway.'

He folded them roughly and stuffed them into the rucksack. The pile on the floor grew.

'Suits. Thank God I didn't buy any more. I'll take this one I'm wearing. Here, this will fit you.'

'Thank you very much, Nkosi.'

'Get us two more beers, Samson.'

They sat down on the floor to drink, amongst the suitcases and the clothing. Mahoney tossed Samson a cigarette.

'Nkosi?'

'Yes?'

Samson looked at his feet. 'My heart is very sad that the Nkosi is going away.'

Mahoney nodded. 'My heart is also sad.'

Samson coughed. 'Nkosi?'

'Yes?'

'Can I not come with you?'

Mahoney shook his head sadly. 'I am sorry, induna. I have already told you.'

'I ask not for wages, Nkosi. Maybe we will make money together, we can hunt crocodiles again.'

Mahoney smiled, 'I have told you that I am not going to hunt crocodiles again, nor elephant, nor look for gold.'

'I ask not for wages, Nkosi! One day the Nkosi must again work for money and then I will be his cook again. Maybe we will find plenty money again.'

'Samson, my friend, I cannot take you. I have told you that I am going over the sea, a long way and I do not know to which lands I will travel, nor if I will come back here. It is impossible.'

Samson played with his cigarette. 'Then – if the Nkosi does stay in another land and he builds a house and buys a wife, will he send for me to be his cook?'

'How could you leave your kraal and your cattle and your wives?'

'Maybe I can bring my best wife.'

Mahoney sighed. 'Maybe, Samson. We shall wait to see the future.'

Samson shook his head. They sucked beer out of the bottles and they were silent. Then Samson said: 'Nkosi, you have told me of the sea, and there were Zulu men on the mines in Johannesburg who came from the sea, and they told me about it, but I have never seen it. It is said it is very big.'

Mahoney nodded, 'It is true it is very big.'

Samson thought, 'Is it bigger than Kariba?'

'Very many times bigger.'

Samson shook his head, 'it is like it was in the valley in this room now,' Samson said sadly and Mahoney nodded. Then Samson frowned.

'The Nkosi has said he will go to England where the Queen lives.'

Mahoney nodded. 'Will the Nkosi eat skoff with the Queen?'

Mahoney laughed. 'The Queen does not know me, Samson.'

'But she knows who the Nkosi is. At Nyamanpofu the Nkosi was the Queen's special representative, he spoke the Queen's words for her. She will remember the Nkosi, I am sure.'

Mahoney laughed gently again. 'The Queen is a busy woman and she has many Native Commissioners, who look after many of her people. I think she has probably forgotten me.'

'She cannot forget. Maybe she does not know the Nkosi has come to England. If you go to her house she will remember and maybe she will make the Nkosi Native Commissioner again.'

Mahoney nodded. 'Perhaps,' he said kindly, 'I will surely visit her.'

'The Nkosi should write her a letter to tell her that he is coming,' he said, 'in case she has forgotten.'

'You are right, induna, I will write her a letter,' Mahoney said.

Samson thought: 'Nkosi?'

'Yes.'

'When you are Native Commissioner in England, who will cook your skoff?'

'There are no Native Commissioners in England, Samson. The Queen herself is the N.C.'

Samson understood. 'Well, even so, when the Nkosi is living in England, who will cook his skoff?'

'I shall have to cook it myself.'

Samson frowned. 'And who will wash the Nkosi's shirts and his socks and his underpants?'

'I will have to wash them myself,' Mahoney said.

'And who will buy the Nkosi's skoff in the shop, and his beer?'

'Me.'

Samson shook his head. 'And who will clean the Nkosi's shoes and his motorcar and bring his breakfast to the Court at eleven o'clock?'

'I will have to do all those things myself, Samson,' Mahoney said.

Samson shook his head. 'Ah!' he said. 'That is no country for a white man.'

Mahoney threw back his head and laughed. It was the first time that he had laughed from his heart for a long time.

Samson looked surprised, then sheepish and then he laughed politely.

'Get two more beers, Samson,' Mahoney laughed.

Samson stood up. 'Nkosi?'

'Yes, induna?'

Samson looked embarrassed, 'I have brought the Nkosi a gift.'

Mahoney blinked. 'What have you brought, induna?'

Samson dug his hand into his pocket. He brought out a lump of crumpled brown paper. He unfolded it and held it out for him to see. It was a piece of carved bone. Mahoney recognised it.

'It will protect the Nkosi.'

Mahoney nodded and he picked up the bone carefully.

'You got this from a witch-doctor,' Mahoney said, and Samson nodded. Mahoney shook his head, 'I cannot take it, induna,' he said, 'it is too powerful a charm. You must keep it to protect yourself.'

Samson looked hurt.

'I got it for the Nkosi,' he said and Mahoney closed his eyes. Suddenly he was very tired and sad and there were tears behind his eyes. He did not want to leave Africa.

'Induna,' he said, 'you took much trouble to get this charm. I take it now and I will keep it to protect me. Thank you, induna.'

Samson beamed and looked embarrassed. Mahoney smiled and put the charm in his pocket. 'Now fetch us the beer,' he said.

When Samson came back with the bottles, Mahoney said: 'What will you do?'

Samson said: 'I will go back to my kraal. I have not seen my wives and cattle for a long time. The drought is bad. I shall not seek the work of another white man. I think maybe I will return to the valley and hunt elephant until the Nkosi returns.'

'That is illegal, Samson.'

Samson grinned, and Mahoney shook his head to show disapproval. 'Do not break the law, Samson. Go back to your wives and cattle and seek money from the land, or go back to the mines in Johannesburg or stay here in Bulawayo and find work in a factory.'

Samson was quiet. Then he said: 'There is drought, I cannot make money from the soil. Nor do I wish to do woman's work in the houses. And there is trouble in the townships. I am a hunter, how else can I live?'

'Trouble in the townships? You mean from the politicians?'

Samson snorted and shook his head. 'Trouble from the politicians ...'

There was the noise of the front door opening and the sound of high heels. Both men turned their heads and listened. The footsteps came down the short passage. 'Joseph?'

Suzanna de Villiers stood in the doorway.

'Suzie.' Mahoney stood up. Samson stood up also. She looked at him steadily with those sphinx eyes. She held a fat brown paper packet and a long brown paper packet.

'I—' she paused, 'I brought you a cooked chicken and some wine. I'm sure you haven't had supper and I know you won't have breakfast and you can take what's left with you tomorrow.'

Mahoney looked at her. She was very beautiful.

Samson slunk quietly round her and down the passage and they heard the back door close behind him.

Chapter Thirty-One

Mahoney woke up with the first light showing on the horizon through the curtainless window. She was asleep beside him on the coir mattress on the floor, curled up on her side, her knees together and held up against her. Her long yellow hair was pulled over her face and she had her back to him. He pushed himself up on his elbow and looked down at her slender shoulders. They were thin. He lifted her hair off her face and looked at her high cheekbones and her wide mouth with her lipstick smeared, her heavy eyelids closed. He took the blanket a little further off her and looked at her breasts lying cradled in the crook of her arm, soft and warm, white against her tanned neck and face and arms and shoulders, the nipples were pink. And Mahoney wanted to cry out in despair and confusion and loneliness and emptiness and fear. He did not want to go away, he did not want to leave his flat and his job and his woman behind, he wanted to stay close to her and have her always, and always be safe beside her in this nice life here in Rhodesia. Nothing mattered any more except Suzie. He dropped down on his side beside her and he put his arms around her and he held her breasts hard and put his face against the warm smooth skin of her back and he stifled a sob.

She woke and turned round.

'Joseph, you're crying.'

He got up and walked naked to the window and looked out of it at the gathering pink in the sky. She lay looking up at him. He looked back at her.

'God, Suzie, this is awful, isn't it?'

She nodded. He looked at her and her eyes were wet.

'I'll make some coffee,' he said.

They sat on the mattress, side by side, their backs against the cool of the wall. The room was bare, just the pile of clothing on the floor and the two suitcases and the haversack and the plate with the chicken bones on it and the empty wine bottle. They sat like that drinking coffee and they looked in front of them and they did not say anything for a long time because there was only one thing to say. He put his hand on her thigh, rather thin it was now, and held it gently, not lasciviously, and let its warm softness soak into his hot palm and she put her hand on top of his and held it limply. He looked at her profile as she stared in front of her and her eyes were wet again and her face was very sad but it was steady. He said, 'I love you, Suzie,' and she looked at him for a long time and then she nodded and kept on looking at him but there was nothing to say, there were no promises that could be made and they both understood this as they looked at each other, 'I love you, Suzie' and she nodded again and then slowly she turned her head and looked away.

She looked about the room sadly and then she said: 'What about your book?'

'I'm taking it with me,' he said, 'in the small suitcase. It'll fit in exactly.'

'Are you going to finish it?'

'Of course.'

'On the ship?'

'I'll find a quiet place on the ship, I'm sure.'

She nodded and then she was silent for a long moment and then she sobbed once and dropped her head into her hand.

'Oh your book! Your book, your bloody book, your beautiful book! If only there wasn't your book.'

He put a hand on her slender shoulder.

She held her head in her hand. 'Another woman, I could compete with that. But your book? Oh, I want it to be good and I want you to be a success at writing because you want that so much and it'll make you happy and if you're happy then I'll be happy. I'll put up with all your irritability about your book and all that. But your book isn't a bond between us, it's a barrier, a barrier, it's a barrier because I can't share that with you, I don't really feel for it, not like you do. So what can I do, I'm an outsider looking in and even that would be okay by me if you were to accept me as just somebody looking in who loves you. But you don't, Joe, you resent me for not being like you. You want somebody like you. Me, I'm not like you. I'm just a nurse, a farmer's daughter, who loves you and you don't accept that, you want me to be like you.'

She broke off and she was still looking into her naked lap and playing with his hand upon her thigh.

'Suzie.'

He sat, not knowing what to say except to say over and over again that he loved her and wanted her and that he did not want to go away.

'Suzie …' She turned slowly and looked at him.

'Suzie – I'm going to explore the Amazon. Then I'll start work somewhere and when I do I'll send for you and if we still love each other then we'll just get married, that's all.'

She looked at him, she nodded but her nod was sad and not convincing. Mahoney clutched at a straw.

'Suzie, maybe you're pregnant.'

She nodded.

'Then we'll have to get married,' he said. She nodded again and then very slightly she shook her head and sighed. 'That's no reason,' she said.

'Suzie! Don't be an idiot! Of course you would.' She looked at him steadily. 'Suzie! I'm going to make love to you now. It's early in the morning and we're both fresh and it's the right time, I want to bind you to me. You can't shake your head at me.'

She looked up at him and she did not resist his strength but she shook her head.

'Oh yes!' She did not flinch and then he rolled on top of her fiercely and then he was inside her. And afterwards she lay quietly underneath him, holding him close and she was quiet and she patted his back, and there had been no passion between them, only bond. Then before they could speak of it, they heard the noise of Samson's key in the back door.

Samson and Mahoney carried the suitcase and the haversack down
the red cement steps of Fortwell Mansions with Suzie's high heels
clicking behind them. They said nothing. They threw the gear into
the back seat of her old Volkswagen and Samson climbed quietly
into the back seat and Mahoney climbed beside Suzie. They drove
off down Fort Street matter-of-factly. It was not yet six o'clock and
Fort Street was quiet. The dogs' urine patches were outside
Hassim's, and the stunted jacaranda trees and the rubber hedges
outside the poor little old Victorian houses were dusty. Mahoney
said: 'I never thought I would be sad to see the back of this street,
but I am.' And Suzie changed gear and said nothing and Samson sort
of coughed.

She took him out on to the Great North Road which led north to
Kenya and south to Johannesburg. They drove through the dusty
quiet surburban streets, then they were heading for the brown
horizons. They drove in silence out past the Drive-in cinema, well
out of Bulawayo, and then Mahoney said: 'I suppose this is as good
as anywhere' and Suzie pulled up on the dry gravel verge.

The bush was brown and dry in the sunrise but it pulled at
Mahoney's guts. Samson unloaded the haversack and the small
suitcase on to the gravel and Mahoney and Suzie leaned against the
little car with the first rays of the sun glinting off it. Samson
Ndhlovu gangled his feet and his arms for a moment then he walked
twenty yards off down the road and he sat down on a milestone and
he faced the rising sun and he lit a cigarette.

'Well – good-bye, Suzie.'

'Good-bye Joseph.'

He had tears in his eyes and his chin quivered. 'God bless.'

She closed her eyes and nodded and then looked again. 'God bless
you too.'

She turned quickly and threw open the door and climbed in.

'Samson!' she called while she looked at the dashboard, but he did
not move. She put the car into gear, and she took one look at
Mahoney, then she let out the clutch and crunched away. She did a

turn on the gravel and she did not look up at him again but he could see the tears running down her face. Then she was gone.

Samson stood up slowly and came back to Mahoney.

'This is not a good place for those who wish to beg to ride in motorcars,' he said, 'it is better if we carry your bags to the top of the hill.'

Mahoney nodded.

They carried the bag and case to the top of the hill and then Mahoney said, 'This is a good place.'

He turned to the black man. 'You should have gone with the Nkosikazi to save yourself a long walk.'

Samson shrugged, 'I have plenty time, Nkosi. I go home now, I do not seek new work.'

Mahoney nodded. He held out his hand.

'Good-bye, my friend.'

'Good-bye, Nkosi. You will seek me out when you return?'

'I will seek you out, induna.' Samson nodded.

He turned and headed back along the tar, through the hot dry bush to the hot dry town.

Part Six

Chapter Thirty-Two

I had a couple of fifty cent beers at Los Angeles airport between planes. I was not excited about returning to Africa. Africa was very far away, now, after three years. America was my home now, I was an American now. I wasn't even excited yet about seeing Suzie again. It was nearly a year since she had left me in New York, and I had gotten used to living without her again. At times I said to myself: You are foolish to go all the way back to Africa to see her, why are you going? You left her in Bulawayo, then you met her again in England but you still could not bring yourselves to marry each other, neither in London nor America nor Paris nor Rusape nor Bulawayo, so what the hell are you going to open it all for? Because you woke up one American morning and found it was spring again and the snow was melting and you thought of the lakes and the fishing and the water skiing and no Suzie, and you found your heart was still breaking, I said. And then you thought of Suzie, warm and golden in the springtime, and snug and soft in the winter, and you realised you had to go back to Africa to see Suzie. But it still did not feel as if I was going back to Africa. It was not until I was on the plane and saw the lights of Los Angeles end abruptly at the black shoreline that it came home to me that I was really leaving America and going home. You're nuts, I said to myself as the boys in the office had said. Why don't you rather send for Suzie? What do you want to go back to Africa for? To get your throat cut? Africa has had it, the Federation has had it, Partnership is a failure, the blacks are whooping it up, there's no future for the white man there any more. No, I'm only going for a visit, I said, and then I'll come back. I

255

looked at the diminishing night light shorelines of Los Angeles and I said: Yes, I'll be back. I'm not going to stay in Africa to get my throat cut, I'm not that crazy.

In Honolulu the Company's man took me on the town. We drank Maitais at two bucks a throw at the Halekelani and ate crayfish Thermidor and drank French wine on the Company. We went down to Sailor Town and we found a couple of Polynesian maidens with waterlilies behind their ears and undulating hips, perched on barstools with their skirts hitched up to their groins and we bought them Maitais too.

'No no no, I'll put it down to entertaining visiting executive from Head Office,' he said when I tried to make a token payment of one round. 'You're coming back to the Company, aren't you?'

'Yes,' I said, 'I'm coming back all right.'

And I was. I was coming back to this land of milk and honey all right.

The Company man said to me: "Scuse me for talking shop, but I've got this Prospect. Worth about a million and a half alive, and one and three-quarters dead. His death tax would be a lot, right? Got a couple of companies and a wife and a few kids. Now I tried to sell him a policy to cover his death tax so his widow would pick up his estate intact. But he doesn't want to know, because his lawyer says he'll only increase his death tax. Now I've got to find a plan so he can cover his death tax without increasing his taxable estate.'

I figured out his Prospect's taxable estate over another Maitai and I produced a stereotype trust and corporate plan whereby this Prospect would kick the bucket extremely liquid, without increasing his taxable estate. The Company man was overjoyed, and prevailed upon me to call round at the office tomorrow and dictate it to his typist. Certainly, I agreed. Whereupon he called for four more Maitais and we turned back to the two Polynesian girls who still had their dresses up to their loins.

'Christ, I think I'll sell this prospect tomorrow.'

I squeezed my girl's thigh and thought how good it was to be a blue-eyed boy of a great American corporation.

In Japan and Hong Kong and Manila and Saigon and Bangkok and

Singapore the Company's men looked after me very well and it felt very good to belong to a great American corporation, and I assured myself I was going back.

At times when I sat with an Oriental barstool under my bum I wondered why I was spending all this time and money going back to Africa to see Suzie. I said to myself: if you never see her again it wouldn't be the end of your world, you are used to going it alone again, you have garnered a new life about you, a good life, you would quite easily get over her completely now if you were to learn that she is married.

Then I thought of the flat we had had together in New York, the waking up in the morning in the warm double bed together, and seeing the icicles as long as your arm hanging outside the window, the trees in the avenue glistening like glass, and the street thick and crisp white, I thought of the warm rustling woman sounds of Suzie getting dressed and the good warm sounds of her cooking breakfast. I thought of the frozen lakes and us skating across them, her long blonde hair flying and her nose and cheeks pink and her eyes and mouth sparkling with joy, of the log cabins and drinking wine by the firelight, snug and happy with each other and then going off to bed while the world was white and frozen and beautiful outside in the moonlight: and I thought of the spring and the new joy in the air, and the new green on the earth and the lakes cracking up, and the hungry fish starting to bite, and the soft paddle of the canoe, and the plop of the bait in the early morning mist on the water and her 'Joey – Joey – Joey—' as her rod bent, and afterwards the love on a hot rock and in the evening the camp fire. And I thought of the summer too, the long hot summer, fishing and sailing and water skiing, the water glistening on her golden full body, and the autumn too, when the forests turn blood red and the sky begins to grey and you see the squirrels begin to scurry across the lawns with their swag in furry mouths and you know that winter is coming – but without Suzie, now, without Suzie to be warm with. And I knew that spring and summer and winter would never be the same again without Suzie, and I was glad I was going back to Africa to find her. And I thought of us in London when I quit the Amazon, and Paris too, and Madrid, and I knew that they would never be the same again without Suzie, that whenever I walked through London or Paris or Madrid or New York, I would always be looking for Suzie, I would always be waiting for her to fall into step beside me and slip her arm through mine and tug it and say: Look at that Joey – isn't it funny? Or: Oh look Joey, isn't it beautiful! A steamy lovely noisy London pub would never be the same without Suzie, wrapped up in her duffle beside me, sipping her flat bitter and telling me about the nut case she saw on the tube today, a Paris sidewalk café would never be the same without Suzie sitting crisp and summery and sleek and elegant, London and Paris and Madrid and New York would never be the same because I would always be looking for Suzie. And I thought of her pulling me aside and pointing into a shop window at a pair of brief panties and saying: Aren't they gorgeous! – how would you like me in those? And I longed for her, even though I knew every inch of her I had never got tired of her saying those things to me. Sometimes I thought of the lounge of the flat and the long long silences between the two armchairs and the boredom sitting brittle upon us and the sense of futility of trying to stir ourselves out of it alone, but only sometimes I thought of this, and not for very long, because so many places would never be the same. And I was glad I was going back to Africa to find Suzie before it was too late.

Chapter Thirty-Three

The night before my ship docked in Durban, South Africa, was Christmas Eve. The ship was very gay. I had been knocking off this Johannesburg bird called Dina, amidst the lifeboats, since our second day out of Perth. You know how it is with birds at sea, and I think Johannesburg birds are more so. They grow up very young in Johannesburg, with all that gold underground. Dina was very good. She was tall and poised and slick, except for the scab on the twentieth vertebra of her back. Every night she rubbed the same spot against the deck or against the lifeboat davit, every morning there was a new little scab, and then every night it was rubbed off again. I think she will always have a little scar there on her twentieth vertebra, about the middle of her back. Some Dina. She said she was coming to visit me in America. She said she would buy me a shack up in the mountains where I could write all day long, or a cottage down on the beach on some Caribbean island, and we would have a boat and we could go fishing for weeks at a time, and the boat would have a special cabin fitted for me with a desk and a tape recorder and a typewriter, and all the books I've always wanted, and I could write. And every year we would fly over to Europe for skiing in the winter, and to Africa to hunt. Dina was something, svelte, soft and full and blonde and silky to touch, and very on the ball, all the answers, Dina. She had been looking for her soulmate, she said. I sat with Dina on a sundeck in my swimsuit drinking good booze and looking at her long blonde gold body with the tiny soft hairs glinting gold on her arms and legs and I thought: she is beautiful, Mahoney, and she has a soul and she wants you and she is rich and she could give you everything you want, you need never work again, you could spend the rest of your life writing and thinking and becoming wise, like George Bernard Shaw was mollycoddled by his millionairess and, actually, you could love her, indeed you could be absolutely smitten if you would let yourself, if you stopped playing it cool and hard-arsed, and let yourself go. If you forgot about Suzie. You wouldn't even have to forget about Suzie, you'd only have to surrender to the fact that Suzie is gone, that she left you a year ago, and admit that you have gotten over her, admit it to yourself, that's all, accept that Suzie and you are no good for each other, otherwise you would never have let her go. Often I thought: you should not see Suzie in Durban to re-open all the old scars, it is not fair to her either, she has garnered a new life about her too now, she has almost gotten over you too, it's not fair to upset her all over again, she is over thirty now, you must give her a chance to find somebody else to love. But on Christmas Eve there was drink and song and dance in the bar and I was gay and laughing because tomorrow I was going to see Suzie, tomorrow I would hold my soft Suzie in my arms again. And then Christmas Day dawned, red, and there was South Africa, silent and vast, Durban rising big and rich and sleepy out of the sea, and I thought: somewhere up there Suzie is lying fast asleep in her bed, warm and smooth and smelling of Suzie, and in her room are her things I would recognise, her dresses and nightgowns, and her hairbrushes and her slippers and her shoes, and I was very excited and very happy. I was very impatient with the delays of docking and clearing customs and immigration. I said good-bye to Dina with a chaste kiss on her cheek and a promise to write and I climbed into my taxi with a laugh in my breast for the joy of Suzie.

It was two o'clock by the time the taxi dropped me off at the back of the house she shared up on the Berea. I left my suitcase behind the back hedge. My hands were shaking. I ran my fingers through my hair and looked at my fingernails. My mouth was dry from licking my lips and smoking since dawn. I walked round the side of the house to the front door. There was laughter and talking coming from within, and a background of music. Oh Christ, a crowd, a crowd of Suzie's housemates and their boyfriends, her new life gathered about her. This wasn't the way I wanted to meet Suzie again after a year, thrust into a jolly party. But maybe it was best. I knocked loudly on the front door. The laughter and the talking continued and nobody came. I knocked again and a male voice shouted: 'Come in if you're good-looking' and through the frosted door I saw a figure come to the door. Even through the distortion of the glass I recognised Suzie's wide red mouth and long blonde hair and her big eyes and my heart seemed to turn over. She threw open the door and her eyes widened and she just stood there.

'Joe!' she whispered.

'Hullo, Suzie.'

'Joe!'

She just stood there with her eyes wide and her wide lips a little apart. She was more beautiful than I remembered her, and she was tanned and summery and well. She was wearing shorts and her legs were long and full and sexy, and I adored her. She stood looking at me and then she cried 'Joe!' and her face broke into her wide Suzie smile. She rushed across the threshold. She slammed the door closed behind her and threw her arms round me and hugged me. She leaned back in my arms and looked at me and there was a glisten of tears in her eyes but she was laughing: 'Oh Joe …'

Then she let me go and held out her hands. 'Look at my hands.' She was trembling. She was grinning and nervous and tearful. Was it nervous withdrawal?

'Oh Joe – I wasn't expecting you for another month, you said January some time.'

She laughed jerkily.

Neither of us knew what to say. A lot seemed to have happened in the year since she had left me in New York.

'Oh darling, it's so lovely to see you!' and she kissed me briefly. She saw all the questions in my eyes and she looked away and took my arm gaily, jerkily, and put her hand on the doorknob.

'Come on! You're in time for Christmas dinner!'

I resisted.

'What's the matter, Suzie?'

'Nothing – I'm just all adither, I suppose – and there're people inside.' She hesitated, then she turned and kissed me hard and short. Then she stood back and wiped her lipstick from my mouth.

'Come on.' She smiled kindly.

The dining-room overlooked the sea and the table was crowded. I was introduced with much jollity. Suzie looked composed and brisk again, but I could tell she was nervous. They were all bubbling with beer and wine and Suzie gave me a tankard and people squeezed up and I sat on a stool next to Suzie. I answered a barrage of bright questions about myself and my trip and everybody tried to make me feel welcome. Suzie looked after my dinner and tankard solicitously. A handsome young man sitting on the other side of Suzie was the life and soul of the party, he was always making jokes, making jokes, and he called her Doll—or was it Darl?—and I wanted to punch him, but I had to be polite.

'Roger's a barrister too,' Suzie said, trying to get us talking.

'Oh yes?' I said, and I thought: I'd love to clean you up in Court, you witty bastard: I suppose your only Court experience is a few dock briefs but you impress Suzie as an all-time Marshall Hall. I put my hand on Suzie's knee under the table to draw her back to me and get comfort from touching her, but she smiled and me and moved my hand away. They laughed and talked about funny things that had happened in their clique in the last year, and when I touched her hand under the table she squeezed it and smiled brightly at me and then let it go. And I got angry and afraid and jealous, but I had to keep gay. After lunch people lounged around the house drinking brandy and liqueurs bloatedly and at four o'clock they started to go home to freshen up for another party elsewhere that night. When Marshall Hall announced his departure Suzie said: 'Excuse me' and she went with him to the front door and was away five minutes. When she came back the other girls tactfully withdrew to the beach.

I was hurt and jealous and as soon as we were alone, I said: 'We aren't going to another bloody party tonight, are we?'

'No. I've just cancelled it.'

'You were going with this Roger chap,' I said.

'Yes.'

I nodded bitterly. I sat down. 'Come here, Suzie.'

She came to me quietly and sat down beside me on the couch and looked very serious. I had so much to say and did not know where to begin. The other people had spoilt it.

'You're looking well,' she said.

I got impatient. 'Suzie, what's the story?'

She looked around for a cigarette and I gave her one of mine. She looked around for matches and got up and walked across the room. I watched her and thought: she's so goddam beautiful.

She sat down again and lit her cigarette. She had stopped shaking.

'Would you like a drink?'

'No. Now tell me, Suzie.'

She took a puff of her cigarette.

'Well. I'm staying here in South Africa, Joe.'

'Why?'

'I like it. It's a good country, it's my country really, I'm an Afrikaans girl really. And it's booming, I've made lots of friends.'

I hated her living a life apart from mine. She had almost lost her Afrikaans accent in America, but it was there again now. Soft and mellifluous, I loved it; somehow it made me more jealous, that she had changed.

'What about America?' I demanded. She looked at me steadily and her eyes were opaque, she was not letting me through.

'What about it?' she said.

'Well, don't you want to come back to America?'

'What for, Joe?'

Christ, she was beautiful. Woman, woman, woman. I would beat this Roger irk to a pulp.

With me.' I sounded harsh. 'For me!'

She looked at me for a long moment and then she shook her head. 'No, Joe.'

It was outrageous. Suzie – my Suzie who had lived with me and slept with me and woken up in the mornings with me for six years all over the globe – that she no longer wanted me, that she had a new life independent of what I thought and felt about, it was outrageous, unnatural, outrageous, unnatural, un-Suzie.

'Christ, Suzie.'

She looked at me.

'What, Joe?'

'Married to me! As my wife!'

She looked at me steadily then she shook her head slowly. Christ it was unthinkable. 'No, Joe, I won't come with you.'

Then Fear. I sat back. 'Why not?'

'Because I don't want to any more. We've drifted apart, now. I don't need you any more now. I don't need you any more now, not like I used to. Too many things have happened, Joe.'

I looked at her and I thought my heart would break.

'I don't want to marry you any more, Joe. And you don't want to marry me, either, really. Otherwise you'd have asked me outright, but you didn't, you only asked when I said I wouldn't come back with you to America.'

But I really did want to marry her.

'We've drifted apart,' she said, simply, with a little shrug. 'I've got used to living without you.'

I got angry.

'Well, I'm bloody well staying right here until you get used to me again, Suzie.'

She shook her head again. 'Don't stay.'

Jesus.

'Why not?'

She was not looking at me. She shook her head again. She was very beautiful.

'Because I'm almost free of you and I don't want to get muddled up and hurt all over again.'

I was very afraid of the unhappiness.

'Look at me,' she said, urgently, 'how well I am, Joe. I've put on weight, I'm happy. I'm confident. With you I was always on edge, waiting for the next explosion, wondering why you found me wanting, lacking something.'

'I didn't find you wanting. You're intelligent.'

'Why didn't you marry me then? Oh Joe, don't be silly, you know we're two entirely different people.'

'Suzie—' All that seemed so unimportant now. 'Suzie, it's true I was critical of you, that was because I was a dreamer, I was trying to write, I was trying to find myself, I thought I could get above everything by my writing. But now I'm not like that. I've written two books and neither has been published and I've given up writing and I've settled for the ordinary things in life, a good job and so forth. I've grown up, Suzie.'

She gave a gentle little laugh, and put her hand on my arm.

'You'll never stop dreaming, darling. You know you'll never stop writing.' She sounded very mature.

I sat back.

'What about this forensic giant Roger?'

'What about him?'

'You know what.'

She looked defensive, 'I like him a lot. He wants to marry me.'

'And you?'

'I don't know. Yet, anyway. I'm going away for a while, on holiday.'

'To think about it, hey?'

She didn't say anything.

'Where are you going?'

'On a sea cruise.'

'Where to?'

'Just up the east coast to Mombasa and back on the *Eden Roc*. Three weeks.'

'When?'

'Next month. End of January.' She got up. She went to the window and looked at the sea.

'That doesn't answer the question,' I said. 'Are you in love with him?'

She did not answer immediately, 'I'm in conspiracy with him,' she said. 'He's divorced. We're in conspiracy to make each other happy. We do make each other happy. Yes, I do love him, nearly. If somebody makes you happy you love them sooner or later.'

Christ.

'I don't make you happy?'

She shook her head.

'No, not properly, *ordinary* happy. And I don't make you happy either. We make each other happy in bed and we make each other happy when we're both lonely and insecure in foreign lands. And when one of us is about to leave the other and take off for the wide blue yonder again we think that we'll never be happy without each other. We make each other happy when we face some sort of crisis and feel insecure. We're neurotically dependent upon each other. By force of habit I suppose. Our romance has thrived off tragedy. But when we simmer down to secure domesticity, day-to-day existence, we don't make each other happy. And that's what life really is: dull, monotonous day-to-day domesticity. Because we've got nothing in common, I suppose, not even a child. You're always struggling for something. I think it's a soulmate you seek. Well, perhaps I'm just not your soulmate. In fact I know I'm not. In fact I think you feel that I stunt your spiritual growth, I stifle you. Maybe when you find a soulmate you'll accept day-to-day monotonous domesticity. But you won't accept it with me, because I'm not your soulmate. But I *will* accept it, with a man who makes me happy, even if he is not a soulmate to me, because I don't need a soulmate like you do. A soulmate is very important to you. You'll never be happy without one. But I'm not like you in that respect. I'm just an ordinary wholesome loving girl who wants ordinary day-to-day happiness. And that's why I can't make you happy.'

'Balls,' I said. 'You *do* make me happy. You're intelligent.'

'Joe-baby – grow up. Don't you realise yet that you cannot change me or yourself. You always think you can mould me, train my thinking. Well, you can't. I've matured sufficiently in the last year to realise that. You should too, and get your young love off your back.'

'Christ, Suzie, what a dreadful thing to say!'

'It's true,' simply.

I had never felt so lonely and afraid of the future.

'Suzie?'

'Yes.'

'Have you slept with him?'

She turned her back and looked out of the window.

'You must not torture yourself with such questions any more, Joe. That is jealousy. I think jealousy is what has kept us together for so long, in spite of our differences, and that's silly.'

'Answer me, Suzie.'

She shook her head. 'We have to stop being jealous of each other some time, and now is a good time to start. I haven't asked you how many girls you slept with in the Orient.'

Jesus. Suzie sleeping with somebody else!

'If I did it was for money, for lust, like buying a meal. No emotions involved.'

I strode over to her and grabbed her arm and spun her round.

'Stop mooning out of the window! Now tell me before I give you a good beating.'

She pried my fingers off her arm and I let her go.

'I should tell you that I have slept with him,' she said calmly, 'to destroy my image in your eyes. But, no, I haven't.'

Relief.

I walked back to the couch and sat down.

'Thank God.' She said nothing. 'Suzie'—despair, helplessness— 'do you love me?'

She turned and faced me again. 'I loved you, Joe. I care very deeply for your wellbeing. I loved you but I realise that it's fruitless. I am getting over you, I'm over the hump. I don't want to weaken to you again. I could very easily. I am intensely attracted to you, I could lie down for you right now, but I don't want to and I won't.'

Hope. I could not face the big wide world. I had to stay close to her. Weak.

'Can I stay here tonight? I'll sleep on the couch. I don't feel disposed to looking for accommodation today.'

'Of course.'

'Thanks. I'll go tomorrow.'

'All right.'

Anger. Outrage again at desertion.

'Christ, how can you say "all right"? I love you, d'you hear. Well, there's only one way to cope with this situation.'

I strode over to her and picked her up.

She kicked. 'What're you doing?'

'Taking you upstairs to rape you, woman, you're *mine*.'

'Put me down!'

She kicked the air. She beat my chest with her hands. I carried her from the lounge kicking.

'Beat me, and I'll drop you on your head.'

She beat me, and I relaxed my arm and she dropped six inches suddenly and both her arms grabbed around my neck.

'That's better.'

'Put me down, Joe! The girls will be coming back from the beach!' She was still kicking.

'Rape doesn't take long.'

I reached the top landing. I was panting. 'Which is your bedroom in this joint?'

'I won't tell you—' still kicking.

'Okay, then I'll do it in the first room.'

'Down the passage!' she gasped.

'Thank you.'

I threw her on the bed and turned and locked the door. She sat on the bed and looked at me sullenly. I put my fingers inside the neckline of her shirt and ripped it open. It tore down to her waist. She grabbed it and I ripped it right off her. She struggled. I spun her shoulders round, gripped the brassiere straps across her back in both hands and snapped it apart. I pushed her back on the bed. Her breasts were white against her tan, and very beautiful. She looked up at me. There were tears in her eyes. I sat down beside her heavily.

'I'm sorry.'

She said nothing.

'You should have fought me, then I could have gone ahead and done it, and everything would have been okay.'

She bit her lip and nodded.

I put my head on her breast and she put her hands around my neck. 'Oh Suzie, I love you so.' She nodded and I could feel her crying.

'It's no good, though, Joe.'

After a moment I said: 'I'll leave in the morning.'

She nodded again.

After a little while I said: 'I've brought you a present.'

'Have you? Thank you. I've got one for you too.'

'Thank you, Suzie.'

'What's mine?' she said.

'A nightie. And some silk.'

'Oh, lovely! Thank you, darling.'

'You can make a dress out of the silk.'

'Yes, lovely. D'you want to see yours?'

'Yes.'

She got up off the bed and padded across to her wardrobe. When she opened it I recognised many of the dresses hanging there. My heart nearly broke. She came back with a package. She put it in my lap and sat down beside me and looked at the package in my lap.

'Open it. Happy Christmas.'

'Happy Christmas, you too.'

It was a sports shirt.

'It'll suit you,' she said.

'Yes, thank you.'

She looked at it in my hands.

'It's a drip-dry,' she said dully.

'Oh.'

She sat on the bed beside me and looked at the shirt. 'And when you wash it you mustn't wring it out. Just put it on a hanger and let it drip.'

'Okay.'

She looked at me. 'Put it on,' she said.

I put it on.

She looked at it and straightened it across the shoulders. 'You look nice,' she said. 'You can wear it to the party tonight, if you want to go. Do you want to go?'

'Might as well.'

'Yes. You look very nice,' she said.

'I'll get your present now,' I said.

I woke up early in the morning. I had no hangover but I felt very bad. It was raining and still dark. I went through to the kitchen to brush my teeth so as not to disturb the girls upstairs. I made a cup of coffee and sat at the kitchen table and drank it and I tried not to think of anything but the open road. I packed my bag and sat in the lounge smoking, waiting for it to get light, but it took a long time. At last it began to turn grey outside but it was the sort of day that would never get very light. Then I went upstairs and scratched on Suzie's door. She came in a dressing-gown. The room was warm and smelt of Suzie's scents and things on the dressing-table.

'It's raining, you can't go in the rain.'

'That's all right.'

'Have you got a raincoat?'

'Yes, plastic job.'

'Wait till breakfast.'

'No, I'll go now.'

'Come in while I put something on.'

'Don't come downstairs.'

'I will.'

'I'll wait downstairs then.'

I waited at the front door. She came down.

'Have you had anything to eat?'

'I don't want anything.'

She stretched up and buttoned the top of my raincoat, as if I were leaving for the office. Then she stood back and said: 'Where're you going Joe?'

I said: 'Rhodesia. Then up Africa to Europe. Then back to America.'

'How?'

'Hitch-hike.'

'You can't hitch-hike up Africa, these days, you're crazy.'

'Of course I can.'

'Joe, listen to me, this isn't the old Africa any more. Africa has changed since you left. Listen to me. You've been away for three years. I've been here a year and we hear more about these things. The Federation is going to be broken up. Northern Rhodesia, Tanganyika, Kenya, they aren't as peaceful as they used to be. Even Southern Rhodesia isn't safe outside the towns.'

'I'll be all right.'

'But only a short while ago a gang of natives stopped that Mrs. Burton in her car and poured petrol over her and her little girl and roasted them alive. Just outside Kitwe.'

'That was ages ago.'

'Not so long ago. And all over the place the natives are felling trees across the roads and when you stop they leap out of the bushes and panga you. Just because you're white. They aren't interested if you are going back to live in America or not.'

'They aren't doing so much of that, any more.'

'Joe, they've only got to do it to you once, you know.'

'I'll be all right.'

Silence.

'Well – I must go, good-bye Suzie.'

'Good-bye, Joe.'

She was looking at the floor steadily. 'And thank you for everything. For six years.' She nodded at the floor.

'Thank you too. For six years.' I wanted to kiss her, but then I didn't want to because she was letting me go. I opened the door. 'Which way to the bus stop to get to the station?'

'Down the road, turn right, next corner.'

'How often do they run?'

'Every half hour or so.'

'Oh well – Good-bye, Suzie.'

She looked up. Her eyes were steady, but they glistened. 'Good-bye, Joe.'

I wanted to run to her arms and weep and beg her to take me back, and never leave her, always stay safe next to her. Then I wanted to beat her for letting me go.

I picked up my bag and opened the door and walked out and closed the door behind me. When I got to the gate, I looked back, with tears in my eyes, but the door was still closed and she was not at any window.

I walked to the corner and after a while a bus came and took me down to Berea to the City Hall. I sat on a bench 'Europeans Only – Slegs vir Blankes'. I thought of the six years and of Bulawayo and Inyanga and London and Paris and Madrid and New York and the winter and the summer and the fall, and I thought of the warm feel and scent of Suzie's bedroom and her dresses which I recognised hanging in the cupboard, and I dropped my head into my hands and pretended I was looking at something between my feet and I cried tears.

Then I crossed West Street to the Railway Station and I waited for the train to take me out of town on the road that leads north to Johannesburg and the Limpopo, and the land of Monomotapa beyond it.

Chapter Thirty-Four

Walking. The best thing to do when you are unhappy is to walk. Walk away into the sunset and never come back. The most difficult thing is to stay behind and catch the same streetcar every day, pass the same pubs, see the same familiar lonely places and at night go back to the same room. You think and remember and you react by habit to things you once shared, but you react alone and that reminds you. But when you walk away into the sunset you at least feel you are doing something constructive, going into a new life,, even if you don't want the new life. You are disciplining your body into going forward, and that helps your mind. When you walk you can look down at your legs carrying you forward, you can watch your legs getting burnt and brown, you can kick stones and sometimes you'll see insects or an anthole on the ground and you can stop and bend down and watch them at work for a little while and you'll think: God, aren't they wonderful little things, how do they know what to do? If you see a dung beetle crossing the road, the vast strip of tarmac desert, heading purposefully for the other side, you'll think, surely: now, why does he want to cross the road? How does he know he'll find anything at all on the other side of the road and whether, if he finds something, it is what he wants? And if he finds something, will he be able to lug it all the way back? Will he be able to find his way back across the desert? What makes him think it is better on the other side of the road than it is on his own side, where his hole is?

And you realise that there is an infinite amount of life apart from your own, and they also have problems, and you can get to love that dung beetle and even talk to it for a while.

And you can look down at your shoes starting to scuff and wear away, and it is good because you are changing, and you can feel blisters, and that is good too because your body is changing. And you can count your steps for a while, estimate distances, how far it is to the big tree, and then pace it off to see how accurate you are. You can look at a hill and wonder what you will see when you get to the top of it, and the hill becomes a goal. And when a car comes along and you thumb it and it doesn't stop you can shout out: 'Fugyoutoo' – which makes you feel better. And when you sleep at night, on a bench, in the bush, and you are cold, you think about being cold and how to stop being cold, which is better than lying in bed thinking about her.

I walked. I walked out of the rolling fecund hills of Natal, rich and green and prosperous, where the Zulus are tall and fat and strong and handsome, through the flat dry Orange Free State and up into the high flat green gold-rich Witwatersrand where the mighty Johannesburg is, where the great mine dumps rise high and yellow into the sky amongst the skyscrapers, and the narrow streets throng with black and white people, hurrying hard and brash about their fortunes. In Johannesburg I threw away my bag, and bought a secondhand knapsack and walked out of the Golden City, north into the boland, the long high golden green plateau of the Transvaal. When I left one car, I walked until another picked me up, and I only stopped for short rests and I slept on benches and behind hedges and in the bush and I ate bread and cheese and fruit. The flesh fell off me, and my body became hard and brown, and I sweated, I began to sweat myself clean, my body and mind and soul clean and empty of all the bad and wrong and unwise things I had done, until all there was left was the grief and the loneliness for Suzie, and it felt that if I walked long and far enough that would be sweated out in the end too, and I would be empty to fill myself with new things. I walked up through South Africa and I felt nothing for the country, I did not feel for the sun and the bush and the black men and the white men that lived in it, they did not feel like my cousins, although I spoke their languages, because South Africa is not my country. I felt like an American. Then I climbed up over the Zoutpansberg mountains, high up over the ceiling of South Africa in the wooded mountains, and when I got to the top I stopped and looked back on the mighty plain below disappearing into the golden mauve of the horizon. Then I swung down the other side of the mountains into the Limpopo Valley, where the bush is hot and brown and grey and more wild, and at last I came to the Limpopo, with Rhodesia, the land of Monomotapa, beyond it.

Chapter Thirty-Five

You know that South African immigration post on the Limpopo, surrounded by the hundreds of miles of flat bush, how the road runs down from the South African gate in a curve through the bush to the Beit Bridge, across the dirty great Limpopo and disappears in another curve up into the bush on the Rhodesian bank? Hot, quiet, lonely. It doesn't seem a long way across, that border between the two immigration posts by car, but it's a long, long walk. I walked across in the height of noon and it was hot. There wasn't a sound except the crunch of my boots on the gravel and nothing to see but hundreds of miles of uninhabited hot thorn trees and hot caked sand and soldier ants. The sweat ran off me and my haversack cut my shoulders and I could feel the sun burning my arms and legs and face browner and my throat was dry. I saw nothing beautiful in the Limpopo, only brown sandy water flowing through hot thorn tree desert. I passed an old tattered African near the bridge and he looked at me sideways for it's not common to see a white man tramping loaded in the sun in that part of the world, but he touched his hat all the same and said 'Molo Nkosi' and I said 'Molo Keghle', which is polite and the correct way to address an old native. I didn't like walking across the Limpopo in the sun into my home country after three years away and being looked at like that by that old African, but do you know that by the time I was halfway across that bridge I began to feel happy. I felt I was coming home.

For the first time since I left New York. I'd been happy in America, certainly, but it was a different sort of happiness, the happiness of affluence and soft possessions. This was a different sort of happiness, of being young and strong. I looked down at my brown sweaty legs carrying me over the hot brown gravel into my home country and it felt good. I felt like a Rhodesian. Not an American.

Outside Beit Bridge I got a lift. West Nicholson, Jessie, Gwanda, names and villages I had even forgotten existed, one-eyed villages, just a hotel and a few shops and a few houses, a police post and a Magistrate's Court and plenty of Africans lounging about in the sun. Miles of flat bush between the villages. Every now and again there were Africans standing at the side of the road trying to sell vegetables and beadwork, holding up their wares as the car went by, and the little piccanins with their bottoms bare and their stomachs sticking out waved to us. The grass was tall at the roadside. I loved every African and thorn tree and turn in the road. Balla Balla, and the sun began to go down and the hot quiet of the sun began to turn into the crick-cricking of the evening and the bush began to turn mauve. Man, there is nothing so beautiful to a Rhodesian as Africa in the late afternoon. Sunset, and we pulled into Bulawayo, my old home town.

Bulawayo.

It looked the same old dump, only more so. Streets wide enough in which to turn an ox-wagon, the sun beating down hot on the streets. There seemed to be more Africans on the streets than I remembered. There were no new buildings. The shops on the main street with their Victorian façades looked as deadly as ever. Many shops windows empty with hopeful To Let signs. The Princess Cinema shut down for good. Empty flats everywhere, especially on the ground floors, easy targets for petrol bombs. It had been difficult to find a flat in my day. 'My day!' I walked past Suzie's old flat, just to hurt myself. It had a broken window with newspaper pasted over it and the cement steps which used to be polished bright red every day were brown and scuffed and a child had urinated on them. I walked to the Italian restaurant in Rhodes Street, where you used to be able to fill yourself up with greasy food for five bob and kid yourself you were having a slice of Continental life, and the restaurant was closed with red To Let signs plastered on the windows. The Cloisters Boarding-House was shut up and empty, and you used to think you were lucky to get into the Cloisters. I walked down to Fort Street, to look at my old flat. I had waited a long time to get into that flat. The fruitshop at the entrance to the block of flats was vacant. I walked through the portals into the fourth-rate courtyard and looked up at my old windows. No curtains, no sign of life. I walked up the four flights of steps and looked in the window. Empty, the floor was dirty. I could see in the kitchen and there was an old newspaper lying on the floor. I looked at the place where my bed had stood, where Suzie and I had first made love. Here, against the window, was where my table had stood, where I had sweated over my LL.B. and later over my book. My prized useless book. I turned and looked out from the block of flats and I saw the red corrugated-iron roof-tops and beyond the brown shimmering horizons of Matabeleland. I turned back and looked into the flat window.

'Serves you right, you bastard,' I whispered, and I walked back down the steps. As I walked I remembered the sound of Suzie's high heels on the steps. I used to be able to distinguish them all the way from within the flat and despite myself I thought: I do believe I would go back to all this for the sound of Suzie's high heels coming from work. You could get your job back and—

And I quickly turned my thoughts to the bloom and frost and boom of America and I walked on down the steps. The next morning I walked up Selbome Avenue till I came to the Magistrate's Court. I knocked on the door marked Chief Public Prosecutor and I walked in.

'Jesus Christ!' Jock said.

'Hello, Jock.'

'Well—Je-*sus*—*Christ*!'

After work I met Jock and some of the boys at the Exchange Bar. After all the cracks had been made about the number of women I must have screwed over the last three years and how beer sales had dropped since I left, and do you remember that case where this bloke did this and you stood up in Court and said … I said to Jock: 'And how's crime these days?'

And he said: 'Jesus' and proceeded to tell me how crime was these days. He pointed to his greying temples: 'See these?' The jails full. Politically inspired crime. Thugs belonging to the black nationalist party of ZAPU, terrorising the people. Political intimidation, beatings up, gangs of thugs roaming the townships at night demanding production of Party identity cards. No card, biff bam powee crunch. Beat him with sticks, bicycle chains, stones, kick him, stone him. Note where his house is, stone it at night, beat his wife and children. Petrol bombs. Fill a bottle with petrol, stick a wick through the top, light it and throw it through the window. The bottle smashes, the room is filled with flaming petrol. Always at night, when the victims are sleeping. Women and children charred and scarred for life. Strikes. Gangs of thugs standing at bus stops dragging workers off buses, beating them up if they refused to observe the strike. Boycotting of African schools. Black thugs standing at school gates chasing the black children away from school, building up an explosive atmosphere. Thugs marching into class-rooms, and shouting at the teachers, threatening them with death, thugs sitting at the back of the class and smiling. Thugs roaming beerhalls demanding Party cards, beating up. Gangs overturning motorcars and setting fire to houses. In the country gangs of thugs burning the schools which the natives had built, gangs burning huts, gangs burning churches. Terrorise the people into following ZAPU, create an atmosphere of lawlessness, give the outside world the impression that an explosive situation exists because we haven't got One Man One Vote. The police working overtime. The courts clogged up.

'See these?' Jock indicated his temples.

Always operate in gangs. Haven't got the guts to do their terrorising alone. Intimidate youngsters into joining the gangs, to give each other courage. That's how we catch the bastards. Catch one member of the gang and he splits on the rest. Gutless bastards.

'I used to be a Liberal,' Jock said, 'but I'm not so bloody liberal any more. I don't mind the civilised ones, but Jesus, I don't want to live under juvenile savages.'

And now it's explosives, dynamite and hand grenades, and sub-machine-guns. Smuggled in over the borders, canoed across the Zambesi, all made in Russia and in Red China. Wide boys trained in Egypt and Russia and in China. Oh, but what tits they are! Trained in Russia and China, but they still take the gang along when they do a job. Trained, but they still leave fingerprints and footprints for us. Trained, but they haven't succeeded in blowing up a shit house yet. Trained, but as soon as we catch one he splits on the rest. Trained but as soon as they're caught they tell us where the cache is. And where it came from. Trained? They couldn't organise a booze-up in a brewery.

'But one day they'll find a few wide boys with a bit of guts,' I said.

'Yes,' Jock said.

'Then what'll you do?'

'We will fight,' Jock said.

'For what?' I said.

'For civilisation. For the rule of law. For moderation. For equal rights for all civilissed men. We'll fight to keep the hoodlums down. We'll fight until the blacks are civilised. The civilised blacks already have the vote. I refuse to hand to vote to a savage. We'll fight for sense in this continent of black ineptitude.'

'You'll lose,' I said.

'The Attorney General'll give you back your job,' Jock said.

'I want it,' I said, 'like I want another hole in the head.'

I visited some married friends in their spacious suburban homes. Toddlers playing on the lawns under nanny's care, the garden boy looking after the lawns, sundowners brought in by the houseboy in white starched uniform. The toddlers hadn't been there when I left. Nor had the bars on the windows.

'—petrol bomb thrown down the road last week. Didn't go off, but there's always a next time,' she said.

'We're safe enough here,' he said, 'The police always catch them.'

'That's what they thought in Kenya,' she said, 'I think we should move closer to town.'

'What, and give up all this?'

'I'm here all alone every day,' she said.

'You've got the servants.'

'It was the trusted family servants who cut the most white throats in Kenya,' she said.

'Amos would never touch you,' he said.

'I'm worried,' she said – 'And what about him?' Indicating the child. 'What do you think, Joe?' she said.

'There have been plenty of changes,' I said. 'Tell us about America, would I get a job easily enough?'

'America is beautiful,' I said. 'And it's got no munts.'

'But I would never be able to sell the house,' he said. 'You can't give them away these days.'

'What's happened to the Davises?'

'He threw in his partnership and went back to England. He saw the writing on the wall.'

'Did you know Jake Jefferson?'

'What happened to him?'

'He's still around. His wife was killed.'

'And the Johns?'

'Gone to South Africa.'

'And the van der Merwes?'

'They went to the States, to Tennessee. They let us practise there, with no further qualifications. Remember the Todds? They left for Australia. So many have left.'

'I'm going back to America, too.'

'Joe, be a good chap and look out for a job for me over there.'

Politics, politics, everybody talking politics.

Christ, there've been some changes. It used to be good here, five years ago, it looked so good here, it was booming here five years ago, remember? There was hope here, we were trying Partnership here, remember? The country was opening up here, there had never been so much money here, the wogs were peaceful here, remember? Well, it isn't like that any more. Britain sold us down the river.

'One man one vote!' is all the rage now. All over the world it's all the rage, now. It's all the rage to be long-haired now. All the rage to shout 'Stop being beastly to the Blacks' at Sunday tea-parties in Chelsea and long-haired booze parties in Kensington, and on the soap boxes at Hyde Park corner now. It's fashionable to get dewy-eyed and intense about one man one vote now. It doesn't matter if they are going to wreck the joint with their one man one vote. Look at the Congo.

Look at Ghana.

One man one vote – once.

Jesus.

Britain? – Jesus. The bastards. The yellow-bellied, two-faced, ass-licking bastards. Was a time when I was proud I was British, Joe. Now? Judases. Judas Iscariots. Sold us down the river. Broke up the Federation when they promised they wouldn't, just broke it up, without even consulting us. We just woke up one morning and there it was. Judases.

Like they did in Kenya.

Harold Macmillan and his Winds of Change.

Bloody shopkeepers. Yes sir, no sir, three bags full. The customer is always right, provided he's black. Very handy to be black nowadays. Great future if you're black and got your Form One. Cabinet Post at least.

Jesus.

Look at Ghana. Call that Freedom? The opposition in chains, in jail. Look at the Congo. Call that Freedom? Murder, civil war, genocide? Look at Kenya. Call that civilised, murder and civil war and genocide? One man, one vote? Yeah, *once.*

Sitting on a lawn in Hillside having a sundowner. What's going to happen here? Look at the Congo – that's what could happen here. Look at Northern Rhodesia: roasted Mrs. Burton alive outside Kitwe.

It'll happen here.

Oh yeah? Sitting in the Exchange Bar having a beer. One man one vote – Oh yeah? Not here. Here it's not like it is up there. There's two hundred thousand of us white down here. There were only fifty thousand in Kenya, only seventy thousand in Northern Rhodesia, only two thousand in Nyasaland. We aren't ruled by Britain like those poor suckers up there, she can't sell us down the river like those poor bastards up there. And if she tries … oh dear.

Politics, politics, pessimism, optimism, realism.

It won't happen here. Here we've got strength, here we've got wealth. Here we've got guts. There're too many of us to be pushed around down here.

And we've got South Africa, South Africa is on our side down here. South Africa is strong, South Africa is rich, they won't let us go under to savages. And we've got Portugal, Mozambique and Angola, Salazar's on our side. The world won't dare push South Africa around, they can't let her gold and diamonds go down the drain. We will be the only stable countries in Africa, the other black states to the North will have tribal wars and civil wars and army mutinies and bloody coups and assassinations, not to mention Communists, you wait and see and in the end the world will see that we were right to fight.

What's going to happen here?

'What do you think, Sergeant-Major?' I said.

The old black policeman shook his head. He was a damn good cop. He insisted on talking English.

'The bastards, sir,' he said, 'they make too much trouble, too very much trouble. They burn my father's house, because his son is a policeman. They frighten my relatives and kill their cattle. You know what they do, sir?'

'What, Sergeant-Major?'

'They cut the tits off the udders of the cows in the night. And they burn the pigs alive in the kraals.'

'Jesus, Sergeant-Major.'

'And they burn the schools, sir. And we African people built those schools with our own hands and our own money, sir. And also they stop the people dipping their cattle, sir, because they say it's white man's magic. And so the cattle die from the ticks sir.'

We were sitting in the multi-racial Empire Bar. The radiogram played Skokiaan over and over again and there was a jabber of voices and young Matabele in their spivvy city clothes twisted and jived with buxom Matabele girls.

'You come back to work in the courts again, sir?' asked the

sergeant-major.

'No, I'm going back to America,' I said.

'America long distance,' he said.

'Yes.'

'You Europeans,' said the sergeant-major, 'are very lucky.'

'Why's that, Sar-Major?'

'You can go away when the trouble comes, sir. We, where can we go, sir? We must stay in our mother country. And when the nationalists take the country, sir, they will kill us because we are policemen.'

'Why should they kill you? They'll need all the trained police they can get, and more, to stop their thugs fighting each other.'

The old black policeman shook his head: 'I doubt too much,' he said. 'Very much. They will kick us out and make the thugs the police. They say we are traitors. They call us Tshombes, because we are like Mr. Tshombe in Katanga who co-operates with the Europeans. You know what I will do, sir?'

'What, Sar-Major?'

'Next year I can retire if I wish it, sir. I think so. I will take my pension and I go home to my kraal. And I will put a high wire fence round my kraal, like it is by the jail sir. And I will buy a shotgun, sir, and all day I will sit with my shotgun. And if any ZAPU boys come to trouble me I will shoot them dead, sir. What else can I do, sir?'

Chapter Thirty-Six

When the boys from the office bundle you half-plastered on to the PanAm jet in New York, and you settle back with a can of Budweiser and you feel that wad of travellers' cheques in your pocket, it's easy to say to yourself: Home was never like this. When you're sitting in the Halekelani knocking back Maitais at two dollars a throw on the Company expense account, it's easy to say: To hell with Africa, I'm an American now and I'm going back to America and I'm going to make a million and to hell with everything else. But when you're back in old Africa seeing all the old things, the tall grass and the sunsets and the afternoon shadows, and you see an elephant crossing the road with her baby hanging on to her tail, and when an old African calls you Nkosi again and a fat piccanin stands naked with his pot belly at the roadside and waves and you hear drums and singing in the sunset and smell the smoke of woodfires and the words of Sindebele which you have not used nor thought about for years come flooding back to your tongue without thinking, then your decision gets you right here, right here in the heart.

I left Bulawayo before light, walking out on the Great North Road heading for Salisbury and the mighty Zambezi. When the sun came up I was way out of town in the bush and the tall grass was wet with dew and the tarmac was cool. The gaunt thorn trees which were brown and blistering and shimmering from my old flat window on a Saturday afternoon were beautiful in the. sunrise, alive. There were cattle among the thorn trees and they were nice-looking cattle, dewy in the morning and some looked up at the sound of my boots on the gravel. Africans passed me cycling into town to work and some of them were whistling jauntily and some waved to me. And I thought: see, what pleasant happy people they really are. I passed an old dip tank, not a hundred yards from the road and the thatch upon the tank was burned and scrawled in crude mud letters on the sides of the tank was: 'zapu puza' which means 'Zapu devours' and I thought: yes, let your coat of arms be an ox-hide shield and round the edge of that shield let there stand the words:

ZAPU PUZA,
ETIAM HOMO SAPIENS,

and let a picture of a petrol bomb be embossed upon the centre of the shield and upon the scroll beneath the shield let there be the motto:

'You're throwing well
When you're throwing Shell'

and the thought made me bitter.

A motorcar stopped for me and we whistled along the tarmac in the morning sunlight. There was mist on the land and it filled the shallow valleys like a still atavistic spirit, and the tops of the thorn trees poked above the mist. It was very quiet and very simple and I had forgotten that it existed. As we passed the long low flat mountain where the Matabele chiefs once held their indabas under the mighty King Lobengula I said: 'There's Thabasinduna!' and the driver said, 'Yes, that's right,' and I felt guilty because I had forgotten about the mountain and I felt guilty because I had never climbed up it in my life, and now I never would.

We drove on and the sun rose bright and hot and the mist was gone and we left Matabeleland behind, and entered the Midlands. And all the way through Matabeleland and the Midlands I looked at the thorn trees and the heat shimmering off the bush and I told myself that I wanted none of it, it was hot and dull and infested with mosquitoes and ticks and savages who were going to destroy the place, themselves and us, that it could not be compared with any state in America, but I could not quite make it. Then we entered the warm fecund Mashonaland where the country rolled and the cattle were fat and the maize stood twelve feet high in the fields and I realised how little I knew my own country and I felt mean and lonely and rootless in my chest. I wanted to tell the driver to let me out so I could walk and feel and reconsider. But we came to Salisbury and I stayed on in the car, heading north for the Zambezi and out of the country, for I had made my decision, which was the only wise one a man could make, and I resolved to stick to it. America has everything, I shouted to myself, great beauty, big money. What d'you want to stay in this desert for and get your throat cut? Look at the Congo. You aren't deserting, you're being sensible. It's the others who're hanging on who haven't got the guts to move. Give praise that you're young and free to get out, that you've had the savvy to see the world and get yourself a great job in a great country. You want to be rich and enjoy life. In Rhodesia you won't get rich and in five years' time they'll kick the chair out from under your arse. You want to be able to fly to Bermuda when you feel like it, and to Colorado for skiing in the winter, to Mexico City for a week, and you want to be able to go down Broadway to a decent show and a night club when you feel like it. What about a week at Miami? Okay, let's go—

But then late afternoon came as we drove through the bush and the thorn trees threw long shadows and the bush turned to gold. At sunset we drove down into the vast wild Zambezi Valley and there were signposts along the road to warn of elephant, and a herd of great elephant crossed the road. The great bull looked at us and whisked his tail and flapped his ears irritably and led his herd across the road and the cows looked agitated because they had their calves jostling beside them. They shuffled off into the bush and melted into the mauve background and now and again one of them trumpeted. The Zambezi river at Chirundu Bridge was vast and silent and red in the sunset and the great sandbanks were mauve and spoke of hippo and crocodiles and great tiger fish and sable and antelope and guinea-fowl coming down to drink. And I nearly cried out loud in the sorrow I felt that I had forgotten these things and

287

would not know them again and because I was deserting them without considering them.

So we crossed the Zambezi into Northern Rhodesia and the next day my friend set me down at Kapiri Mposhi, a trading post in the middle of the bush, where the dirt road for Tanganyika begins.

At Kapiri Mposhi it was very bad. I walked many miles up the road to Tanganyika, then I sat down in the tall grass on my sleeping bag. I spent thirty-six hours at that place because not many vehicles travel that road to Tanganyika. I didn't mind not getting a ride, not even when it rained. The rain beating down was a suitable penance. I drew figures in the gravel and I watched the soldier ants and at night I made a small fire and lay looking up at the stars. Once a car passed me and I did not even thumb it because I did not want to talk and I did not want to leave the place. Occasionally Africans passed. Sometimes they glared at me hostilely and did not greet me and I ignored them, and sometimes they greeted me by lifting their hands and saying 'Moni-moni' and I raised my hand and said 'Moni-moni'.

Some of them stopped to ask me where I was going, but I could not converse freely with them because I do not speak Chinyanja and I kept breaking out into Sindebele, and every time I found myself thinking in Sindebele I felt more sad.

And I remembered so many things I had forgotten about and I could smell the smoke of woodfire under the sadza and the warm human smell and sounds of old servants chatting round the fire in the backyard at night and the wonderful tales of the jungle and of their kraals far off about which they told me, and my heart cried out for Africa.

I walked all next afternoon and on after sundown, because there was no point waiting in the vast anonymity of the bush, and it was better, I suppose, to be ninety miles from Mpika than a hundred miles from Mpika. I did not see any people that afternoon but I did see fresh cow dung across the road which showed that there were kraals not far away into the bush. Nor did any vehicles pass along the road. When the moon was high I grew tired and I imagined I saw strange things lurking at the side of the road up ahead. I thought of lion and leopard. Sometimes I heard a strange crash in the bush and

I started and stared. I though of animals and I though of ambush parties and once I shouted out in kitchen kaffir: 'All right, you, come out of there!' But there was only silence thereafter and the cricking of night insects and I continued on my way. Often I thought I saw something flit across the road way up ahead. I weighed up the things a man should do: If I lay down to rest and lit a fire I would scare away any lions and leopards: but I would attract the attention of any wandering groups of terrorists. I thought: You'll look funny in America with your throat cut. The company is so particular about the appearance of its executive officers. And I thought I would one day write a story entitled: *The Inconveniences Resulting From Having Your Throat Cut*. At last I grew very tired and I moved fifty paces off the roadside and built a fire. I built a large fire with thick logs that would glow long after I fell asleep. I lit the fire and as it took hold on the thick logs I pushed them deeper into the flames, and I watched white ants and black beetles scurrying desperately from the heat and the thick smoke that was permeating through, their cracks and passages and burrows. Some ran towards the fire, scurrying here and there frantically for cool crevices, sticking their heads and antennae into every place they came across, then withdrawing frantically and scurrying on. They bumped into each other and trampled over each other, each man for himself. The flames crept further down the log and cut them off from the retreat and they ran around in a smaller area. Some of them toppled off the log into the flames but not one of them chose a quick death and jumped off. Instead the flame crept up round the log until they were imprisoned on a narrow strip and they stood blindly, their antennae twitching. When the flame came against them they shrank back but then they could shrink no further and then a tongue of flame licked over them and they suddenly jerked and then they crumpled and then they shrivelled up. And the flame took hold and destroyed both them and the log. And further down the log where the flames had not yet reached, some were making for safety right off the log, but some still dithered and milled around scurrying from the heat but not having the sense to get the hell right out of it. I sat with my back against a thorn tree and I opened my haversack and pulled out the brandy bottle. I drank at the brandy from the bottle and I watched the flames and the dying ants and beetles and I thought: there go I. And I smelt the wood smoke and the crackling heat of the fire and I listened to the cricking of the crickets and the other still African night noises, and I looked up at the vast sky through the thorn branches and I felt very sad. At last I lay down in my sleeping bag with the weariness of Africa's dirt road on me and the tired glow of her sun on me and I fell asleep.

I heard the car when it was a long way off. The sky was turning pink. I scrambled out of my sleeping bag and ran through the bush to the road. I stopped and listened. The hum was coming from the south. I ran back to my camp and picked up my haversack and my bag. I jumped over to the fire and urinated on to it. Then I picked up my gear, and raced back to the road trailing my bag behind me. The hum was closer. I rolled up my bag as the big Ford Fairlane came round the bend travelling at ninety miles an hour. The big body heaved gently as she whined round the bend. I stood back and gave it a long sweeping thumb. There was one man in the car and he slammed on the brakes and shot past me to a halt. I picked up my gear and ran after him.

'For Chrissake,' he said, 'what are you doing here?'

'Same as you,' I panted, 'heading north.'

'Get in,' he said.

'Thanks,' I said.

I threw my gear on to the back seat. He hunched over the wheel and before my door was closed the great car surged forward.

'For Chrissake,' he said – 'Do you know where you are?'

'Northern Rhodesia, about ninety miles from Mpika.'

'That's right,' he said. 'And do you know where you're also ten miles from?'

'No'

'The Congo border. And d'you know what was on the news last night?'

'No,' I said. 'Didn't listen to the news last night, regrettably.'

'Good thing you didn't, I suppose. It was on the news last night that bands of Congolese savages have crossed the border and are whooping it up along this road. Boundaries mean nothing to these chaps. That's quite apart from the local political enthusiasts. They're also whooping it up along here.'

The car was doing ninety again.

'Hell,' I said.

'This is the real hot spot round Northern Rhodesia these days. Kenneth Kaunda himself comes from these parts.'

'But Kenneth's all right,' I said.

'Kenneth's all right, but some of Kenneth's followers aren't as all right as Kenneth.'

Ninety miles an hour over the long dirt road, swaying at the bends, hunched over the wheel.

'What're you going north for?'

'Business,' he said. 'Cattle. Bloke selling up lock stock and barrel for a song.'

'You buying the ranch?'

'Ranch, hell, nobody'll buy the ranch. I'm after his cattle.'

And as we came round the bend we saw it, the great tree lying across the road, the stump end white and freshly hacked. It was sixty yards ahead of us, right across the road, the branches crumpled and sticking out.

'Oh Jesus,' he said – 'here we go.'

He slammed his foot on the brake. Eighty – seventy – sixty – fifty – and the tree loomed closer, the bush flashed by crazily, weaving. The great car swayed on the dirt. I put my hands on to the dashboard then I remembered and I dropped my hands to the seat and tried to sit limp. Forty, thirty, twenty yards to go, forty, thirty miles per hour. The tree was very large now, swinging across the road in front of us. Thirty miles an hour. Words came to my mouth automatically, words that I had not said since I was a schoolboy, words I do not believe in, but as I said them I believed them: 'God surrounds us.' At twenty paces they emerged from the bushes on both sides of the road, twenty black youths scrambling through the bush with shouts and in their hands were rocks and sticks and stones and spears and pangas. They waved their sticks and pangas and shouted and scrambled towards the road and on their black faces were smiles and shouts and creases of glee. Fifteen paces and he tried to make for the bush at the right hand side, and the great car went into a skid, into a broadside and she heaved and keeled. She broadsided on to the tree, crushing the branches and she banged against the trunk. She teetered and she dropped back to her wheels. And they swarmed over the tree and round the car with their jumping and their brandishing and their sticks and the world was full of the crashing of their weapons and the metallic crunch of the car.

'Doors!' the driver shouted and we slammed down the lock buttons.

A rock loomed through the air and shattered the windscreen.

'There's a monkey-wrench under the seat,' he shouted. 'Beat the hell out of any one who sticks his head in!'

The engine roared as the rocks clattered on to us.

'Jesus, you black bastards!' he screamed.

He let out the clutch and the car bucked alongside the side of the tree tearing itself free from the branches. A spear bounded through the broken windscreen and ricocheted into my leg, but it was a shallow jab.

'You bastards,' he screamed. He drove the car straight into the black jumping bodies. They scattered and beat at the car with their sticks. He drove straight for a man with a rock poised for throwing and knocked him down.

'Got you!' shouted the driver, but I could not tell if we rode over him. The back of the car was taking the beating now. The back window went in a crash and they chased behind us throwing rocks. They ran behind, swiping with their pangas. My window smashed and I held the spear in both hands and jabbed it out the. window. He drove the car straight into the bush. It heaved across the sand and grass. He swung the wheel round the top of the fallen tree and put his foot flat on the accelerator. He rode over saplings. Trees bent and crumpled and beat the shattered glass and crumpled sides. He headed her back for the road and charged the road. She lunged into it and jolted over it. They leaped over the tree and ran to meet our flank. He swung her hard left and pressed the accelerator to the floor. And with many knocks and rattles she surged off down the road and we left the Africans behind waving their sticks and looking disappointed. I leaned over the seat and looked out the window and stretched out my hand and gave them the V sign. Then I remembered that God had surrounded us and I stopped doing it.

'Well,' I said, 'you saved our lives.'

'Look at this,' he said angrily and waved his hand round the car. He drove until we were a mile from the scene then he pulled up at the side of the road. The Africans were mere dots on the road behind us. He motioned me to get behind the wheel.

'Keep her ticking over,' he said. He looked at the car. There was a panga wedged into a long cut in the door. He pulled it out and slung it into the seat beside me.

'Keep it handy,' he said. He filled his lungs and faced down the road and bellowed the gravest African insult at the black dots. 'Your mothers' privates,' he yelled in the vernacular.

Then he chuckled and went to the bonnet and opened it and looked at the engine.

'Radiator's got a leak,' he said. 'And I've got no water.'

'Then we'll both piss into it,' I said, 'I, for one, have got plenty.'

'Good idea,' he said.

I leaned over to my haversack and pulled out the brandy bottle. I took a slug and my hands were shaking and then I passed him the bottle. That night we slept at the hotel at Mpika and he and I got pretty drunk together. I got talking to a young farmer and after a while he said: 'Keep going north.' He put his finger to his lips and said 'Pfftt—' and shot his finger through the air like a missile. 'Right north,' he said, 'till you're off this godforsaken continent.' For the next four days I rode on native buses north, and so I came to Arusha, Tanganyika.

Chapter Thirty-Seven

Politics.

Sitting at the Arusha Hotel, drinking cold Tusker. Politics in the bars, on the hotel verandahs drinking tea and cold Tusker and gin-slings, over the dinner table, at the Club, over shop counters, in the newspaper – politics, politics, politics. Everybody waiting, everybody hoping, everybody thinking: what's going to happen to me and mine? The Safari Hotel? – closed down by the Government because the guests didn't stand up when the Minister of something came in. Get your money out of the country, send it back to England, back to India and Pakistan, down to South Africa. Lorries coming down from Kenya, farmers' lorries loaded high, the backs built higher with planks and netting wire, loaded with furniture, beds and mattresses and stoves and refrigerators and food for the road, children curled in nests among the furniture and mattresses and sacking, all heading south to the haven of South Africa. Uhuru's coming in Kenya, it's come in Uganda and Tanganyika, flee from Uhuru. Abandon your farm, give up your green acres, sell your cattle for what you can get, put a match to the homestead so at least they won't have it, throw your maize to the chickens and pigs and eat as much as you can: it's a long haul to South Africa. Thank God for South Africa and old Hennie Verwoerd—

Sitting at the Arusha Hotel: I'm sick of politics.

Look at this, just look at this will you, what it says in the paper: this M.P. asks why are we being flown to parliament by white pilots? It's not wise to entrust the safety of our M.P.s to white pilots, he says. And why, asks the same M.P., have we still got some white magistrates? And here it says another M.P. asks: And when is private enterprise going to be Africanised? Why is the manager of a large oil company still white? Politics, politics, I'm so sick of politics.

'So I went to the police station. I said to the sergeant: I want to report a trespass, Africans have taken to walking across my garden in broad daylight, trampling over my flower beds and so help me, they sit down in my backyard and have a crap. And the sergeant leans across the counter and he says to me: "I don't quite hear you, white man." So I say: "Africans are trespassing and buggering up my garden." And he says: "I still don't hear you." So I get the message and I slip a pound across the counter. And he says "I hear you a little better, but I still don't quite hear you." So I slip him another quid. And he says: "I hear you much better, but I still don't hear you quite properly." So what can I do? I slip him another quid. And he says: "Ah, now I can hear you nicely." So I have to go through the pantomime of telling him all over again how the munts are trampling across my garden and he says he'll see what he can do. That's a week ago and they're still crapping on my doorstep.'

'It's a hell of a set-up,' I said.

'I tell you,' he said, 'keep going north, right north. Or right south.'

Politics.

And the labourers thought that they would be given the factory. Sort of share it out. And when they found the old management still in control they were as injured as hell. And when the management threatened to sack the whole damn lot if they didn't pull up their socks, the Trade Union comes down like a ton of bricks and threatens seven kinds of strikes. And the Indian shopkeepers! Jesus, they're having a time of it. They hate the Indians, you know, and they thought they would get the Indian shops. Now they're boycotting and throwing bricks—

Lorries coming through from Kenya heading down south, the sad salvage of a lifetime piled on the back of one lorry, caution thrown bitterly to the winds with an angry cry over the shoulder, getting the hell out of it.

'—iron bars on my windows: that's what I'm putting on. Iron bolts on my door. I won't let my kids cycle to school any more. I sleep with a .38 next to my bed. That's a nice way to live, isn't it? And me forty-three years old. What can I do? How can I sell my house? Who'll pay a cent for it? And even if I sell my house, where'll I get a job? And if I get a job, what kind of bloody job? Or maybe I can get a job. But then, how can I sell my house? All my money's tied up in that house. Hell, I don't want to start all over again living in some poky flat in South Kensington—'

'Quite,' I said.

'So what do I do, just tell me what do I do—?'

Then I climbed around the slopes of Mount Kilimanjaro, just some miles from Arusha. I walked up the approaches to Kilimanjaro from the town of Moshi, and the sun shone warm and fecund and golden on the warm green grass, still wet in the morning's freshness. The sun burned my body and there were no people to be seen, no houses, no streets, no trinkets and chromium plating and Madison Avenue, no Wall Street, just vast green empty spacious great forevemess, pregnant and primitive and exciting and virgin and even dangerous under the great vast blue sky – I walked up the long slopes of Kilimanjaro through towering trees and bush veld pregnant with the lazy sounds of Africa, I came to the cool green slopes and places where ice-cold rivers tumble and froth and grass grows thick and tropics vie with winter shades, I walked and walked up the winding slopes where it grew so green and dark and the very air vibrated with that hot cool life of Africa, with birds and palms and creepers and jungle leaves, where paths cross streams and tumbling brooks. I walked and black men and women and children came out of the jungle huts and smiled and waved and shouted: Jambo! And the children gambolled beside me and smiled and laughed and begged to be allowed to carry my haversack – I walked in the lengthening shadows of the afternoon up the winding paths of Kilimanjaro, through the mauving jungle and the evening nesting noises of all the things that live and throb in the African evening. 'Rest well, Bwana, has the Bwana enough to eat? My huts are near and there is there food and warmth, and shelter for the Bwana.' And I walked up and around Kilimanjaro and I passed through tiny villages of black men and many fell into step beside me and we went to nearby huts and shacks and we drank kaffir beer and sat in the sun, and it was very warm and friendly. And in the evening I sat at my fire and watched the flames and the coals and the flickering shadows in the middle of great dark green Africa and I listened to the great quiet noises of Africa in the night, the noise of insects and the great silence and the faraway sounds and shouts of village life, and I smelt the woodsmoke and I knew that never again, nowhere else, was all this to be recaptured. And I was very sad, for I knew my life was changing and would never change back again.

And then I strode back down the mountain, back on to the plains of Tanganyika and I set out on to the road to Ngorogoro where the wild animals and the Masai people live in a great lush crater so big that the old volcanic walls are distant mountain ranges. And I spread my sleeping bag in the camping site near the log cabin rest huts at the top of the crater and in the evenings I sat in the grass at the lip of the crater and I watched the sun go down on Africa in furious red and orange, and I watched the animals in the great crater below go down to the watering holes in turns, to drink, and it turned mauve down there below, and you could hear the distant squeal of elephant and the roar of lion. When the sun had set I went into the log cabin bar and sat at the wooden counter with the tourists and drank cold Tusker and I thought: 'Never more.' And in the mornings I went down into the crater in the back of a Land Rover and bounced and churned over the great jungle plains below and watched the animals. I felt the heat and sweat and smell and languor of midday, and the lengthening shadows in the afternoon and the movements of animals down to the waterholes to drink and the bush turning mauve and the night noises starting. I watched a pair of lions making love on a green hill. The sun was hot and they had full bellies and they were very happy with each other. She lay on her side, growling and her tail flicking and he climbed all over her, growling. At last she got on to her stomach and she flicked her tail aside and he got down on her, his giant paws and mighty legs astride her back and gripping her, his great back haunched and shuddering and his muscles and thighs bulging. And he groaned and pounded at her, his great mane and head bent down to her ears and she pressed her rump up to him and she whimpered as a woman whimpers. Their bodies beat each other savagely and rhythmically and he looked as if he could not get enough of her, nor she of him. And when it was all over he rolled off her, and sat down heavily beside her and she toppled back on to her side and lay panting in the sun. He looked at her very tiredly and gently and he yawned and she yawned and she stretched out her great paws and stretched her claws, and her tail was no longer flicking. I thought: You will never see it again. And I felt very bad. And when I sat at my fire that night I wanted to make up my mind to get up with the dawn and pack my gear and set off down the roads of Tanganyika and south again, back to Rhodesia to find Suzie and say: 'We're going to stay where we belong.' But I did not. After three days I packed my gear and set off down the road back to Arusha, to the road that leads north to Kenya, the Mau Mau territory whence the farmers were fleeing. And from Arusha I took a bus to Nairobi. And with that bus, Africa, my Africa was gone.

This is it, I said – you're an emigrant. And it got me right here, right here in the heart.

I got myself a seat at the very back of the bus, in the corner, and the bus filled right up about me.

There was a notice: 'This vehicle is licensed to carry 32 seated passengers and 12 standing passengers.' As we pulled away from the bus terminus in the mid-afternoon there were thirty-two seated passengers and twelve standing. As we pulled through Arusha the driver honked his horn for passengers. He turned down side streets honking his horn and searching for passengers. He stopped wherever he was flagged down and he jammed them in, one on top of the other and then two on top of one. He sat them in the aisle, he sat them four to a double seat, sitting on each other's laps. And what made me mad was that the passengers did not mind. And still the driver drove round the blocks honking for passengers. And what made me madder than all hell was that those passengers were helping him: they were leaning out the windows with big smiles and shouting encouragement, shouting: 'Come on! We're going to

Nairobi!' All night on the bus I thought about my decision to quit Africa, and I hashed over all the things I had seen and done and heard in Africa.

I looked round at the wogs jabbering in the bus and picking their noses and spitting, black and woolly-headed and ignorant and primitive, and I liked them. I realised I loved Africans. I was used to them, but I do not want to be ruled by them, I am an Anglo-Saxon and I want to be ruled by Anglo-Saxons, by Anglo-Saxon standards. You are doing the right thing, I shouted at myself. When the dawn came we rattled into beautiful Nairobi, tall new elegant buildings rising up white out of the jungle into the dawn, built by white men and now lost. Spacious avenues carved through the jungle and I cried to myself: See—see! The same will happen to Rhodesia, and to the whole of Africa in the end. I walked from the bus terminus to the nearest travel agent while my anger was still hot. I had intended going overland through Uganda to the Sudan, and taking a Nile steamer to the Mediterranean, but I was so up to here with Africa and Africans and African politics, I bought myself a ticket on the next boat sailing north out of Mombasa through Suez to Europe in ten days' time. Then I went to the Stanley Hotel and drank cold Tuskers very angrily and I washed my hands of Africa.

That day I took a train down to Mombasa, then a bus a hundred miles up the East African coast to Malindi, and I checked into the hotel there, on the palm-slung white beach. Might Suzie be waiting for me in Mombasa? She had planned on arriving in Mombasa on the *Eden Roc* at about this time. If so, I would be safely out of the way when Suzie's ship came in.

Mornings I lay on the beach trying not to think about Suzie, or about Africa, trying not to think about anything except the million I was going to make in America in the noble subject of Death Tax and the Life Underwriter. There were a number of American tourists staying at the hotel, resting up for or between or after their passion-wagon package-deal safaris. Whenever I thought about Africa I went up to one of these Yanks and started asking him about his home in Hartford Connecticut or Buffalo New York or Boise Idaho, and we yapped about what a great country the ole U.S.A. is, how it's saving the world for there is nothing a Yank more dearly loves to talk about than how they are saving the world. I used all my Dale Carnegie on them and I became great buddies with them and I got a number of invitations to make nice long visits to Hartford Connecticut and Buffalo New York and Boise Idaho. One of them was a millionaire and one evening when my heart was breaking for Africa I went straight up to him and started talking about the Estate Tax problem his poor widow would have when he kicked the bucket and he said 'Tell me more,' and he gave me a list of his assets and I figured out his death tax and told him his little woman would have to flog most of his shares in his corporation, so his post-mortem income would be all shot to hell, along with him, and she'd have to flog the mansion and the yacht and move into an apartment and sonnyboy wouldn't be able to vote himself president of the corporation, nor any of the subsidiary corporations of which his corporation was presently major shareholder, and he said to me: 'What do I do, Joey-boy, just tell me what I do?' with tears in his eyes. So I said: First of all we decrease your New York State Succession Duty by forming another company in Alberta, Canada, where they ain't got no Succession Duty, and you become major shareholder of the Alberta Corporation, and you flog your shares in your New York company to your Alberta company and then for New York Succession Duty purposes your New York company will be legally situated in Alberta, Canada, and not in New York, and therefore it would not be subject to New York Succession Duty, but only to Canadian Federal Estate Tax which is lower than New York Succession Duty and on a million bucks that's a lot of potatoes. He was very impressed. Then, I said, you insure your life through my company, to an amount equal to the balance of your tax, which is now only two hundred and fifty thousand dollars, so that when you slip off this mortal coil your little old lady can pay the death tax with the insurance money and then she can go right on enjoying your loot. Say! that's a great little old plan you got there, Joe-boy, he said. And we made a date for me to visit him in Buffalo New York in ten weeks time and I would write him up. I figured my commission on the policy would be over nine thousand dollars in the first year, and with a few beers inside me, and the prospect of that kind of potatoes and the trips to Miami and Bermuda, I was glad I was going back to America. Whenever I found myself thinking of Suzie, I went straight up to one of the dolls and turned on the charm, brittle, hard-arsed, bedward charm. In the evenings it was not very hard to stop thinking about Suzie and about Africa, because there was the sundowner hour that went late into the night, and I concentrated on the problem of trying to lay a different bird every night, and if I didn't make it, at least I went to bed drank; but in the mornings when I woke up, I remembered the soft woman feel and smell of Suzie and I remembered her dresses I recognised from America and London and even from Bulawayo, hanging in her cupboard, and I remembered the warm woman sights and sounds of Suzie getting up in the morning and getting dressed and getting breakfast, I remembered the soft sweet bulge of her breasts and the long smooth line of her legs, and I thought of the summer and the fall, and the winter and the spring of America, the sunshine and the snow, but no Suzie waking up with me in the morning. I thought of Suzie, waking up to the sounds and feel of Africa without me, in another man's bed, not even thinking about me any more: and it felt very bad. And I felt the warm smell and feel and familiarity of Africa, and it felt very bad in the mornings.

When the sun was getting high in the late morning, and it was time for the bar to open, and the women were getting languid and salty in the seaside palm-slung sun, it wasn't so hard. But on the morning before the ship Suzie might be on was to dock in Mombasa, a hundred jungled miles away to the south, it was very bad. I started drinking early that morning, but I could not bring myself to be hard-arsed and brittle and charming, I just sat on the hotel verandah and stared at the sea, and drank beer and just cried inside for Suzie, my Suzie, Suzie, Suzie, my mate, my lover, my love, my sweetheart, my darling, my dearest person, and I felt that I was torn and bleeding and would never be the same again, nothing, the whole world, the air, the sun and the snow, a bottle of wine, the mornings, the sunset, a million things would never be the same again.

I drank all that morning, and all that afternoon and late into the night, but I did not get drunk, and after midnight I walked up the bush path at the back of the hotel to the servants' compound and I beat on the door of the headwaiter's hut, who I knew owned a motorcar, and I gave him ten pounds to drive me then and there to Mombasa. I knew I should not do it, I didn't even know what I was going to do when I saw her ship. I didn't even know for sure if she was on the ship, perhaps she had changed her plans, she may already be engaged, and she may even have slept with him already, she may even be married already – I didn't know what I was going to do, I knew I should not go to Mombasa, but I am an emotional man whose heart rules his head.

Ezekiel, the headwaiter, dropped me off at the dock gates just before dawn, very pleased with his ten quid. It was warm and it was sleepy and it was very African at the docks, and the crickets were still chirping among the palms and the jungle. I walked down to the quay where the *Eden Roc* would dock, and I sat down on the dirty concrete and hung my legs over the side and I sat there trying to think straight in the silence. After a long time the sun came up over the jungle coast, very red and very beautiful. When the red was gone and the sun was bright on the early morning sea, and the black stevedores were coming into the docks, the *Eden Roc* appeared on the horizon and I gave up all the thinking I had been trying to do, and I gave myself over to a tired nervous sad excitement. When the tugs went out and hitched up with her the harbour was alive and I got up off the quay and I went round to the side of the warehouse where nobody aboard would notice me. I leaned against the corner of the warehouse with my hat pulled down low over my eyes and chain-smoked and I was very excited, though I did not know what I was going to do, except that I just had to be there, and I peered at the faces lining the rails of the ship. There were hundreds of faces. I ran my sandy eyes over them again and again, over the same rails. My heart contracted as I came upon a face. But I could not be sure. I noted the position of the face and I moved my sandy eyes on. And my heart contracted again. I went back to the first face to compare it, and it would be gone, lost as people moved about and waved and shouted hullo. And I found third and fourth and fifth and even more faces. I could not recognise the dresses of any. I searched through all the faces and then more came and many moved and went away. Then many people left the rails.

It was now breakfast time and people went and others came. There was a long delay before people began coming ashore down the gangway to see the sights of Mombasa. As they came down, in ones and twos I grew excited and moved a little closer, round the corner of the warehouse to make sure I could see each face. They collected round the bottom of the gangway, then they moved off down the quay towards the taxis and the buses, they walked past within twenty paces of my corner of the building. I was in a good position. At nine o'clock more passengers came down. My heart skipped many times as people came to the top of the gangway into the sunlight. By ten o'clock the flow had turned to a drip. I waited until half-past ten, trying to think what I should do. Then I thought: if you go aboard and you find her it will break your heart and hers all over again, it will do no good because nothing can come of it, she has made a new life and you are making a new life – and if you find she is not on the ship, it will break your heart because you will be sure she has decided to marry the man – it is best to go away not knowing. And I turned away from the quay and I walked back out of the docks, and I went to the first hotel and I walked into the bar.

'Give me a cold beer, please.'

'What kind of beer?'

'Any kind of beer is all right.'

He was an old white man with a kind lined face. He poured the cold Tusker very carefully. The beer purged my mouth and throat clean, like cold acid, and it made the cigarette taste good for a change, like food.

'You off the ship?' he asked kindly. There were only two of us in the old colonial-style bar. The ceiling was high and there was a big overhead fan and there were palms growing outside the big old windows.

'No,' I said, 'I'm waiting for a ship to America.'

'You don't sound like an American,' he said.

'I'm Rhodesian,' I said.

He looked at me. 'You emigrating there?' he said, and the word got me right here.

'Yes,' I said.

He nodded and looked at me.

'Things are bad in Rhodesia,' he said. 'They're bad here too. They're bad all over Africa. But what I always say is: what chance has the country got of staying stable, if all the young people go?'

'Give me another Tusker here,' I said loudly, and he gave it to me and then he moved down the bar and read the newspaper. And I sat and looked out of the window on to the palms and the sea, and I drank lots of cold Tusker and I tried to think straight. I tried to think about the beauty and prosperity of North America, about the money I was going to make, and the holidays in Miami, and Bermuda and living happily ever after as a good successful corporation man. I tried to think straight for a long time, I shouted at myself, but I could not really think, I could not feel like an American, I felt like an African. And I did not want to go back to North America, all I wanted to do was walk out of the bar on to the ship and sail down the coast and throw myself down on the shores of Africa, and stretch my arms and legs out into the sand of Africa, and cry my pain and unhappiness and tiredness out into her warm familiar soil. 'What chance has the country got if all the young people go?' the man had said. I drank the beer and it flooded my system like a balm, and slowly a laugh built up in my chest, then into my throat, a bubble of happiness, then a smile across my face. And I realised that the most important thing in these three score years and ten is to do what you feel is good, good for your heart, to live and sweat and feel and love and die where you belong. And I threw my last beer down my throat and I picked up my haversack and I waved to the barman and I walked out into the sun. I swung down the road back to the docks and there was a spring in my step and a laugh in my throat, and I looked at the blacks in the street and I smiled at them and my happiness was infectious and they smiled and waved to me. 'Jambo!' I laughed and they laughed, white teeth flashing in black chubby faces: 'Jambo, Bwana!'

I walked up the gangplank of the ship into the Bureau Square, and I went to the Purser's Office.

'Any berths to Beira?'

'Yes, sir,'

'You're hired,' I said, 'to take me to Beira—'

'Sir—?' the Purser's Mate said.

I pulled out my traveller's cheques. Only then did I hesitate, and only for a moment: Maybe Suzie is married, how could you live in Africa without Suzie—

'Have you a passenger list?'

'Yes, sir.'

'Have you a Miss—?'

He waited. 'Miss who, sir?'

Christ oh Christ, Jesus Christ in a tea kettle, you can't go on eating your heart out forever, you have made your decision independent of Suzie, and that is the best way.

'Nobody,' I said, and reached out for his pen.

'All I want to do is sleep,' I said, and the Purser's Mate looked at me curiously.

I went to my cabin and fell down on the bunk. When I woke up it was dark, and the ship was rolling and we were far out to sea.

Chapter Thirty-Eight

I showered and shaved and asked a steward for the time. Eight o'clock. I put on my crumpled suit and made my way aloft to find the bar.

I sat in a corner of the bar, where I could see everybody who came and went. I scanned all the faces. No joy. I waited until the second dinner sitting had come up, until the bar was full, but still no joy. At nine-thirty the band struck up and people started dancing. At ten o'clock I went aft to the bar lounge. I went to the smoking room and to the library. I went to the sundeck and along the promenade and I disturbed many couples as I walked along. Each deck, each corner, each figure brought a surge of excitement, then disappointment again. At eleven o'clock I sat down in a deckchair and acknowledged that Suzie was not aboard.

I sat in the deckchair and I looked at the sea, silver in the moonlight, and at the long black jungle coast, vast and dark and pregnant between the silver sea and the starry sky, and I thought: Suzie is still in Durban, a thousand miles away from Rhodesia and she is in love with the man and she is going to marry him, she has slept with him already, and you will have to forget about her as she has forgotten about you. Even now she is lying in his arms, naked and loving and she does not care about you any more, she is no longer your woman. And I wanted to jump up and shout and shake the ship apart. I sat in the deckchair a long time, and then I wiped my sleeve across my eyes and I got up and walked back to the bar.

I found her in the shadow of a lifeboat davit, leaning over the rails and watching the silver sea and the black coast, and her long gold hair was blowing wispy in the wind. I stopped and stood looking at her and my heart was knocking and I could feel the tears behind my eyes again and I was very happy. She did not turn around. I put my hand upon her shoulder and she turned with a small cry and she had tears in her eyes.

'Why are you crying, Suzie?'

Her eyes opened wide and she stared at me. Then she dropped her head against my chest and pressed herself against me and wept: 'Oh no! Oh no no no for Christ's sake!'

I took her hands as she wept against me and on her left hand I felt the ring. She sobbed and put her arms round me and squeezed me. Then she ran her hands up my chest and held my face. She looked up at me with tears running down her face and she shook me between her hands and she said: 'Oh God, Joe, whatever is going to become of us?'

Later she unbuttoned her coat and unbuttoned my suit jacket and put her arms around me, and pressed herself flat against me.

'I'm trying to graft on to you,' she said, 'to become part of you. Maybe then I'll be happy as a nonentity.'

She pushed the ring round and round with her thumb. 'For a while,' she said, 'I knew such peace. Ordinary surburban honest-to-goodness happiness. Not trying to keep up with him, not needing to keep up with him, I didn't have to. I didn't feel I needed to be better or different, just me. He wasn't smouldering to be any better or different, and it didn't cross his mind that I should be. He was complete and mature, a nice ordinary man and he made me so too!'

'Why were you weeping?'

'I was weeping at the deathbed of my soul, although I wanted it to die. My soul was with you, behind the hinterland of Africa, wherever you were, sleeping in the bush, trudging north through the jungle up out of Africa to America, every day getting further and further from me. My soul was stretching out between you and me, wherever you were, stretching thinner and thinner, like an elastic band with each turn of the propellers. And it was about to snap, and my soul would die, and then I would be free.'

Later she said: 'I knew you would come back to Africa. You were doing very well in America, but I knew you would come back, you would never be happy as a corporation man, no matter how much money you made.'

Later I said: 'Private practice in Salisbury. That's what's going to become of us. We'll buy some land, and put down some roots, and we'll bloody well stay, come hell or high water. The country needs all the young men of goodwill it can get.'

Part Seven

Chapter Thirty-Nine

It was a hot night. There was a high moon shining big and bright and still and there was no wind at all, the only sound was the muffled whoosh of the bicycle's slow tyres on the tarmac road and the creak of the pedals and the noise of the night insects singing in the bush. There were no lights but the bicycle's rickety lamp weaving as African Police Reservist Tambudza pedalled slowly along in his blue uniform to report for his night duty, but you could see him coming from a long way because of the moon. He had only a truncheon and a police whistle and a pair of handcuffs upon him.

'Here comes one.'

The young men lay flat in the grass in the wide ditch alongside the road. They held sticks in the grass, and stones that they had picked up at the side of the road. They lifted their heads to look down the road and the moon shone on their black sweating faces and on the white of their eyes. They lowered their heads and waited and the black police reservist came cycling along.

'Tshombe!' The black policeman swerved and braked and put his foot to the ground and his hand went for his tmncheon.

'Tshombe – Tshombe – sell-out' and the gang was upon him and the rocks hurtled through the air and the policeman ducked and threw his arms over his face. The stones pounded on his head and his shoulders and his chest and he reeled away from the bicycle, crouching, and his arms were over his head and the rocks smashed into him. One hand went to his truncheon again, but before he could get it off his belt they were on to him with their sticks.

'Tshombe—' They beat him from all sides with their sticks, on his head and on his neck and on his shoulders and his legs, and they swiped and hit each other they were so thick about him.

'Sell-out—!' and African Police Reservist Tambudza went down unconscious. His scalp was broken open and his nose crushed and his teeth were broken. He lay spread out bleeding onto the tarmac and the youths jumped about him and lifted up their sticks and swiped down at him and they kicked him in the head and the chest and the face and in the guts.

The tall man turned from the body and he trotted down into the ditch. He picked up a gallon can from the grass and he trotted back to the body. His gang was still beating the body and he shoved them aside. The African Police Reservist was making frothy sucking noises in his throat. The tall man unscrewed the cap off the petrol can and he tilted it over the body and splashed the petrol all over it. The gang stood back. They were panting hard from the exertion and the excitement. The tall man took a box of matches from his pocket. He struck one and he stepped back and the gang stepped back also. Then the tall man threw the match on to African Police Reservist Tambudza. There was a whoosh of flame five feet into the air and the petrol burned on the tarmac also and it threw a big light and long jumping shadows in the bush and it lit up the black grinning faces and flickered white on their teeth and on the whites of their eyes. African Police Reservist Tambudza came to, and he rolled over in the flames and he tried to get up and he clawed his face with his burning hands and he screamed. The youths turned and scattered and ran away into the night.

They ran through the bush and down a dirt path. From a long way away they could see the flames on the tarmac. They ran until they came to a dirt road and then they walked into the African township to the branch office of the Party. They sat round a fire in the backyard and ate porridge with their fingers and they laughed as they told the boss of the Party branch what they had done. And the boss said they had done good work, for Police Reservists were Tshombes, and he gave them each a shilling.

The young white man with his girl friend found Tambudza on the road. The flames were nearly finished and the uniform was gone and the flesh was peeling back and the bones were showing through and Tambudza was still crying. The young man stifled the flames with his jacket and he examined the man in the car lights. He turned to the girl and said: 'Go and fetch the police and an ambulance.'

The girl roared away in the car and the young man sat down on the tar next to Tambudza and he held his head. There was no light save the moon and no sound but the cries of Tambudza and the singing of the night insects.

'Tell me who done it,' the young man said.

But Tambudza only said: 'Holdi my handi, Sah, Ah em dying.'

Chapter Forty

Out in the country there were the gangs carrying sticks and stones and axes and wearing fur hats on their heads and slogans on their lips, the press-gangs marching through the hot dry bush swaggering through the villages and beating on the doors and dragging out the people and demanding to see their Party cards and beating and killing and burning their huts and trampling their crops and maiming their catue. In the bush there were the meetings, the round-ups of the people, the young men and women and the old people and the children, the young men with their sticks driving the people along the paths to the meetings, the fur-hatted ones shouting the slogans: 'Every person must join the Party! Every person must fight for the Party! Any person who does not join is a Tshombe. Find who are Tshombes and burn their huts and kill them and destroy their cattle and their crops. Kill! Burn! Action, boys, Action! One man one vote! Burn the diptanks in which the Government makes us dip our cattle. Burn the white farmers' houses. Burn the mission schools. Burn the churches. Action, boys, Action! Make petrol bombs: Burn – Burn—!' And in the nights there were the flares of matches and then the roar of burning thatch and the crackle of burning timbers and the screams of women and children and the screams of burning pigs and goats, and the footsteps of the gang running away in the night. And there was the shattering of glass and the whoosh of burning petrol and the screams of men and women and children beating their burning flesh, and the sounds of the feet of the gang running way into the night.

In the African townships round Salisbury and Bulawayo it was very bad. The grey Land Rovers rumbled down the dirt roads with their searchlights flashing and in the back were black and white policemen in their riot overalls and they carried shields and long truncheons and in every Land Rover there were Greener shotguns. There were wire mesh screens on all the windows of the Land Rovers and over the headlights and the stones and rocks came hurtling through the air from behind the hedges and from over the roof-tops of the houses and from the knots of youths and men and young women. The gangs roved the townships stoning the houses of the Sell-outs and the Tshombes and throwing their petrol bombs through the sleeping windows and challenging people to show their Party cards. And if they could not show their Party cards the gangs chased them and stoned them and beat them and kicked them and then the gang ran away. The gangs went into the beerhalls and through the beergardens and they kicked over the tables and they knocked over the mugs of beer and they chased the people out of the beerhalls. And in the early morning the gangs lay in wait for the people who were Tshombes because they were going to work and they drove them home again and they threw stones at the buses carrying the workers. And in the evenings they waited for the Tshombes who had gone to work and they beat them. And now policemen rode on the tops of the buses with Greener shotguns and there were policemen with dogs at the bus stops and the Land Rovers rumbled through the townships. And the courts were crammed.

The Party thugs did not trouble Edward alias Phillimon alias Wiseman alias Moyo, however. Nothing troubled Edward, except maybe the ignition wires on certain models of Continental cars he hadn't quite got the hang of yet, but Edward preferred American jobs anyway and he had their ignition systems licked. The only thing about the Party thugs that troubled Edward was all those cops around with their roadblocks and their checkpoints. That cheesed Edward off so much that he punched up every Party thug that came his way on principle. Once when the shebeen he was holing up in was raided by a gang Edward got so mad he pulled out his .38 pistol, arrested six of them, tied them up, went to the public telephone, and called the police anonymously to come and fetch them. Party thugs and the police had a hard time catching up with Edward because he didn't stick around in one place long. Every second day or so Edward hijacked another car and moved to the other end of the colony just for the hell of it.

Edward Moyo was driving very fast out of Bulawayo on the Salisbury road in a new Ford Thunderbird he had found. He did not propose going as far as Salisbury unless he had to, because he had just come from there: he was trying to shake off the police Bee car that was chasing him. Edward had no doubt that he could lose the Bee car because he knew the Bee car could only do about ninety whereas he was doing a hundred, but he was worried about staying on the main road because he knew the police would radio the next town and they would throw up a roadblock. He took a chance and slowed down to eighty and swung off the tar down the dirt road. He heaved round the bend on two wheels and then back on to four and the big T-bird heeled on to the other side of the road. He swung her back to the other side and then he put his foot on the accelerator again. The Bee car was five hundred yards behind him. Then he picked up the police roadblock in his headlights, three hundred yards ahead.

They had barrels across the road and there was a Land Rover parked at the side and there were five policemen in riot kit. They trained their spotlight straight into his windscreen and they waved their arms to flag him down. There was nothing else for Edward to do. He kept his foot flat and he leaned on his hooter and he charged the roadblock at a hundred and ten miles an hour.

The policemen at the roadblock scattered. The Thunderbird hit the barrels with a clap like thunder and the barrels crumpled and flew through the air, six forty-four gallon barrels flew through the air like slugs out of a shotgun. The big blazing light of the Thunderbird went out in a clatter of glass and there was the crack of its big body denting. It heaved in the road and there was a drum crushed under its wheels and it caught under the big chassis and it made a screaming noise on the road. The Thunderbird swayed across the road at a hundred miles an hour and Edward heaved her back and then she was swaying the other way. And then she went into a broadside. She was doing seventy miles an hour. She roared off the road with the police Land Rover spotlight trained on her, and she went over the shoulder of the road and her offside keeled over and her nearside came up, and she rolled. She rolled seven times through the long grass and the bushes with a great noise of metal and crashing bushes. Then she came to rest on her hood.

The Bee car screamed up to a stop with its spotlights beamed on the wreckage in the bushes. The doors opened and the sergeant jumped out with his Greener shotgun. The police from the roadblock came running up.

'Okay, Edward, take it easy,' the sergeant shouted. There was no reply.

'He's dead, for Chrissake,' the constable said.

'You don't know Edward,' the sergeant said.

He started walking through the grass towards the wreckage with the Greener. When he was fifteen paces off the door creaked open and Edward crawled out.

'Stop, Edward!'

Edward got to his feet and started to run. He pulled out his .38 and fired one shot behind him. The sergeant dropped to his knee and he raised the Greener and he fired.

The slugs hit Edward in the back but he kept on running flat out. He was gone into the black bushes and there was only the sound of his running.

The sergeant held up in his hand.

'I got him in the back. He'll pitch up at a hospital in a day or two and we'll nobble him.'

It was a week, actually, before Edward took himself to the hospital. A witch-doctor had cut eleven slugs out of his back with a dirty razor blade and the witch-doctor smeared his own special muti into the holes and they had festered. Edward's back was a hump of swollen flesh before he staggered to the hospital. The cops nobbled him. But it was two weeks before they could move him to the prison to interrogate him, which was the only safe place to interrogate a tough cookie like Edward, and it was several days before the cops could find time to deal with him.

Edward accepted it philosophically. He had had a bloody good time and it was a fair cop. I admit, he said, while he chain-smoked the policeman's cigarettes.

'Were you alone each time?' the policeman said. The cop had never had it so easy.

'Sometimes I was with my friend,' Edward said. He leant over the table and took another cigarette. The policeman passed him his lighter.

'Who?'

'It is very troublesome in prison without cigarettes,' he said.

The policeman pushed the box over. 'Take the lot,' he said.

Edward picked up the box and put it inside his tunic absently.

'Who is your friend?'

Edward pulled on the cigarette.

'When the box is finished my craving will be very bad.'

'Okay, Edward,' the policeman said, 'I'll bring you some more tomorrow, I promise.'

Edward did not blink. 'His name is Paradise Mpofu,' he said.

The policeman wrote it down. 'And where is he now?'

'How many cigarettes will you bring?' Edward asked.

'A hundred,' the policeman said. Edward shook his head.

'A thousand,' he said.

'For Chrissake, Edward,' he said, 'how am I going to smuggle a thousand cigarettes in?' Edward shrugged and said nothing.

'Okay,' the policeman said. 'A thousand, I promise.'

'What kind?'

'Any kind,' the policeman said, 'this kind.'

Edward shook his head. 'Lucky Strike,' he said.

'Okay, Lucky Strike for Chrissake.'

Edward nodded. 'He is already here in prison for another crime,' he said absently.

'Here?' The cop stood up and he went to the door and opened it and he said to the prison sergeant: 'Bring me Mr. Paradise Mpofu.' The sergeant came back with number 7635, Paradise Mpofu.

'Are you Paradise Mpofu?' the policeman said. Samson Nhdlovu alias Paradise Mpofu nodded. 'Your nice friend Edward says you stole lots of cars with him. What do you say to that?'

Samson Ndhlovu looked unabashed. 'Have you any cigarettes?' he said.

'Sure.' The policeman felt in his tunic pocket and brought out a new packet of twenty. Samson took the whole packet.

'When will we go to Court?' he said.

The policeman was pleased with Samson's attitude.

'That depends,' he said pleasantly. 'The courts are very full these days. This case must go to the High Court. Maybe in two months. First there will be a preparatory examination in the Magistrate's Court.'

Samson nodded thoughtfully.

'Well?' the policeman said. 'Do you admit?'

Samson looked at him. 'Maybe I admit,' he said, 'but maybe I forget to admit.'

The cop nodded. 'How many?'

'A thousand,' Samson said.

'Yes, and what kind?'

'Benson and Hedges Kingsize,' Samson said.

Chapter Forty-One

Mahoney drove his beat-up Vauxhall west along the black road carved through bush. He held the wheel with his right hand and his left hand rested on the neck of the cold beer bottle on the seat. There were three more cold ones lying on the seat next to his black gown and his wig tin. The beers vibrated together and Mahoney leaned out and stuffed his gown between them. Then his hand went back to the opened beer and he lifted it to his mouth and tilted back his head and watched the road down his cheeks as he swallowed. Then he put the beer down on the seat again and felt for the packet of cigarettes, took one out and lit it. The two empty beer bottles rolled between his bare feet at the pedals and he cursed softly and heeled them back under the seat. He started humming tunelessly again, the same old tune, 'Volare.' Then he deliberately cut the tune in mid-hum and he pulled on his cigarette and frowned as he searched for a new song to sing out loud, a new catchy song to stop him brooding. He felt under the gown for a new beer and opened it with his teeth. He began to sing:

> 'Where have all the flowers gone?
> —Long time passing—'

His eyes were crinkled up against the glare of the sun on the bonnet of the car. The bush was brown and hot and the sparse grass was short and brown and the ground was hard and dry for he was approaching Matabeleland now and the drought was very bad. There were very few cars on the Salisbury-Bulawayo road. There were some black people every few miles walking along the road in old white men's clothes, sitting at the side of the road with their bundles waiting for the kaffir bus to take them out there into the brown ocean of bush to their pole and mud and thatch kraal and their thin cattle.

'Where have all the maidens gone?
—Long time passing—'

He pulled on his cigarette. Then he found himself singing 'Volare' again. He stopped himself, because 'Volare' was Suzie's song. He did not want to sing 'Volare' and he did not want to go to Bulawayo to prosecute at the High Court Criminal Session because both reminded him of Suzie. Suzie's ghost was in both of them. He hummed something else tunelessly just for the sake of the noise. Then he was staring through the windscreen thinking again. Then he put his thumb and his finger to his eyes and pressed. 'Suzie where the hell are you?' he said aloud.

'What's the matter?' he had said brusquely.

She was sitting in the only armchair in the big lounge of his house in Salisbury. The floor was red cement and there was one grass mat on it. There were no curtains in the windows and the grass outside grew higher than the window sill. There was a dining-room table ten feet long with eight dining-room chairs which he had picked up at an auction for ten bob. One end of the table was cleared for dining purposes but the rest was stacked with his papers and his books. He was sitting at the table writing with a quart of home brew beer beside him.

She was staring through the front door at the jungle that was the garden. Her face was steady and expressionless and her eyes were hard and sad. That look always unnerved him a little. He knew it from Bulawayo and London and New York. She blinked when he spoke to her and then she turned and looked at him and shook her head.

'Nothing,' she said.

'Oh for Chrissake.'

They looked at each other. She shook her head again.

'You see,' she said, it's no good.'

'What's no good?' But he knew what she meant.

'Us.' She was still looking at him steadily with those hard sad eyes, her long legs curled underneath her in the only armchair.

'I should never have come back,' she said, it has achieved nothing. We're just the same as we were, Bulawayo, London, New York, everywhere and now Salisbury. Fine in bed and b-all to say to each other either before or after. Unless we're half sloshed, which we are half the time.'

'You mightn't have noticed,' he said crisply, 'but I'm writing a book. And I've got a kingsize job on my hands as Crown Counsel!'

'You've been writing one book or another ever since I've known you. And you've always been doing some kingsize job or another. Oh'—she closed her eyes and she waved her hand—'I'm not saying you shouldn't write your book or do your job. It's just that we don't get on, that's all. We fight. You're clever and I'm dumb.'

'You're not dumb—!'

'You're always telling me I'm stupid.'

'Because you say some goddam stupid things sometimes,'he said harshly. He was still at the table, glaring at her. 'Why don't you get with it, for Chrissake, instead of staring into space brooding about how we don't get on? Why don't you try to get on with me? Why don't you study something, any goddam thing. Psychology, yoga, politics, any bloody thing just so long as we can talk about it before and after. Here—' he leaned across the table and grabbed a fistful of manuscript and shook it at her. 'Why don't you read my book I'm writing if you want to get on with me? Then maybe, just maybe, we can talk about it before and after. Why don't you read the last bloody book I wrote—'

'I did,' she said tremulously.

'Did you hell! You read the first ten pages and you gave up—'

'I didn't understand it—' she cried.

'Because you didn't try to understand it! Why didn't you try to discuss it with me if you didn't understand it? That might have given us something to talk about before and after—'

'I wish you'd drop this "before and after" bit—' She was rubbing her hand across her forehead.

'You said it, kid. You didn't read that book because there wasn't enough story in it to hold your butterfly mind—'

'Is that a crime?' she said softly. 'Why does the average person read a book? Why wasn't your book published?—'

'I'm not talking about the average person, I'm talking about why we don't get on! If you read a book for something more than mere entertainment maybe we'd get on a bit better. Have you ever stuck at a book that doesn't amuse you—'

'And if you didn't get half sloshed every night trying to write your book we'd get on better!' she shouted. 'You're like a bear with a sore head the whole time. Your book's the slobbering of a drunken man—'

'*Christ!*'

He was on his feet, he smashed his fist down on the table. He could have struck her in his anger, but he did not.

She dropped her head.

'I'm sorry,' she said softly, 'I really am.'

He sat down. He took a gulp of his beer and then he ran his fingers through his hair.

'I'm sorry I shot my mouth off too,' he said.

They sat in silence. The bare house was empty. The insects were singing in the night outside.

'Why aren't we married?' she said softly to her lap. 'I loved you so much. We should've got married in Rusape that time. We'd've had children by now to talk about. Other couples our age have children to hold them together, we have nothing except memories.' She looked at him. 'Why haven't we had a baby?' she said. 'I've tried hard enough.'

He studied her. She was so goddam beautiful.

'Why didn't you marry me when I first came back to this desert?' he said softly. 'A trial period was your idea.'

She plucked at the stitching in the armchair, 'I know, I'm a mug,' she said sadly. God, she was beautiful. Her long golden hair hung straight down the sides of her face as she looked at the stitching she was picking at and her face was miserable and she had tears in her eyes.

'I'm in such a pickle,' she said.

'Suzie?'

She looked up at him and sniffed. 'What?'

'Let's get married then. Give it a bash.' He got up and he went and sat down on the arm of her chair.

'Tomorrow,' he said. What the hell. It couldn't be worse than living like this. 'We'll buy some bloody furniture and get a decent cookboy and clear the goddam jungle from the front door—'

She looked up at him with a startled dreamy look. Then she put her fingers through his hair.

'Don't be daft, darling. What we need is a divorce.'

She looked at him. 'You know that if we agreed now to get married tomorrow we'd both wake up in the middle of the night in a cold sweat.'

She got up out of the chair and held her hand out to him. He took it and she bent and kissed him.

'Come on, leave your book, it's bed time. I've got a feeling tonight's my night for getting a baby.'

She kissed him again.

'That'd fix us,' she said into his lips.

Later as they lay inert in the double bed she said into the darkness: 'Maybe I just need a holiday at the seaside. I'm a bundle of nerves and so are you.'

Half-past four on a Sunday afternoon at the Que Que Hotel. Criminal Sessions starting tomorrow at ten a.m. sharp in Bulawayo and he had to be on the ball. One hundred and forty miles of flat dry Matabeleland bush to go to Bulawayo and he still had his goddam briefs to swot up when he got there. And in Bulawayo of all godforsaken places.

Hot. His skin was greasy as he sat at the round tin table on the hotel verandah. The sun beat on the tin roof of the hotel verandah. The tar road through the town was hot and dirty. Across the road in the bare brown park the natives sat in the sun chattering and picking their noses and the babies had snot encrusted on their lips and flies in their eyes.

They stood on the gravel sidewalks and chattered and laughed and shouted at each other. There were the town boys and women dressed in their Sunday best white man clothes and there were the rural natives in their white man's tatters. The dull red cement of the hotel verandah was warm from the sun and his dented Vauxhall was hot and his shirt stuck to his back. Dogs had cocked their legs on the pillars of the verandah. There was a dartboard at one end of the verandah and there was a poster of a luscious black-haired woman with perfect teeth saying against a palm beach background: Things Go Better with Big Big Coke, and there was another poster of a lion sitting on a beer-barrel licking his chops and saying: Lion Cheers, Rhodesia is Lion Country. And outside the hot verandah of the hot hotel was the wide flat white-blue sky with nary a cloud over the vast flat bush.

The locals sat at the tin tables on the verandah drinking beer. Hot, strained, sweaty, unkempt faces red from the sun and the dust and the years of drinking beer under the sun. Unlovely women, heavy and hot and red and sweating at the armpits and thighs. Podgy, possibly flabby, possibly smelly, but thighs, thighs enclosing a crotch, a crotch to be splayed on a hot summer bed in a hot summer land, a bed that is used to sweat. What else is there to do? There is nothing else to do.

Beer, cigarettes and sex. What else is there to do? What else to do but lie wet upon each other with sweat like oil sealing and sucking and plopping bellies and loins together, hairy chests matted against wet flaccid breasts, the hair on the back of the neck in wet small ringlets, hot beer breaths and pants and heaves and up and down and thump and grind and faster and quick and deeper and more and if and now and guts and explosion: and then the sad sticky descent and the heavy disillusion, the waste, the emptiness, the roll off, the rich acrid smell, the lack, the slattern sleep. What else to do?

Even in the rich green of Salisbury.

That was all they had done together, all they could do: Suzie sitting in a clearing in the garden at Sunday noon in her bikini, peeling the potatoes, sipping cold wine, her full golden body glistening with tanning oil, her yellow hair long and shining in the sun, the demijohn of wine tucked into the shade of the tall grass: the portable radio singing out the request tunes, he sitting in the deckchair in his swimming trunks with his floppy blue Police Reserve hat on his head drinking cold beer and reading or maybe scribbling notes for his book on his lap, chain-smoking. Getting a little drunk in the Sunday sun together in the jungled garden before the big lunch. Sunday noon in the sun was a kind of half-holiday. They got mellow and fulsome in the sun. Then they could talk. They talked emotionally and nostalgically then about London and the States and they talked about the Club they belonged to, who was sleeping with who and what somebody at the office had said on Friday, and doesn't this tune take you back to those glorious skating week-ends up in Vermont? And they were sorry for being so bitchy to each other last week and she asked him to read her bits aloud out of his book and maybe out of a book of poetry he had been reading. When they were half sloshed in the sun in the garden on Sunday they talked all right, mellow and excited at the knowledge of what they were going to do after lunch. Then at about two o'clock they went inside to cook lunch and sometimes he undressed her there and then in the kitchen that dwarfed the tiny electric stove and they cooked lunch happily together and sometimes they made a little love right there and standing up in the kitchen, just a little, enough to tantalise each other. Then she cleared his papers off the big table in the lounge and she laid it and bedecked it with the frangipani and the chrysanthemums that gloried in the garden and they sat down, very happily, and drank cold wine and ate the roast chicken – it was always roast chicken on Sundays – and her full breasts were white against the brown of the table and the gold of her shoulders and the gold of her hair and the yellow-pink frangipani she always wore behind her ear on Sundays and her red mouth was wide and loving and happy. And then afterwards they went to the big sultry bedroom and he lay down and she came on top of him with her hot sultry kisses and her long hair brushing his face and her breasts flattened against him and she wriggled and worked herself down on to him. And it was all the different ways on Sunday afternoons, revelling in each other's beauty, and then at last the long soaring searing release: and then the panting, sweating sun- burned quiet, and then the long drugged sleep. And when they woke up it was already dark and quiet and the world was dull and empty and there was nothing to do or say and nothing to look forward to, not even each other for they had wrung and sucked everything out of each other. And another week gone.

Mahoney sat on the verandah of the Que Que Hotel. The sun was going down over the mauve bush in a flood of red. His eyes were a little red and he knew he had five beers inside him but he was steady enough. He snapped his fingers at the waiter and he bought two hot pies and a cold beer to take with him and he carried them to the car and he set off down the long dusty road into Matabeleland.

It was late as he drove into the wide dry familiar streets of Bulawayo. Empty streets, empty windows, empty shops, empty flats. He tried not to look at old landmarks as he drove to his hotel, but every corner, every silent café, every closed bar shouted Suzie! at him.

Chapter Forty-Two

Lots of empty shops and flats with 'To Let' chalked over the windows, no new buildings, and a lot of the old ones looking more run down, fewer cars, more natives: but the tarred roads just as wide and black and dusty and hot and the sky just as mercilessly blue and the bush just as infinite and brown and flat. And the High Court just as deadly and much busier. The only joints that had plenty of business, indeed much too much, were the courts and the cops. But Mahoney had no time to brood. He had showered and shaved and taken two of his red buck-up pills and eaten breakfast with his briefs open on the table while he ate. Being Crown Counsel on the opening day of Criminal Session was as unpleasant, he reflected as he humped his robes and books and briefs up the familiar old stone steps of the High Court and down the bleak passage to the door labelled Crown Counsel at eight o'clock, as being director producer stage-manager prompter hero villain and noises-off in a badly casted unrehearsed under-propped play with a lousy plot on its opening night before a highly critical audience armed with slings and arrows. The harbinger of further alarm and despondency was the police orderly standing outside his office who now came forward with a cheery perspiring smile and immediately began to harbinge.

'Good morning, sir, you the prosecutor? Inspector Goodman, sir, your orderly. Hot enough for you, sir—?'

'Come in,' Mahoney said, 'and tell me what's gone wrong.'

He sat down in the hard chair and put his hand to his head and looked at the inspector.

'Now, about case number two, sir, the witness Dlijah is missing, just couldn't find him at his kraal, sir. Tribesmen in the area haven't seen him for three weeks, rumour that he's gone to Bechuanaland. Case number four, the witchcraft merchant, the woman Nxquashe is in hospital having a Caesarian. Case five, the doctor is going on overseas leave, ship passage booked and everything, must hold the case before next Tuesday. Also, none of the exhibits have arrived here yet. We'll find them, don't worry, sir, but it takes three days to get them in here by bus. Also, in that case Constable Porter is getting married, next Saturday, says can we please please please hold the trial before then so he can go on honeymoon. Case six, everything in order. No, I'm not kidding, sir. Case seven, only trouble is that Inspector Jones is on a refresher course in Salisbury and says can we please not bring the case on until three weeks time, after his exam, sir. Number nine, the schoolteacher is away visiting his sick mother. They're expecting him back any moment but nobody knows quite where his mother lives. Number eleven, three witnesses missing. We sent a truck out to find them and they just disappeared. We think they've been got at by relatives of the accused. Number fourteen, the accused has escaped. Yes, perhaps that is the first piece of good news, sir. Now, in number fifteen there are three doctors involved. One is on transfer, the other quitting his job at the end of the month and the other is the only doctor at the hospital and cannot come unless a relief is sent out to his bush hospital because he's got an epidemic in his district. I'm trying to arrange for a relief with the central hospital but they can't spare a doctor until the end of the month. They've got an epidemic too. Sixteen, the defence counsel phoned me day before yesterday and says he'll be out of town for a fortnight, can we please postpone his cases, that is number six, ten, thirteen and twenty until he comes back. He has already left, sir. Difficulty is in case number twenty, the farmer who had his barn burned down is going to start reaping his crop and it's going to last for the next month and says for God's sake he just can't leave his reaping in the hands of his native labour for two days because they'll ruin it. It'll take him almost a day to get into town and a day to get back. Can't you do without his evidence, sir? Number nineteen, the witness Sixpence has died, sir, somebody chopped his head open at a beerdrink. Same in number twenty-four – the old girl Soquomasi died last week of natural causes. Was she a very important witness? Twenty-eight everything okay. Twenty-nine everything okay except that African Constable Mprofiti was stabbed in the chest last night trying to arrest a thug. We can hold court in the hospital, just for his evidence. Thirty-four one of the petrol bombing cases, Inspector McGladdery will be phoning you. He's having a hell of a job keeping the witnesses away from the political thugs who'll intimidate them and says can you please hold the trial early …

'Otherwise, everything okay, sir. What case do you want to bring on first, sir?'

'Situation normal,' Mahoney said.

Then the registrar telephoned from upstairs: The Chief Justice wants to know what cases you're bringing in front of him and when. He can only sit for three days this week because he's going to Salisbury for five days on Thursday. So don't start anything in front of him which you can't finish before Wednesday night. You'll have the other judge while the C.J.'s away but when he comes back next Tuesday he'll take over your Court again, so try not to start anything before the judge which you can't finish by Monday next. Then the following week both are sitting on appeals so I'm flying a judge from Salisbury for you, but only for five days, so for God's sake—

'For God's sake,' Mahoney said.

He stripped the cellophane off his third packet of cigarettes since Que Que, lit one and began to cough.

'First we'll take the pleas. Then lay on Edward and whatsisname for trial,' he coughed to the inspector.

He was feeling dizzy.

'Now let me go and pay the Attorney General's respects to their Lordships,' he said, 'before the bun fight starts.'

At nine o'clock the black crowds began to collect outside the High Court. They came from the African townships of Mzilikazi and Tshabaala and Mpopoma in their Sunday best and they gathered in the sun outside the locked gates of the public entrance and round the side where they could see the prisoners arriving. There were the sullen-faced youths and the fur-hatted gentlemen with their carved walking sticks moving about among the crowd.

At nine-fifteen the two prison trucks arrived, heavy blue Ford monsters with stout wire mesh over the windows and black woolly faces peering through and grinning and waving and the black prison corporals in their khaki and green uniforms scowling. You heard the prison trucks coming as they turned into Lobengula Street behind the High Court two blocks away. The prisoners were chanting, deep-chested melodious thumps that rose and fell, rose and fell: 'Za-pu pu-za! Za-pu pu-za! We are going to have the Country.' It was loud and deep and clear as the trucks rumbled into the yard at the side of the Court and the crowds sent up a shout of cheers and waves and laughs and the answering chant.

'Za-pu pu-za—'

The police were in a gauntlet from the trucks into the cells. 'Quiet – Toola – Toola—'

The prisoners climbed out and walked down the gauntlet waving and smiling but still chanting. The heavy metal doors clanged shut behind them in the dark cell corridor but the chanting rose deep and muffled, ringing up from below and reverberated through the Courthouse and the chattering rose like a cloud of bees from the crowd.

The gates of the public entrance were unlocked and the crowd filed in a thick stream up the steps and along the corridor and up the steps to the gallery as excitedly as a circus crowd. Two white constables and a policewoman stood at the top of the steps frisking them for weapons.

At twenty to ten Mahoney pulled off his tie and clipped on his high white collar and his white cravat and pulled on his gown and shoved his wig on his head. He picked up his stack of briefs and walked down the corridor and into the Criminal Court.

The big panelled courtroom was crowded. Policemen, clerks, lawyers, press, witnesses, public. There was an expectant buzz, the chanting rang up from the cells below and from the gallery the wall of black faces staring down. Mahoney turned and looked up at the gallery. Then he called the inspector.

'Inspector, tell those gentlemen up there to take their goddam fur hats off. Tell them it's bad manners to wear hats in a building let alone in a Court—'

Wish we could throw the bastards out, Mahoney thought. They're only here to intimidate my witnesses.

The inspector came back. He nodded his head and Mahoney followed him outside into the corridor. One of the black gentlemen was standing handcuffed between two constables and he was trembling. The policeman held out his hand.

'Look what I've found.'

'Christ,' Mahoney said.

It was a khaki chunk of metal the size of a tennis ball.

'Hand-grenade,' the inspector said. 'Russian made.'

'Where?'

'Under our friend's fur hat.'

Mahoney looked at the object and then he turned to the black man.

'Please, sir,' the black man jibbered – 'I didn't know, sir—'

'The hell you didn't! You were going to lob that thing into a crowded Court. That's going to cost you twenty years, chum. And—' he lifted his finger and jabbed him in the chest, 'you're going to tell us where you got it from and who else has got 'em, you bloody murderer—'

'Take him away,' the inspector snapped.

'We're not starting Court,' Mahoney said, 'until you've searched every man-jack of them again.'

'Sabotage Section are already on their way here,' the inspector said.

'The inconvenience of being blown to bits is considerable.'

The chanting from the cells rose to a crescendo.

'And look,' Mahoney said irritably – 'we can't hold court with that din. Who's making it, just the political hoods or everybody?'

'Everybody,' the inspector said, 'even the nice wholesome non-political rape artists.'

'Well we can't hold court with that din. We'll have to bring 'em up from the prison one at a time.'

'Leave it to me. I've just had a brainstorm,' the inspector said.

He strode into the courtroom and into the dock and down the staircase to the cells below. Mahoney walked back into Court and sat down at the bar. Suddenly the chanting stopped. A minute later the inspector climbed back up into the dock and came to Mahoney. He was smiling.

'How d'you do it – promise them ice-cream?'

'Dogs,' the inspector beamed, 'I put a police Alsatian in each cell and told them it would bite if anybody speaks above a whisper.'

The prisoner's dock was behind the bar and Mahoney had his back to it. Mahoney seldom looked round at the faces of the men he was prosecuting to jails and the gallows. And today he was too tired to turn his neck unnecessarily.

It was mid-afternoon. The pomp of the opening of the Criminal Session was over. The police brass and the counsel and the attorneys and the magistrates who packed the Court at the opening ceremony to show their respect had gone back to their jobs and now Mahoney and his Lordship and the Assessors were getting on with theirs. It was hot and sweat trickled down from under Mahoney's wig and his gown stifled his suit and his suit smothered his shirt and his shirt stuck to his wet skin. His head was thumping and he had a fluttering sensation from time to time in his chest. But the case was going smoothly enough, thank God. He was glad he had chosen this one to start the session, for he felt in no shape for a scrap today. He had more than twenty witnesses to lead, but Edward Moyo and Paradise Mpofu were letting them go through the witness box unchallenged. Edward Moyo and Paradise Mpofu were indeed being perfect sports about the whole business. Edward Moyo was reading a Superman comic with a puckered frown, his thick lips mouthing each word slowly, and Paradise Mpofu was fast asleep. If their disinterest in their own trials included a measure of contempt of Court, the Court did not mind and Mahoney was very relieved. He could not understand why they had pleaded Not Guilty, but he wasn't bothering his sore head about it.

It was not until three-thirty when Mahoney said to the Court: 'I close the case for the Crown, Milord,' and sat down gratefully, thankful for a lucky day and the fact that within one hour he would have a tall frosted glass of beer in his hand, that he turned around in his chair and looked back at the two prisoners. His chest fluttered again.

'*Samson*,' he breathed, but nobody heard him but Paradise Mpofu alias Samson Ndhlovu.

Samson was fatter. He got more food and did less work in prison than he did at large, which wasn't very often these days. His big head had the shaven baldness of the hard labour prisoner and he wore a moustache and a little beard that encircled his mouth. He had just been woken up by the interpreter and he was standing up and blinking a little owlishly at his Lordship. He heard his name whispered and he glanced at Mahoney and frowned. Mahoney stared at him. Then he lifted up his wig and smoothed his matted hair with his hand and Samson's eyes widened and his mouth opened and then he beamed at Mahoney.

'*Mambo*' – he said out loud.

Mahoney grinned at him and then he turned his back. He rifled through the police docket until he came to the list of criminal convictions in the name of Paradise Mpofu. It read:

Contravening Section 10(1) Wildlife Conservation Act, Elephant Hunting: 3 months i.h.l.
Contravening Section 10(1) Wildlife Conservation Act, Elephant Hunting: 6 months i.h.l.
Contravening Section 24(1) Firearms Act, unlicensed possession .303: 2 months i.h.l.
Contravening Section 10(1) Wildlife Conservation Act, Elephant Hunting: 12 months i.h.l.
Contravening Section 3(1) Gold Trade Act: 3 months i.h.l.
Contravening Section 3(1) Gold Trade Act: 6 months i.h.l.
Contravening Section 3(1) Gold Trade Act: 2 years i.h.l.

'And now you're pinching cars, you stupid bastard,' Mahoney whispered. His lordship was speaking: 'Mister Interpreter, ask Edward if he has any witnesses to call in his defence.'

The interpreter spoke to Edward.

'I have no witnesses to call,' Edward said tiredly.

'Do you wish to give evidence yourself or do you wish to make an unsworn statement, or do you wish to say nothing? If you take the oath and give evidence you will be cross-examined by Counsel for Crown. If you make an unsworn statement you cannot be cross-examined. Evidence on oath carries more weight than an unsworn statement.'

The interpreter relayed it to Edward. Edward looked bored. He knew Court procedure, his face said.

'I wish to say nothing,' Edward said.

'Very well,' said his Lordship. He turned to Samson.

'Ask Paradise if he has any witnesses to call.'

Samson straightened a little. He did not look at Mahoney.

'Yes, I have a witness to call,' he said through the interpreter.

'Very well,' his Lordship said. 'Call him.'

'His name is Mr. Green,' Samson said.

'Yes,' said the judge. 'And where is he?'

'He is at the prison,' Samson said apologetically.

The judge grunted. 'Court will adjourn for five to ten minutes to enable Mr. Green to be fetched from the prison. Mr. Mahoney, will you instruct the police to fetch him.'

'Certainly, milord,' Mahoney said.

Court adjourned and Mahoney hurried to his office. He lit a cigarette and he waited for the knock on his door. It came.

'Come in.'

A black constable came in.

''Scuse me, sah, but the accused Paradise wish to see you sah.'

Mahoney smiled. He took four cigarettes from his packet and handed them to the constable.

'Give these to Paradise and let him smoke them now if he wants to. Tell him I cannot see him until after the case is finished because I am the prosecutor.'

'Yassah.'

Mahoney smiled sadly to himself as he finished his cigarette. He was thinking of a dark river at night and the sweep of the hunting lamps and the yellow cat's eyes gleaming in the black water and the panting wait, the rifles trained in the blackness. The big black frame of the man kneeling beside him in the boat, then the explosion, the jolt, the stars, the deafness, the falling, the cold terrifying bite of the water, the panic, the thrashing, and then the sudden plucking out of the water, the wet crumpled heap of himself in the boat again.

'I'm sorry, old boy,' Mahoney said to himself, 'but there's nothing I can do to keep you out of prison and it's going to be a long long time—'

The inspector put his head in the door.

'Mr. Green's arrived.'

'Right,' Mahoney said. He flicked his stub into the corner and put his wig back on.

Mr. Green stood in the witness box and took the oath looking bewildered.

'Mr. Green,' his Lordship said, 'who are you?'

Mr. Green looked nervous. 'I'm the assistant superintendent of the Prison, my Lord.'

'I see,' the judge said. 'And do you know the second accused?'

Mr. Green peered across the courtroom at Samson. Samson was beaming at him hopefully.

'Yes, my Lord,' Mr. Green said. 'He is a prisoner at my jail. I think his name is Paradise Something.'

'Yes,' the judge said. He turned to Samson.

'Well, Paradise, what questions do you wish to ask Mr. Green?'

Samson cleared his throat and smiled cheerfully. He spoke to the interpreter and the interpreter said: 'Mr. Green, do you know me well?'

Mr. Green nodded bewilderedly. He turned to the judge. 'Quite well, my Lord. I see him almost every day at the prison.' He turned to look back at Samson.

'For how long have I been in your prison, Mr. Green?'

Mr. Green shook his head. 'Oh, I can't say, my Lord, without looking at the records. But quite a long time.'

Samson nodded.

'Have I been in prison for the last twenty months?'

The judge and Mahoney both sat up.

'Yes, about that I'd say,' Mr. Green agreed.

'What? As a hard labour prisoner?' the judge said.

'Yes, my Lord,' Mr. Green said.

The judge looked at Mahoney and Mahoney looked at the judge. Then they both looked at Samson.

'And have I ever escaped from prison?' Samson said.

'No, he hasn't, my Lord,' Mr. Green said.

'I am being prosecuted,' Samson said stiffly, 'for the crime of stealing some cars four months ago. Is it possible that I'm guilty?'

Mr. Green looked very bewildered.

'No, it isn't,' he said.

'Thank you,' Samson said. He sat down with dignity.

The judge looked at Mahoney and Mahoney was staring at the ceiling and a smile was spreading across his face.

'You old bastard,' he whispered.

'Well Mr. Mahoney,' his Lordship snapped, 'it would appear that the accused has made a fool of the Crown.'

Mahoney got to his feet and bowed: 'So, my Lord, it would indeed appear. What is called the cast-iron alibi.'

Later, the policemen standing in the corridor grinned at each other as they heard the belly-shaking laughter of Samson Ndhlovu and Joseph Mahoney coming from behind Crown Counsel's closed office door.

Chapter Forty-Three

Just two beers. Just to unwind me. Just two beers so that I can bear to sit down at that bloody table afterwards and read tomorrow's briefs.

Mahoney walked into his hotel, smiling tiredly to himself. He was very white and his hair was still flattened and matted from his wig. Selbome Avenue was hot and flat and wide and dry, his suit was dank, and his lips were salty and the sky was pitilessly blue and the palms of his hands itched like they did in the old days but he was smiling to himself because Samson Ndhlovu alias Paradise Mpofu had made fools of them all.

He went straight from the street into the hotel cocktail bar.

He liked this bar. He used to take Suzie here often. He shut his mind from her. The bar was empty and the barmaid smiled at him very prettily as she gave him the cold Lion.

'This is new,' he said, 'having a barmaid in here.'

'The boss started it about a year ago. Business was so bad, it helps business. A man prefers to have a woman serve him, than a munt. Most of the cocktail bars have barmaids now.'

'White girls?'

'Oh yes. Men wouldn't want to look at black girls '

Mahoney nodded. 'The Battle of the Barmaids.'

'Oh well – cheers,' she said.

'Cheers.' He smiled at her into her eyes and pulled out of his beerglass. It was like food. 'To Paradise,' he said.

She thought he was toasting her eyes, she lowered her eyelids coyly.

'Paradise Mpofu,' Mahoney said, 'an old black friend of mine.'

'Oh.'

'It was very funny,' Mahoney said. 'You see, this chap Paradise – his real name is Samson, Paradise is his underworld name – he used to work for me.'

He told her the story.

'But why did he do it?'

'To get a holiday from jail, he told me. He knew he would have a few days off hard labour while the trial was going on, and he'd see something of the outside and he'd see some girls, maybe, and so on. So when he saw his old buddie Edward in jail he just said to him: If you're going to confess, just implicate me and then I'll confess and we'll get some cigarettes out of the swines and I'll get a few days off hard labour.

'The cops are busy people these days. The jails are so full. It quite often happens that a cop catches up with a chap when some other cop arrests him at the other end of the country for some other crime. The cop was just too delighted.'

The barmaid laughed.

'That's quite a good story.'

The beer was making him feel good. It was taking the tight tiredness out of his chest and shoulders and head.

She gave him another beer. Two men came in and sat down at the bar. Mahoney took a long pull out of his glass. Nectar. Balm for his ragged nerves. This was the stage he liked best – the second beer alone. He liked it alone. When you get on to your seventh, that's the time to start talking the usual crap to the bloke next to you, not before. On his second beer he could begin to think clearly. It was too valuable to waste in bar talk. He liked to be alone in a crowd. The bar was filling up. Men in office suits, women in office dresses, coming from the sweat of the office into the cool ether of the cool green cocktail bar for the time-honoured custom of the sundowner. Mahoney ignored them. He recognised a few of the faces, a few years older, but he did not want to break his solitude with smiles and handshakes and ransacking his memory for names and talking about the bloody Situation. The bloody Situation, he was sick of talking about it. Independence, Independence – he was sick of hearing the same old cliches trotted out with the conviction of fact. 'We can't drift on like this—' Like how? 'Like we are now.' But we're running the country ourselves now. 'Yes, but Britain'll hand us over to the blacks like she did in Kenya and Nyasaland and Northern Rhodesia.' No she can't – our constitution is different to Kenya. 'She'll do it all the same.' But don't you see that Britain can't do that without breaking the *Law*, for Chrissake, if we break the Law by declaring independence we'll be outlaws and then she will be *entitled* to step in and hand us over like Kenya, but if we stay as we *are* Britain can't do a bloody thing to us. 'What are you, a kaffir lover or something? You want to see the country handed over to the blacks?' Oh for Chrissake—

A hand fell hard on his shoulder.

'Well if it ain't old Honeytalk Mahoney—'

'Good God – Max—'

And there was Max, a bit fatter and grinning all over his handsome face.

'I recognised the suit,' Max grinned pumping hands.

'It happens to be a very good suit—'

'It must be to last all this time—' He caught Mahoney's wrist and inspected the cuffs. 'Yes, and still using paperclips for cuff-links, the haberdashers don't make much out of you, do they, Honeytalk? Christ, what are you doing back in town, boy? Last I heard of you you were canoeing down the Amazon. Where're you living?'

'In Salisbury. What'll you have, mate?'

'Scotch, since you're so pressing. What you doing back in town, boy—'

'I'm prosecuting the Criminal Session here.'

'Still a prosecutor, hey? Jesus,' Max shook his head, 'that always amused me. Old Joe, the hardest case of them all and he's a custodian of the public conscience! I'll never forget the time you kidnapped the snake-charmer from the circus for Ian's bachelor party—' Max was shaking.

'And I'll never forget how you chucked the snake-charmer's crocodile in the public swimming pool to the alarm and despondency of the Municipal authorities.'

Max laughed out loud. Mahoney turned to the bar. 'Honey—' he called to the barmaid, 'give us a cold one and a Scotch.'

'Honey,' Max leaned forward to her. 'Beware of this man, always keep the bar between him and your belly-button.'

The barmaid giggled. Mahoney grinned at her hopefully.

Max took a big sip of his whisky.

'Now tell me about it,' Mahoney said quickly. He did not want to talk about himself, 'I take it you're not married.'

'Certainly I'm married.' Max patted his stomach. 'Pillar of Society, me—'

'*Married!*'

Max looked a little lame. 'Two kids,' he said brightening. He brought a Kodak envelope from his pocket and pulled out two colour photographs.

A woman crouching on a lawn. She was holding a small baby and she had her free arm around a toddler. Their faces were puckered up against the sun and the baby's face was screwed up in a bawl. There was a corner of a white house with a splitpole fence behind it and a wheelbarrow and one end of a washing line. The girl was a little plump and her hair looked as if she meant to wash it today. A Sunday morning shot.

'Pretty girl,' Mahoney said politely.

'She was better before the kids were born. The rest are of the house.'

It was one of those new three-bedroomed jobs in the newer suburbs on a third of an acre with every window in the expected place and a red tiled roof and the neighbour's washing line and servant's kia over the splitpole fence.

'Do you rent it?'

'Bought it. Property's cheap these days.'

Mahoney nodded. 'Well, fancy Max a heavily committed suburbanite.' But he felt envious all the same.

Max put the photographs away. 'And what about you, what happened to the luscious Suzie?'

'Suzie.' Mahoney took a drag on his cigarette. 'Old Suzie, you know – she's gone overseas again.'

'Where overseas?'

'I don't know.'

'Is it all off between you then?'

'I don't know, Max.'

'Okay, we'll change the subject. Honey—' he called the barmaid, 'give us the same again here.' He turned to Mahoney and grinned and punched him lightly on the shoulder. 'Hell it's good to see you again Joe-baby, we must have a party one night. I can jack us up with a couple of jumpers.'

'What about your wife?'

'I couldn't take my wife on that kind of party, could I?' Max grinned.

'Fix me up, Max. But I want a push-over. I'm getting too old for the high-powered wining and dining warm-up.'

'I've got just the doll for you. Big and strong, could kick-start the VC.10.'

'That's the doll. You fix it up.'

'Leave it to me,' Max said.

Mahoney took a sip of beer.

'And what you been up to these five years, Max?'

'Well, had a trip to England a few years ago. What a ball—'

'Belong to the Overseas Visitors Club?'

'Too true – and do those girls give of the freedom of their loins.' Mahoney nodded.

'And on the ship going over! I swear, that's why the ship rolled so much, too many people poking at once. The parties and shacking-up! Midnight nude swimming parties, the works. Women go mad at sea.'

Mahoney nodded.

'And in Earl's Court? All those colonial sisters living like sardines, fornication spreads like an epidemic. I tell you it's catching—'

Mahoney laughed.

'And then I did a very sensible thing, you must try it next time. Joined a Marriage Bureau. Join a Marriage Bureau, see, costs a fiver. Then the Bureau fixes you up with a string of women to try out.

You impress the Bureau no end with your colonial status, dashing young bwana from Rhodesia, huntin', shootin', fishin' type don'tcha know, shoots lions before breakfast and rides around his estate in a pith helmet and jodhpurs cracking his sjambok over the backs of the niggers. And. you tell the Bureau the type of dolls you want to try out, thirtyish, who know what it's for, and they fix you up with a wagon load of women just panting to come out to sunny Africa and be a pukkah memsahib. And you screw them all and they bludgeon each other to death over you. Then you phone up the Bureau and say No, I don't fancy any of those, send me another selection. Marvellous. Never sleep alone.'

Mahoney was laughing.

'Old Max.'

Max grinned. 'And how's things with you, Joe-baby? Have you many cases to do here?'

Mahoney shook his head: 'Jesus.'

'What kind of cases?'

'Half of it's political crime. Politics, politics, politics. Political murders, petrol bombings, mob violence, intimidation. Mostly black versus black. Zimbabwe African People's Union thugs murdering and blowing up Zimbabwe African National Union and vice versa. Both parties killing and blowing up and intimidating other blacks who won't join their party.' He puffed his cigarette. 'Very democratic souls, ZAPU and ZANU.'

'Freedom lovers,' Max said. 'Can you imagine what it would be like living under them? And yet these are the people Britain wants to hand the reins of Government to.' He shook his head. He stubbed out his cigarette impatiently, 'I tell you, Joe, the sooner we declare ourselves independent the better. Go it alone. Stand up for ourselves against those arse-licking British politicians, this is our country, we made it—'

Mahoney shook his head.

'Max, Max, Max.'

Max glared at him. Mahoney had never seen Max glare before.

'What? Do you say we should just drift along like this and let Britain, our dear Mother Britain, sell us down the river? Like she did in Kenya and Tanganyika and Northern Rhodesia, like she did to our own Federation—?'

Mahoney sat back. He spoke flatly.

'Max, a unilateral declaration of independence won't work.'

'*Why* won't it work, huh? *Why* won't it? It'll work if we stand up for ourselves and fight for what is ours, the Rhodesians will fight.'

Mahoney leaned forward.

'The Rhodesians will fight, Max,' he spoke softly as if explaining something to a young person. 'But an army marches on its stomach, Max, that's why it won't work, Max. On its stomach. If we declare independence the first thing Britain will do is strangle our economy. She won't send the Tommies in straight away, Max, she won't have to: she'll just put an embargo on our tobacco crop, and on our sugar crop, Max, and we won't be able to sell our sugar, or our maize or our beef, she won't buy anything of ours, Max, and nor will any other Commonwealth country, and nor will America or most other countries. And Britain won't sell us anything either, Max, nor will most other countries and she'll freeze our London assets so we won't have any foreign exchange. And we won't be able to get any petrol because Britain will stop all our oil supplies. And how're you going to run a modern state without petrol, Max?

'Britain could kill us, or half kill us with trade sanctions alone, Max, without firing a shot. But that would only be half our troubles, Max. While our economy is grinding to a halt the wogs would be whooping it up. Every black state in the North would be sending their terrorists in to fight us. And our own black hoods would be busy too, the saboteurs that ZAPU and ZANU are shuttling to and from Peking and Moscow to be trained as James Bonds. So we won't only be fighting economic sanctions and external invasion, we'll be having civil war as well, Max—'

Max snorted impatiently. He spoke softly with half-closed eyes:

'We'll fight, the Rhodesians can fight. Moishe Tshombe cleaned up Christ knows how many thousand Simba with a couple of hundred white mercenaries—'

Mahoney closed his eyes, and shook his head.

'For *years* you'll have to fight, Max. For ever. Because even if

Britain gives up after a couple of years and makes some kind of deal with Rhodesia, even if she recognises Rhodesia's independence after a while, the black states to the north of us will *never* give up. For those blacks, majority rule is a mania, a craze, a huge matter of face. And Moscow and Peking will always be egging them on, Max, and there'll be a never-ending supply of blacks to send in, it won't matter if the white Rhodesians ran their asses off for years shooting them, there'll always be plenty more to send in. Look, Max: the Portuguese have got eighty thousand soldiers fighting the black guerillas in Mozambique and Angola, and those soldiers come from Lisbon, Max, they're out here doing their national service, they don't come from the suburbs of Mozambique and Angola. The Rhodesians could not raise more than ten or twelve thousand soldiers, Max, and they would be men from the suburbs and if you call them out to fight the country's business grinds to a halt. Max, in this country, we have only two hundred thousand whites – counting women and children, and the aged – occupying a jungle three times the size of England, with four million wogs in it. There are more people in a Lisbon or Birmingham suburb, Max, than there are whites in Rhodesia. That's why it won't work, Max.'

Max was nodding gently, firmly, tough. He looked at Mahoney steadily. 'What's the alternative? You tell me.'

Mahoney took a slow deep breath. He was beginning to feel a little drank, and he was very tired. 'There's only one alternative, Max.'

'And that is?'

Mahoney sighed. He knew what Max would say. 'And that is Partnership, Max.'

Max looked at him as if he had said something totally irrelevant. 'Partnership?'

Mahoney sighed. 'Partnership, Max, while yet there is time.'

Max's face was creased up in a smile-frown.

'Partnership, the man says—' He appealed to the ceiling. 'Partnership!' He looked at Mahoney. 'We've *got* Partnership here already, for Chrissake, we had Partnership in Federation for ten effing years, and where did it get us—?'

Mahoney nodded tiredly.

'And why did it get us nowhere, Max? Because despite all their nice words, the whites did not practise Partnership, Max, that's why. Sure, we passed the laws that enabled educated wogs to vote, and so that in the dim and distant future they would all be entitled to vote, but did we *treat* the wog any different, Max? Did we hell!' He held up his hand to silence Max. 'We just sailed straight on being Bwana.'

Max was nodding his smile-frown. 'So you say the way to stop the gangs of ZAPU and ZANU thugs and to stop Britain selling us up the river to them, is to start being nicer to the wog—'

Mahoney was shaking his head peevishly.

'For Chrissake, Max! There's a lot more to it than giving them a bit more human dignity. For Chrissake, what the bloody white Rhodesian can't realise is that the wog is *going to rule Rhodesia,* Max. The hard fact is that the wogs outnumber us twenty to one, and everybody else in the world is behind them, Max. We're stuffed, Max. *Stuffed.* And the best we can do for ourselves is try to get the best terms for ourselves and try to ensure that when they take over the joint they don't make too much of a shambles. And that means a couple of hundred thousand whites have got to try to create a middleclass of munts, who are conservative and surburban and reasonable, with a sense of responsibility instead of believing that everybody will have a car and a white man's house when Uhuru comes—'

'Joe-baby,' Max said softly, 'and just how are a mere two hundred thousand whites going to achieve this?'

Mahoney's eyes were glinting, and his face was hard.

'By playing it cool,' he said slowly. 'By diplomacy. By keeping our traps shut about declaring ourselves independent, by stalling, by lying if you like, by prolonging negotiations, by saying yes yes yes maybe yes, by playing Britain at her own bloody game and leading her up the garden path.'

He paused. He held up his finger and prodded Max's shoulder.

'But that's not all, Max. While we're gaining time, the whites will have to work hard, individually as well as collectively. organise themselves into committees and action groups. Teach some school at night, the white women give domestic science classes and hygiene and birth control clinics, the men promote the sort of philanthropic activity like the Round Table and the Rotarians do. And at the same time, train every able-bodied white man as a soldier or police reservist, so that we can police the country rigidly and constantly, but quietly and discreetly. And the whole time, keep playing it cool with Britain, keeping our fingers crossed. That's the alternative, Max. But the whites will have to really work, Max – like the Israelis work—'

'And keep our fingers crossed.'

Mahoney nodded. Max's face was thoughtful.

'And what are you doing about it, Joe-baby?'

Mahoney grunted. He spoke quietly, a little defiantly at first.

'I've got some land. I bought fifty acres fifteen miles out of Salisbury, cheap as hell these days. It borders on the Native Reserve. Well – I'm trying to teach the natives how to farm—'

'*Farm*—?' Max said.

Mahoney nodded firmly. He took a pull of his beer.

'Agriculture. I'm no great agriculturist, but I know something about land husbandry, and I know the wog. The wogs there are just scratching a living from the soil, they aren't growing cash crops that they can sell, they grow only enough to feed themselves. For the rest, they have scrawny cattle which impoverish the land, because they keep too many, because they count their wealth in cattle. Well, if we want to turn the wog into a businesslike farmer, who makes a bit of money and adopts civilised standards, we've got to make him change his farming habits: get rid of his herds of useless cattle, and get a few good ones. Government is doing a lot, but it's a hell of a big job. Individuals should help. So, for a start, I've bought a decent bull. He's no prize champion, but he's good beef stock. I've put a word out around the Reserve that my bull Ferdinand will serve any native cow for a sum of one shilling, satisfaction guaranteed or your money back. Well, this season Ferdinand shagged a couple of dozen native cows. In a couple of months' time there'll be some fair calves in the district, better stock than last year. I won't make any money out of Ferdinand, not at a shilling a shag, but I feed him off my land,

and I'm prepared to invest a little money in goodwill, Max. So should a few more farmers. So should blokes like you, Max: you could spare a contribution of ten guineas towards a fund which will buy bulls and distribute them about the Reserves. So could every man in this bar.'

Max nodded. Mahoney sipped his beer, energetically now.

'Esprit de corps, Max, that's what we need.' He waved his hand. 'Chickens. You know what deadbeat birds kaffir chickens are. Well, I bought myself a real champion Leghorn rooster, kingsize chap. Called Cocky. I've got Cocky, a dozen good Austrolop hens, which are good eating birds, and some kaffir hens as foster mothers. I take the eggs and put them under the kaffir hens to hatch and, by Christ, I've got chickens all over the place. And again I've put the word out in the Reserve that I'll swap my young roosters for kaffir roosters. Straight swap. My high-class roosters are out there in the Reserve improving the native birds. Christ, these wogs could use good chickens, both for their own food and for marketing. Pigs – I'm getting up a similar scheme for pigs.' He rubbed his chin rapidly.

Max had his chin in his palm and he was watching Mahoney's eyes. 'What else, Joe?'

Mahoney waved his cigarette enthusiastically.

'Pigs, as I've said. And sheep. Get rid of the native goats. They've got goats running all over that goddam Reserve and they're no good to man or beast. There's a good market for mutton and wool. I've put out the word that I'll provide a good ram for stud purposes if ten kraal heads will each buy one ewe, and I've offered to help them sell sufficient goats to get the cash to buy the ewes—'

'And have the ten kraal heads come forward?'

Mahoney shook his head.

'No, not yet. Three have said it's a good idea, and they're going to talk to the others about it, but so far nothing's happened.'

'How long ago did the three kraal heads say that?'

'About two months ago, now.'

Max nodded.

'What else, Joe?'

Mahoney took a sip of beer.

'Well, cash crops. These wogs only grow enough to feed themselves, they don't think of growing enough to feed their livestock, let alone growing enough to sell. So I'm trying to make my land a small model farm. Already I've got the place breaking even: it feeds me and my servants and my animals. But I've put out the word that the local wogs can come and discuss things with me. I've held a few indabas on my place, and I showed them round and showed them how they could do the same thing—'

'And how many have followed your example?'

Mahoney shrugged.

'These ideas take a bit of time to catch on with the natives—'

Max nodded.

'The important thing, of course, is to get the other white farmers in the area to do the same thing, help to teach the natives how to farm. We'll get Government backing, organise a country-wide campaign to build the natives up into a stable farming nation—'

'Joe—'

Mahoney stopped and looked at him.

'Joe. It won't work.'

Mahoney snorted defiantly. 'What—?'

Max held up his hand.

'It won't *work*, Joe. Oh Christ, it's an admirable plan, it is even a clever plan, I mean that, I admire your initiative and generosity. But it *won't work*, Joe, because the wog is just not interested in hard work that's *why*, Joe. He would rather sit in the sun and drink tshwala and let his wives do the work and look at his scrawny cattle, than get up off his backside and use his head. For a year you've been running your farm and you've made a success of it, and you've encouraged your black neighbours to follow your example – but have they? No, they haven't. And they won't ever follow it, Joe, unless you go and stand over them and *supervise* them. You've offered to help them replace their goats with sheep. But will they? No, Joe. Because the wog *likes* goats, Joe, he counts his wealth in the number of goats he owns. He doesn't *want* to sell his goats or eat his goats, he just likes to look at them, and the fact that he can't buy a shirt for his back or food for his family with his goats is irrelevant to him, because he doesn't *want* to get rid of them anyway. Your chicken scheme – sure some wogs will come along and swap their kaffir roosters for your good roosters, Joe – but why? Because it's something for nothing, it requires no hard work, does it? But you know, as well as I do, what will happen to the chickens, Joe: the wog doesn't feed his chickens, he lets them forage, so they won't get big and fat and they won't lay many eggs, Joe. And the wog doesn't keep his chickens in a fowl run, so the hens will still mate with the kaffir rooster from the kraal next door. So your good roosters' blood will be dissipated, Joe. Your Ferdinand the bull. Sure, some natives will bring their cows along to Ferdinand to be serviced. That much a wog can understand. But what will happen to Ferdinand's calves? I'll tell you. The heifers will grow up and they'll be shagged by the kaffir bulls in the communal grazing areas, and all your good deeds will have been undone.' Max leaned forward. 'Your Ferdinand will just be a drop in the ocean, because the kaffir bulls outnumber him a hundred to one, Joe. The only hope for improving the strain of kaffir cattle in any given area, is to get rid of every goddam mangy kaffir bull in the area, and put one or two Ferdinands in their place. But will the wogs get rid of their bulls—?'

Max snorted cigarette smoke out of his nostrils, 'Joe, the only way to get rid of that bad kaffir stock is to send the *army* in to *shoot* all the kaffir bulls and the goats and the goddam kaffir roosters. And *make* those natives share the use of Government-owned bulls. But how is the wog going to like *that!* I tell you, he'll scream like hell. And what will the political boys say about it? Christ, they'll love it, they'll shout and scream murder and robbery and incite violence, and the next thing the United Bloody Nations will be screaming about how the whites are stealing bulls.' Max waved his hand, 'it won't work, Joe: the political blacks will see to it that it fails. The political blacks don't want to see the whites being good scouts, they don't *want* to see the black peasant grateful to the whites – they don't *want* harmony Joe, because it's detrimental to their campaign of unrest. Do you think for one moment those political blacks will let you succeed? Will they hell! They'll go out into the Reserve and say it's a white man's trick to enslave them, to steal their land, to pull the wool over their eyes, to put a magic spell on them, etcetera. The political boys would incite them to kill your Ferdinand, Joseph. Christ, it's happened before, all over Africa – the first people to get their throats cut in Kenya and the Congo were the nuns and the missionaries – right here in Rhodesia how many mission schools and mission farms have been burned, hey? – *dozens,* Joe ...' Max snorted. 'Humph! That's why it won't work, Joseph.'

Mahoney's face was white with frustration.

Max nodded, maddeningly, kindly wise.

'That's why it won't work, Joseph: because the wog is too idle to make it work, and because the political wog will be determined to make it fail and because the white farmer is too fed-up to try to cooperate with your plan very enthusiastically, I'm afraid. And right or wrong you can't bloody well blame them. For the last ten years all the farmers have seen in Africa is trouble from the black and appeasement and ass-licking from the British: all the black has to do is to get up in front of a microphone and start screaming slanderous and seditious statements in bad English to a mob of ignorant savages, about what shits the British are in general and the local whites in particular, organise a campaign of violence and murder – and the British invite him over to London and give him the country as a present: the British wine him and dine him and lick his ass at Lancaster House and they reward him for his sedition and his slander and his murders and his terrorism by making him Prime Minister. *King* – for Chrissake. They make him Prime Minister knowing full well that he is *not* going to promote democracy, but his own dictatorship, knowing full well that he is going to destroy the rule of law by declaring his opponents outlaws and locking people up without trial, knowing full well that he is going to give all the important jobs in Government to his own black pals, simply because they're black, knowing full well that he is going to ruin the efficiency and impartiality of the civil service by Africanisation, by kicking out the tried and tested white civil servants and giving their jobs to blacks simply because they are black, knowing full well that he is going to make the army and the police force his own political tools – knowing full well, in fact, Joseph, that he is going to turn a well organised colony into a dictatorship, with a one-party rubber-stamp parliament, and a corrupt and inefficient civil service.'

Max was a little red, and his eyes were hard, and his mouth was hard. He tapped the bar counter with his finger, tap tap tap tap.

'Joe, the whites in this country have seen too much. Granted the whites have not been angels themselves, far from it, but they have at least been hard-working, and their governments have observed the rule of law, and their civil service has been efficient and honest and their judges have been high-class impartial lawyers, and the whites have turned this country from a jungle into a prosperous organised state. And they have seen too much of how willingly Britain gives in. The whites here have seen the Mau Mau of Kenya, the murders and the plunder and the savagery – what happens? Britain encourages the white farmers to settle, to fight, then hands them over to the tender mercies of their own murderers. The whites have seen the white Kenya farmers sold up the river, *seen* the Kenya farmers who turned a wilderness into a garden being forced out, driving right here down Selborne Avenue, with one mere lorryload of all they can salvage – they have *seen* the Congo chaos, and the genocide and God knows what, they have *seen* the Belgian refugees driving into Bulawayo. They have seen the dictatorship and corruption in Ghana, the parliamentary opposition thrown into jail, they have seen the murders and the marauding in Northern Rhodesia, blacks murdered, whites murdered, Mrs. Burton and her baby roasted alive in her car outside Kitwe. And what does Britain do? She breaks all her solemn promises to us and breaks up our own country, the Federation, and gives it to the blacks – without even consulting us, without even having the guts and decency to tell us beforehand.' Max's upper lip was curled.

'And,' he tapped the counter again, tap tap tap, 'she'll do the same thing to us in Rhodesia, Joe. Don't kid yourself, Joseph. Don't kid yourself with legal arguments that she won't sell us because we've been a totally self-governing colony for forty years. The fact is, we're a *colony*, Joseph, and she'll sell us up the river, because it's easier and cheaper to do so than to have to listen to the screams of the tinpot black states that control the once-mighty British Bloody

Commonwealth.'

He leaned forward.

'The Rhodesians are bitter, Joe. They are determined that the line is going to be drawn. At the Zambezi. And the only way to draw the line is by independence. And if Britain won't give it to us, the only way is to seize it, Joseph. And to defend it, Joseph. With our very lives.'

Mahoney was listening, stubborn and silent. He snorted.

'And *that,* Max,' he jabbed the air, 'is precisely what we'll have to do. Defend it with our lives. And we'll *lose,* Max, and the country will be in ruins. And then the blacks will have it. And there'll *be* no more Rhodesia, Max.'

'Oh Jesus!' Max banged his glass down on the bar and slid off his barstool. He walked out the door.

Mahoney slid off his barstool, and strode down the bar to the toilet. He was shaking. He splashed cold water on his face. He looked at himself in the mirror. Pale, his face was pale. And some lines now, round his eyes, and on his forehead. No longer a youthful face. He knew he should have dinner and go to bed. But Max had made him too angry. Political blindness. Blindness begets blindness. Violence begets violence. He walked back to the bar.

The bar was full. You'd think the bloody country was booming. Gentlemen in well-cut suits shoving up the gins and whiskies, women in office dresses being one of the boys. The regulars, the noontimers for whom the bar was a second club. Living on hire-purchase in mortgaged suburban villas and jazzed-up flats with a view of the brown horizon. None of the rugged Harris-tweed-in-Africa huntin' shootin' fishin' types of Kenya. Too close to the Golden City of Johannesburg to the south and the Copperbelt to the north. Business people – *kupella.* Not one of them had been on a bloody safari in their lives. Peel off their suits and their dresses and they're lily white underneath. Or if they've got a tan they got it down at the Municipal swimming pool in Borrow Street or drinking gin-slings round their own suburban swimming pools, or at Sunday golf at the Club, not from taming the wilds of Africa. The bush-tunicked, felt-hatted, leopard-skin-banded, bush-breaking, belt-tightening Rhodesian pioneers who'll happily eat sadza, my poor aching ass.

Louis Peterson the real estate agent was there. Mahoney recognised him from the old days at the Club. He was with Mrs. Peterson. Jesus, is business bad. You can't sell a house for love nor money. Offices, he's got more vacant office space to let than you can shake a stick at. And flats? Two months rent free and you still can't let them. He's got executive-type houses on his books, five bedrooms, two acres, tennis court, swimming pool, the works – and you can't let them for peanuts. You couldn't get them for eighty quid a month five years ago. I tell you, the sooner we take independence and put these black bastards to the north of us and the British Government in their places the better. Mrs. Peterson was on her fifth gin and beginning to get along with it. She must've been quite a looker in her day, Mahoney decided. Forty-fivish now, too much gin and cigarettes and sun for too long showing through creases round her mouth and eyes and her neck was a bit leathery. She was talking in a gay high-pitched very English accent. 'Traitors,' he heard her say, and 'Communists' and 'sadza' and 'should be deported.'

Two black men walked into the cocktail bar. They were dressed in suits. They walked past the bar heading for the farthest corner table. A moment of silence fell in the bar and then Mrs. Peterson's high voice sang out:

'Get out you bloody kaffirs—' The two looked at her and hesitated, then kept on walking.

'Get out you bloody kaffirs,' Mrs. Peterson shouted, 'go to your own damn bars!'

Mahoney turned angrily and leant out and touched Mrs. Peterson on the shoulder.

'Mrs. Peterson – please!'

Mrs. Peterson spun on him. She wondered if she had heard correctly.

'You leave me alone, you kaffir-lover. Who do you think you are – addressing me—?'

'It's an offence to use abusive language in public,' Mahoney snapped, 'and if you don't shut up I'll run you in—'

'Who're you to preach to me—?'

'Don't you talk to my wife like that.' Mr. Peterson was glaring at Mahoney.

'Kaffirs aren't allowed to drink in here,' Mrs. Peterson shouted, 'it's against the law—'

'Not yet it isn't, Mrs. Peterson. Kaffirs can drink anywhere. It's for the manager of this hotel to decide who he lets into his bar—'

'It's against the law,' Mrs. Peterson shouted. 'You should be deported, you kaffir-boetie, I'll see my M.P. about you.' She turned and shouted down the bar: 'Get out to your own stinking bars—'

The two black men were standing in the corner. A black waiter was arguing with them. Everybody in the bar was looking at them. Two young men in sports coats were striding down to them. They shoved the waiter aside and grabbed at the Africans' collars. The Africans stepped back and fended off the white hands and there were shouts.

'Don't you touch me, you kaffir—'

Mahoney jumped off his stool angrily.

The manager was striding down the bar.

'Gentlemen – gentlemen—'

He stepped between the two young men and pulled them back.

'This is my bar—'

The young men glared at the two Africans. The owner straightened his collar.

'Now will you two gentlemen please leave. I'm afraid the right of admission is reserved in here and we don't serve Africans.'

'Chuck 'em out,' Mrs. Peterson shouted.

'We have got money—' the African shouted.

'I'm sure you have, gentlemen, but I'm afraid—'

'I'm going to the police,' the African shouted, 'for a case of assault—'

'You do that,' the manager said quickly, 'but will you please—'

'Jesus—' the young white said. He began to take off his coat – 'I'll give you something to go to the police about—'

The black waiters were milling round. The manager shoved his arm out across the white youth's chest. 'You get out too,' he snapped. He took a step forward and took the nearest black man by the elbow.

'Now please, gentlemen – before there's any more trouble—'

The black man shook his elbow free and straightened his jacket. They walked down the bar with the manager following behind them.

'And stay out,' Mrs. Peterson called.

The black man turned and wagged his black finger.

'When we rule the country—'

He was drowned in shouts and boos and laughter. The manager put out his hands and eased them out through the door.

The gabble and the laughing took up again. Mrs. Peterson leaned over towards Mahoney.

'And *you* get out too. Go and drink in the kaffir bars with your black friends—'

Mahoney just looked at her. She wagged her finger under his nose.

'*You,*' she said, 'should be *deported*. You're a bloody *communist*—'

Mahoney turned his back on her. He walked out of the bar and looked up and down the street. He saw the two Africans a hundred yards away. He strode after them.

'Excuse me—'

The African turned round and looked at him.

'I apologise for the bad behaviour of my own race—'

'It is too late,' the African said.

Mahoney turned and walked back to his hotel. By Jesus. Ugly. Bloody ugly. He stopped outside the hotel. 'Fuggem,' he said. He turned and walked up Selborne Avenue.

He got into his dented Vauxhall and drove slowly up towards the intersection, through the lights. The shop windows were lighted except the empty ones. The empty streets shouted Suzie! Suzie! at him. He drove out on to the Great North Road to the Ranchers, and the strip Show. At least he would not be alone at the strip. And as he drove he thought as hard as he could about Jackie in Salisbury, of her lovely red mouth and her big dark brown eyes that told him she would love him forever.

The tables were full, men in open-neck shirts were making a great deal of noise and the African waiters were having a hard time getting between them. There were half-a-dozen cowgirls dressed in green bikinis and green diamond mesh stockings, high boots and little woodsy jackets with tassels on their pockets and on their heads they wore red stetsons. They were also serving drinks.

Mahoney made his way to the bar and competed for a beer, then he jostled back into the hall with it. Then the manager appeared in his dress suit and threaded his way through the tables and as he went he signalled to the waiters to leave the hall, for it would not be right for them to see a white woman strip, and the waiters made their way out of the hall into a room at the back where they would remain until the show was over. The crowd started cheering and whistling and banging their beer bottles. The drummer played a roll to command silence and a spotlight came on the manager and he smiled gratified round at the audience. He held up his arms.

'Ladies and Gentlemen,' he shouted. 'Ladies and Gentlemen, thank you, thank you, thank you. Ladies and Gentlemen, I wanna thank you for being a wonderful audience. And now, Ladies and Gentlemen, the moment you have all been waiting for. Tonight I want to introduce you to that lovely lady you all know so well, that lovely lady all the way from the Golden City of Johannesburg – who has just returned from her brilliant worldwide tour of South America – where she was internationally acclaimed as the Sweetheart of the Strip – Ladies and Gentlemen – let's have a big hand for that lovely lady – the star of our show – the beautiful – the one and only – Gina Michlieu.'

A burst of clapping and whistling and a roll of drums, the spotlight clicked colours to passion pink and swung on to a side door, the band struck up and Gina Michlieu, alias Katie van der Westhuizen, swathed in cloak and evening dress and a flurry of sequins and feathers and high heels swirled through the door with a bright smile all the way from the Gold City and her worldwide tour of South America and got down to her bump and grind routine.

As the music thumped Gina bumped, as it whined she ground in a flood of passion pink spotlight, her hips and breasts undulating and her lips pouting purple. Off came her stole and her elbow length gloves and then her dress in sections with appropriate orchestration. Then she sauntered and bumped and ground her way round the ringside tables choosing a guy to unhitch her bra. Loud whistles and stamps and cheers. Then she wanted her two-way unhitched. She rubbed her crotch meditatively on the corner of a ringside table while she leered around. Then she wanted her stockings unhitched and she lifted her knee and placed her foot on a chair and presented her thigh and one buttock to the man and as the music thumped she hollowed her back and protruded her bottom and ground it round and round as he bent forward to unclip her suspender. She strutted into the middle of the floor dressed only in panties, high-heeled shoes and one stocking and she planted her feet apart and threw back her head and bumped and swivelled her hips and groin back and forth and round and round. The long muscles on the inside of her legs stood out smoothly from the apex of thighs, her legs were hairless and waxen in the spotlight, her belly was rippling and her panties so small you could see that she had shaved away her pubic hairs. She stretched her arms up to the ceiling and her breasts lifted and they vibrated with her tension. Then she thrust her arms down and stroked the inside of her legs upwards, up over her crotch, her belly, breasts, over her neck, through her long hair, then she extended her arms and reached for the ceiling again. And the whole time her hips were going back and forth and round and round.

Finally she slithered to the floor and her blonde hair was scattered out and round her head and her eyes were closed and she bent her knees and opened her legs and she rubbed the top of her crotch and she cried out and wriggled and threw her head from side to side and clenched her teeth. Her breasts shook big and she arched her back and pushed her thighs and crotch right off the floor and she started to beat the floor with her buttocks while she clasped her arms across her breasts and her cries rang out. Then she gradually calmed down, her ups and downs became slower and more peaceful, her cries sighs. And the spotlight clicked out.

As the overhead lights came on and the crowd burst into whistles and shouts and thumps, Mahoney ducked back into the bar. What he wanted, as he put it to himself, was a good shag. The second man in was a police inspector. They recognised each other from the old days.

'What's a nice boy like you doing in a place like this, Inspector?'

'I'm on duty,' the inspector said. 'Actually I am here to see that Gina doesn't contravene our decency laws. I love my job,' he leered. 'What's your legal opinion, Mr. Mahoney? Was Gina indecent?'

'I'd have to look at the law.'

'Well she went through the motion of sexual intercourse, didn't she?'

Mahoney nodded, 'I envisage certain practical difficulties if you bring her to Court.'

'Such as?'

'Well, what witness are you going to produce to prove she went through the motions of sexual intercourse?'

The inspector leered.

'Me.'

Mahoney nodded.

'Okay, let's have a dummy run. You tell your story as you'll tell it in Court and I'll cross-examine you as if I were defending our Gina, Sweetheart of the Strip.'

'Thank you, Mr. Mahoney, that would be very helpful.'

'Right.'

'Right.' The inspector grinned. He cleared his throat and put on his professional witness face. 'On such and such a date Your Worship I attended at the Ranchers Hotel. The Ranchers, Your Worship, is a public place, approximately two hundred members of the public were also in attendance, Your Worship. At approximately ten fifteen p.m., Your Worship, the accused made an appearance in the centre of the dance space. She was clad in decent if extravagant clothing. To the sounds of music, Your Worship, she systematically and suggestively disrobed until she was reduced to a pair of high-heeled shoes and a pair of very brief pants, Your Worship. At this juncture, she sought to simulate a woman of sexually passionate disposition—er—caressing her body in a most sensuous manner,

Your Worship. Thereafter she lay down upon the floor. May I refresh my memory from notes which I made at the time, Your Worship?'

'Yes.'

'She …' the inspector flicked through his notes. 'She lay down, Your Worship, in the spotlight, she parted her knees, Your Worship. Thereupon, Your Worship, she began to move her hips up and down through the motions of sexual intercourse. I was shocked in my modesty, Your Worship.'

'That's a lie.'

'Yes.'

'Right. Now I'll cross-examine you on behalf of Gina.'

'Right, sir.'

'Here goes. Inspector, I understand you to testify that in your opinion and experience the motions executed by the accused were the motions of sexual intercourse?'

'Yes, Your Worship.'

'Tell me, Inspector, you are married, I suppose?'

'Yes, Your Worship.'

'For how many years have you been married?'

'Nine years come April, Your Worship.'

'Is your wife a passionate woman, Inspector?'

The inspector grinned. 'Well, I—er—I'm not sure what you mean, Your Worship.'

'Does she like sexual intercourse, Inspector—'

'Well, really, Your Worship.'

'Answer the question, Inspector. You see I need to know how much you know about sexual intercourse.'

The inspector put on a straight face. 'Well—er—Your Worship – yes she does. No more, no less than the average woman, I suppose, Your Worship.'

'Is she, in her sexual habits, an average woman, Inspector?'

'I would say so, yes, Your Worship.'

'You suppose so?'

'Yes, Your Worship.'

'And what, Inspector, is your knowledge and experience of the Average Woman?'

The inspector rubbed his chin. 'Tricky,' he said.

'We'll turn to your practical experience. Have you made love to *many* women, Inspector?'

The inspector burst out laughing. 'Your Worship, I object.'

'Inspector, we are entitled to know what your experience is, so that we can evaluate your opinion. Now, please, Inspector. How many women have you made love to?'

'I don't know, Your Worship.'

'Twenty?'

'Possibly. I haven't exactly kept a list, Your Worship.'

'Of course not, Inspector. No gentlemen ever does. And were they Average Women, Inspector?'

'I would say so.'

'Why would you say so?'

'Well …'

'These incidents all took place over nine years ago, I presume, *before* your marriage, Inspector.'

'Of course.'

'Quite. You remember each incident clearly?'

'Well hardly, Your Worship. I mean some of them.'

'Quite. It is rather a characteristic of sexual intercourse that one is not really aware of the details of what is going on, one is rather more preoccupied with the sensations induced, I believe?'

'That is so, Your Worship.'

'Now tell me, Inspector, how many of these incidents can you remember in detail, clearly?'

'Well, I don't know, Your Worship, I mean …'

'I know it's difficult. You would really have to sit down and think hard about it first, wouldn't you, Inspector, in order to be halfway accurate?'

'Yes.'

'Quite. So you haven't thought much about it for the purpose of giving evidence in this case?'

'I didn't expect to be asked these questions, Your Worship.'

'Right, Inspector. Now let us move on to the details of what you actually saw the accused do. You say she lay down upon the floor.'

'Yes.'

'And you say she sought to simulate a woman of sexually passionate disposition, caressing her body in a most sensuous manner?'

'Yes.'

'In your opinion she pretended to be sexually passionate?'

'Yes.'

'Did any of the fifteen or so women of your experience behave like that, Inspector, without you actually being in contact with them?'

'No.'

'I see. So you are *not* speaking from experience?'

'I am speaking from my general knowledge of life. I know sexual passion when I see it.'

'I see, what *actually* did you see her do?'

'She touched her private parts.'

'How?'

'With her hand.'

'Of course it was with her hand, Inspector. It is unlikely that she touched it with her foot. In what manner did she touch her private parts with her hand?'

'She placed her hand against her private parts.'

'Over her private parts?'

'Yes.'

'Have you ever seen a woman masturbate, Inspector?'

'No, I have not, unfortunately.'

'So you don't know what that looks like. Never mind. Perhaps the Crown will be producing somebody as a witness to tell us what that looks like. Perhaps a nice policewoman. In any event, Inspector, what else did she do?'

'She moved her hips up and down. It loses a lot in the telling, Your Worship.'

'I see. Would you then please step out of the witness box and lie down on the floor and go through her motions so we can clearly see what you mean.'

The policeman threw back his head and laughed.

'You may take your jacket off if you wish, but not your trousers, Inspector. I would also like you to show how she touched herself in a most sensuous manner, to quote you. I'm afraid we can't provide the orchestration but you may hum to help you get with it.'

'Have another beer,' the inspector said.

He walked out of the Rancher's and got into his car and drove back to town. The city hall clock struck a quarter to twelve. It was high time he went to bed and slept off some of the beer inside him before Court tomorrow, but he didn't care about Court, he wanted to go to the Victoria. He used to take Suzie to the Victoria. He took the elevator up to the top floor. The cocktail lounge was in darkness, but the light of the city was all there. He walked through the dark cocktail bar to the end, up the spiral staircase to the grill room. It was still open, but there were no couples dining by candlelight and the band was not playing. A wine steward came to him.

'Can I just have a beer in there? I don't want to eat.'

The wine steward's black face widened.

'Mambo!' he said. 'How is the Mambo?'

'Goodness me, Amos, you still here?'

Amos beamed across his black face, and laughed a deep delighted giggle at being remembered. 'Yes, Mambo! How is the Mambo? Many years we don't see the Mambo.'

'I've been away, Amos.'

'Is the Mambo still big in the Court-i?'

'Enormous, Amos.'

'How isi the Madam?'

'You remember her too, Amos?'

'Too muchi I remember the Mambo and the Madam. Hasi the Mambo got plenty piccanins now?'

'Not yet, Amos, not yet. Listen Amos,' Mahoney broke into Sindebele, 'can I have a beer and drink it downstairs in the cocktail bar? I won't put on any light.'

'Of course yesi, Mambo,' Amos said in English.

'Bring me two, Amos—'

Mahoney sat in the dark cocktail lounge at the window looking out on to the hot quiet night lights of Bulawayo. He had sat at these windows, perhaps in this very chair, with Suzie. And with a score of other women in between. A hell of a lot of water had passed down the Zambezi, a hell of a lot in five years. A lot of things had happened to a lot of people. Solly Berger for one. Solly Berger, back in the gutter, a down-and-out alcoholic again, hangman again, executing the sentence of death at Salisbury Central Prison on Fridays so as to keep him in grog. Max, a small-time adulterous suburbanite with a mortgage bond and an overdraft. And himself? Back on the same hot dry itchy bank he had started from. Still feverishly writing his dark thoughts and chewing up the midnight oil and his lungs and his youth trying to write. And drinking himself to death.

I know an old man, Mahoney thought. I know an old man, once he was young and vibrant and clever and full of frustrations, which was good when he was young. He was a good lawyer when he was young and he loved and laughed and drank and worked and he had a beautiful girl. But the girl was never good enough for him, so he thought, and he worked and drank and worked and drank and after a while the girl left him and he was not such a good lawyer any more. And he did not know it, or if he knew it he did not care. And all his life he worked on himself and he drank and the world passed him by and he got nowhere, but he didn't know it, or in the seldom sometimes that he knew it, he did not care. And in the end he became an old man who had thought and written many million of words and they were nothing and the world had passed him by already and his girl was gone now. But still the old man did not know it, or refused to know it, he did not care, or he told himself he did not care and still he kept writing and hoping and figuring. But he became a nothing, nothing but a drunken old man whom the world passed by. And all the time he was lonely.

I know that old man, Mahoney said, and I fear he is me.

Oh Suzie – where the hell are you Suzie? Why, why, why did it happen? Where and why was the rot?

Only in my mind? – or also in fact? In my fanciful conceit, or also in my bones, or hers?

Oh Christ a thousand memories.

The evening silence between two armchairs. What happened at the office today already told, grunted at, gone back to where it belongs. Nothing, nothing to talk about, nothing that hadn't already been talked about a thousand times before. Unhappy eyes. Unhappy silence. Discontented silence of impermanent lovers.

'We would talk about our children,' she said, 'that's what we would talk about. That's what nature intends two people to talk about.'

'But we don't make each other happy, do we? We fight.'

We fought. Oh why, why did we fight? Because we lived only off each other's love, and off each other's bodies, having nothing to share, except our bed and our love? Oh why, oh why wasn't love enough? Because I am a dreamer, and she is not?

'Because you are a dreamer,' she said, 'and I am not. I do not understand your dreams – what it is you want. I can only be patient with them and be available to you when you awake to humour you. That's my role in life, to humour you. It was always the same, in Bulawayo, in London, in the States.'

The barefoot days. I telephoned her from a girlie bar in Buenos Aires on Christmas Eve – five years ago. A whore was rubbing her breasts against my shoulder and her crotch against my hip, and the atmospherics were very bad. I had not seen Suzie for one year. 'Come to England, Suzie,' I shouted, 'I am going to be back there in six weeks, and I love you', – and when I hung up I laid the whore. Suzie was in London when I got back. It was winter and it was snowing and cold and Suzie was plump and silky and lovely and all muffled up in her sweaters and duffle coat. Sitting in those glorious steamy London pubs drinking bitter and cider and eating bangers and pies and singing bawdy English drinking songs. We were very happy. And afterwards, going back to her crummy digs, tiptoeing up the stairs so her landlady wouldn't catch us, her little room warm with the gas fire and the smell of her and her things, and the warm narrow bed, and her eager excited laughing surrender to me, arms and mouth and legs open to me: and waking up in the morning nourished to the marrow by having lain warm and close to her all night, and the snow on the window sill and the bustle on the streets, and the warm sounds and smells of breakfast and Suzie getting dressed, and all her familiar things hanging in the cupboards and on her dressing-table – Oh God.

We bought an old car, and drove to Scotland. Suzie sitting muffled in the front seat, lighting my cigarettes and passing me chocolate. Wayside inns at lunchtime, bitter and bangers, the country brisk in thawing snow, the buds coming out, the brooks and streams tumbling, frothy and good, snow fights in the fields. Nights warm and snug before the fire in little inns, fire flickering on our faces rosy from the cold and the landlord all cheery and the locals making a great fuss of Suzie because she was beautiful and laughed with them, they all fell in love with Suzie: and afterwards, climbing the rickety stairs to bed with bellies full of hot food and beer, into the low-beamed chamber, shivering into the double bed with its warm patch of hot water bottle, warming each other enough to take off her nightie and make love. And in the morning the heather of Scotland, the lochs and the sea and the mountains and the sheep and the woolly cattle and the road map at the breakfast table, and coaxing the old car to start.

But – London again. Holiday over, the old car's battery going flat in the dismal sleet outside our windows. Suzie and I going off to the office in the morning, coming home cold and late to the bedsitter. Going down to the corner pub for a pint of bitter, then back to the bedsitter. The long silence between the two armchairs. Pen to paper again, the scratching of my pen, the desultory sounds of the woman's magazine pages turning.

For Chrissake don't leave me, Suzie.

Let's go to America – get out of these crummy digs and live like white men and make our fortunes.

A new purpose. Visits to travel agents, to the American Embassy, medicals, advice booklets, leaflets.

Subterfuge.

Winter week-ends in America, the forest thick with white, the sun glinting in a million spectrums off the ice-glassed trees, streaming across the lakes on skates, long blonde hair flying, her nose red and her eyes sparkling, muffled up against the cold; whooping down the snowy hills on skis, then rum and beer and a log fire, and roast chicken, faces glowing in the fire warmth. Summer week-ends on the lakes, the morning mist sitting on the water, the soft sound of the paddles of the canoe, the soft plop of the lines in the water, the breathless grunts and wriggles and struggles of the strike; then the gathering heat of the noon, lying on a hot rock, cold beer and fried trout, and Suzie's orange-coloured panties and black bra in a heap, skins glistening in suntan oil, love with the grass crushed green underneath us, the smell of grass and Suzie, and fried trout and the sweet clean taste of her wide mouth, long golden hair lying in the green grass, rounded brown thighs, white belly on the green grass.

'A baby a baby Oh give me a baby—'

But – New York. The long winter evenings, the world muffled by snow, home from the office, a bath, a beer and two armchairs again. The silences. The desultory sounds of the library books and magazine pages turning, then the scratching of the pen trying to scratch-capture dreams, the frustration, the agony. The sad faraway eyes staring at the window. Why haven't I got a baby? I've tried hard enough. So – the television set.

'You work,' she said, 'at your desk, like a man possessed. You shut me out of that part of your life, you don't try to tell me what you're doing, what you're thinking, you live unto yourself, you're self-sufficient. Then you come up for air, but you're still in your dream world, I try to enter it, but I can't, and in the end I don't even try any more.'

Sitting in our apartment in New York, icicles on the window, snow deep in the streets, the trees in our avenue heavy with snow and ice; an essay: 'Advantageous Aspects of Apartheid,' another: 'Problems of Partnership,' another: 'Estate Taxation and Life Insurance,' the frustrated quest for creation, expression, the rejection slips pasted on the wall to mock me: the television murmuring in the next room, Suzie's head coming round the door.

'The Late Movie's on—'

'I'm busy, Suzie.'

Too busy. Always too busy. Too busy to let her invade, to take the time to take her hand and explain the process, the reasons, the need, the result. The only way she could get in was to demand and fight her way in, but Suzie was no fighter. 'Come here, Suzie,' I should have said. 'You come here now, and sit down and damn well listen to me. I'm going to tell you what it feels like, what I want, what I'm trying to do, and you must think about it and feel it too, and read what I do, *share* it with me Suzie, help me Suzie, you must *try* Suzie, for God's sake *try* to be my soulmate—' But I did not. Because it wasn't even very clear to me, in those days. And Suzie was no fighter. She was a waiter. She was scared of me. The long silence and no baby, no matter how hard she tried.

One day Suzie coming home from office, sad face, sad eyes, Suzie saying: 'I am leaving you Joseph, I am going home. I have been tried and found wanting—'

Suzie don't leave!

But I did not stop her going.

Would that I had.

Then why do you come back to me? Because I love you.

Then why do you say you won't marry me? Because you'll never accept me into your dream world.

Then why don't you try to force your way in? I can't, I don't know how to. You've got to *try*. I have tried.

You haven't, you're idle, you just let me get on with it.

How can I try when you won't accept me? We know each other too well, we're too used to each other's habits, I know you won't accept me, you know I won't try. If only you could accept me and marry me for what I am, you've got a built-in resistance to me—

Back together again on the farm in Salisbury, the garden overtaken by jungle, creeper growing in the windows, the tattered lounge suite I got for thirty bob at the auction, only one window curtained. Another trial period. 'Let's try to get on, let's try to be soulmates.' Impermanence again. No carpets on the huge floors, no curtains in the big windows, rattling around the big house, echoes echoing impermanence. The table in the big lounge with its pile of papers dominating our lives, scribbles, stories begun and unended, new stories begun. The long silences, the pen scratching, Suzie curled up in the armchair reading, Suzie staring out the uncurtained window at night.

Why aren't we married, Joseph?

The brown horizons. The long dry infinite horizons, the hot dry feeling of sameness, for ever, silences for ever. But I am free now, I can seek, I can try, there are such things as soulmates.

Guilt.

The escapes. Wine in the sun on Sundays. Suzie lying in her bikini in the tall grass, her little transistor singing, me sitting in the shade, writing, beer and wine in the sun. Sitting in the sun sipping chilled wine, flesh getting warm and soaked with sun and wine, flesh warm and brown and full, long gold hair down over her shoulders, long legs, wide mouth moist with wine, sun's warmth sitting on flesh glistening on her brown belly, on her breasts. Sipping cold wine, chill glass to warm lips, the smell of the warm grass, happy together, pleased with each other, talking of love, of London, New York, steamy English pubs and Scottish lochs in the early morning, frozen lakes and fishing trips. Talking about my book, my stories, thoughts warm and sweet and flowing clear with the wine and the sun, thoughts thick with colour and action and emotion. Looking at Suzie, chill amber glass to wide red lips, glistening, talking happily, laughing, remembering, feeling, hoping. God, Suzie, you're beautiful, stroking her warm brown flesh; her arms, her legs, her breasts, full and soft and perfect under my fingers.

'Take your bikini off.'

Naked in the sun in the secret spaciousness of the tall warm green grass, drinking wine, talking, laughing, stroking, feeling, the little transistor singing, flaunting maleness and flaunting femaleness, long sucking kisses, tasting of wine and a little bit of salt, trailing fingertips, playing, rosy with the sun and the flesh and the wine in the tall warm grass, the taste of her flesh and her wide mouth on my mouth, the sweet joy of depth, of sucking flesh, the long slow revel glowing in the sun and the wine, waiting, tantalising, enjoying, stopping, starting, lingering, sipping wine in the sun. Then picking a chicken, hot succulent meat, roast potatoes in fingers, smeary mouths and long sips of wine and beer, then the long animal loving, long legs splayed and interlocked, hips twisting and pounding. Then the long surfeited animal sleep, drugged by love and the sun and the wine.

And then the awakening, the late afternoon, thick with sleep and the sun and the wine, sexless unsexed reality. The brown horizons and the curtainless windows and Suzie's faraway stare, and the silence again.

'Why haven't I had a baby? Then we would have to get married, we'd *have* to accept each other. Why haven't I conceived? I've tried hard enough.'

Sad, anxious Suzie, worried about getting her baby before it's too late.

'I'm *going* to have a baby.'

Suzie determined. Fussing in the kitchen every night, cooking up an exotic meal – *feed* the brute. Candles and a tablecloth every night, seductive Suzie coming on to my half of the double bed every night, Suzie with her thermometer taking her temperature every morning, counting days, Suzie telephoning me at the office and suggesting we drive home for lunch so we could make love, Suzie lying very quiet and still afterwards, with her legs raised on a pillow to retain her baby.

And why couldn't I make the decision for myself?

'I'm going to get my own flat in town,' she said, 'I must make a new life for myself—'

I always let her go, I never held her hand and made her stay.

Oh! Why didn't I?

Suzie's bachelor flats in town. The sad empty pretences of making a new life, a home, her own curtains, her own mats, her things spread out along the window-sills. Suzie vowing she was going to stop seeing me, Suzie telephoning to tell me anything important. Suzie telephoning me just to say hello. And my empty house emptier, the evening more silent. Putting my toothbrush in my pocket and driving into town to Suzie's flat. The relief of her familiar sleeping form against me, the fretful impermanence of waking up in the morning knowing tonight we do not share a bed.

'This can't go on. We must make a clean break.'

'Yes.'

But it went on. The clean breaks lasted a week. Then the week-end, Friday afternoon after Court, Come and have a drink with me, Suzie. The silent week-end stretching ahead, the empty house on Sunday quiet and empty and sultry, crying out for Suzie's footsteps.

'Come, Suzie.'

She came, with her things in her week-end bag. Friday night, party night, happy to be together. 'We get on so well when we don't see each other every day.' Saturday mornings, the early African Sunrise, the grass dewy in the big garden, Suzie singing in the kitchen, going shopping in the village, eggs, bacon, sugar, coffee, biscuits, chicken, wine, Suzie humming while she shopped. Sunday morning early morning tea in bed, sharing the newspaper: then the wine in the noonday sun. The drugged sleep – reality. Driving Suzie back to her flat. Sitting silent in the car.

'Here we are.'

And another week gone. And nothing solved. The unnaturalness of carrying her bag inside, switching on the lights in the dark flat, opening the windows. The unnaturalness of parting.

'Good night, Suzie.'

Suzie standing in the middle of her little flat. 'Good night, Joseph.'

Kissing her once, the look in our eyes: this can't go on. Good night, Suzie. Turning to the door, looking back,

Suzie standing in the middle of her flat, her things on the window-sills.

No promises of phone calls, no dates, nothing said. Driving back to the empty dark farm on Sunday nights.

This can't go on.

This can't go on. But it went on. The High Court circuits, the escapes, thinking: next month I go away on circuit for six weeks, we won't see each other for six weeks, we will break clean then. Suzie's faraway eyes thinking: next month he goes away on circuit, when he comes back I won't let him back into my life. Driving away on circuit, the problem shelved for six weeks. Six weeks of sweat, everybody wanting to get home to Salisbury, the Judge, myself, the registrar, the shorthand writer. Six weeks. Six weeks of driving around a jungle three times the size of England, looking forward to getting home. How many cases left, how many Court days?

Circuit Sessions drawing to a close, the last week, the last day, the last case, the last witness, the last judgment. The last party, the last handshake from the Mayor, the Magistrate, the District Commissioner, the Commissioner of Police, the open road. The relief, the excitement, the open road, the small towns, stop for a beer, driving on through the bush, thinking Suzie, Suzie, Suzie. Happy as I drive over the last range of hills, and there is Salisbury. Irresolution, excitement, pleasure, the long silences forgotten. Driving to Suzie's flat, looking up at the windows. Yes – the light burning! Drive home Mahoney, drive home, have guts, go back to your dark empty house, have the guts to pay the price for wanting a soulmate – but soulmates don't matter when your heart is breaking for your mate. Running up the stairs to Suzie's flat, knocking on the door, breathless, waiting for her footsteps. Footsteps coming, the door opening.

'Joseph!'

Oh, the laughing and the hugging and the kissing, the joy, all good intentions forgotten. It went on.

'High Court circuits,' she said. 'That's why I haven't had a baby, you're always in Umtali or Gwelo or Fort Victoria when it's the right time for me to get my baby—'

Circuits, homecoming, Friday night parties, wine in the sun on Sundays. The pretences, the attempts. Taking a girl to a movie, seeing Suzie at the movie with a man. 'We're finished Joseph, we can't go on.' Meeting the boys for a sundowner on Friday at the Long Bar: I saw your ex out with a chap last night, is it really all off between you? Lying awake at night, wondering, imagining, hating, loving. Getting drunk, jealousy. Getting drunk, driving round to Suzie's flat, the windows in darkness. Jesus! Waking up in the morning in the big empty house – the mornings are very bad. Driving the long way round to the Courthouse, so as to pass her flat.

Weeks and months. Seeing her at restaurants, in cocktail bars, at night clubs, nodding to each other across the room, our hearts in our eyes.

'Suzie?'

'Yes?'

'We're going to try again—'

'We've tried a dozen times.'

'Who is this chap, what does he mean to you?'

'Who are all these girls I see you with?'

'They mean nothing.'

'He means nothing.'

'Suzie, I'm picking you up at the office at five.'

Silence.

'Suzie!'

'All right, Joseph.'

Another Sunday in the sun, another six Sundays in the sun.

The shock.

Suzie sitting upright in the chair, very sober, very still, her long legs crossed, long golden hair down, very groomed, very beautiful, talking very quietly. My car parked outside her flat hot from the two-hundred-mile drive from Fort Victoria, the dust of the long hot road still on me, my books and my robes and my suitcase still in the car. Shocked, the fear pulling at my guts, believing only too well.

'It had to come, Joseph. You've been back a year, it's been on and off for a year, it's been both our faults. But love has been dying. Love must be nurtured, not starved and pulled about, torn apart.'

Standing fiercely in the middle of the room, anger and jealously and fear.

'But do you love him?'

She spoke carefully.

'Yes. Not blindly, passionately, restlessly like I loved you. I love him calmly, soberly, I'm grateful to him.'

'*Grateful!*'

'Don't mock me Joseph. Yes, grateful. He accepts me for what I am, he doesn't want me to be any different, he doesn't make me feel stupid, he makes me feel confident, he makes me laugh and I make him laugh, we share things. And he wants to marry me as I am.'

'But you've only known him for five weeks, for Chrissake, how can you love him?'

'Five weeks is long enough when it's the right person. I understand now what you mean when you talk about soulmates. Somebody who *feels* with you. He is my soulmate, he *feels* with me, I *feel* with him.'

Jesus. Outrage, disbelief, jealousy. That she could even think about another man was emotional adultery, let alone stop loving me.

'*Jesus*.'

Suzie sitting very still. Legs crossed, her chin on her knuckle, speaking evenly as if rehearsed, as if justifying herself.

'I'm entitled to happiness, Joe. We've been unhappy so long. We don't make each other happy except in bed. We're happy for a little while, then we get claustrophobia, or you do. Brian makes me happy. And I want a baby soon, soon I'll be too old to have a baby, it's like the call of the wild, Joe—'

'Christ!' Suzie in another man's bed with her legs open, another man sucking her breasts, Suzie kissing another man's loins with her wide mouth, Suzie taking another man's baby. Outrage, apprehension—

But still I did not seize her hand.

'But how can you stop loving me in five weeks?'

'It hasn't been five weeks, Joseph. Love has been dying for two years, ever since you let me go in New York.'

'And is it dead, Suzie, dead dead dead?' She shook her head.

'I love you still. I am you, and you have killed me. Now I have been brought back to life by another man. And I am going to pursue this life, Joseph, I am going to feed it and water it and give it a chance. I am going to see him, confine myself to him, to see if I can get to love him properly, completely, and if I do I will marry him, Joseph. And you must not try to stop me, Joseph, you must not interfere, you must not create a scene. You are honour-bound to let me try to find happiness, Joseph, if you love me at all—'

Standing fiercely in the middle of the room. Not knowing what to say, what to do, incomprehension. You are honour-bound to let me try to find happiness, Joseph, if you love me at all. Suzie rising from the chair, walking up to me, putting her hands gently on my neck, looking up at me.

'It had to come, darling Joseph.'

Suzie's eyes wet with tears, her wide mouth moist. The call of the wild, she said. Her babies. Suzie's sad eyes, some lines round them now, some lines on her face now, and in her hair some glints of grey. The call of the wild.

'Joseph, don't interfere. Don't stop me. Give me a chance, darling.'

The drinking. The empty house, dead and empty, echoing memories of Suzie. The drinking, coming out of the Court reckless, going down to the Long Bar, meeting the boys, long hard pulls at the beer, heart hard and angry and weeping, ready for fight, images of Suzie: Suzie kissing another man, Suzie kissing another man's loins. Wanting to fight. Driving home at midnight to the empty dark house, empty. Sitting in a cocktail bar waiting to keep a rendezvous with a girl called Jackie, a man sitting next to me, asking for a match. Jackie sitting down beside me, ordering her a drink, making polite small talk, comparing her to Suzie, wishing she was Suzie, Suzie kissing another man's loins. Looking up, heart contracting, there is Suzie, sitting with this man, heads close together, whispering. So this is the bastard, the great Brian – Jesus. Good Jesus Christ. Oh Jesus. Suzie looking up, looking straight into my eyes, unblinking, soft, afraid, imploring: Don't hit him Joseph, don't bully me, don't louse it up Joseph. Turning back to Jackie, hands trembling. Jackie putting her hand on mine. Take it easy, Joey, let's go somewhere else. But refusing to go somewhere else, not wanting to go anywhere else, wanting to sit right here and torture myself, watching Suzie and her lover, hating Suzie and her lover, *lover* – Jesus – sitting, heads close together, images, Suzie going back to his hotel, Suzie taking off her clothes for him, standing naked for him to adore her. Images of Suzie with her long high-heeled legs planted astride, and her head thrown back as the bastard kneels before her, Suzie spreadeagled on a bed, long blonde hair across a pillow, eyes closed, mouth open –

Jesus Christ, I'll kill the bastard. Unreal, a bad dream, the un-Suzie, the unnatural. The guy turning to me: So you're Joseph Mahoney, how do you do, I heard a great deal about you, Joe. Jesus Christ, a Yank, such a nice guy, such a nice wet effusive pain in the ass, make one false move you nice wet effusive pain in the ass, and I'll flatten you right here – Suzie's eyes imploring: Don't louse it up, Joseph, don't be mean, don't be a bastard, be honourable *please* Joseph darling – What are you drinking, Joe? the nice wet effusive pain in the ass offering me a drink if you don't bloody mind. Wanting to say, stick your bloody drink right up your All American Boy ass: but wanting to talk so I can assess him, wanting to be near Suzie, torture myself, somehow win her back, not wanting her back because her wide mouth is soiled with this bastard's loins. So accepting his drink, getting drunker, the whole time pumping the All American Boy for information so I know what kind of tit he is, Suzie talking nervously, politely to Jackie, the whole time her eyes flickering back, imploring: Don't humiliate him, Joseph. Protective Suzie, hand on his arm, murmuring something, intimacy, protectiveness, new Suzie, un-Suzie, Suzie another man's woman now, whispering something unnatural, outrageous, leaving their barstools now – 'Good night both of you.' Suzie going home with another man for Chrissake, walking out the door, his woman now, Suzie's flesh his now, Suzie's arms and legs and breasts and moles and freckles adulterated – Christ!

Jackie's hand on my arm, big soft deep eyes, suffering. Take it easy, Joseph.

Everywhere, Suzie, everywhere: crossing a street, Suzie standing on the corner, sitting in the cinema, Suzie walking down the aisle, seeking out new bars where Suzie is unlikely to go, Suzie and lover walking in, Suzie everywhere, in the flesh, in my mind, Suzie lying on her back in my dreams kissing his hairy flanks, Suzie's ghosts echoing in the big cold empty house in the night. Drinking, moving, drinking, talking, drinking, drinking too much, because when I stand still I hear Suzie's voice, see Suzie's eyes, feel Suzie's flesh, hear Suzie's steps. Waiting for the telephone to ring, putting my hand out to the telephone, clenching my teeth, holding my head: Be honourable, Mahoney.

And another day, another week, another month went by and it did not get easier.

Sitting in the empty lounge of the empty house, strewn papers, wet empty beer bottles, drunk pen scrawlings, trying to lose myself in the agony of writing, hating, loving, lost – a taxi bouncing up the long dirt drive, long flashes and shadows through the curtainless windows, car door slamming, light running feet. Getting up from the table, going to the door, Suzie running up the dirt drive, long hair swinging, skirt swirling my heart beating – Suzie stepping into the light from the curtainless windows, breasts heaving, tears running down her face, a cry, running into my arms, clutching, crying her heart out into my chest. Oh Joseph, Joseph, *Joseph*—

Oh why why why didn't I take her back, why couldn't I take her back, why couldn't I open my heart to her again? Oh, would that I had!

The bitter unreal half-life for a week, the sombre silences of sundowners, the half-forgiveness, the anger flaring. Suzie packing up her gear, buying her ticket. Driving in silence to the airport, unloading her gear, black porters carrying it to the weighbay, going up the stairs to the cocktail lounge, sitting in silence, Suzie's sad hard face, gentle hard, eyes red, sipping a brandy.

'Suzie?'

Turning her head slowly, looking at me with her steady unhappy eyes.

'Suzie, I do believe you, that you didn't sleep with him.'

Suzie's little stare then her little shrug. 'You don't.'

'I do.'

Suzie turning slowly away. 'Maybe in three months when I come back we'll be all right again.'

'Yes.'

Suzie staring, then shaking her head: 'No, it will never be the same.'

The scream of the Boeing coming in, the bustle, the loudspeakers, standing up, heavy heart, pushing through the crowd, people looking at Suzie, one brief kiss, one heartbreak, gone through the swing doors of the transit lounge. Standing back up on the balcony, the big Boeing lying big and heartbreaking in the floodlight, Suzie walking across the tarmac, tall, straight, long gold hair blowing, turning once, a wave, up the steps. The big Boeing screaming down the night tarmac, a hundred anonymous windows twinkling, anonymous Suzie somewhere, sitting in a seat, unidentified, flying away into the night. The Boeing screamed and lifted, up into the African night, up over the bush, up up higher higher, cabin lights gone now, diminishing into the night, further and further, red tail light blinking, blinking, blinking smaller smaller smaller in the black night, smaller, gone. Suzie gone.

Six months ago. No letter, no address.

Mahoney sat in the dark lounge on the roof of the Hotel Victoria, looking over the night lights of Bulawayo. There, far below, was Tregar House. He counted four floors up, three windows along. Suzie's old flat of long ago, a light burning.

Maybe it was because he was very tired and very drunk, but tears were running down his face.

Part Eight

Chapter Forty-Four

Mahoney was whistling as he drove his beat-up Vauxhall back to Salisbury. He was always happy when he was going home again at the end of a circuit session. It was like finishing a six-week oral examination. On the whole, he thought, it had gone off pretty well. A couple of clangers when he had had a hangover, but no guilty man had got off the hook. Five out of seven he had expected to swing had swung and the other two had got fifteen years.

Death Row must be pretty full these days. Mahoney did not keep a record of the number of men he sent to the gallows, but he knew he must have done about two-thirds of the stretcher cases currently awaiting execution in Death Row. Occasionally he read in the newspaper that a man had been hanged and usually he had to think hard to remember the name and the facts. Then: 'Oh yes, he's the bloke who chopped up his Auntie to get medicine for the witch-doctor.' Occasionally he met Solly Berger in the street or in a bar and Solly would say: 'I gave one of your boys the big jump today, Shadreck something-or-other,' and Mahoney would say, 'Shadreck? The name rings a bell, what did he do?' 'He's the chap who set alight his neighbour's hut and roasted him alive because he wouldn't join the Party' or 'He's the one who ...' Suzie had grown accustomed to it. But Jackie never got used to it.

'How can you take it so lightly?' she demanded. 'How can you sit there quaffing beer and saying casually. "Oh really, did you, how did he take it?" Don't you feel terrible?—'

'Paddy,' he said, 'if I got my bowels in an uproar every time I prosecuted a swinger I'd be a shuddering wreck. I don't enjoy getting a man sent to the gallows any more than the judge likes sending him there, but I can't allow myself to feel personally responsible because the law says that murderers and petrol-bombers must hang. I don't exactly go along and watch the execution you know.'

'But how can you approve of the death sentence, anyway? It's a barbaric system—'

'Honey, when I was a starry-eyed law student I was also opposed to the death sentence. But let me tell you that usually only the *bad* boys hang in this country. This country has got the most lenient judges when it comes to murder because they know that murder is almost the national sport among the wogs. They're always chopping each other up. They pull out their knives and their battle axes and start using them where you and I only get mildly annoyed. Go to a beerdrink, get into an argument over whose mother eats owls or whose rooster laid the hen that's sitting on the eggs and – crunch. Exit one wog. Try that sort of thing in England or America and you'll find yourself taking the big jump. But in this country they only get ten or fifteen years because the judge knows they only just dropped out of the trees. You can take it that if a man is sentenced to death here he bloody well deserves it. He's either planned the killing or he's done it for motives of robbery or he's chopped up his granny to give her liver to the witch-doctor for medicine to make him lucky at gambling.'

'But what about petrol-bombers?' Jackie demanded. 'Why should they be sentenced to death even when their silly old bomb doesn't go off and nobody even gets hurt?'

'Because, Paddy,' Mahoney said patiently, 'it is necessary to deter others. Petrol bombs are vicious things. How would you like your children to be roasted alive? And the black politicians are encouraging their boys to lob these bombs at anybody who doesn't belong to their Party. And at the white man to create a reign of terror. They're so easy to make, you've *got* to put a stop to it. Petrol bombing is about the easiest and the sneakiest and the cruellest and the most cowardly way to kill anybody. That's *why*, kid—'

Bastards. Cowardly bastards. You don't think the same way as me?

Okay – boom! No luck, Charlie, on you and your umfazi and your piccanins. *Cowards.* But when he was hanged and his body handed over to the relatives to bury the Party organised a big funeral procession and the party thugs chased the men and women out of their houses with sticks and threats to join the mourners and the Party bosses stood around the grave in their fur hats and delivered funeral orations for the brave martyr who had been persecuted to death for his people. And there was usually some long-haired foreign correspondent of some overseas cheese-wrapper to take down the drivel and the next week the United Nations were yapping about 'this martyr'. And the Party bosses drove away in their plush cars and instructed the Party cells to incite some more martyrs to die.

Mahoney shook his head. It didn't take much clairvoyance to realise there was a lamp post marked out for him if the blacks took over the joint by force.

But Mahoney was happy. The session was over and he was going home. He had no hangover. He was looking forward to his bare house and his huge shoulder-high lawns and his chickens. It was a jolly good house, even if it had no furniture and the creeper grew in through the windows. Rose bushes everywhere. Fifty acres on the outskirts of town and Mahoney paid only one thousand pounds for it. Five years ago, it would have fetched five thousand pounds.

And he was looking forward to seeing that long-legged red-lipped Miss Jacqueline again, one hundred per cent girl girl girl right down to her chewn fingertips, very soft and fragile underneath even if she was the last word in executive-secretary efficiency with her red-brown hair groomed up on top of her head and her steady heavy eyes. 'Me ole Myopia' Mahoney called her. Her high cheek-boned face had an ascetic no-nonsense look. But after work she wore her glorious long red hair loose down to below her shoulders, or sometimes in a plait, and she wore no eyeshadow on her slanty eyelids and her brisk efficiency was gone and she was all shy feminine sparkle and ups and downs and her dark eyes misted with emotion and smouldered with enthusiasms very easily. She made him laugh more than any other woman had done. Always brooding about something of the greatest importance, always demanding his opinion on some obscure subject. A great one for passions, our Long-legs Hot-lips Paddy: one week it's Mythology, then it's History of the Arts, then it's how she's going to make a million pounds, then it's Politics, then it's how she's going to turn his book into a Nobel Prize-winner. All very undigested, but it was there all right.

But there was no getting drunk in the sun on Sundays with Paddy, no reckless Sunday afternoon passions hot from the sun and wine, no glorious breasts dipped in wine for him to suck. She sat with him while he got drunk in the sun, but he went to bed by himself afterwards. Which, Mahoney smiled wryly to himself, was a hell of a thing when getting drunk in the sun and taking your woman to bed was the national sport and birthright. What else is there to do on Sundays?

He was still happy when he pulled up outside the Gatooma Hotel at lunch time and went into the cocktail bar for a beer.

The Gatooma cocktail bar was rather a smart joint. Nobody, to Mahoney's knowledge, had ever put up a good reason for Gatooma being just there. It had a police station, a magistrate, a railway station, a hotel, a cinema, and a row of corrugated-iron-roofed general dealers squatting under the Central African sun, and that appeared to be it. Mahoney said that some pioneer's granny must have suddenly got the hell in with the ox-wagon and announced that she was bloody well going no bloody further. But the Gatooma had glass swing doors, air-conditioning, edge to edge carpeting of rosebud persuasion, comfortable foam-rubber barstools, BOAC and UAT ashtrays, and all the usual trinkets and booze and at night it had subtle concealed lighting. It was smart and neat, and the sort of pub for which you felt you had to put on a jacket and tie. indeed because he was wearing sandals and shorts and a shirt with no buttons Mahoney intended having his beer on the verandah, until he saw that the cocktail bar was filled with sweaty, dusty, brown-legged men in khaki shorts and open-neck shirts. He pushed open the glass door and worked his way up to the bar. He had to shout his order above the noise and across two layers of shoulders. A middle-aged brown-faced farmer next to him grinned at him, khaki bush hat resting on the back of his head.

Mahoney poured his Lion between jostling elbows. 'What is it, market day or a lynching—?'

'UDI,' the farmer grinned. He had a detribalised Cockney accent. He threw back his head and shouted: *'Yahoo—'*

Mahoney lowered his glass. 'What d'you mean?'

'The Prime Minister's giving a nationwide broadcast at one-fifteen. Ain'tch 'eard, mate? Says everyone's gotter listen in—'

'Nationwide broadcast?' Mahoney stared. Then he waved his hand. 'So what, he's given nationwide broadcasts before, he isn't going to declare independence. This is just to tell us that we got to be patient—'

'Says we *gotter* listen in,' the farmer crowed, ''e ain't ever tol' us that before. All employers gotter give their staff time orf to listen in, all the school kids gotter get 'ome for lunch early so they can listen in. What's 'at mean if it ain't UDI?'

'He wouldn't dare,' Mahoney breathed, '—it's suicidal.'

'What's 'at?' The farmer cocked his ear close to Mahoney.

'I said I doubt it,' Mahoney raised his voice.

The farmer transferred his glass to his other hand and stuck out his chest.

'I tell yer somep'n mate,' he grinned, ''e *is*. And if 'e doesn't 'e'll be *out*.' He jerked his thumb over his shoulder. 'Somebody's gotter stand up ter these British bastards. Lyin' cheatin' bastards. I tell yer somep'n—' he leaned forward again. 'Was a time when I was *proud* ter be British. Even voted Labour, I did, back 'ome. But I tell yer the British Guvment these days—' he stuck out his lips and made an anal noise: 'Stink,' he said.

Mahoney nodded impatiently.

'Tell me, what do you grow, mate?'

'Terbacco,' the farmer said, 'and maize and a bit o' everything.'

'How you going to sell the stuff if Britain imposes the trade sanctions she's threatened—?'

The farmer looked at Mahoney as if he wondered if he had heard right.

'Pah!' Hostile now. 'Sanctions? Don't make me laugh. Sanctions? D'yer really *b'lieve* that crap about sanctions?'

Suddenly everybody in the bar was saying 'Shh – shh – shh—' and suddenly there was dead silence and everybody was craning forward to listen to the radio on the bar counter and the sober cultured voice of the announcer was saying '… announcement by the Prime Minister, the Honourable Ian Douglas Smith.'

There was a moment's blank and then the flat Rhodesian accent of the Prime Minister came through sombrely and slowly and loud and clear and there was not even a shuffle in the tiny crowded bar.

The Prime Minister spoke for a long time. And he ended: 'I call upon all of you in this historic hour to support me and my Government in the struggle in which we are engaged. I believe that we are a courageous people and history has cast us in a heroic role. To us has been given the privilege of being the first Western nation in the last two decades to have the determination and fortitude to say "so far and no further".

'We may be a small country, but we are a determined people who have been called upon to play a role of worldwide significance. We Rhodesians have rejected the doctrinaire philosophy of appeasement and surrender. The decision which we have taken today is a refusal by Rhodesians to sell their birthright, and even if we were to surrender, does anyone believe that Rhodesia would be the last target of the Communists and the Afro-Asian bloc?

'We have struck a blow for the preservation of justice, civilisation and Christianity, and in the spirit of this belief we have this day assumed our sovereign independence.

'God bless you all.'

There was a moment's silence then a man threw back his head and shouted *yahoo!* – and the bar was suddenly roaring with shouts and slaps and laughs and handshaking. *Yahoo!* – Good ole Smithie! – Attaboy Smithie! – God bless Smithie! – and men began to sing and stamp their dusty boots and thump on the bar.

'Give every man a drink!'—a five-pound note slapped down on the counter—'Here's a toast to Smithie!' – 'That'll teach those Commie bastards!' – 'Here's a toast to Wilson!—' and the anal noises filled the bar and everybody was laughing.

Outside in the hot dusty road it was quiet, dead quiet, only the distant noise from the bar. There was nobody on the streets, not a moving vehicle. Mahoney climbed into his old car and started her up. He patted the dashboard.

'Congratulations, honey,' he said. 'Your value has just gone up a hundred per cent, dents and all, 'cos nobody will sell us any cars now. Not that we'd have the foreign exchange to pay for them.'

He put her into gear and drove off slowly down the quiet street.

'I'm sorry, honey,' he said, changing gear, 'on second thoughts you're almost worthless. There isn't going to be any juice in the country to run you on. And, boy, do you love petrol—'

He turned on to the main Salisbury road and he lifted the bottle of cold champagne to his lips.

'Might as well go down with a flourish.'

Chapter Forty-Five

Nor had there been any rain in the capital of Salisbury while Mahoney had been away. But the countryside of Mashonaland was green and there were kopjes and gentle hills around Salisbury and the soil upon which the city spreadeagled itself was rich and the big suburban gardens were green and bright and the avenues were thick with trees. After the rains the city would be a gentle purple from the jacaranda trees and a bright scarlet, and the pavements would be trampled mauve and vermilion from the fallen petals. Mahoney grinned when he drove over the last ridge of hills and saw the tall office blocks and flats rising high and white and modern out of the jungle. Salisbury had quite a skyline for a city of only one hundred thousand whites, and out in the big old rambling downs of Highlands and Borrowdale and Umwinsidale it was beautiful and the old homes were gracious. 'The last bastion of the white Bourbons north of the Limpopo' the pink journalists were fond of calling it. You could actually walk around downtown all Saturday morning and not see anyone you knew.

It was four o'clock and he met some of the homeward bound traffic. Cars were hooting gaily like they did on old year's night. There was not a soldier to be seen. The office men and girls were emerging from the buildings, the black white-sleeved constables were on traffic duty as usual. There'd be some pretty heavy drinking tonight. Not only Friday night but UDI night. The bars would be full of the overseas press types and the jubilant Rhodesians. There'd be a few punch-ups tonight, by God. Rebels versus anybody who didn't fancy sadza.

He drove up Jameson Avenue, through the traffic. He was feeling pretty jubilant himself with a bottle of champagne inside him. The constable on point duty recognised him and saluted him and waved him through. The perks of being a Grade Six Crown Counsel in a Revolutionary State, he grinned to himself. He was looking forward to the drinking tonight. He hoped he was around when some of these long-haired overseas pressmen who were infesting every hotel in town rubbed some of the rebels up the wrong way.

He hesitated at the traffic lights of Jameson and Second Street. He could turn left to Jackie's house or he could drive straight up Jameson and out of town to his farm. He wanted to turn left to the welcome of Jackie. She didn't even know he was coming home tonight. She might have another date, but she would break it for him. He hesitated while the traffic lights showed red against him. Why're you bursting a blood-vessel to see her? he demanded of himself. All the time you're in Bulawayo you're brooding about Suzie, so why are you bursting a blood-vessel to get to this doll? You're still brooding about Suzie even now. If Suzie was in her old flat in Westminster Court – oh, if Suzie was in her old flat in Westminster Court … The homecoming from circuits when Suzie was here – the excitement. The joy as he rode up in the elevator of Westminster Court. Relief to get away from each other when he left town on circuit but the joy of coming back, all forgiven, all forgotten, the dinner and the wine and the love-making—

So why hurry to Jackie? It's not responsible behaviour. Jackie's in love with you – sure, she'll break her date if she's got one, because she's in love with you. It's not responsible to hare around to her place the moment you hit town as if you can't bear to be apart from her for another minute. What's the matter with you, why must you always have a woman to hold your hand?

The traffic lights changed to green and he turned left to Jackie, and drove out to Borrowdale.

He turned in at the big white gates. A head appeared at an upstairs window, white face, long red hair and a wide red mouth. She peered and then her wide mouth broke into a smile and she waved energetically and she disappeared. She came running out of the house as he climbed out of the car. She ran up to him and grabbed both his hands and pumped them.

'Hi.'

'Hi, you big fat slob—'

She flicked her fingers over his chin.

'Aren't you shaving till we get One Man One Vote?'

'That's it.'

'Well!' she flicked her head to get her hair off her face, but it was a nervous movement: 'Welcome back, come in—'

'Are you doing anything tonight?'

'Yes,' she said. 'I'm going on the town to listen to the fighting talk with a big fat slob called J. Mahoney – Esquire—'

He dropped his arms around her and pulled her against him and bit her neck and he dropped his hand to her bottom and squeezed hard.

'Hey,' she wriggled free, grinning. 'Are you ready?'

'I'm bathed, just let me change—'

As they drove out to his house she sat apart from him.

'So what d'you think of UDI?'

'I'll give you the benefit of my learned opinion later. Right now you slide your fat bum closer to me.'

'You're rude,' she said, sliding up close to him.

'When're you going to decide to sleep with me?'

'Golly, you're so *rude*—' She glanced up at him then she stretched and kissed his cheek quickly.

'No,' she blushed.

Mahoney changed the subject.

'Have you been out to my house regularly?'

'Once a week,' she said, 'I was going again tomorrow. Goldilocks has got twenty-two eggs! They're due out today or tomorrow and Mrs. Nkrumah's got fifteen she's been sitting on, they're due out in ten days ...'

'Good for old Cocky! How is he?'

'Cocky as ever. Golly, what a menace, I have to take a broom to keep him from getting me with those wicked spurs when I go to check up on the maternity ward. And he flies out of the run the moment I drive up and chases the car. I'm terrified of him.'

They were leaving the gracious houses behind and now they were in open rolling country. He turned down a dirt road at the bottom of the valley and then in at a wooden gate. There was a long drive up to the house and the rose bushes along the drive stood among tall grass. The house was obscured by two frangipani trees and there were two great msasa trees.

Ferdinand the bull and Pregnant Wife were grazing on the lawn. He parked in front of the house and hooted for his servant.

'Tickey's not here,' she said, 'I haven't seen him once all the times I've been here.'

'Swine. He's hopeless. I'm going to fire him anyway, my old boy Samson I've told you about's coming back at the end of the month.'

'*Is* he?—'

'It's quite funny, I'll tell you about it later. Will you open the house?'

'I *love* this house—' she said.

It was a good Rhodesian house. The roof was thatch lashed to wooden rafters and the four rooms stood in a long row with a red cement stoep running the length of it.

They walked into the lounge. It was a big room with a red cement floor and the walls were sprinkled with battle axes and spears, murder weapons that Mahoney had collected from bloody trials.

'Hey, what's this?'

The tattered old lounge suite Mahoney had picked up at an auction sale was a different colour and the tears were patched up.

'I haven't dyed it, I gave it a good scrub with that furniture cleaner stuff.'

'Did you? Thank you, Ugly-mug.'

'I'm not ugly.'

'Ugliest girl in town,' Mahoney affirmed as he walked ahead down the passage into his study: 'Hey, *curtains*—'

There were curtains on his study windows.

'I dug them out of Mom's storeroom.'

She was standing admiring her work smugly. He kissed her.

'Thank you, Hotpants,' he said.

She stepped back, 'I am *not* a hotpants—'

'I can tell a hotpants a mile off.' He kissed her on the nose and walked through to the kitchen. It was big and there was the old electric stove in which Tickey had built a wood fire the first time Mahoney had told him to boil some water.

'I am *not a hotpants—*'

Mahoney turned the key in the back door and swung it open.

'I am *not—*'

She was facing the door as it swung open and her eyes opened wide and her fingers shot up to her mouth and she screamed.

He spun around and faced the door.

The white Leghorn rooster was hanging on the outside of the back door by its neck. It was dripping blood and the small noose was made of string. The word 'Hokoyo' was daubed underneath the door in blood.

They stared at the big white bird. Then he put out his arm and touched it.

'He's only been dead a little while.'

'What does "Hokoyo" mean?' she whispered.

'It means "Danger" ...'

Chapter Forty-Six

Samson Ndhlovu was pure-bred. His father was a growing youth when the mighty Lobengula's word was law in Rhodesia from the Limpopo to the Zambezi. His grandfather had been an induna, senior warrior, under Mzilikazi, who was Lobengula's father, who in turn was the General of Chaka, king of the Zulus. Mzilikazi had rebelled against the Zulu Chaka and had led his fighting people north from the lush seasides of Natal, up across the Limpopo and settled in the flat cattle plains of Matabeleland. Every year when the impis of Mzilikazi and Lobengula set off on their plundering expedition from the royal kraal of Bulawayo they brought back many strange captive women. But there was no strange blood in the veins of Samson Ndhlovu. He was all Zulu. Being, therefore, a gentleman, Samson Ndhlovu hated no man. Other tribes, not excluding the white man, were just not worth worrying about. Samson did not want to be a white man, he did not want a white woman for his own, he did not want to drink in white men's bars and he did not care who ran the country as long as nobody pushed him around. He treated the authorities with the distant politeness he expected from them. He was not interested in the fur-hatted politicians and he had ignored the Party thugs until it was impossible to ignore them, whereupon he had retaliated. When he had been beaten up three times Samson had joined the Party for the sake of peace, carried his Party card as a warrant of safe conduct, and he ignored the Party again. He did not believe the promises of the politicians and their thugs that when they ruled the country every black man would be a boss with car and refrigerator and a white man's house and a white wife. Samson would have liked a car and a refrigerator but he was not interested in living in a white man's house with a white wife. He wanted to live in his kraal with a few buxom black wives and drink beer and sit in the sun and watch his cattle until it was time to go hunting again. That was the way for a Matabele gentleman to live. He liked the city only because it gave him much opportunity to drink beer and to copulate.

When Samson Ndhlovu had left Mahoney standing on the road to Johannesburg, he had no intention of working for another white man as a servant. He had walked back into Bulawayo, packed all his belongings in his cardboard suitcase, counted his money and gone on one last fling of the beerhalls and shebeens. Two days later he left Bulawayo with two split lips and broken teeth, a black eye, a gash in his head, a delightfully tender penis and the satisfaction in his heart that he had sorted the men from the boys and the women from the girls and had left a good few broken hearts behind him.

When he arrived at his kraal ten days later he found things were very bad. His women had ploughed the lands and planted the mealie pips but the rains had not come and the cattle were thin. He sat on his haunches in his bachelor hut and thought and then he collected up his spear and his knobstick and his axe and he had set off for the Zambezi Valley again to hunt elephant and crocodile.

But—ah!—it was not the same valley. The valley was now full of water and the animals and the people had moved to new pastures, and the elephant were scattered far and the shores of the lake were so wide that it was not easy to find crocodiles any more. What he needed was guns and a boat, like the Nkosi had had, but he had no money. Ah! He wished the Nkosi was here now. The Nkosi had plenty of money and he would buy another boat and it would be like it was in the old days. Samson dearly wished he had not spent so much money in the shebeens in his two years in Bulawayo. For a month Samson followed the game spoor and lay in wait along the lakeshore, but it was not like the old days and then he had returned to his kraal and packed all his belongings in the cardboard suitcase again and he had set off walking to Northern Rhodesia, faraway across the Zambezi to the copper mines where he had heard that a black man could earn forty pounds a month, to earn the money to buy a boat and an engine and some rifles.

It was good on the copper mines but the Party was there too. In fact there were three parties and three armies of thugs. Samson Ndhlovu had his head kicked in three times and then he got tired of it and he joined all three parties and carried three different party cards. Samson Ndhlovu, quickly distinguishable in a crowd by his six foot of black muscle and with the reputation he earned as a hard-hitting, hard-drinking Casanova, did not manage to deceive all three parties for long. He took the beating of his life from a gang of the smallest and newest party, who left him for dead in an alley, he spent six weeks in hospital and when he came out he took the sensible course of openly espousing the biggest party, which happened to be the original Party he had joined in Bulawayo, becoming One of the Boys and making the minimum contribution possible. It was after this the Party moved in on him. He was making time with a chubby little half-crown whore over a mug of beer at the Mine Compound beerhall when the messenger tapped him on the shoulder.

'Ndhlovu, the Vakuru – the big ones – wish to see you.' Samson looked peeved.

'Which one?'

'The Branch Secretary,' the messenger said in English. He pronounced it 'Brunji Sekiturry.' Samson was irritated.

'I will come on Monday,' he said. 'I have been working hard under the ground and now I am drinking beer.'

He turned back to the girl.

The messenger went away and twenty minutes later four young men came back.

'Ndhlovu – why do you trouble the Vakuru—?'

Samson went with them peevishly. He was not interested in the Vakuru and he had had nothing to do with them before. Besides, the Branch Secretary was a Mashona by tribe and Samson considered the Mashona the lowest form of Bantu life. Had not the Mashona been slaves to the Matabele in the days of Lobengula?

The Branch Secretary was a short spindly man with a broad flat nose and crisp curly hair brushed straight up. He wore a dark blue suit with a yellow tie with a white girl in a bikini painted on it. With him in the plush office was Kamisu, the young scarred thug with thick lips who was recognised as the Officer in charge of the gangs, who held the rank of organisational Secretary and who had been trained in Peking as a soldier. The Branch Secretary did the talking.

'Ndhlovu, you are a lucky man. You have belonged to our Party for only a short time, but already the Party is going to reward you. We are going to send you on a scholarship to a university over the sea.' He spoke in Sindebele except for saying 'ma-Party', 'ma-scholarshi', 'ma-university', and 'ma-sea.'

Samson's mouth opened and his eyes widened. He had only heard these words when he first came to Zambia.

'Ma-*scholarsheep*—?' he said. 'But I do not know anything about the ma-university—'

Samson considered the Branch Secretary beneath contempt, and he had no desire to mix with the Party thugs more than was necesssary for his well-being, but the idea of going over the sea, possibly even in an airplane, intrigued him.

'Therefore you must learn these things,' the Secretary said.

'But,' Samson said, 'I do not know how to read and how to write, only a very very little which I learned when I was a small boy, how can I go for the ma-scholarship?'

'They will teach you those things at the ma-university,' the Secretary said, 'and many other things too.'

'What other things?' Samson demanded.

'They will teach you'—the Secretary hesitated—'to be a good farmer.'

'Aah—' Samson said slowly.

'When we rule our country,' the Secretary said quickly, 'every man will have a big farm and it will be a good thing that you know how to be a good farmer.'

Samson nodded. It made good sense to be a good farmer. 'The ma-scholarship is given to you by the u-Government for America.'

'*America*—' Samson said slowly.

Kamisu spoke for the first time. 'Do you agree?'

'I will tell you tomorrow,' Samson said curtly. He had no time for

Kamisu, whom he considered a bully. Kamisu was a Manyika which was only one up from a Mashona.

'You must decide now,' the Secretary said.

Samson shook his head firmly.

'I have many things to think about. I have been saving my money and I now have almost enough to buy the things I need. How long will I be at the ma-university?'

'Six months,' the Secretary said, 'and the Americans will pay you some money too. You must decide today.'

'How much money?'

'Seventeen pounds each month—'

Samson turned and walked to the window. Seventeen pounds each month for learning ...

He turned back.

'I agree,' he said.

Samson Ndhlovu did not go to America. It was not until he was met at Cairo airport by the resident Party official that he learned that he and the other nine scholarship winners were going to Russia, and not to America. They did not go to a university, but to a house forty kilometres outside Moscow. They were not taught to read and write, nor did they learn land husbandry: they were taught Leninism and Marxism and they were trained as saboteurs.

Chapter Forty-Seven

In fact, Samson Ndhlovu thoroughly enjoyed himself in Russia. He enjoyed learning how to clean and assemble and fire sub-machine-guns, rifles and half-a-dozen kinds of pistols and he was a crack shot; he enjoyed learning how to make explosives and how to blow up bridges and buildings and railway lines, how to tap telephones, use radio, how to use trick cameras and invisible inks, unarmed combat, how to track and how to smuggle, how to blackmail and how to kill. It was all very interesting and Samson Ndhlovu was good at it. His Russian instructors praised him. He was well fed and clothed, the seventeen roubles per month pocket money that the Russian Government gave him was enough to keep him in cigarettes and vodka, and the Russian girls liked him, particularly the girls who came to the camp every day to cook their food and clean the rooms. In fact the white Russian girls liked the black Freedom Fighters in general and Samson Ndhlovu in particular so much that the Russian boys of that neck of the woods got cheesed off and there was a punch-up one Friday night outside the camp in which Samson Ndhlovu dispatched two Russians to bed for a week with concussion. The Russian authorities, embarrassed by this exhibition of racial hostility and anxious to keep favour with their black comrades, arraigned the Russian youths before a People's Court and dispatched Samson and his fellow Freedom Fighters to Uzbekistan for a week on holiday. The Russians saw to it that Samson Ndhlovu and his black comrades had a good time in Russia and Samson made the most of it. But he did not understand half the lectures on Leninism and Marxism and what he did understand he did not think a good idea at all. Samson Ndhlovu had two wives and fifteen head of cattle and a hundred and twenty-three pounds in the bank and he intended buying a rifle and a boat and an outboard motor and he didn't propose sharing all that with anybody and he didn't propose letting any Party official, not even a Matabele let alone a Manyika or Mashona, tell him how he should spend his time. Samson Ndhlovu did not propose becoming a Freedom Fighter in Rhodesia or anywhere else: he proposed making a lot of money as a hunter and a fisherman and then sitting on his buttocks in the sun drinking tshwala and watching his cattle and his wives and his daughters grow fat.

When they returned to Zambia the Party officials met them at the airport and hustled them to the Party Headquarters. They were given a hero's welcome. After a week they were given their orders by Kamisu. They were to return to Rhodesia, each to a specified town, they were to find civilian employment, then organise cells of saboteurs and start blowing up things. Caches of arms and explosives would be supplied them by the Party. Samson Ndhlovu nodded co-operatively and said he would do all those things. Kamisu drove them to the north bank of the Zambezi and arranged for them to be ferried across the river in dugout canoes by fishermen. The group split up and Samson Ndhlovu sprinkled his farewells with appropriate Party slogans and 'comrades'. And Samson Ndhlovu melted into the bush. He made his way up the south bank to Kariba, he bought himself an old boat, an old outboard motor and an old rifle and he chugged out towards the mauve horizon. He set up his base camp two hundred miles away to the west near the mouth of the lake, only fifty miles from his own kraal, and the Party never heard of him again.

The police and the Game Department rangers heard of him, however. Four months later Samson Ndhlovu was in jail for contravention of the Wildlife Conservation Act, and for unlawful possession of firearms. He told the police his name was Paradise Mpofu, lest the Party got to hear of him. The authorities confiscated his gun and ammunition and when he came out of jail the Native

Commissioner refused to give him a licence to buy another and refused to give him a concession to hunt crocodile. Paradise Mpofu took his boat across the lake to the northern bank and bought himself another gun and three months later he was back in jail. After coming out of jail the third time Paradise Mpofu decided to go in for something less noisy than crocodile and elephant hunting. He went in for illicit gold buying and selling. He had to journey to Bulawayo to sell his unwrought gold and in Bulawayo a Party man eventually recognised him. He was waylaid outside a shebeen before he had got rid of his swag. He woke up in hospital under arrest for unlawful possession of unwrought gold. From then on Paradise Mpofu was a marked man, both by the police and by the ma-Party.

Chapter Forty-Eight

Personally, Samson Ndhlovu was glad that the white men had declared independence – whatever that meant – because they had cleaned up the townships and restricted the thugs to remote areas at the same time. Samson Ndhlovu came out of prison full of hope. The white man had sorted things out at last, the Nkosi had a job for him in Salisbury. Salisbury was a big place, like Johannesburg people said, the townships were big and the women and the beerhalls many. And maybe the Nkosi would decide to buy a boat again and return to the valley and then it would be like the old days again and they would make plenty money.

Samson Ndhlovu whistled as he swung the panga sideways over his shoulder and slashed at the tall rough grass that grew in Mahoney's garden. The grass fell under the slash and he carried the panga through and up over his other shoulder and slashed down again. It was Friday, the last day of the month, pay-day, and the post-dated cheque the Nkosi had left behind when he left last week to hold court in Fort Victoria fell due. At about noon he would get on his bicycle and ride into town and cash the cheque at the bank. And from the bank he would ride on to Harare, the best African township for beerhalls and dancehalls and women. Friday night, pay-day night, there would be plenty of beer and women in Harare tonight. A-haa-ah—!

Samson Ndhlovu was pleased with life. It was a good job he had working for the Nkosi. The Nkosi had made him bossboy over the little farm, to look after the animals, and he would get a bonus on any profits. Together they would make money on this land. He only regretted that the Nkosi spent so much trouble in trying to help the people in the Reserves. The Nkosi was very foolish about that, because any Matabeleman knows that the Mashona are very stupid and idle people. Half the time and sometimes more the Nkosi travelled very much to Fort Victoria and Umtali and Gwelo and Bulawayo with the ma-High Court-i. The Nkosi said it was because he had no wife that the u-Guvmenti sent him around the country so much. That was a good thing too, the Nkosi having no wife. It was good because the u-Guvmenti sent the Nkosi away very much and there was no washing and ironing and cooking to do for the Nkosi. He liked the Nkosi very much, the Nkosi was an induna, but no man likes washing, ironing and cooking. And the white men's wives were very troublesome people. They were not docile people like the Matabele wives. Samson could not understand why the varungu let their wives be so troublesome. A Matabele would never stand for it. A Matabele would give his wife a good beating and if she did not mend her ways he would return her to her father and reclaim the cattle he had paid for her and then the father would give her a good beating too. But the varungu were not sensible people like the Matabele. The varungu let their wives command their houses. Sometimes the wives could shout at their husbands and yet the husbands did not beat them.

But the Nkosi was sensible, almost as sensible as a Matabele. The women knew they could try no nonsense with the Nkosi not even the woman Jek-i who came to the house very often. She looked after the Nkosi like a Matabele woman. She was always looking at his clothes to see if they were needing buttons or sewing, which was a good thing because otherwise the Nkosi would have him sewing things. The umfazi Jek-i was a little bit troublesome sometimes when she came into the kitchen and started giving him orders about the skoff but for a varungu umfazi she wasn't too bad. He approved. She was better than any of the other women he sometimes found in the Nkosi's bed in the mornings. The varungu women were strange people.

And the Nkosi himself was a strange one. The Nkosi had some strange spirits in him. He was not like other white men who were always seeking pleasure and money. He was not a happy one, the Nkosi, not a very happy one. It must be an evil spirit maybe that bedevilled him. He drank very much tshwala, the Nkosi, but he did not drink like the other white men at the hotels and at ma-club-i. He drank in his ma-study while he sat at his table and wrote all his words on the paper. Always he was sitting at his table writing on the paper. Sometimes in the early mornings the light was still burning in the ma-study and when the Nkosi left for the Court-i his face was white and his eyes were red and a man could see that he had been writing his words all the night. Sometimes Samson looked through the window late at night and he saw the Nkosi sitting at the table and staring across the room for a long time with his pen in his hand. And in the mornings all the ashtrays in the ma-study would be full and the floor would have many cigarette ends on it and sometimes the Nkosi's skoff would still be in the oven the next morning. When he found the Nkosi still working very early in the morning he knew that the following morning he would find a woman in the Nkosi's bed. But never the woman Jek-i.

Samson Ndhlovu paused in his swiping and felt in his pocket for a cigarette. He found one and put it in his mouth. As he finished lighting it he saw the man standing on the roadside outside the gate. He was leaning against a tree and he was watching him. It was the same man who had been standing in the same place yesterday.

Samson held the smoke in his lungs as he studied him. Then he let the smoke out and he spat carefully on his hands and he turned his back and began swiping the grass again.

Samson Ndhlovu was drunk, happy drunk. The Ma-Petticoat Cocktail bar was a good place to be drunk in on a Friday night, pay-day night. The Ma-Petticoat was full of beer and noise and music and laughing and dancing and full of those fat black bouncing-breast five-shilling whores. There was an impromptu band of two guitarists and a drummer and a trumpeter competing with the canned music of the loudspeakers and there were two groups of thumping bumping sweating dancers and there were gambling schools.

Samson Ndhlovu was a good-looking man. His was the tall loose-limbed muscular blackness that a white tee-shirt and a pair of faded jeans became, the type of nigger who in London would always have a blonde Maisie or Violet or Betty hanging on his arm. He looked very good tonight with the sweat glistening on his broad black grinning face, his long legs and back and arms swinging and undulating to the thump of music. He danced by instinct, to the rhythm that thumped in the air and his Zulu veins. Samson Ndhlovu was immensely pleased with life and with himself. And he was pleased with the big shiny-faced woman dancing with him. She was the best-looking umfazi he had seen in a long time and she was all his for five shillings, a sensible way for a man to spend five shillings. And she spoke Sindebele.

'Let us go now,' she shouted.

Samson stopped dancing and grabbed her arm and pulled her through the thronging beerhall. She followed laughing and shouting to her friends. He led her outside into the big enclosed dirt yard. He pulled her behind a lavatory wall and shoved his hand on to her breast and pinned her against the wall.

'Let us go to my house,' she giggled fatly.

'Let us go then.'

They staggered happily across the enclosure to the main gates. She was laughing and shouting to her friends sitting on benches outside, Samson was humming to the music blaring out from the hall.

'This way.'

They passed through the gate into the darkness of the gravel road. The streetlights were dim and a long way apart and the old houses on the sides were in patchy darkness. There were dim forms of people walking and now and again they passed through the dusty pools of yellow streetlight. She led him down a dirt lane with patchy rubber hedges on both sides. He had his left arm round the woman and his right hand was on her breast.

'How much further is it to your house, woman—'

'It is near.'

The black forms stepped out of the rubber hedge from both sides and Samson turned to face the movement. Before he could lash out a knobstick crashed down on his head and he went down. As he lay on the ground they beat him on the head. Then they picked him up by his arms and they carried him down the lane and into the backyard of the woman's house and in through the back door.

'Tshombe—!'

The black hand swiped across his face and jerked his head to the side. He fell sideways off the chair and lay in a heap with his wrists tied behind his back.

'Sell-out – Vatengesi—!'

The youth behind him kicked him in the back and Samson grunted. The short man yanked his head up and then punched him in the mouth.

'Tshombe—'

Then they stopped and the big man came and stood over him. 'Now tell us who you are.' Samson looked up at him from the floor. 'I am Paradise Mpofu,' he said through fat raw lips.

'You are Samson Ndhlovu.'

'I am Paradise—'

'You are Samson Ndhlovu. The Party sent you to Russia to learn how to fight for the country. And instead you are a Tshombe.'

Samson closed his eyes and shook his head and waited for the kicks. They came and then the big man told them to stop.

'The way to this man's tongue is through his testicles. Put him on his back.'

Samson bucked on the floor and twisted and kicked out and screamed and shouted but they held him down on his back and they held his legs apart.

'First I will kick you not very hard.'

The shoe came back and it jabbed between his legs and Samson screamed.

'Who are you?'

The sweat was wet on his face and chest and the pain was screaming between his legs. '*Samson*—' he shouted. 'Samson, Samson—' The black faces grinned.

'The Party sent you to Russia?' The black shoe was hovering

between his legs.

'Yes – yes—'

'You are a sell-out—'

'Yes – yes.'

'Put him back in the chair, boys.' They heaved him up into the chair again. He sat hunched forward with his head on his knees. 'Are you suffering, Tshombe?'

'Yes,' he groaned.

'Do not hit him any more, boys. We want him alive, not dead.' He turned to Samson. 'Do you like your life?'

'Yes,' Samson said between his knees.

The big man paced up and down the room.

'The Party wanted you to take action when you came back but instead you are a Tshombe.'

Samson said nothing.

'Do you know what has happened to the Freedom Fighters who went to Russia with you?' Samson shook his head.

'Some are in jail waiting to be hanged. The others are in jail for many years.'

Samson waited.

'You are the only one who has not done his duty.'

The big black man bent down and grabbed Samson's head and yanked it back.

'Now it is time for you to do your duty,' he said into his face.

He shook the bleeding head from side to side.

'Do you understand?'

'Yes.' The word was shaken out of his head.

'And if you do not do your duty we will catch you again. And if you run to the police we will inform them that you are a trained Freedom Fighter and you will go to jail for many years'—the man was still shaking his head and his words were coming out in jerks—'and even in the jails we will get you, for the jails are full of our men—'

He stood back snarling and his fist crashed into Samson's face again. The chair crashed over and Samson sprawled. They picked him up and put him back on the chair.

'Are you alive, Tshombe?'

Samson nodded.

'Do you like your life?'

Samson nodded again.

'Then listen to me. Even when you come out of jail we will catch you again. And when we rule the country you will be burned alive with all the other Tshombes. Do you understand?'

Samson nodded.

'And your wives and your children will be burned alive, do you understand?'

Samson nodded.

'*Do you understand!*' he screamed.

'Yes,' Samson said, 'I understand.'

The man squatted on his haunches in front of Samson and peered up at him.

'Now I will give you your orders,' he said. 'Are you listening carefully?'

Samson looked him in the eyes.

'There will come soon a night which is called the Night of the Long Knives. On that night every man will kill his employer, and his employer's wife and his employer's children. There will be no white men left, and then we will have the country. And men like you will have to fight the police and the soldiers. The Night of the Long Knives is near. You will be told about it. Before that, you must take some action. Your first action will be to throw a petrol bomb.'

Samson nodded.

'It will be good action, Ndhlovu. It will show the varungu that the people of Zimbabwe are very unhappy about their country. You will throw it into the house of a man who has been responsible for many of our Freedom Fighters being hanged by their necks. That will frighten the varungu very much.'

Samson nodded and waited.

'Do you know whose house you will throw your petrol bomb into, Ndhlovu?' Samson shook his head.

'You will throw it into the house of your own master, Ndhlovu.' Samson's eyes widened.

'And if you fail to throw it, Ndhlovu, we will kill you and somebody else will burn your master, as we burned the policeman Tambudza—'

Chapter Forty-Nine

'*Samson*' – rap rap rap went the knocking on his door – '*Samson—*' rap rap rap. 'Where are you, wake up – vuka vuka – why aren't you working—?'

It was dark in his hut, only slivers of light coming in through the cracks and under the door. The door was rattling. Samson woke up and lifted himself on to his elbow and he winced. His head was thumping and his whole body ached. He opened his mouth to speak and it was dry and fat. From the chinks of light he could tell it was late in the morning. He remembered the beating of the night before in a flash.

'Vuka, Samson—'

He recognised the woman's voice. The woman Jek-i, the Nkosi's woman. He shoved himself up on his elbow again and answered her but his voice was a croak.

'Okay, Nkosikazi—'

'Wake up, Samson,' the voice came through the door, 'it is late and you aren't working. The Nkosi has telephoned me from Fort Victoria to say he is coming home tomorrow early and the house is not ready—'

'Okay, Nkosikazi—'

He heard her turn and walk away down the back path to the house. He swung his legs to the floor and he winced again. He was very stiff and aching and his head was thumping and he could feel his left eyelid fat over his eyeball. He put his hand to his head and rested his elbows on his knees. He remembered it all now. He remembered them unblindfolding him and their footsteps running away into the night and when he got the scarf off his eyes he was in the middle of a dark lane somewhere in Harare.

It had been dawn when he found his quarters. He remembered his instruction and his stomach turned over but he shoved it into the background. He stood up and straightened himself experimentally. Then he went to the cracked door and unbolted it and pulled it open. The sun broke into the dark smoke-stained room, on to the old ashes of his cooking fire and on to his rickety iron bed and his paraffin boxes on which stood his things. He screwed up his face against the light and he winced again. He saw the woman Jek-i's car shining in the sun through the bamboo thicket. The hens with chickens were resting with them in the shade of the wild rose hedge that grew round the side of the chicken run. The kitchen door was open. He looked up at the sun. About midday. He turned and picked up the chip of mirror from the paraffin box and examined his face. It was swollen and his mouth was encrusted with dried blood. He pulled on his tunic and picked up a handful of cold ashes from the fireplace and went to the garden tap and scoured his teeth with his finger and the ashes and he doused his face and then he walked down the kitchen door.

'It's very naughty of you.' Jackie had her back to the door as she ran her eye along the pantry shelf taking stock. 'Just because the boss is away it does not mean that you can take a holiday—oh!—' She looked at him. '*Samson* – what's happened to you?'

Samson grinned sheepishly and then winced when it hurt.

'It is nothing, Nkosikazi, I have just been fighting.'

'Samson – you look terrible …' She stepped up to him and touched his face lightly and peered short-sightedly at his puffed face. 'You must go to a doctor—'

'It is nothing.'

'But—' Jackie studied him, 'are you sure?' She peered at him again.

'Sureah, Nkosikazi.'

'Whatever have you been doing—?'

Samson hung his head and looked around for something to do. 'Some boys fight too much Friday,' he said.

'Well, you must report them to the police—'

Samson tried to grin again and stopped when his lip cracked open. He shook his head.

'No,' he said. 'Police send me to jail—'

Jackie put her hands on her hips and sighed. She decided he was all right.

'You and the master—!' she said and she grinned. 'You are both very bad men, that is why you like to work together, hey? Too much women, hey Samson? – you fight over the umfazis?'

Samson was relieved.

'Too much tshwala, Nkosikazi—' he said trying to look sheepish.

'Yes, well—' she dropped the kitchen kaffir and said in English – 'I have no sympathy.' She moved to the electric mains and switched on the refrigerator.

'In my car,' she said, 'there is a box of beer. Bring it in, please.'

Samson came back with the box. It hurt him to carry it but he dared not show it in case she insisted on taking him to hospital. Then the policeman on duty at the Outpatients Department would start asking questions.

'Put them in the fridge, please,' she said, 'so the boss has some cold beer when he comes in—'

She was packing tins of food on to the shelves. Samson squatted down in front of the fridge and groaned out loud. She turned and looked at him. Then she went to her handbag and took two Veganin tablets from the phial she carried for her period pains. She picked up a quart of beer and snapped the cap off it and held them out in her white hands.

'Here you are, big boy,' she said. 'On behalf of the Nkosi who is most sympathetic to drunks—'

Samson took the tablets and the bottle with a wince of a smile. Jackie nodded to the back door.

'Go'n sleep it off,' she crisped, 'I'm going to play golf now. When you wake up come back here and make everything nice. The boss is arriving first thing in the morning. See that everything is tidy for him because he is very tired. Too many skellums in the Court in Fort Victoria—'

Chapter Fifty

Samson felt better when he had finished the quart of beer but his hands were still shaking and he felt very nervous. Jackie had gone. He went down the path to the kitchen and took another beer from the refrigerator. He reckoned that the Nkosi would not mind if he knew what troubles he had. Then he remembered the bottle of red pills in the bathroom, the pills the Nkosi took when he had been working all night and still had to work all day, the pills he had tried in Bulawayo. He swallowed two and went back to his kia and sat down on the bed and thought.

He thought again about going to the police and he realised over again it was no good. The Party would see to it that he went to jail, if they didn't kill him first. There was only one way of doing it so nobody got hurt. It had to be done tonight, before the Nkosi came back. If he waited it might be many days before he had another opportunity. Tonight it would be safe and nobody would be hurt and maybe the Party would be satisfied. Maybe the police would even catch the Party men. Then he realised that was even worse than he telling the police first, for the Party men would report him first and then the police would surely never believe him.

'Tonight is the only chance,' he said aloud to the smoke-stained wall of his kia.

The two red pills and the two bottles of beer were making him feel much stronger. He was even feeling calm and almost happy.

He thought about petrol. It was impossible for even white men to get petrol these days. Paraffin. He went to his primus stove and shook it but there was very little in it. He poured the paraffin from the stove into the empty beer bottle. Then he went to the kitchen again and he took the bottle of benzine off the pantry shelf arid carried it back to his kia. He poured some into the beer bottle. He pushed a hole through a cork and he pushed a piece of string through the hole. He lit the string and let it burn a little and then he snuffed it out. Now it looked real. He pushed the cork and wick into the bottle and examined it critically. It looked real. He smiled sadly. It would frighten the Nkosi all right. Then he looked around for a sock. He carefully wiped his fingerprints off the bottle with the sock. Then he slid the sock on to his right hand like a glove. He picked up the bomb with his socked hand and he went through the motions of throwing it experimentally. Then he returned the benzine bottle to the pantry and he put the bomb and the sock under his bed to wait till dark.

At eight o'clock he stood in the garden under his master's dark bedroom window. He held the bottle in his socked hand. He did not light the wick again. He aimed for the centre window pane and he drew back his arm and he flung the bomb through the glass. He heard it shatter against the far wall. He ran round the house to his kia and he jumped into his bed and after a long time he went to sleep.

The police found six things linking Samson Ndhlovu to the crime. On the broken glass bottle they found four wool fibres corresponding exactly in thickness, colour and substance with the sock in Samson Ndhlovu's kia. From that sock the forensic scientist recovered .127 of a cubic centimetre of a mixture of benzine and paraffin and traces of the same mixture were found amongst the fragments of beer bottle in Mahoney's room. The name of Mahoney's grocer was stamped upon the label of the beer bottle. In Samson's room was a length of string identical to the charred wick found in the broken bomb. On Samson's floor were fragments of cork identical to the cork found in the neck of the bomb. And in his primus stove was the paraffin and in Mahoney's pantry stood the benzine.

Samson Ndhlovu denied all knowledge of the crime. He said he had spent the night with a woman in Harare. He did not know the woman's name and he did not know her address.

Chapter Fifty-One

It was a bright fresh Rhodesian morning under a sparkling blue sky and the sun shone golden on long thick green grass and the earth was damp and rich after the rains. The Borrowdale Road was busy with late model cars, despite petrol rationing. Salisbury looked gracious and luscious and prosperous. Not, Mahoney thought, on the brink of bankruptcy. Or was it on the brink of bankruptcy? It bloody well should be in view of all Britain's sanctions, but everywhere life seemed to be going on as normal. No riots, no extraordinary crime wave, no soldiers to be seen. The black traffic constables still stood at the pedestrian crossings and waved the whole city to a halt so that half-a-dozen school children could cross the road.

'i hate harold' the sticker said on the rear window of the car ahead of him. Every second car in Rhodesia bore 'I hate Harold' stickers. The other common sticker read: 'Thank You South Africa-Dankie Suid Afrika' on a background of a petrol pump.

I hate harold. Mahoney shook his head. How bloody childish. But how bloody true! Everybody hates Harold. Even me, now, Mahoney thought, even the stable moderates, the ones with a bit of nous who had been dead against UDI were now all behind Ian Smith because Harold was being so beastly. You couldn't help hating Harold. Harold stopping old Rhodesian ladies' pensions, Harold stealing all our London money, Harold invalidating our passports, Harold stopping all our oil, Harold stopping us from selling our tobacco, Harold refusing to sell us anything. Harold this and Harold that.

And now Horrible Harold had held a special Commonwealth Prime Ministers' Conference in Nigeria, for Chrissake. What was

Great Mother Britain coming to? The British Prime Minister held to ransom by tinpot black states over Rhodesia. Tinpot black states threatening to chuck Britain out of the Commonwealth, for Chrissake. Ghana and Tanzania severing diplomatic relations with Britain, yet Britain still pouring in millions of pounds in aid, for Chrissake. And Britain selling arms to the Viet Cong and the Cubans! What kind of set-up is this? For Chrissake.

The Borrowdale Road traffic swept round the bend, past Government House. Gracious palatial Government House, looking a bit sick now. His Excellency the Governor was now in law the sole legal Government of Rhodesia, appointed so by Horrible Harold, but looking very sick. Ian Smith had taken away all his trappings, his guards and his cars and his salary, he had even cut off His Excellency's telephone. Now Ian Smith was charging His Excellency rent for Government House.

'Sick sick sick,' Mahoney said aloud.

He pulled up outside the huge old colonial-style High Court. He bought a newspaper on the corner and walked upstairs to his office and sat down. He put his knee up on the desk and opened the newspaper. Then he straightened as he read the headlines:

MILITARY COUP IN NIGERIA

A smile spread across his face as he sped through the item then he scrambled off his chair and went out of his door and across the corridor.

'Hey, Phil, you see there's been a military coup in Nigeria—?'

Phillip grinned at him.

'Yeah, it was on the morning news. Beautiful, isn't it?'

'And only last week Horrible Harold was holding his precious Prime Ministers' conference there on how to restore law and order in Rhodesia—'

'Isn't it beautiful?'

'Hell, why didn't it happen when Harold was there? *That* would have been beautiful. Imagine if they had captured Harold and held him to ransom.'

'Held him up for auction—'

'In his underpants.'

'Yes, in his underpants. There would have been some pretty high bids from Rhodesia.'

Mahoney shook his head.

'The showpiece of Africa!' he said. 'God, it makes a laughing stock of Britain. All those gentlemen shouting the odds round the conference table about how the Rhodesian rebels should be put in their places, and outside the door their own rebels are whetting their spears.'

'Ian Smith must be grinning all over his face—'

'He sure must be.'

Mahoney turned and crossed the corridor back to his office. He took off his suit jacket and slung it over the chair and he started taking off his tie. He put the paper down on the desk and glanced at it as he fiddled to loosen the collar studs. There were white blanks dotted all over the front page where the Government censors had chopped out news items likely to mislead the unsophisticated members of the public and cause alarm and despondency. Mahoney put the court collar round his neck and snapped it over the studs and flicked the newspaper to the front page to see if there was a report of his case. Yes, there it was, front page news:

COURT TOLD OF RUSSIAN SABOTAGE TRAINING:

'The trial of the twenty-four Rhodesian Africans charged with having undergone sabotage training in Moscow in contravention of the Law and Order Maintenance Act entered its twenty-second day in the High Court today.

'The Crown alleges that during the period between April and October 1965 the twenty-four men were recruited by ZAPU officials in Zambia to undergo courses in sabotage and intelligence in Russia, Communist China and North Korea ...'

The door opened and Peter came in. He was also wearing a court collar and white cravat.

'Morning, Joe—'

'Morning, Pete—' Mahoney said.

Pete sat down. He felt in his pocket then held out a packet of cigarettes.

'Thanks,' Mahoney said. He lit it and started coughing. 'Excuse me.' He sat down and looked at Pete.

'How's your case going?' Pete said.

Mahoney shrugged. 'Okay. Enough to make an undertaker sick.' He flicked the six-inch pile of paper with the back of his hand. 'Look at it. Those are just my notes of the cross-examination so far. The brief is another six inches high.'

'Much law in it?'

Mahoney shook his head. 'Not much. The law's straightforward. Just mountains and mountains of fact. How's your roll going in B Court?'

Pete nodded. He shifted in his chair.

'I'm starting your boy Samson's case today.'

'Today? I thought you weren't starting it till Monday—'

Pete nodded. 'I've decided to bring it forward a bit.'

Mahoney was silent a moment. 'Oh-huh,' he said, nodding. He fiddled with his pen.

'Is it true that you're paying Mike's fees?'

'Yes.'

Pete shook his head. 'Unusual situation,' he said. 'Crown counsel has his house bombed, then hires the best defence lawyer to defend the accused.'

Mahoney looked at him. 'It's not so unusual when you bear in mind that, he saved my life once.'

'But he tried to kill you.'

'He didn't try to kill me. He knew I wasn't in the house.'

'Well, he tried to burn your house down, then.'

Mahoney grunted, 'Yes.' He got up and pulled on his jacket and sat down again. Then he stood up again and turned and looked out the window, 'I'm not so sure he did,' he said, 'there's more in this than meets the eye. Samson wouldn't burn my house, he's not interested in politics—'

Pete grunted.

'You can't believe your faithful servant would do it to you?' he said flatly. 'Well I can. Old Mau Mau trick. Happened many a time in Kenya that the trusted cookboy who had been with the family for twenty years and dandled all the bwana's children on his knee was the one to slit his bwana's throat. And his memsahib's throat, and the kids' he'd dandled on his knee. The Mau Mau made them do it because the more horrible the murder the more Charlie cookboy felt bound to the Mau Mau, like Macbeth. Having waded so far into the blood to turn back is as tedious as go o'er. It's a kind of initiation ceremony with these chaps—'

Mahoney waved his cigarette irritably.

'I know that,' he said. 'The point is that whoever intimidated him wanted to get me, obviously. Yet Samson threw it when I wasn't there. So? He was obviously pulling a fast one on the intimidators—'

'That story won't help him,' Pete said flatly, 'because he still threw it into a residential building and that's a capital offence even if nobody was in it.'

Mahoney closed his eyes till the interruption passed.

'And if he was pulling a fast one on his intimidators he could have thrown a fake bomb too. Hell, if he really wanted to burn the joint down he would have gone back when he saw the bomb didn't work and put a match to the thatch.'

'You've forgotten one thing, Joe: the wick on the bomb was burned.'

'He could have done that beforehand to make the job look authentic'

Pete stood up and put his foot on the chair.

'Yes, well, that's a theory,' he said, 'but it's no good to him if he doesn't say it.'

Mahoney shook his head.

'The stupid bastard,' he said, '—if only he would tell the truth.'

'Have you been to see him?'

Mahoney waved his hand.

'I've been down to the prison with Mike to see him umpteen times. But every time he insists that he didn't do it, says he knows nothing about it. Stupid bastard.'

Pete shrugged.

'Have you explained your theory to him?'

'I've explained everything to him a dozen times in his own language. He still insists he didn't do it. He just sits there with that wooden expression on his black face. You know the wog,' he said, 'you can talk till you're blue in the face. He gets the idea into his head that when he's in trouble the best thing is to deny. Deny everything. Deny your fingerprints. Any port in a storm. Maybe he doesn't even trust me when the chips are down, thinks I'm trying to get him swung maybe.'

Pete looked around for an ashtray.

'Use the big one,' Mahoney said, nodding to the floor.

'Yes, well, he'll swing all right if he sticks to that one,' Pete said calmly.

Mahoney nodded.

'Maybe the Executive Council will reprieve him,' he said, 'it's not a very serious case.' Pete's eyebrows went up.

'I think it's very serious when the ZAPU thugs start the Mau Mau stunt of getting the trusted servants to butcher their own masters.'

Mahoney nodded, 'I suppose so.' He paused. 'Listen Pete – I've kept my nose out of this case, but do me a favour: go easy on him if he gets into the witness box. He's a dead duck already. Try to bring out all the mitigating features in the case for the benefit of the Executive Council.'

'Okay, of course I will—'

'And Pete? If he gives evidence and you bring him to his knees in cross-examination, give him a chance to admit that he did it but threw a fake bomb. Put it to him in so many words and see what he says—'

'Okay, okay,' he said stiffly, 'of course I will.' There was a pause.

'You see,' Pete said, feeling for his cigarettes '—I'm in rather a different position to you. I don't believe this trusted servant lark. I don't believe you can trust these chaps further than you can kick them. They'll cut our throats as soon as it suits them. It happened in Kenya, it'll happen again here. These long-haired liberals overseas don't appreciate that there's only one thing a wog understands and that is a swift kick in the backside when he steps out of line. That's the way he was treated fifty years ago by his chiefs, that's the way it'll always be. Give him power and he'll abuse it. Look at Nigeria. Look at Ghana.'

Mahoney nodded.

'I don't believe for one moment,' Pete continued, lighting his cigarette, 'the wogs would ever let us stay if they ever got to power here, even if we were born here. And as for you and me who have prosecuted most of their heroic petrol-bombers and saboteurs,' he nodded out the window '—they'll hang you and me from those lamp-posts out there. I mean that. Especially since UDI. You and I have been so much in the daily news prosecuting their heroes, they'll lynch us publicly. You and me'll be among the first to go, and don't kid yourself about that one, chum.'

Mahoney nodded.

'I don't kid myself,' he said flatly.

Peter blew out smoke.

'So I'm not awfully sympathetic towards your pal Samson. As far as I'm concerned he's your cookboy who tried to kill you for no rhyme or reason other than that you're white and you've done your duty, and I don't want the ZAPU thugs to get the same idea about my cookboy—'

A distant chanting noise came through Mahoney's window, from way up Third Street. Pete cocked his ear and listened. Mahoney did not turn. The chanting drew closer, a deep throated melodious up and down up and down. Pete moved to the window and looked out. The chanting was loud now. Through the jacaranda tree tops outside the window he glimpsed the big blue prison truck rumbling along Third Street towards the back entrance to the High Court. There were two police Land Rovers escorting it, loaded with armed policemen. A crowd of African men, women and children were gathered on the roadside and they were waving to the prison truck and some of the African women were wiping their eyes.

'Here come your twenty-four Red-trained hoods,' Pete said.

The chanting was very loud now, as the trucks turned across the road towards the Court building.

'Yes,' Mahoney said, without looking up. 'It's the same every morning. They sound very brave, don't they? It would be quite moving if you could forget that almost every one of them confessed to the police the moment they were caught.'

'Yes,' Pete said out the window '—James Bond wouldn't think much of this bunch. Therein, my friend, lies our salvation. What is it they're singing?'

'I'm not much good at Chisezuru,' Mahoney said turning slowly to the window. He put a cigarette in his mouth: 'Something about, "We are going to rule the country." ZAPU is going to have to wait a long time if they're going to rely on tits like that. Imagine trained saboteurs re-entering the country with their pockets bulging with evidence of My Trip to Moscow and Peking.'

Pete snorted. The prison truck was trundling slowly out of sight past the corner of the building.

'Twenty years, boys,' he said, 'that's what your little holiday to Moscow is going to cost you.'

Mahoney turned from the window and puffed on his cigarette vigorously.

'Except Samson Ndhlovu,' he said. 'He's in that truck, too. He only threw one dud bomb and it's going to cost him his life.'

Chapter Fifty-Two

The next day was Friday, and at four o'clock there were black thunderclouds hanging low in the sky and it was very close and warm and dusky and counsel's robes were hot. A Court adjourned at four o'clock and the twenty-four black men were filed down to their holding cells below the Court room. Mahoney slung his gown and wig on to a chair and hurried down the corridor to B Court. He tiptoed down the aisle and slid on to an empty bench and sat down.

Pete turned his head, saw Mahoney in the gallery and nodded briefly. Mahoney nodded. Samson had his back to Mahoney, sitting upright in the dock with an African policeman sitting beside him. Mike was on his feet addressing the Court. It sounded like the tail end of his argument. He didn't seem to be saying it with much conviction – what could he say? Mahoney thought. The red-robed judge was bent over his notebook, listening tiredly with his hand shielding his eyes. The assessors on either side of him were sitting back in their chairs.

Well, that looks like that, Samson my boy, Mahoney thought.

Mike finished his address and sat down and sat back and looked at the judge. The judge nodded absently, squinted at the clock at the back of the courtroom then he turned and whispered in turn to each assessor. Then he looked back at the bar and Mike and Pete stood up.

'Well, gentlemen – the Court will deliver judgment in, say, half an hour? We will take some tea and resume in half an hour or as soon thereafter as possible.'

The judge pushed himself to his feet and everybody stood up.

'Silence in Court!' the orderly bellowed, and the judge and assessors walked to their private door. Everybody stood still until the judge disappeared and then counsel stood easy and Pete took out his cigarettes and tossed one along the bar to Mike. Mahoney caught Samson's eye as he was led off to the cells below and they nodded to each other. Mahoney went to the bar and took one of Pete's cigarettes without asking. Mike shuffled over to him.

'Well, what d'you think?' Mahoney asked both of them.

Mike tilted back his wig and shrugged.

'He's a goner,' he said and Pete nodded. Mike shrugged again and lit his cigarette. 'Sorry, Joe, but what could I do?'

'Did he give evidence?'

Mike nodded, exhaling smoke.

'Yes, and he wouldn't admit a bloody thing. He made an idiot of himself in the box.'

'He *is* an idiot.'

He turned and walked to the dock. He opened the little gate of the dock and peered down the stone steps, and then he looked around for a policeman in the Courtroom.

'Come and open the cells for me,' he called, 'I want to see the accused.'

The black policeman preceded Mahoney down the steps to the bottom and juggled the key in the thick wooden door.

It was a long dark cellar with the dark thunder-clouded afternoon shining dully through the iron bars at the far end. There were two cells side by side and a dim electric light burning overhead. An African constable sat on a stool struggling to read a newspaper. He stood up when he saw Mahoney and straightened his khaki tunic.

'Which cell is the accused Ndhlovu in?'

'This one, sah.'

'Open it.'

The constable swung the big iron door open. Samson was sitting on the bench under the small iron grid. He looked up listlessly as Mahoney entered. He shuffled to his feet. The cell was dim and the walls were painted brown with many scratch marks on them, and there was a dented latrine bucket in the corner. The cell smelt of yesterday's disinfectant overlaid with today's sweat and latrine bucket.

'Kunjani?' Mahoney said.

Samson looked at Mahoney's nose, not his eyes.

'Ngiyaphila. Ngingabuza wena?' he answered quietly.

'Ngiyaphila. Be seated.' They both sat down on the wooden bench. Samson rested his elbows on his knees and clasped his hands between them and leaned forward and looked at the cement floor beneath his feet and waited.

Mahoney leaned back and looked at his profile. The man's face was wooden, giving nothing away. He was breathing slowly and his eyes were surly and hooded but there was moisture on his forehead and on his lip and a long thick rivulet of sweat ran down the side of his face from his ear and glistened in the dull light from the grid. The light shone on the back of his black woolly head, and between the short tight curls sweat glistened on the chocolate scalp.

Mahoney felt in his suit pocket for his cigarettes and held the box out to Samson.

'Thank you.' Samson took one. Mahoney sat back and blew smoke out.

'Eh – eeh,' Samson said slowly.

'Eh – eeeh.'

Samson nodded between his knees and blew smoke onto the floor. 'So I am going to die, Nkosi?'

Mahoney watched his profile as he pulled on the cigarette.

'The ma-judgi is still considering the verdict,' he said emptily.

Samson shook his head shortly and put the cigarette back to his mouth, still looking at the floor between his feet. He took the smoke deep and spoke as he exhaled it.

'But I am going to die,' he said, 'the ma-judgi will find me guilty.'

Mahoney didn't answer. Samson twisted his head round slowly and looked half-upwards at him, waiting for an answer. The rivulet of sweat shone down his chocolate neck.

Mahoney looked him in the eye. He nodded.

'Yes, old man.'

Samson turned his head back to look at the floor.

'What are we waiting for then?'

'The ma-judgi is thinking out his words.'

Samson nodded slowly to the floor. Mahoney opened his mouth again to speak but Samson took a breath to say something and frowned at the floor like a man about to mention something that has always puzzled him but which he has never got around to asking before.

'But I will be hanged even though the Nkosi was not in the house? If the Nkosi was not in the house, how could I injure the Nkosi's body?'

It was his first indirect admission that he had thrown the bomb.

'Yes,' Mahoney said.

'Why?'

'That is the law, old man. The ma-judgi has no choice in the matter.'

Samson nodded again.

Mahoney pulled on his cigarette.

'But,' he said, 'you still have a right of appeal. And, thereafter, the high ones in the Government reconsider the ma-judgi's sentence and they can lessen the sentence.'

Samson did not look up. He gave a small shrug.

'I am without hope of that,' he said matter-of-factly.

Mahoney did not contradict him. They were silent for a moment, then Samson said tonelessly: 'The boys in the prison, they say that soon the Government in England will send soldiers here and defeat the white man here. Then they will give the Government to the black men and we will be liberated and we will be made heroes. They say we will be given plenty of money and farms and cattle, and those of us who are already hanged they will make statues of us and put them where the statues of Rhodes stand in Jameson Avenue.'

Samson looked sideways at Mahoney to see his reaction.

Mahoney nodded. 'That could be,' he said.

Samson smirked wryly.

'The wise ones in prison say that then they will hang all the white men who put them in jail. And the African police will have to go back to Europe with the Europeans.'

Mahoney nodded.

'What else do they say in the prison, old man?'

Samson shrugged.

'They say Britain will now do all their work for them in getting the country from the white men. They will not have to fight too much now because Britain will send the soldiers. They say it is very good for the black man that the white man has stolen independence because now the white man is finished, like a man who masturbates does not have the strength to take a woman afterwards.'

Mahoney nodded again.

'What else?'

'Nothing much. They are youths with big mouths who say the same thing over and over again. They say that when the black man rules the country we will all be very rich, we will all have motorcars and plenty money and white women.' He shrugged again.

'And what will they do if Britain does not send soldiers?'

Samson twisted his head to look at Mahoney again.

'Then it will be the Night of the Long Knives,' he said slowly. 'They say that then every black man will kill his master and his master's wife and the children all in one night. And we will break out from the jail and fight.'

Mahoney pulled on his cigarette.

'When will this be?'

Samson shrugged.

'We will be told.'

'And you, old man? What will you do?' Samson snorted softly.

'I will already be dead, Nkosi,' he said. 'But if I were alive—' he sighed and shrugged, 'I would fight too, so that I can escape the gallows. But,' a thin wry smile flickered once, 'I will not kill the Nkosi. The Nkosi is like my elder brother or my father.' He shrugged again.

They were silent for a moment.

'Old man?'

'Yes?'

'Listen, old man. You have admitted a short time ago that you had thrown the bomb. Listen'—he held up his hand to silence the black man—'Listen, old man, what I am about to say is very very important. It will save your life. Are you listening?'

Samson was looking at his feet.

'I am listening, but I did not throw the bomb.'

Mahoney continued: 'This is important. If the ma-judgi finds you guilty, the law says he must sentence you to death. But before he passes sentence he must also ask you if you have any reason why you should not be sentenced to death. Now this is very important. When he asks you that question, you should tell him three things. First,' Mahoney looked at Samson steadily and ticked them off on his fingers. 'First, that you are very very sorry for what you have done.' He paused. 'Second, if you were forced into doing this thing, you must tell him you were forced, and you must tell him all the details about how you were forced. Third, if the bomb was a fake you *must* tell the judge now. It is your last chance.'

Samson shook his head.

'I have heard. But I did not throw the bomb.'

'Samson,' Mahoney said sharply, 'the time for lies is finished. If you tell the judge the truth, then there is a good chance that the high ones in Government when they consider the question of mercy will decide not to hang you. A very good chance, because we do not like to hang people. Do you understand?'

Samson nodded.

'I understand, but I did not throw the bomb.'

'Christ,' Mahoney said in English. Then in Sindebele: 'Don't be a stupid fool. Do not lie to me!' He raised his voice angrily.

A voice echoed through the cell corridor. It was the European Court orderly.

'Bring up the accused—'

Mahoney took hold of Samson's shoulder.

'The judge is ready now.' He squeezed the shoulder. 'Good luck, induna. I will be sitting directly behind you. Here—' He lit a cigarette hastily and put it in Samson's mouth. Then he stuffed the rest of the pack and a box of matches into Samson's jacket pocket. 'Have a few puffs quickly. Now—' He shook Samson's shoulder urgently, 'hear me! Tell the judge what I told you! Do you hear me?'

Samson nodded quickly.

'Do not think that because you have denied you must continue to deny. Lawyers are used to people changing their stories. Tell the *truth,* for if you do not you will *die—*'

They were standing. The African constable was turning the key in the cell door. Samson puffed hard on the cigarette. His face was masked again but his hands were trembling. The door swung open and the African constable was in the doorway. Mahoney glanced at the constable and then turned to Samson. He punched him lightly on the shoulder and he turned and walked out past the constable and up the dim corridor.

Outside the sky was very black with rain and it was hot.

It was very quiet in the big courtroom, quiet so that the judge's voice fell heavily loud. It was dark and still and heavy outside and the streetlights were burning, and in the courtroom the overhead lights shone yellow and old on the panelled walls. The gallery was full of black faces. Everything was very still in the courtroom, but for the shorthand writer's pens and pages. The judge leaned forward and spoke steadily into the middle distance.

He paused at the end of every sentence and the black interpreter translated sentence for sentence into Sindebele. Samson Ndhlovu did not move, he did not look at the interpreter, he stared at the wall behind the judge.

Mahoney sat, legs crossed and chin resting on his hand, listening carefully. It was a good judgment, the old boy overlooked nothing, he chose his words carefully and slowly. It was the only judgment he could deliver. It was a hanging judgment all right.

The judge sat back in his big high red leather chair.

'Accordingly,' he said, 'I find you guilty as charged.'

'Samson Ndhlovu,' the young registrar was on his feet speaking now, and Samson Ndhlovu stood up in the dock and the black constable sitting beside him shoved his helmet straight and stood up beside him, '—Samson Ndhlovu, you have been duly competed of the crime of contravening section 37, sub-section i, sub-paragraph b, sub-section i of the Law and Order Maintenance Act, Chapter 39, as amended.' The young registrar spoke tonelessly, a little nervously. He cleared his throat. 'Do you have anything, or do you'—he glanced at a piece of paper he was holding—'do you have anything, or do you know of anything, why the Sentence of Death should not be passed upon you according to the Law?'

The judge sat back looking at the ceiling. The interpreter translated it to Samson. Counsel sat very still. Mahoney craned forward, looking up at the side of Samson's neck.

Say it, he willed. *Say what I told you, for God's sake.*

Samson looked steadily at the registrar while the interpreter translated.

Say it.

Samson dropped his eyes for a moment and shuffled his feet once and then said to the interpreter: 'Yebo.'

'Yes, my Lord, I have something to say, please,' the interpreter said out loud. Mahoney closed his eyes and breathed out.

'Yes?' the judge said. 'What is it you have to say?'

'Speak,' the interpreter said.

Everything, Mahoney willed, *tell him everything—*

Samson blinked slowly again, and he straightened up and cleared his throat.

Everything—

Samson Ndhlovu spoke to the interpreter and Mahoney sat back with a groan and put his hand to his forehead.

'I have only this to say,' the interpreter said in English: 'I did not throw the bomb.'

The judge nodded.

'Anything else?'

Samson shook his head.

'No, my Lord,' the interpreter said.

The registrar stood up again and twisted his head round and looked at the judge. His Lordship nodded briefly. The registrar looked across the courtroom at the Court orderly and nodded. The orderly was on his feet and he began to chant in a deep Irish accent.

'Hear ye, hear ye, hear ye. All persons are charged to stand and keep strict silence while the Sentence of Death is passed upon the prisoner at the bar.'

The two counsel stood up, and the registrar and the judge and his two assessors.

'The sentence of the Court,' the judge said flatly and slowly, 'is that you be returned to custody, and that the Sentence of Death be executed upon you according to Law.'

Samson Ndhlovu listened passively to the interpreter, and then he blinked once and nodded his head once to the judge.

It was dark, but the stars were hidden behind the thunderclouds. The judge had gone home, the counsel had gone home, the High Court was in darkness but for the electric light burning in the cells and in the police orderly's office. The police staff were waiting for the truck to come from the prison to fetch Samson Ndhlovu.

Mahoney walked slowly up and down the dark courtyard, smoking and thinking. He was thinking, strangely, of Hong Kong. He was thinking of pulsating life and lights throbbing in crowded streets, of the jangle and jostle and bars and cars, of ships standing in the harbour, of harbour lights twinkling on the water, of the breath-taking fairyland dazzle from the top of Victoria Peak, of the salty wind on his face as he rode on his chopping junk out to the islands, of week-ends in tiny white bays with palms. He was sick sick sick and tired tired tired; he was thinking of that cell below the High Court with that solitary sweating man sitting in it waiting to be taken to Death Row, in the heart of landlocked Africa. He was sick sick sick and tired of the vast landlocked prison of darkest Africa, of the vast sullen mass of ignorance and fear and hatred.

Honk Kong, America – anywhere. How strange life is. If I had not come back, if I had gone back to America I would be rich now and Samson Ndhlovu would not be sitting in that cell. What good has come out of it? I came back to—why did I come back? I came back to, well, take part in—in evolution I guess, in a little piece of history, to be in on something worthwhile. And what have I got to show for it? A bad liver bludgeoned by drink, a couple of hundred quid, maybe, in the bank, a thick tome full of criminals I have sent down, Suzie gone and—and Samson Ndhlovu sitting in the cell. What have

I contributed? At least in America I would have made lots of widows rich when their husbands kicked the bucket. There is something to be said for that.

What, indeed, have I contributed?

Hong Kong, America – I am sick of primitive smouldering Africa. A seething swamp that needs to be drained, a swamp as big as Africa. I have contributed nothing, admitted, but what could I contribute? What can a man contribute – it's like trying to empty the ocean with a teaspoon. If every single white man in Rhodesia did his little bit, it would be no more than trying to drain the ocean with a kiddies' beach bucket. That man sitting in the cell – it was no good feeling sorry for him. It is like hearing the death screams of an animal in the bush at night as a leopard gets him. It is part of the life in the jungle – animals come and animals go and they are forgotten, for they are incidents in the life of the jungle. Necessary incidents. The antelope serves the purpose of the leopard. Samson Ndhlovu has served his purpose, he is finished, it is his death scream you hear in the night. It is but a small incident in the lifetime of the jungle. It is no good feeling sorry for him or trying to crash in there and pull the leopard off him. The only way to stop those death screams every night is to gather an army and go in there and clean up the jungle of the leopards.

That's not a bad idea, at that. But it would take one hell of a big army, for the leopard does not hunt alone. He uses the fox and the wildcat and the snake and the scorpion and the wasp and the bloody termite too.

But it's worth a try.

Mahoney shook his head.

'Hong Kong,' he said aloud, 'or America. You can't empty the bloody ocean with a teaspoon. Get away from it all—'

The prison truck arrived. The police orderly's door opened and a long shaft of light fell into the courtyard.

'Oi-Oi, Mac,' the prison officer said,'—come to fetch the stretcher case.'

'Okay, Mac'

The orderly put his head back inside his door and bellowed down the cell corridor. 'Tagwisa—!'

From down the corridor the distant hollow voice of the black constable: 'Sah?'

'Bring the Death Sentence boy.'

'Yassah.'

The prison officer flapped the collar of his tunic. 'Cor-er, 'ot ain't it?'

'Yeah,' the orderly said.

'Pity to have to make this special trip down 'ere to fetch this chap, what wi' petrol rationing an' all,' he said.

'Yeah,' the orderly said.

The orderly spotted Mahoney's cigarette glowing in the darkness. 'That you, Mr. Mahoney? I thought you'd gone home!'

'No,' Mahoney said, walking forward into the light.

'Evenin', Mr. Mahoney,' the prison officer said, ''ot enough for you, sir?'

'Just about.'

'Fink it'll rain then?'

The orderly cleared his throat.

'Did you see your boy all right, sir?'

'Yes,' Mahoney said, 'I've just left him, I've only been waiting out here a few minutes.'

The prison officer looked at Mahoney.

'Wot – is 'e your boy, then?'

'Yes,' Mahoney said.

'Cor-er,' the prison officer said.

'Treat him gently,' Mahoney said quietly, 'he's a good chap.'

The prison officer looked surprised.

'Okay, sir,' he said slowly. 'Don'tcha worry about that. They get V.I.P treatment until they're dropped. Special food and cigarettes and all.'

'I've given him about sixty cigarettes,' Mahoney said. 'Let him keep them on him, at least for tonight.'

'I'll try, sir,' the prison officer said, surprised.

The big gate at the end of the cell corridor rattled and the prison officer said: 'Well, better be gettin' along, then,' and climbed up into the truck and started it and revved the engine over. A black prison corporal was standing at the back of the truck at the door.

The iron gate of the cell corridor swung open and Samson Ndhlovu stepped through with his hands manacled in front of him. He stepped out into the darkness of the courtyard. He saw Mahoney standing there.

Mahoney walked over to him. The truck was grumbling.

'Well – good-bye, induna.'

'Good-bye, Nkosi.'

They stood awkwardly for a moment, with the orderly and the black constable hovering in the background. Then Mahoney put his new cigarette in Ndhlovu's mouth. Then he clapped his hands quietly and Samson patted one hand with the other.

'Stay well, induna.' It sounded a silly thing to say.

'Stay well, Nkosi.'

Mahoney shifted his feet and then he nodded to the orderly. The orderly came forward.

'Okay, Samson,' he said gently.

Samson coughed and started walking to the truck. The black corporal took his elbow and helped him climb up because he could not use his hands very well. He crouched into the dark truck and the corporal clanged the door shut behind him and the prison officer revved the engine.

'Farewell all,' the prison officer called out the window.

Mahoney moved round the back of the truck. He could see Samson sitting at the wire mesh. The truck gave a big growl and began to rumble forward. Then Samson turned and shouted to Mahoney above the roar.

'Nkosi—'

'Yes?' Mahoney waved to the orderly. 'Tell him to cut the engine.' The engine cut. 'Yes?' Mahoney said.

Samson cleared his throat. He spoke down through the mesh.

'Nkosi? – can I still appeal?'

'Of course, induna,' Mahoney said.

Samson cleared his throat again.

'Nkosi,' he said, 'can you please give me a note in the Nkosi's handwriting, for the prison, to tell them I am going to appeal—'

Mahoney shook his head.

'It is not necessary, old man.'

'But,' Samson frowned – 'if you do not they will hang me.'

Mahoney shook his head.

'Not yet, old man.'

Samson frowned worriedly.

'But are they not going to hang me tonight?'

Mahoney's stomach contracted. You poor bastard, you poor old bastard! Have you been sitting in that cell thinking you were going to get the chop tonight? And all you do is ask for a note. Christ. This is Africa. Give me a note, Bwana. Give me a note, the white man's magic, the thing that opens doors, the thing that explains everything, the passport from one white man to another. Give me a note to the shopkeeper telling him you want a pound of sugar. Give me a note, Bwana, to the hospital telling the ma-dokitari that I have a pain in my stomach. Give me a note to the prison, Bwana, explaining to the Bwana at the prison that he mustn't hang me tonight.

Mahoney nodded.

'They will not do anything to you for at least three months, old man. But,' he nodded kindly, 'I will give a note to the driver now, just to make sure. Do not worry.'

Samson looked relieved.

'Thank you, Nkosi.'

Mahoney raised his hand.

He went to the front of the truck.

'Tell the boy if he asks you that I have given you a note for the superintendent,' he said.

The officer winked and started the engine. The truck coughed and rumbled away down the dark alleyway.

He stood in the darkness watching the big blue shape disappear. He could not make out the man in the back behind the wire mesh. Then the truck got to the corner into the lamplight. The light shone on the wire mesh and he could see Samson Ndhlovu. He raised a hand and waved and Samson raised his manacled wrists once.

Good-bye, you poor old bastard.

He turned and walked back into the courtyard. His eyes were burning.

Christ, he thought, I want a beer.

He put his knuckles once to his eyes and squeezed, then he walked into the orderly's office and picked up the telephone and dialled a number.

'Get your fat ass down to the Long Bar, Paddy,' he said brusquely, 'we're off the wagon,' and he hung up without waiting for a reply.

He walked up the alleyway and turned right into wide Jameson Avenue. The streetlights were burning cheerily yellow and down the bottom the neon lights were flashing. Fly BOAC. Fly CAA. Fly UAT. *Fly, fly away, my boy, while yet there is time.* He looked at the statue of Cecil John Rhodes standing in the middle of Jameson Avenue and he wondered why the old buzzard was facing west instead of north, like all his other statues. Cape to Cairo Rhodes. Then he smiled grimly and gave a short laugh. *Why, of course – Rhodes's facing West because the country's going that way.*

He crossed and walked along and turned down into the Long Bar. The first person he saw sitting on a barstool was Solomon Otto Berger, very red and bulbous in the nose. He dropped his hand on his shoulder.

'Where you bin these last three months?' Solly demanded.

'On the wagon,' Mahoney said. 'Doctor's orders. Ulcer, liver, the works. *Barman—*'

Chapter Fifty-Three

'Fight?' Mahoney said. He was a little drunk. He snorted-laughed. 'Hah. Sure we *can* fight. You can put up a magnificently heroic show *fighting* it, Solomon, sure. But can you *win,* Solomon? And if you win, can you kill it, Solomon? 'Cos if you can't win the fight, Solomon, or if once you've won you've got to spend the rest of your life watching out for a stab in the back, there's no sense in fighting in the first place, is there, Solomon?'

Jacqueline's attention was divided between arguing with Mahoney and worrying about the beer. He had had eight already, she wanted to get some food inside him.

'The Jews are fighting successfully in Israel,' she said.

'The Jews, my dear girl,' Mahoney said, 'happen to number three million. And the Jews are fighting *external* aggression only, not internal *and* external. Mrs. Cohen in Jerusalem isn't afraid that little Izadore will have his throat cut by the cookboy. Mrs. Cohen does her own cooking. And most of the world is rooting for little old Israel, not trying to push her under. And the Jews, my dear girl, are tough cookies. They all get with it on kibbutzim and things, and the dollies tote guns against their tanned bulging thighs. They don't live on two acres in Greendale with four servants and two motor cars.' He took a long pull on his beer.

'Well,' Jackie said – she wriggled on the barstool defiantly – '*I'll* stay and fight.'

Mahoney leaned out and patted her unkindly on the back.

'You do that, girl. You do that small thing. But first let me tell you the kind of fighting you're going to be doing. There'll be no beating of drums, no stirring tramp tramp of boots through the streets as the soldiers march off to war. There'll be no boom of cannons at the front, no Florence Nightingale stuff for you to do up there in the trenches; there'll be no sandbags and machine-guns in the Main Street. The war you're going to fight is going to be a scream in the night, pulling your gun out from under your pillow when you hear a roof timber creak in the night. The way you're going to fight is with bars on your windows and your kids sleeping in the same locked bedroom as you. You're going to fight it with your pistol next to your soup plate in case your cookboy chops open your head when he brings the meat and potatoes to the dinner table. You're going to have your pistol balancing on the wash-basin when you sneak into the bathroom to put in your Dutch cap at nights so you don't have babies—'

Jackie blinked.

'—you're going to fight this war by driving your children to and from school because you daren't let them cycle. And there'll be no Sunday drives and picnics, I'm afraid. And your husband – well, you won't see your husband very much, I'm afraid. He'll be out most nights patrolling on Police Reserve duties, if he's lucky, or more likely he'll be out there in the Zambezi Valley trying to shoot guerillas.

'You *see,* Jacqueline, it's not going to be a *real* war like the Spanish Civil War or like Tshombe's war in the Congo. You aren't going to *see* much of the enemy. There's not going to be much to *shoot* at, Jackie. It's going to be a war of terror, Jackie. You fighters will knock off one or two, even maybe one or two thousand over a year, but it won't make any difference, Jackie, because there'll be plenty more where they came from. Look at my friend Samson Ndhlovu. They *made* him do it, Jackie. So Samson Ndhlovu gets the chop. So what? There are plenty more Samson Ndhlovus in this world for the wide boys to use.'

Mahoney took a sip of his beer.

'It's going to be like Kenya, Jackie,' he explained maddeningly – 'it's not going to be like Israel or like the wars the pioneers fought in their laagers. In our case it's going to be *worse* than Kenya, Jackie, much much worse. Because the Kenya settlers at least were doing their fighting *legally*, Great Mother Britain and the rest of the civilised world were on their side. Britain even sent troops to help. But not us, Jackie. We're outlaws. Everybody's against us. The wog who throws a petrol bomb in your child's bedroom window and burns him alive will be applauded by many for attacking the outlaws. And even if – and I repeat *if* – Britain and the United Nations don't actually send soldiers, they'll still be imposing sanctions. We'll be ground down economically and physically. And mentally. *That's* the kind of war you'll be fighting, Jackie. That's the worst kind of war. It is much better to have soldiers to fight against. And shall I tell you something? You can't win, Jackie.'

Mahoney took a long pull out of his glass. Jackie was glaring at him.

'I wish,' she said slowly, 'that you would not speak to me in that maddening way as if I were a child—'

'Sorry, kid—' Mahoney said coolly.

'*Why* can't we win?' she cried. 'Why, why why? – we've got *right* on our side—'

'Sure, Jackie, we've got most of the right on our side here. We've got a multi-racial society, or almost multi-racial, the wogs can go to our cinemas and into our pubs and there's nothing to stop a black man becoming Prime Minister right now provided he can gather the votes. Etcetera, etcetera. But don't you see honey, that what is right or wrong doesn't happen to *matter* at the moment. It doesn't happen to matter to the *politicians*. What matters to the politicians is *money* and *power*. And it happens to suit their purpose to make this the decade for Let's Stop Being Beastly to the Blacks, so that they can make money *in* Africa and keep the Communists *out*. It's more profitable and easier to be *nice* to the wogs than beastly at the moment. So if all the black countries say they want to see black men rule Rhodesia, okay, everybody else'll back them to keep all palsy-walsy—'

'Why doesn't everybody else bombard South Africa, then, to keep in palsy-walsy with the blacks?'

'Because South Africa is too important at the moment. Nice gold and diamonds. Strong army to keep the Communists at bay. South Africa'll become expendable in due course, too, but it suits the overseas politicians to be reasonable with the South Africans at the moment and just say Shame-on-you to them every now and again to keep the blacks happy.'

Jackie was looking at him intrigued, then she shook her head.

'Oh come on, now, Joe, it is not as simple as that, don't believe it. There is some sincerity in this politics business.'

Mahoney laughed softly. 'You think so? At dear old ladies' tea-parties, yes, and among those students at their bloody college debates, yes. Even among the parliamentary back-benchers, maybe. But not, *not*, my girl, in the front benches where the brass sit. *Not* in the conference room at No. 10 Downing Street. Not in Wall Street and Threadneedle Street. Not even in the Kremlin. What matters in those inner temples is *money*, kid, and how to keep making it. Why is Britain selling arms and ammunition to Cuba? To the Viet Cong for Chrissake? To South Africa? America and Britain are big friends and America is at war with the Viet Cong and at war with Cuba! But Britain is selling arms to the Communists! Why? Because it suits Britain's purpose, and her purpose is to make money. It doesn't matter that people will get killed. Britain hopes America will win the war in Vietnam, because then she'll be better able to trade in the Far East, but in the meantime she'll help the Commies fight the Yanks because it's good business. Britain doesn't want Cuba to undermine America too much, but Britain likes Cuba needling America 'cos then Britain can sell arms to Cubans. She'll only stop selling arms if the other side looks like winning, because if the Yanks actually lose, then Britain'll lose a good trading partner. The Yanks would do the same to Britain, given a chance. Don't think for one moment, my girl, that the British Government has got its bowels in an uproar about the sorry lot of the poor black man here. The British Government only wants to keep the black Commonwealth happy so they can still get their cocoa beans from Ghana and sell their trinkets to Tanzania. Until she gets into the European Common Market.' He turned to Solly. 'Right, Solly?'

Solly nodded his head. 'I guess that's pretty much right,' he said.

'Sure it's right,' Mahoney said.

He turned back to Jackie. He tapped his forefinger on the counter.

'There'll *never* be any peace now, Jackie, you'll always have your pistol dangling at your podgy thigh, my girl. You *can't* win. Not even the South Africans can, let alone little old us.'

He looked at her.

'And,' he said, 'I'm not going to beat my brains out trying. I'll sit back somewhere and read about your efforts in the newspaper.'

Jackie was looking steadily into his eyes and her eyes were hard.

'So!' she said. 'So. That's that. What exactly *are* you going to do, pray?'

Mahoney shrugged and snapped his fingers for the barman.

'Same again here, Alfonse.'

'Do?' He sat back on his barstool and held his arms out and made an airplane noise. 'Get the hell out of it, that's what.'

'To?'

'Hong Kong,' he said, 'or Jamaica.'

'Jamaica,' she said scornfully. 'Hong *Kong*. And do what?'

'Lawyer,' Mahoney said complacently. 'Magistrate or Crown Counsel or something. Write. That's what I'll do, write. Get a soft job as a magistrate and write. Wonderful life, Hong Kong. No wogs.'

Jackie looked away.

'Wonderful life is right. Drink, you mean. Women, you mean. That's what you'll do in Hong Kong. All the nice English girls will love you with your blarney and all the nice little yum yum girls too. You'll go to the dogs and end up a no-good whisky-tanned colonial servant. Excuse me—'

She jumped off the stool and picked up her handbag and walked down the Long Bar to the Ladies' room.

Part Nine

Chapter Fifty-Four

It takes about three months to get around to hanging a man, from the day he's sentenced, to that Friday morning at nine o'clock sharp. There is a lot of red tape. First, the shorthand writer's record must be transcribed, then the appeal has to be argued, then the Executive Council has to consider granting the Royal Prerogative of Mercy, warrants have to be signed and countersigned, then the condemned is given some time in which to make his peace with his Maker. A lot of things happen to a man in Death Row in three months.

Death Row in Salisbury Central Prison is a two-storeyed rectangular fortress. There are two floors of cells in Death Row, on either side of the building, and at the far end is an exercise yard with very high walls. At the end of the south row of cells is the gallows chamber. The gallows occupies two floors; they take you in the upper door and they carry you out the bottom. The cells on the top floor look across at the stout wooden doorway of the gallows chamber. Nearly every Thursday evening a man was taken from his cell and put in the holding cell next door to the gallows chamber, nearly every Friday morning the condemned men heard the hangman arrive early. They went to the grids of their cell doors and peered through and they saw the hangman enter the gallows chamber and close the door behind him. Then they listened and they could hear him shuffling around in there, rigging his rope, and then they waited and they heard a loud clanging thud as he tested the trapdoor once. Then they saw him come out again and lock the door behind him and tramp down the iron staircase and they heard the iron door clang behind him as he went out to wait and have a cup of coffee, maybe. Then they waited a long time. There were people coming and going, priests and warders, and sometimes they took the man out of the holding cell to the lavatory, for there is no lavatory in the holding cell lest he find a way of injuring himself with it. Then they heard the big iron door open again and the heavy tramp and the clanging of boots climbing the stairs and then the senior prison officials and the doctors and the hangman again came into view, and they opened the gallows chamber and filed into it and closed the door behind them. Then the other prisoners started singing and wailing and chanting. Then at one minute to nine o'clock the gallows chamber door opened and the hangman came out with a priest and two prison warders. They opened the door of the holding cell and sometimes there was the sound of a struggle and sometimes shouts. And then they brought him out of the cell with his hands cuffed behind his back and they marched him through the gallows chamber doorway, and as soon as they had passed through the door was shut again, and everybody stopped singing in the other cells. There was half a minute of silence, then the big loud clanging bang again, and a moment later a thud. And the wailing started again, and you could hear it even outside the prison walls.

A lot of things happened to Samson Ndholvu in those three months. He was in a cell upstairs in Bomb Alley. The ordinary murderers were kept in the cells downstairs. There were three men to a cell in Death Row and there was what the prison warders called a 'fluctuating population' of roughly thirty men in the Row. Some of the Bomb Alley boys had been there for a year, their lawyers staving off execution with appeals to the Privy Council on rare legal points. The Privy Council dismissed one appeal and the lawyers found another and everything in Bomb Alley on Death Row waited for another while whilst it was argued.

The grid on Samson Ndholvu's cell door was directly opposite the gallows chamber. He had a view of the top of the steel staircase, of the gallows chamber door, of the holding cell door, and of the door of the padded cell next to it where the boys who went off their heads were put. Samson Ndhlovu had watched through the grid and he had seen many men make the second last shift to the holding cell, then the last shift the next morning to the gallows chamber. Most of them had gone quietly, some of them had gone down fighting and kicking and screaming. He had heard the trapdoor bang across the alley many times. Every time it happened he was waiting for it, waiting for the bang a week before, and every time he heard it he closed his eyes and when he opened them he was covered in sweat. That was the worst part, the waiting for the bang. It was very bad during a man's last three weeks, after the superintendent came to say that an appeal had been dismissed, during the time the man waited and counted the days being eaten up slowly, one by one. It was very bad during the last Thursday, waiting for them to come and take him to the holding cell. It was very bad but it was not yet the end, for anything might yet happen, there might suddenly be the noise of an explosion, as the political ones said, the sound of the outer wall being blasted open and the Freedom Fighters breaking in to rescue them. Or there might suddenly be heard the sound of the airplanes and the faraway boom of the cannon as the English or the Americans or the Zambians came to fight the white men, as the political ones said. Or the white men might find they have no more money left, as the political ones said, and they would have to surrender and then the English would come and liberate them without a shot being fired. It could happen. The political ones said that the longer they managed to delay the execution by the appeals, the better chance they had. But at the end of the last Thursday when they came to fetch you and they took you across the alley to the holding cell with all the others shouting good-bye to you and you listened for the footsteps in the early morning and then waited to hear the bang, then it seemed that you were right in that holding cell also. And you realised that soon it would be you in that holding cell. Waiting for the bang was the worst part.

Samson Ndhlovu heard many things in his three months. He heard many screams in the night, a lot of things cried out in sleep, a lot of confessions. And he had heard a lot of politics. And the only real thing to talk about, because it was the only thing in which hope lay, was politics. And he found that if he hoped to live he had to hope for the English to come and for the white men to fall, for the Freedom Fighters to come and for the Night of the Long Knives.

Samson Ndhlovu studied the business movements in Death Row. He studied the procedure engaged when shifts were changed, when food was brought, when exercise was given. He studied the structure of Death Row and he examined the bars and wall and the door of his cell but he found no weakness in them, nothing even that a man could work loose and use as a weapon or a tool. Every day Samson Ndhlovu took exercise in the yard with the high walls with his two cell-mates. Every day he looked at the high walls. Every day he looked again while he was waiting for his turn to wash under the shower in the corner of the exercise yard, lest he had missed something last time he looked, but every day he saw only smooth sheer concrete up which not even a monkey could climb.

Then one day Samson Ndhlovu was standing under the shower. As he turned the tap with soap in his eyes his fingernails scraped against something on the wall. It was one of three iron brackets which held the shower pipe to the wall. Samson Ndhlovu stood with his back to the yard under the falling water and fingered the bracket. It was not very firm in the wall for the constant water had loosened its fitting. He worked on it with his fingers. Every day for two months Samson Ndhlovu worked on the bracket for five minutes as he stood under the shower. After two months it came away from the wall and Samson shoved it quickly into the cleft of his buttocks.

That night Samson Ndhlovu started work on the bracket. It took many nights to straighten it and to file it sharp on the floor of the cell in the middle of the night.

He did not yet know how he was going to use the dagger, but it was a good thing for a man to have.

Chapter Fifty-Five

A lot of things happened in those three months. Joseph Mahoney was ordered by his doctor to relax completely for a week and to go back on the wagon for six months. Mahoney went on the wagon, but he only relaxed when he heard Jackie's car coming up his drive. He sat at his table and worked on his book. A gang of six youths set fire to the church and pigsty of the Holy Cross Catholic Mission. The African Commonwealth countries again threatened to expel Britain from the British Commonwealth unless Britain used force to conquer Rhodesia. The British Commonwealth Secretary decided to reprieve two petrol-bombers awaiting execution on Salisbury's Death Row. Matthew Mapunga strangled the second-born of his wife's twins. Tickey stabbed Ninepence in the heart at the Ma-Petticoat Beerhall because Ninepence alleged that Tickey ate owls, a most offensive thing to say. Evi was raped and so were Mary, Olive, Violet-i, Janice, Joan-i, Farewell and Mafuta, to name only a very few. The four terrorists who called themselves the Leopard Gang put up a roadblock on the Umtali Road, held up the car driven by the Turnbull family, stabbed and stoned Mr. Turnbull to death and poured petrol over Mrs. Turnbull and Miss Turnbull and burnt them alive. Mahoney wrote to the Jamaican Government saying he would accept their offer if they paid him more. Shadreck Matumbeni fell off a bus. The British Prime Minister stopped shipment of maize bound for Rhodesia for famine relief of Africans. Samson Ndhlovu lost his appeal. Jacqueline Josephine Riley still refused to go to bed with Joseph Mahoney. There was a military coup d'etat in Ghana, and four days later Britain recognised the new regime. Jacqueline

Josephine Riley still stoutly resisted going to bed with Joseph Mahoney. Shadreck raped his six-year-old daughter because the witch-doctor told him it would cure his syphilis. The Jamaican Government offered Joseph Mahoney more money. Joseph Mahoney became very restless about Jacqueline Josephine Riley. Joseph Mahoney wrote to the Jamaican Government accepting their offer. Joseph Mahoney took to brooding much about Jacqueline Josephine Riley. Joseph Mahoney resigned from his post as Crown Counsel in the Rhodesian Government, placed his farm lock stock and barrel on the books of an estate agent and booked a passage for one adult to Jamaica. Joseph Mahoney spent three sleepless nights and then changed the single passage to Jamaica to a double passage to Jamaica and spent two more sleepless nights thinking about it. Joseph Mahoney spent another week thinking about it. Joseph Mahoney became engaged to be married to Jacqueline Josephine Hotpants Paddy Riley.

Chapter Fifty-Six

It was a beautiful Sunday morning. Beautiful, Mahoney thought, as only Africa can be beautiful in the early morning. Why think that? he asked himself – *don't* think that. There are many places that are beautiful in the morning; Hong Kong, the States, a million places. You think only Africa can be this beautiful in the morning, or beautiful *like this*, because it is your home, because you feel it belongs to you and now you're leaving it. Well it's *not* your home, chummy, get that straight, it's not your Africa, get that straighter: it belongs to the blacks. And they are going to get it by hook or by crook. And if they don't get it *given* to them, they are going to cut your throat to get it, chummy. Get used to the idea for God's sake, like the Kenya boys had to get used to the idea, like the Zambia boys are having to get used to it, like even the South Africans will have to get used to it one day. Only you're being a bit smarter than the Kenya boys: you're getting out *before* the balloon really goes up.

There was a knock on his bedroom door, then Arthur, his new cookboy, came in with the tea. He put it down without looking at Mahoney and walked out.

Mahoney didn't like him, he was sorry he had taken him on. He did not trust him. He looked *exactly* the type to panga you at the dinner table. Come to that, Mahoney thought, not for the first time, that probably is precisely what he's here for: he's probably been sent by the Party to panga you. Why not? If they were interested enough to get Samson Ndhlovu to petrol bomb you, why should they stop now?

Mahoney swung his legs off the bed. He poured tea into a cup and he took it to the window and stood there naked as he drank it. God, but it *was* a beautiful morning. A brisk summer-winter morning. The two frangipani trees were still blooming and the wild roses were blooming pink and the grass was green and thick and the sun was a ball of gold in a sparkling blue sky. There were birds singing. Space, beautiful space. And so far as he could see, shrubs and trees and bushes. Not a soul in sight. He could walk out into the garden now stark bollock naked and not a soul would see him.

Mahoney put the cup down and stared out the window at the frangipani tree. Then he turned and walked to his bedside and lit a cigarette. He blew the smoke out in a physical effort to disperse the thought, but it didn't work: he still saw Suzie sitting in her deckchair under the frangipani tree. He saw her sitting in her bikini with her leggy busty body golden from the sun, glistening a little under the tanning oil. Her long gold hair was hanging straight down below her shoulders under her wide sunstopping straw hat and her wide red mouth was smiling as she lifted the frosted wine glass to her lips. Sunday in the sun with Suzie.

He pulled hard on his cigarette and strode naked through the house to the bathroom. He ran the tap in the basin and started humming loudly.

Sundays in the sun with Suzie—

He did not look at his face in the bathroom mirror until he had the lather ready. Then he looked at himself and he stopped humming.

He liked what he saw. His eyes were clear and his face had a healthy colour to it. The hand that held the razor was not trembling like it did a couple of months ago. 'Gad, but you're a healthy good-looking bastard, Mahoney,' he said aloud. 'You're such a healthy good-looking bastard you should *never* get married. You should stick around single and shag yourself to death. It's all this no-drinking that does it.'

But it was no good. He started shaving but his eyes moved from the mirror to the window, back to the mirror, back out the window as he scraped his face.

Sundays—

Well forget it, chum! There just aren't going to be any more Sundays in the sun either with Suzie or anybody else, not in Rhodesia. You can't go through life mooning around in the past. Stop feeling so bloody sorry for yourself. This time Sunday after next you'll be safely married and there *can't be any looking back*.

This time Sunday after next you'll be waking up in your train compartment for two rollicking down the coast to catch a slow sugar-boat honeymoon at the expense of the Jamaican Government, count your blessings for a change. You're getting out of this desert before it's too late. You're being smart. Like that bod you spoke to in Tanganyika said: Get going north, right north till you're off this godforsaken continent. In two months' time you'll be sailing your boat on Sundays, out in the sparkling blue sea, making for an anchorage off one of those palm-slung Caribbean islands, and you'll have a beer in your hand and you'll have Jacqueline. You'll laugh with Jackie and argue with Jackie and have intelligent discussions with Jackie. You'll have a goddam wine in the sun with Jackie – Mahoney closed his eyes.

But it won't be quite the same with Jackie, will it!

He opened his eyes and looked at himself. Then he put the razor down slowly.

No, he said slowly into his eyes, it won't be the same, Joseph. It never will be the same. Your second love, your third, fourth and subsequent loves, none of them are ever quite the same as your first real love, Joseph. Better maybe, more suitable maybe, but never the *same*, Joseph. Not when that first love was Suzanna de Villiers anyway, Joseph. So get used to the idea, Joseph.

He lifted a towel slowly and dragged it down one cheek. He wiped the other side of his face and then he dropped the towel.

Jackie will make you a good wife, Joseph. You need a good wife, Joseph, if anybody does. You *love* Jacqueline, Joseph, but you're *in* love with Suzie. Whatever the hell that means.

Well, there aren't going to be any more Sundays, not like there used to be. Doubtless a good thing too – look how fit you are since you laid off the demon drink. Don't moon out the window at that frangipani tree.

There aren't going to be any more Sundays, Joseph, so get used to the idea. This time Sunday after next you'll be married.

This time Sunday after next you'll be gone.

He turned and shouted as loud as he could.

'Samson! – enza lo breakfast kamina—'

Samson? *Samson!* Oh Jesus. This time next Sunday Samson Ndhlovu'll be *dead*.

He pulled on a pair of short trousers roughly and stumped down the passage to the kitchen.

'Arthur – enza lo breakfast kamina quickly please—'

He went to the lounge and switched on the radio. He wanted to fill the house with noise.

Wish Jackie were here.

He walked back to his bedroom and started getting dressed. He felt like just wearing shorts and sandals and a tee-shirt but he decided he had better not if he was going to have lunch with Jacqueline's old folks. More than somewhat pukkah souls, Colonel and Mrs. Riley.

Chapter Fifty-Seven

It was *supposed* to be a nice quiet little Saturday morning wedding, Mahoney thought as he turned in the Riley's drive, but it wasn't going to be by the looks of things. If he had had his way they would have sneaked off down to Enkeldoorn or Umvuma or Rusape or somewhere and had the District Commissioner solemnise the union. But oh no. You can't pull that one on a girl. Oh, they'll sleep on bare boards for you, they'll follow you to the ends of the earth etcetera etcetera, but they draw the line at District Commissioners. The old folks had nearly choked when he had hopefully put the suggestion up. It *had* to be a white church wedding. Jackie had shot him a little smug look and a wisp of a smile when the Old Girl said that. Well, fair enough. It would be only a small wedding, that was agreed. After all, there wouldn't be *time* enough for a *big* wedding, as they were getting married only three weeks after their engagement. Just close friends of the family and some of Mahoney's buddies, say fifty or sixty people or so. What a pity, but what could you do, as they were getting married in such a rush? Quite, Mahoney said sympathetically. And the planning had started off small. But soon there was this business friend of the Old Man's and the old boys he played bowls with and the people from the Club and there were the Old Girl's bridge cronies and the old dears from the Women's Guild. And more rare relatives than you could shake a stick at. And then there were the blokes from Mahoney's office and then most of the lawyers and then even *judges*, for Chrissake. Mahoney had enough of judges in his professional life to want to avoid them as lepers in private life, but what could you do? And all the jokes. And the wedding presents, for Gawd's sake! The wedding presents first made Mahoney alarmed, then embarrassed. It really makes you feel that you're a goner when the wedding presents start rolling in. Tea-trays and ice-buckets and cutlery sets and dinner services. And those mumsie tea showers and tablecloths really give a sensitive young man the heebie jeebies. Mind you, the cheques were rather a different story, but how the hell were they supposed to get all this junk to Jamaica, anyway? And now, this Sunday morning as he turned in the Riley's drive, there were tables and chairs scattered over the huge lawns, and there was a lorry off-loading more chairs. The Riley's were having a dummy run to see how the seating accommodation for the garden reception was going to work out. Must be three or four hundred chairs, Mahoney reckoned moodily.

He pulled up behind the lorry at the side of the big house and stepped out. The Old Man was at the other end of the garden supervising two gardeners spreading the chairs. He waved and Mahoney walked across the lawn to him.

'Good morning, Joseph, my boy, you're around early.'

'Good morning, sir. Yes it's all this clean living.'

He was a decent Old Stick. He and the Old Girl had been a bit alarmed when their one and only had taken up with him – 'Hasn't he got rather a reputation, my dear? I mean he *has* got rather a reputation as a—a rough diamond. *Do* be careful—' But they had been very decent when he said he was marrying her and taking her to the other end of the earth. And the Old Boy had given them one hell of a cheque as a wedding present.

'How's the old liver?' Colonel Riley said.

'When I die,' Mahoney said, 'they'll have to beat my liver to death with a stick.'

The Old Man laughed.

'You two enjoy yourselves last night?'

'Yes, we had a quiet meal and went to see this latest James Bond flick.'

'Heard anything about your book yet?' Colonel Riley said.

'Not yet,' Mahoney said, 'it's only been with this agent fellow three weeks. Jackie up and about yet?'

'She's just five minutes ago driven down to the Greek to get this morning's paper. Go up to the house and see if you can get yourself some tea.'

As he walked up the path Jackie's car came swirling in the drive. She was taking the gravel drive very fast and as soon as she saw Mahoney she leant on the hooter, a long blast and then three short ones. She was beaming behind the steering wheel. She scrunched to a halt and flung open the door and came running across the lawn to him. She was waving the newspaper.

'Joey – Joey – wonderful news—'

She flung her arms around him and then stepped back.

'Guess what?'

'What?'

'*Samson's been reprieved*,' she cried.

'*Samson—!*'

'It's in the paper.'

Mahoney snatched it from her.

'Centre page. It was on the news last night too but we were at the flick—'

Mahoney scrambled through the pages.

'Good God, he was going to be hanged on Friday—where, here it is.' He read aloud:

'London, Saturday. The Commonwealth Secretary announced in London today that Her Majesty the Queen had extended the Royal Prerogative of Mercy to three Africans presently awaiting execution in Salisbury Central Prison. The announcement came six days before the three men were scheduled to be executed. All three men had been convicted of different crimes of 'petrol bombing' which carries a mandatory death penalty in Rhodesia. The Commonwealth Secretary warned that if the three men were hanged on Friday as scheduled all those Rhodesian officials who authorised and assisted in the execution would be guilty of murder. The three men are Samson Ndhlovu, Phineas Matubeli, and Eros Bande ...'

Mahoney dropped the paper to his side.

'Good God—'

'They'll never dare to hang him now,' Jackie beamed breathlessly, 'it even warns them there they'll be guilty of murder if they do.'

'Good God,' Mahoney said, 'Phineas Matubeli and Eros Bande.'

'What about them?'

Mahoney frowned. 'They were reprieved at the same time. They're two bad bastards, they're this Leopard Gang I've told you about. The ones that put up the roadblock and then poured petrol over the Turnbull family and set them alight.'

'So?' Jackie demanded. 'They're two bad ones, but I don't care if they get off just so long as Samson does.'

'That's just the point,' Mahoney said bitterly.

'What do you *mean*, Joseph?'

Mahoney snorted. He waved his hand. 'Can the Rhodesia Government *afford* not to hang the Leopard Gang? As far as the Rhodesia Government is concerned they were properly tried and properly sentenced to death. They deserve to hang and they must be made an example of. The British Commonwealth Secretary has no power to reprieve them, as far as our Government is concerned. If our Government is intimidated by the Commonwealth Secretary into *not* hanging these blokes it'll be a sign of weakness and the political wogs'll make enormous capital out of it. There'll be petrol bombs flying in all directions. As far as our Government is concerned it's *vital* that this Leopard Gang be hanged.'

'So? It's not vital that they hang Samson.'

Mahoney turned with exasperation.

'Isn't it? Even if they don't want to hang him, haven't they *got* to show the British who's boss out here? If they're going to defy the British Government over the Leopard Gang haven't they *got* to go the whole hog? How can they obey them, as it were, in respect of one case and defy them in the others, especially when it all comes in one announcement?'

Jackie stepped in front of him.

'Oh Joe! But look what your Michael lawyer friend said outside the flick last night. He said the Cabinet were bending over backwards—'

Mahoney tapped the newspaper angrily.

'Neither Mike nor the Cabinet knew about this last night.'

'But Joe! They can't do it. They'd be guilty of *murder*. They couldn't make a political football out of Samson!' Mahoney snorted softly.

'Couldn't they? Oh couldn't they just! What do you think Britain's doing with Samson Ndhlovu but making a political football out of him? Britain couldn't care if Samson hangs or not, they just reprieved him, *and* the bloody Leopard Gang, to embarrass Rhodesia. To put Rhodesia on the spot. Britain can't lose one way or the other. If we hang these blokes they'll hold us up to the rest of the world as bloody murderers. If we don't it shows we're weakening.'

'But, *Samson* …' Jackie said desperately.

Mahoney snorted angrily, 'if the British have made a political football out of poor old Samson Ndhlovu, what *can* the Rhodesians do but kick him?'

'Oh, Joe!' Jackie had tears in her eyes.

'If the bloody British played it clean instead of playing with a man's life, I'm bloody sure the Cabinet would've let him off the hook. But now'—he thumped the paper with the back of his hand— 'I'm bloody sure Samson Ndhlovu will hang. On Friday.'

Chapter Fifty-Eight

On Thursday night Joseph Mahoney sat in the darkness of his house verandah, holding a glass of beer. His first beer in nearly three months, he thought. But by God he needed it. He stared out into the night, into the bush that was his garden, and he was angry and weeping at the same time inside. Samson, oh Samson, my friend. And he wanted to shout: Damn you all you rotten stinking political bastards, you bloody English and you bloody black hoodlums, damn your eyes you profiteers of human misery, you stinking hypocrites and you smash and grab swines, oh Samson – the cigarette trembled in his hands as he puffed it and his throat ached.

A bloody political football—

Five minutes, that's about all they had together. That was about all they wanted. There had been very little to say. Samson had been already waiting in the small cell on the ground floor of Death Row, sitting at the end of the small table with a black prison corporal on either side of him, the light bulb behind the iron mesh casing shining above his head.

'Kunjani, induna?'

Samson said quietly: 'Kunjani wena, Nkosi?'

'I am well.'

Samson was sweating a little. There were beads of perspiration at his hairline. They looked at each other down the length of the table, the black corporals looking woodenly, self-consciously, in front of them. Then Samson lowered his eyes and waited.

'Do you have everything you want?' It sounded a silly question.

Samson breathed in deeply as he nodded his head once, slightly.

'Yes, thank you.'

'Here,' Mahoney opened his packet of cigarettes and lit two. He stood up and held one out down the length of the table. Samson stretched out both hands and took it. His wrists were manacled.

'Here,' Mahoney pushed the packet of fifty down the table. 'And'—he felt in his suit pocket and brought out the other packet of fifty—'I got these for you.'

Samson nodded.

'Thank you, but it is not necessary. They give us as many cigarettes as we want tonight.'

'Take them,' Mahoney said.

The two packets stood in front of Samson.

'I wish I could have brought you some tshwala,' Mahoney said, 'but it is not allowed.'

Samson shook his head. 'They give us tshwala too.'

'How much?'

'I do not know yet,' Samson said. There was an awkward silence. 'They give us good skoff tonight,' he said, trying to make conversation. Mahoney blinked. He knew the prison regulations. 'What have you chosen?'

'Fish and chips,' Samson said. They were silent a moment and Mahoney felt the tears catch behind his eyes. 'I am very fond of fish and chips,' Samson said lamely.

Silence again. Then Mahoney said. 'Induna?'

Samson looked up. 'Nkosi?'

Mahoney waved his hand, 'Is there anything you want me to do? Tomorrow?'

Samson shook his head.

'About your property? Your wives and cattle?'

Samson shook his head again. 'My younger brother will inherit my wives and cattle,' he said, and Mahoney nodded.

'There is only one thing I would like,' Samson said self-consciously, 'and that is to be buried at my kraal. But I am afraid the Nkosi cannot help me, I must be buried in the prison.'

Mahoney nodded slowly. 'Yes, I am afraid so. It is the new rule.'

Samson nodded. There was silence again. Mahoney could think of nothing sensible to say.

Then Samson smirked once.

'What is it, induna?'

Samson shook his head, 'I was just thinking,' he said, 'of the valley. Of Kariba.' He paused and smiled. 'Of the many good times we had. It was very good round the fire, hey, Nkosi?'

Mahoney's nose was tingling at the roots.

'It was very good, induna.'

Samson nodded. 'We were young and strong and free, then. And we made plenty money,' he said.

Mahoney could feel his chin wanting to quiver. He pulled on his cigarette hard.

Samson sighed and looked up and his eyes were glistening too.

'I think it would be a good thing if we had stayed in the valley, Nkosi.'

There was a pain in Mahoney's throat. 'Yes, induna,' he said, 'we should have stayed.'

He wanted with all his heart to be in the Zambezi Valley now with Samson Ndhlovu.

Samson breathed out through his nostrils and blinked and he looked at Mahoney.

'And now the Nkosi is getting married,' he said.

Mahoney nodded. 'Yes.'

Samson looked him in the eye. 'I am glad,' he said, it is a good thing you are getting married. Now your soul will be rested and you will have the joy of children. Children are a great pleasure, you know, Nkosi.'

'Yes?'

'A great pleasure. I am glad for Nkosi. The woman Jek-i is a good woman. I think she will look after the Nkosi very well. Some of the women the Nkosi has had have been rubbish, but the woman Jek-i is a good woman.'

Mahoney screwed up his eyes once to force the tears away. 'Thank you, Samson.'

Samson looked at Mahoney seriously. 'Nkosi?'

'Yes, induna?'

'The woman Jek-i is a good woman. The Nkosi must not grieve any more for the woman Suzie, for that will make the Nkosi unhappy and the woman Jek-i too. The woman Suzie was a good woman too, but you must not grieve for her. You must be pleased with what you have.'

'Do I grieve for her, induna?'

Samson nodded. 'Yes, Nkosi, you did. You grieved too much. It is not good for a man to dwell in the arms of a dead woman.'

Mahoney nodded obediently, 'I will remember what you say, old man.'

'The woman Suzie was a good woman,' Samson said, 'but she was no good for the Nkosi.'

'Why is that?'

'Because you quarrelled too much, Nkosi,' Samson said awkwardly, 'I do not know why that is, but it is so.' Samson cleared his throat embarrassedly and decided to say it. 'I do not know for sure why it is so, I only think. But I think it was the Nkosi's fault. The Nkosi has an unhappy spirit. Do not make the same trouble with the woman Jek-i, Nkosi.'

Mahoney closed his eyes. When he opened them Samson had looked away.

'I wish,' he said, 'that I could be at the Nkosi's wedding. I could have helped serve the tshwala.'

Mahoney felt the tip of his chin tremble again.

'I wish it too, induna,' he said.

Samson looked up and his eyes were glistening again and he tried to make a joke.

'Perhaps it is a good thing,' he said, 'I would only have got drunk and disgraced the Nkosi.'

Mahoney snorted to clear the burn out of his eyes.

'Nkosi. Do one thing for me, for the sake of the valley. For the sake of Kariba.'

'What is that?'

'Tomorrow morning at nine o'clock, drink a glass of tshwala. And when you drink it, think of the valley.'

Mahoney screwed up his eyes and put his thumbs in the corners. The pain in his throat was bad. Then he took his thumbs away quickly and opened his eyes.

'I will do it, induna,' he said, 'I promise you.'

Samson coughed and cleared his throat. It seemed as if there was nothing left to say.

'And now,' he said awkwardly, 'the Nkosi is going far away.'

It tore at Mahoney's guts.

'Yes, old man,' he said, 'far away.' And he wished with all his heart that he was not going. He wished he was there in the Zambezi Valley.

'It is a pity,' Samson said.

'Yes,' Mahoney said, 'it is a pity.'

'Then why do you go?'

Mahoney closed his eyes. 'Because I deem it best.'

'Why do you deem it best?'

Mahoney fidgeted. 'Because, old man,' he said loudly, 'the troublemakers make too much trouble. This will be no home for the white man.'

Samson snorted softly. 'This will always be the Nkosi's home, whatever happens. There is always room enough for an induna.'

Mahoney closed his eyes again. What was there to say? 'It is true,' he said.

'It is true,' Samson Ndhlovu said.

It seemed as if it was finished. There was nothing more to say. There was a silence, then: 'Eh – eeeh,' Samson said.

'Eh – eeeh.'

They looked at each other. Then Samson said: 'There is nothing more to say, Nkosi.'

'No, Samson,' Mahoney said, 'there is nothing more to say.'

He stood up slowly. He leaned down the table and stretched out his hand. Samson stood up and took his master's hand in both of his. There were tears in both their eyes. They shook hands and then they clapped their hands softly.

'Stay well, induna.'

'Stay well, Nkosi.'

Mahoney stood at the far end of the dark verandah of his house. He lifted up his big beer glass. 'Stay well, induna.'

He lifted the glass to his mouth and he drank it down. He flung the glass against the wall of the verandah and it shattered.

Chapter Fifty-Nine

They hardly slept all night. They had not talked much at first because they knew all about each other and they had talked it all out over the months. Then they had played a couple of games of draughts, the only game Samson had learned on Death Row, with one of the warders to make up the two boards. The priest had come but none of them had wanted to see him because none of them were Christians. But he was on duty all night and they could send for him if they wanted. Then they got tired of the draughts. There was a large guard on watch in the corridor. They had sat around in the cell with their backs to the wall and talked a little. Then Phineas had broken out in a sweat and he had started calling for the priest and they took him out to the padded cell and sent for the priest. Phineas had been to a Mission school for two years when he was a boy. Then Eros had fallen into a doze and Samson was left by himself.

He sat gingerly against the wall, resting slightly on one side so his buttocks were squinched together to keep the small dagger wedged in the groove. He had nicked himself twice when he moved and there was a small patch of blood on the back of his khaki pants but he pulled his tunic down to cover it. He had practised carrying the dagger wedged into his buttocks for a long time but it was awkward when he sat down. And he had not bargained for the warder staring in at him the whole time. The warder looked at Samson the whole time because he was the only one awake. The dagger was uncomfortable but he dared not fidget too much lest it work loose. He pretended to scratch his buttocks and managed to ease it. He did not trust himself to close his eyes for long in case he fell asleep. He was very tired, for he had not slept well this last week and his nerves were screaming. And his arms and legs and buttocks were aching from sitting in this position all the time. It would have been very good to stretch out on the floor or even to get up and walk around but he dared not.

'What is the time, old man?'

The warder looked at his watch.

'Nearly four o'clock,' he said.

He heard the shouting begin as the hangman was halfway up the stairs. It was not the usual wail the boys in Death Row put up.

'Murderer – Murderer – Murderer—' they shouted through the grids of their cell doors. 'Soon you too will hang when Britain comes – murderer – you too will hang—'

They screamed it at the tops of their lungs, they hammered on the cell doors and beat their feet upon the floor. It was heard all over the prison and in the hard labour blocks the political boys took up the chant and the wail:

Murderer – Murderer – Whoo – Whoo – Whoo—

Solly Berger clenched his teeth angrily and pulled his hat lower over his eyes and went quicker up the stairs. His chest was pounding from the exertion. The warders on the top landing stood up and saluted him. The shouting and wailing reached a crescendo. He nodded to the warders and fumbled for the key of the gallows chamber. They were screaming and trying to spit through the grids at him now. The warders were shouting and walking down the cells beating on the doors with their batons. Solly flung open the chamber door and slammed it closed behind him and leant back against it. *Christ—*

The shouts and the wailing were muffled and trailing off now. Christ, what an antiquated building, where the poor bloody hangman has to run the gauntlet every time. There should be a separate entrance for all this dirty business. He knew it was coming but not as bad as that.

He bent and unzipped his bag. He pulled the three stout ropes out feverishly and the ball of white string and the little pair of nail scissors and felt for the brandy bottle. He pulled it out and uncorked it and lifted it up and took three swallows out of it. He sighed and then he corked the bottle and shoved it back in the bag.

Well, get on with it.

He looked up at the stout beam above the long stout trapdoor. It was built to take six ropes at once. He felt in his pocket and took out a piece of paper and looked at the first measurement. Then he picked up the first rope and put a foot gingerly on the trapdoor and pressed down to make sure it held. Then he stretched up and lashed the noose to the hook on the beam. The noose lay in a heap at his feet. He went to the ball of string and nipped off six inches with the scissors. He took it back to the noose. He felt in his pocket and brought out the three cardboard labels. He took the one with 'Samson Ndhlovu' printed on it and tied it to the rope near the top.

He turned and went back to the other ropes and he felt for the piece of paper again. He coughed.

Samson heard him cough. 'What's the time, old man?'

'Five minutes pasti sixi,' the black warder said.

Samson stretched his left leg out carefully and he jerked a fraction as the dagger nicked him.

He wanted very badly to go to the lavatory but he dared not because they watch you, even in the lavatory.

They heard the heavy iron front door open and clang and the noise of feet, several pairs of feet, and the shouting started again and then the wailing.

'Murderers – Murderers – Whooo – Whooo—' and the thumping on the cell doors.

The priest was in the cell kneeling with Phineas and murmuring prayers and Phineas was on his knees too with his hands over his face and he was shuddering as he wept tears. Eros was sitting in the corner with his arms folded tight round his knees and his forehead was resting on his knees. He had been like that a long time but he was not shuddering. Samson Ndhlovu was still sitting. His eyes were hooded half-closed and he stared straight ahead of him, breathing fast, through his mouth, his mouth dry and his lips chapped from constant licking. He was sweating, the sweat glistening on his forehead and on his chest and when he let go of his knees he trembled. He shifted position with a jerk and his calf muscles bounced and his knee quivered and he clasped it back tight against him. He felt very weak, not strong enough for the task. When he heard the footsteps and the shouts he wanted to scramble to his feet and scream and charge right now. The waiting was very bad and it was hard to keep the head clear, hard to keep concentrating. *The priest*. His breath came in short pants – he could do it to the priest, anybody would do, it didn't matter who, just so long as he stabbed him. Even if he failed to stab him properly, even if he made a noise to warn the priest and the priest warded off the knife, even that would probably be enough.

No, not the priest. He might kill him and the priest did not deserve to die. It was also no good pretending. He had to do it properly, stab him properly, if he only injured the person slightly they might not bother to try him. Even if he injured the man seriously they might not bother to try him. They might say it does not matter. It would be better to kill, it was very important to kill so that it was a very serious matter and they had to take him to Court. The white men treat death as a very important matter and they will delay the hanging to try him. It takes a long time to try a man, maybe two months. The British will come before two months. Surely the British would not hang him for defending himself against his murderers.

But he must be careful. He must be quick. One good stab, that is probably all he would have time for. Then they would grab him. When do they tie you up? I must be careful for that. Do they speak first and then tie you up? Do they come around the back? Or do they catch you and then speak? They must say something before they hang you. As soon as the door opens, that must be the time. But they must not get behind my back. I must be in this corner where I am now and I must let them come to me. But I must not arouse their suspicions that I am going to struggle because then they will be ready. I must pretend to be very meek and frightened. I am frightened, very frightened, but I must look weak as well so that maybe they come to me nicely—

'What is the time, old man?'

'It is three minutes before nine o'clocki.'

The shouting – ah, it tears at a man's sinews. But it is good, it makes noise, it gives a man courage. Three minutes. Now it is time to stand up. Stand up, Ndhlovu, stand up quickly. Stand up carefully; Ndhlovu, because of the knife. Hark, the creak of my muscles as I stand up. I am weak, very, very weak and I am shaking. My kneecaps they are shaking, I am very weak. Quickly, now, the knife, do not fumble it, the knife in your hand behind your back, the other hand on your face like a man in great fear of death. Peer through the fingers. Ah, but I am shaking, like a woman.

'Samson, do you wish anything of me, my son?'

The priest standing in front of him now, looking at him kindly. Ah, it would be so easy now.

Samson shook his head behind his fingers.

The priest saying prayers for him now, with eyes closed tight, muttering aloud and the noise of the shouts. 'Murderers, murderers, murderers—' But not the priest.

'May the Lord have mercy upon your soul, my son—' Samson nodded. He did not understand him. The priest moved on to Eros.

'Eros, my son—'

The shouting was very loud now, it was a scream now, thirty men screaming in cells, they must be coming now. The knife is well in my hand, it is slippery. Maybe it is my own blood. I think I have cut myself. *Here they come—*

The black warder was unlocking the cell. The prison superintendent standing at the gate in his green uniform and two other white warders behind him and three black warders and two men in suits. Yes, one is the hangman, the man I've seen many times. Open the door, and in they come.

They advanced on him abreast, the superintendent and the two men in suits. They stopped in the centre of the cell with the warders behind them, and a black prison sergeant beside them. The strange man in the suit spoke. He had a document in his hand.

'Are you Samson Ndhlovu?'

Samson nodded through his fingers.

'I am the duly deputised Sheriff of the High Court of Rhodesia. I have here a warrant for the execution upon you of the Sentence of Death.'

The black prison sergeant interpreted.

'Do you wish to see it?' The sheriff held out the document. Samson shook his head through his fingers.

The sheriff turned slightly.

'Are you Eros Bande?'

Now—

Samson gave a loud scream and charged. Solly Berger spun in shock and raised his arms and reeled. A scramble of black and white and khaki and green and batons. The shouting outside, a continuous thumping scream. The shouts in the cell, the shock, the jumping, the flailing of batons. Samson Ndhlovu lashed out and spun, and then a crack of thunder in his head and blackness. Solly Berger lay spread on the floor with blood running out of a hole in his neck.

Samson Ndhlovu had just enough time to realise where he was. He was held upright, strapped to a board, leather straps all the way up his body binding him to the board. A white man in green uniform facing him, six inches from him, arm outstretched holding him vertical. A rope around his neck. A line of faces against the wall. A movement, a sudden plunging, a deafening bang.

Chapter Sixty

The empty house was full of the noise of the radio, music, market reports, women's gardening hints succeeding each other at full volume, blaring out of the house over the garden. Mahoney sat at his table, chin in palm, staring out the window, sucking from the whisky glass. His mouth was dehydrated, with no saliva to give it, but he didn't care. He was not really drunk, and he should be, he thought distantly; noori – he'd been drinking all night, on an empty stomach. He didn't care about that either, he didn't care about anything, he felt reckless of himself, he felt only hate pumping. The noon-time news came on, the announcer's cultured voice shouted through the house but it bounced off Mahoney: another American bomber raid on Vietnam, American protests over a new shipment of arms by Britain to Cuba, a prison officer was fatally stabbed when a condemned prisoner made a bid to escape in Salisbury Central Prison today – the words bounced off the walls, reverberated out over the grass. The telephone rang in the passage, but he did not bother to answer it. Mahoney's eyes were dull – steady, hate throbbing. He didn't feel sorry for Solly Berger, he no longer felt grief for Samson Ndhlovu. You're dead, Samson, dead dead dead. He only felt anger. You're dead, Samson, because of the rotten stinking loathsome fecund manoeuvrings of politics, the sneaky nasty hypocritical savagery of politics, the buy and sell of politics, the manoeuvring, the wheedling, and the big-stick waving and the ass-licking, you're a babe in the woods of politics, Samson, a babe sent into the jungle as cannon-fodder, used by the British so they can dangle you as a pawn for their own clever ass-licking ends. A political football, Samson. You and a million others, Samson, not just you, Samson, before you and after you there have been and will be a million babes in the wood, pawns for the wide boys, you are not the last, Samson, the rotten stinking business will go on for ever until the whole of Africa is destroyed, a hotbed of corruption and inefficiency and tyranny, with a few black dictators sitting on the ruins, puppets of Moscow and Peking. I grieve no more for you, Samson Ndhlovu: I only loathe the forces that used you. And I am glad, glad with all my heart that I am leaving, I can wash my hands of the stink and slime and taste of backstabbing and corruption: I grieve only for the suckers, the pawns that are to follow you, Samson.

Mahoney got up slowly from the table and filled his glass, while the telephone still rang. He carried the glass to the passage and picked up the receiver.

'Hello.'

'Joe, are you still all right?'

'I'm all right, Jackie.'

'You sure you don't want me to come out?'

'Quite sure, Jackie.'

'Darling?'

'Yes?'

'Cheer up.'

'Yes.'

He replaced the receiver and walked slowly through to the kitchen. He stood still and surveyed the concrete floor, the walls, the thatch roof, the stout rafters. His works, his money, he had built it: he felt reckless of the loss, indifferent, he no longer loved it, they could have it – one day, one day in the not too distant future the forces of Anglo-African politics would steal it from him anyway, like they did the land of the Kenya farmers: fuggem. He moved through the kitchen and out into the sun, and screwed up his eyes and looked about him at his kingdom; the chicken runs, the hens with the new rooster, the grazing paddock, Ferdinand and the kaffir cow and the one calf: it was a good little calf, stout and strong, it was an object lesson to the natives in what a good bull was worth. It would work

if he stuck at it, if he kept on talking and spreading the word about
– he shook his head: let somebody else break his back with good
works. He looked over at the pigsty, the champion boar and the
kaffir sow and the ten piglets squealing: good porkers, five pounds
sterling each in four, five months, fifty quid: what wouldn't a native
farmer do with an extra fifty quid per annum, and if enough of
them did it, Christ, it would change the face of the whole district …
He shook his head again. He tossed the whisky down his throat and
turned back into the house. He stopped at his table and poured
another shot into the glass, and strode over to the shouting radio
and spun the knob. Music, music, let's have some bloody music.

He did not hear the motorcar on the gravel drive, the footsteps
mounting the concrete stoep, he did not see the silhouette fill the
doorway. Then he sensed it.

He snapped the radio off and turned round, one movement, fists
bunched at the hips, half crouched. He stared, then he dropped his
fists and straightened slowly.

'Hello, Joe—'

His mouth opened around the name, his eyes frowned, his heart
was beating very fast, then joy and tears pumped up to his throat.

'Suzie!'

She stood in the doorframe, long hair down, stood hesitant in the
doorway, eyes nervous, lip trembling in uncertain smile.

'Yes, it's me, Joe—'

'Suzie.'

He took a step forward, unsteady, heart beating in his ears, his
eyes unbelieving, tears coming up, eyes crinkled against the light,
joy knocking in his chest. He walked unbelieving across the room,
he stopped three paces in front of her and he stared at her. She
looked into his eyes, shaking, breathing very hard.

'Suzie, you've come back!'

'Oh—'

He strode, she ran, clutching each other, clutching, arms clutching
each other, squeezing, fingers digging, tears, tears into shoulder,
hair across her face, tears wet on her face, salty kisses, smooth flesh
wet, cries, oh oh Joseph, my darling, my darling love, my love, my

love, my darling Joseph, tears and gasps, blonde hair sticking to his salty face, clutching.

'Oh Suzie, you've come back, you're back, you're back—'

She cried, she held him back at a distance, and looked at him, tears running.

'How are you, my love?' Her hand felt his face, fingers buried into his hair, fingers trailed his eyebrows, his cheek, his lips, feeling him.

'Suzie, you've come back—'

She clutched him, cried against him:

'I heard, I tried not to come, darling, I heard about your engagement, I heard about the bomb and Samson's trial, read it all, then that you were leaving, then your engagement to Jackie, and I didn't come, Joseph, I wept for you, but I didn't come, I ached just to see you, to hear your voice, I so wanted just to speak to you, to wish you luck, to tell you I love you, but I didn't, because I thought it best, I didn't want to start it all over again. Then I heard about Samson today and my heart cried out for you—'

He held her, dazed, she sobbed it out into his shoulder.

'Suzie, you've come back—'

She shook him gently, fingers digging into his arms, sobbing. She shook her head, no no no Joseph – she held him back again, arms straight, she bent her head back, and her hair fell off her wet face.

'No, Joseph. Because I'm married, darling. I'm married, *married,* darling—' she shook him gently.

'Married?'

'Yes, darling. To Jake Jefferson, darling,' she tossed her head and laughed, tear-gay, a loving tear-laugh. 'To Jake, I'm a policeman's wife now, darling, a nice little wife in a nice little Government House, having tea with other Government wives and talking about babies and dinners and the price of butter darling, nothing else, darling.' She shook him gently, firmly, tearfully, her fingers felt his face, his lips – 'I'm happy, darling, don't you see, I'm ordinary, I'm a nice ordinary girl married to a nice ordinary man talking about nice ordinary things—'

He looked at her, dazed, tears in his eyes. 'Jake Jefferson?'

She shook him.

'Darling, don't you see, it's all for the best, I'm no good for you darling, no good, I'm too different from you, Jackie is good for you, she's your soulmate, she feels with you, she breathes with you, I've seen the way she looks at you, I'm not your soulmate, I wanted to be but I couldn't be, I didn't know how, I tried and I failed, I'm just an ordinary girl and now I'm happy living an ordinary life in an ordinary marriage, no ups and downs no moods no creative anguish, no frustrations no arguments, dull ordinary suburban, don't you see, darling Joseph, one of us had to make the break—'

Mahoney looked at her.

'Suzie—oh Suzie why didn't you come back to tell me?'

'Darling, because you know what would have happened, you'd have abandoned Jackie and I'd have abandoned Jake—Jackie and Jake, isn't that a coincidence, darling?—and we would have started all over again—'

He still looked numbly at her: 'Suzie?'

'Yes, darling?'

'Have you got a baby?'

She closed her eyes and shook her head. 'No, darling.'

Mahoney closed his eyes. 'Suzie, are you happy?'

She bit her lip and nodded, yes yes yes.

'Suzie?'

'Yes, darling?'

'Where are you living?'

'At Kariba, Jake's stationed up there because of the emergency. Oh Joseph, it was hell, sometimes, knowing you were just two hundred and fifty miles away—'

Her eyes were closed, he looked at her, he shook her gently.

'Suzie'

'Yes, Joseph?'

'Do you love me?'

She opened her eyes and looked at him.

'Oh I still love you, I have always loved you, I will always love you—'

He held her tight against him, clutched her, he shook, dry sobs of grief, loss, a hundred anguished regrets. She held him tight against her, calmer now, her hand holding his head, stroking: Cry my love, cry cry my brooding love.

His hand took a bunch of her hair gently, and he pulled her head back, they looked into each other's eyes, he picked her up, she held on to him, acquiescence in her body, love, compassion, softness, giving. He carried her down the passage, still she clung soft and giving to him, looking at him, he laid her down on the bed, quivering, aching, crying inside, he held her to him, she held herself against him, sobbing, crying, giving, weeping, desperately loving, he rolled on top of her, she gave herself to him, soft hips pressing up to him, softness and love and succour, her dress rode up her thighs, they fumbled with each other's clothes, pushed them off each other urgently, whimpering, giving, the searing, sobbing bliss of reunion, the joy, the heartbreak.

Oh my love my love my love my love – afterwards they lay very still, holding each other, wet with each other's sweat, wet with each other's tears, wet with the seed and flesh of each other. She held him, rocked his head against her breast. He slept.

It was dark when he woke. He sat up quickly in the dark, listening, sensing, the night insects singing outside his window. He jerked his arm out and felt for Suzie: he felt only the rumpled blankets. 'Suzie.' It echoed shortly in the passage, muffled in the thatch. 'Suzie!' He jumped off the bed, pulled on a pair of shorts. Foreboding. What had wakened him? 'Suzie!' He crossed the room to the light switch, flicked it on. Nothing, the room remained black, only the patch of night light from the window, the noise of the insects, eerie. He felt himself blanch, a knocking in his ears, No *lights,* lines cut!

'Suzie!'

He dashed across the room to the wooden box, rattled the lock. He felt feverishly for keys, found them, the padlock shook in his hands as he undid it, he pulled out the revolver. He broke the breach, felt the cartridges, snapped it to. He strode to the door, then stopped, listened. Only the insects and his own breath. He put his head carefully round the door and looked into the passage.

Murky, nothing.

He stepped into the passage, three four five paces to the

telephone. He put his back to the wall, lifted the receiver, listened. Nothing, dead. He dropped it. So the lines were cut. The blood rushed up his neck.

'Suzie!' he screamed.

He howled, the howl of a beast protecting its mate, he rushed down the passage, gun first into the lounge. 'You savages—'

He stopped, panting. Nothing. He kicked open the door of the dining-room. Nothing. He ran into the kitchen, nothing, back into the passage, down to the study. He flung open the study door and rushed in.

Nothing.

He saw his Winchester torch on the table. He grabbed it, switched it on, and turned back to the door. The beam fell on the table, a note scrawled on a piece of paper. He grabbed it.

Good-bye my love, my Joseph. Take care, Suzie Jefferson.

He slumped against the wall. He forgot about the lights and the telephone. He sobbed a dry sob. Suzie Suzie Suzie Suzie Jefferson.

He heard the faraway bellow of the bull, and he did not move. It came again, muffled far away, a bellow of anguish, he listened, holding his breath. Why was the bull crying at night? He listened, his hand tight around the revolver, no bellow came again, only the noises of the night insects. He pushed the chair back, stood up slowly in the dark, listening. Silence. He stood still, then he walked quickly into the passage, stopped, listened, strode into his bedroom. He pulled on a shirt, sat on the bed and put on his shoes. He listened, strode back to the passage and picked up the telephone again. Nothing, still dead. He put the receiver back. He walked quickly, lightly back down the passage, into the kitchen. A thin moon was rising over the black kopje, shining dull on the black silent bush. He went to the back door and stood listening. Only the insects. He drew back the bolt and swung the door open and stood back against the inside wall. Nothing happened. He looked at the door in the moonlight and his eyes widened. He stared at the door, a pounding in his ears, a cry stifled in this throat. He heard the bellow again, clearer now, he recognised the thing dangling there, pinned to his door, ragged, oozing, dripping blood, the bull's testicles. He let go his breath.

'You savage bastards—'

He plunged out the door, teeth clenched, he ran crouched across the yard, stopped, panting, behind a bush. He listened, peered, he ran on down the long path towards the paddock. His footsteps pounded the earth in the night, he ran crouched low, tensed for the black shape to leap out from behind a bush, panga upraised glinting in the moonlight. But only the thudding of his running and his heart and the night insects. *Bastards!* He crashed on down the path. He ran at the fence of the paddock, stopped against it, panting, searching the darkness.

The bull bellowed, a long groaning cry. Mahoney vaulted the fence and ran to the black shape. He flicked on his torch and his eyes peeled back.

Aarr—

The bull was standing, head low, eyes rolling, long ragged coils of intestines hanging down into the grass, ragged flaps of muscle hanging down, blood pumping out, the green grass black with blood. The bull stretched out his neck and his nostrils dilated, and he gave a bellow, dry and hissing and weak and air bubbled red and slimy out of the long hole in his guts. The kaffir cow lay on her side, a big round raw flat hole where her udder had been, her guts hanging out. She was breathing, blood pumping out with each breath, quivering. The calf lay twenty yards away, dead, in a tangle of its own intestines.

'Christ!'

Hate, teeth clenched, he brought the revolver up between the bull's eyes and pulled the trigger. Crack, the shot filled the night, the bull crumpled. 'Bloody murderers—' Crack, another shot, the cow kicked and was still. He filled his lungs and screamed.

'You bloody murdering bastards, I'll get you!'

He looked around him, in the dark paddock, and then he ran across the paddock towards the pigsties. He ran twenty paces and then stopped, his eyes wide: there was a new light and a new noise in the night, the whoosh and flash of petrol fire leaping up into the night sky, and the screams of pigs and the shrieks of chickens on fire. He stood still in the paddock and stared, his mouth panting open, tears of hate flickering in the leaping firelight. Then he gave a howl and he charged.

He ran across the paddock, he vaulted the fence and fell, he scrambled up, cursing, and ran towards the fires. He crashed through the bushes, branches tearing at his arms and clothes and face, he fell, scrambled up and ran on, swerving, blood from scratches running down his face, across his chest. The heat of the fire was on his face, leaping on his wild face. He crashed through the last belt of trees and bushes and stopped. The heat of the flames seared him, he shielded his face. The pigsty was ablaze, great flames leaping in the air, pigs screaming. The thatch above the housing was gone. The fire had caught the bushes in front of the sty, gaunt branches, red coals. He ran around the side of the sty, he ran to the wall, the fire threw him back. The boar was screaming, charging across the pigsty, petrol burning on his back, flesh on fire, the kaffir sow was caught in the sty, a burning beam filling the doorway, up to her udder in burning thatch, flesh burning, piglets kicking and screaming and running, on fire, screaming, keeling over, the stink of burning flesh. Mahoney ran back, and then charged the wall, feet up, kicking, he feel back on to the ground. The wall still stood. He got to his feet, tears running down his face. He raised the revolver, took aim, fired. Crack, crack, the boar and the sow dropped into the coals. He turned and ran on to the fowl runs. Chickens running, on fire, beating the air with their flaming wings, small birds shrivelled up, stumps of legs and wings twitching.

'*Cowards!*'

The fire was well into the bushes, a million sparks leaping up into the air like the devil's spawn, flames leaping on to bushes, fire running towards the house. He ran towards the boys' huts. 'Arthur— Arthur, where the hell are you – for God's sake why aren't you helping—?'

He ran through the dark into the compound, he kicked the hut door open, the light of the raging fire leapt into the room. His things were there, his blankets strewn aside. But empty.

He turned and made for the house. As he rounded the kopje he saw the fire had reached the house. The house was blazing.

It was nearly midnight. He was calm, he felt dead, dreamy, reckless, hate-filled, calm. It was very nice in its dead dreamy way, not to care any more, to be reckless, to be indifferent to others, indifferent to himself, save his determination to carry out his resolution, to be deadly, recklessly determined. It occurred to him that he was a coward, that he was escaping again from responsibility, but that didn't matter either. Nothing mattered. He sat on the barstool, dry streaks of blood on his face, coal ashes on his face, scratches on his legs.

'Barman give us two more Scotches here.'

Jackie sat tense beside him, very white, big brown eyes, wet, deep wet, face very white. She put her hand on his knee, he did not move.

'Joseph, come home.'

He turned his head and looked at her, his eyes were clear and hard. He said tonelessly: 'Jackie, I've told you I made love to her. Not twelve hours ago. I love her. I *am* her, Jackie. She may be having my child. I cannot marry you, dearest, sweetest Jackie, because I love her. I cannot come home with you.'

She looked at him steadily, a new tear in each eye, and she gave a tiny nod.

'Come home anyway. You need to sleep.'

'Jackie, today I slept in Suzie's arms. Do you know what it means to sleep in your love's arms, Jackie? I will not be able to sleep in your arms, Jackie, nor in your house.'

She looked at him, very white, full red lip trembled once.

'Where will you stay?'

'Right here, until the sun rises, drinking Scotch.'

'I'll pick you up here in the morning.'

He looked at her steadily, he spoke dreamily.

'In the morning, Jackie, I am going straight down the road to Army Headquarters.'

She closed her eyes desperately.

'But what about your job in Jamaica?'

'I don't intend working for a bunch of bloody two-faced British.'

Her eyes pleaded. 'Please come home and sleep on it. It'll seem different in the morning.'

'I've told you, Jackie.'

She opened her eyes.

'But you're a good lawyer, Joe. If you stay in Rhodesia there are more important things for you to do right here, you can be of greater service right here. It's people of your calibre who're needed here now to fight for sense and moderation in this mess—'

Mahoney did not blink, he shook his head dreamily, once.

'Jackie, there is nothing more important, there is only one important thing left to do. And that is to fight. There is no more time left for moderation. There is no more room left for moderation and moderates. The black nationalists don't want moderation in Rhodesia. Peking and Moscow do not want moderation in Rhodesia. Moderation is compromise, and, therefore, moderation is weakness. You cannot fight the enemy with compromise and weakness, Jackie, you must fight with all you've got. That is the tragedy, that is why there was UDI, that is the tragedy of UDI – you are forced to choose between black and white, you are driven to take up your cudgel in one camp or the other. The Rhodesians have made a stand. Now they must fight for it. First things first, and the first bloody thing is to kill the enemy before he kills you. Then when we have won, it will be the time for moderation. If there is anything left to build on, but ruins.'

She put her hand back on his knee.

'Please, Joseph. Come home.'

He shook his head.

She looked at him, very white, full red lip trembled, 'I will always wait for you, Joseph.' He nodded once. He squeezed her hand. She slid off the barstool and walked very fast out of the bar.

Part Ten

Chapter Sixty-One

It was hot in the Zambezi Valley, pregnantly hot. The thunderclouds were black, low, making the afternoon dark. We met elephant and buffalo and also some lion that afternoon: the lion padded away into the jungle when they saw us but one of the prisoners said they were fanning out to hunt us down and they were so nervous I thought they were going to try to run away, handcuffs and all. We came to a good place to rest, behind the little kopje, and the sergeant put two of the lads on guard and we broke out our ration packs. The three prisoners sat in a row. The big one, Barnabas, was sullen but the other two were nervous and they were polite. We gave them a ration pack each and the two smiled nervously and clapped their hands but Barnabas just stared sullenly at the ground and refused to eat.

'Okay Barnabas,' the sergeant said and he took the ration pack back.

We sat back and had a smoke. There was another deep rumble of thunder over to the west. The sergeant looked at his map.

'When we get back to the farm, get on to questioning these three right away.'

I nodded.

'You won't have any trouble getting the story from the two small ones,' he said, 'but friend Barnabas will take some time.'

'He'll talk too,' I said, 'they all talk, as soon as one talks they all start blaming each other.'

'Don't leave any marks,' the sergeant said.

'I won't need to clout anyone,' I said.

The sergeant nodded.

'You're a good interrogator, DA,' he said. The sergeant could not get used to having a lawyer under him. The boys called me DA, from seeing Perry Mason on the television.

'It's not that I'm such a good interrogator,' I said, 'it's that these blokes aren't good terrorists. They aren't trained enough or dedicated enough. And they're dumb.'

The sergeant had the prisoners' suitcase next to him. He opened it again and pulled out their clothes and looked at their three sub-machine-guns again. Two were Russian and the third was from Red China.

'Cheap stuff,' he said.

'But they kill you just as dead,' I said.

The sergeant shook his head.

'Can you believe it?' he asked. 'Three terrorists sneaking through the jungle into Rhodesia and instead of each man carrying his own gear so he's travelling light, they put all their gear and their guns into one heavy suitcase so that they can only stagger along. Ask them why, DA.'

I beckoned to the small one called Lazarus. He stood up and came over to us, his hands cuffed behind his back. His face was sweating and his legs were trembling. I asked him. He said 'Ah—' and looked embarrassed and then he told me. I turned to the sergeant.

'He says it's because the Party doesn't trust him and the other one. He says lots of others were tricked into being trained. They were told they were being sent to America to learn engineering but they were sent to Peking instead and trained as saboteurs. The Party thinks they may defect so it sends blokes like him back into the country in threes with all their personal belongings in one suitcase and the man the Party trusts keeps the suitcase so the other two will stick with him.'

The sergeant and the lads were laughing. Lazarus looked embarrassed.

'Very well, Lazarus,' I said, 'go sit down again.'

He looked relieved and walked back to his tree. The sergeant shook his head.

'I feel quite sorry for him,' I said.

'Don't feel sorry for him,' the sergeant said. 'He'd kill us if he was given a chance. I reckon we should shoot the bastards instead of handing them over to the police.'

'Savages,' Willie agreed.

'I mean it's pathetic,' I said. 'Lazarus here probably isn't a bad chap. You can see he isn't. He's just dumb. The Party is just using him for their own ends. They fill his head with stories and slogans he can't understand, they bully him into supporting them and then they bamboozle him into fighting for them, doing their dirty work for them.'

'I don't feel sorry for them,' the sergeant said, 'coming in here to create a reign of terror. Murders and bombings and Christ knows what. Life means nothing to these blokes, except their own. Christ, look how they're always murdering and burning their own people if they don't support them. Christ, Britain thinks these people can rule Rhodesia? You'd think they would've learned from what happened in the Congo and Ghana and Nigeria and Uganda and Christ-knows-whereall.'

'Sarge,' I said, 'the British are not so stupid as to think these people can rule themselves. The British *have* learned that much. It's just that it happens to suit Britain to give Rhodesia to the blacks, to get the other black states off her back. It suits Britain because if she makes herself unpopular she'll lose trade.' I nodded at the three blacks. 'You say life and death means little to these blokes—' I nodded at them again, 'but it doesn't mean much in Washington or Moscow or Peking, when money and power is at stake, mate, nor in Westminster. Particularly in Westminster. And that's what power is, Sarge: trade and money. The whole world is a jungle, Sarge. The guys I hate are not the likes of Lazarus here, who shriek with glee when they come to chop my head open, it's the rotten stinking money-grabbing politicians at the top who use him. They appeal to his savagery, they use him as a cannon-fodder. Lazarus is just a football. Money rules the world, Sarge, not ideals. The British ain't that dumb.'

The sergeant frowned. He was a Cockney, see, still had his old folks in London.

'Aw,' he said, 'the British ain't as bad as that, DA. They're just misguided, like—'

'Sarge—' I opened the suitcase and pulled out one of the sub-machine-guns. I held it out to him. 'See this, Sarge? This is a Chinese machine-gun, isn't it? What does that mean?'

'It means the Red Chinese are helping these blacks,' Sarge said.

'That's right, Sarge. And why? Because by helping the blacks the Chinese will extend their sphere of power. Right?'

'Right,' Sarge said.

'Right. Now the Americans and British are allies, aren't they, and the Americans are fighting the Commies in Vietnam, aren't they? But if you and I were American servicemen and this were a Vietnam jungle and we were capturing communist guerillas, Sarge, do you know what we would see on those weapons?'

'What?' Sarge said.

'*Made in Birmingham,* Sarge, *Made in England.*'

The Zambezi ran through gorges for many miles from the Kariba dam wall down to Chirundu Bridge. The river ran hard and deep and wide and green and treacherous there, and the gorges were steep and very hard to climb and the land beyond them was rugged and very wild. Then, near Chirundu, the gorges sloped off and the great river ran out into the long wide Zambesi basin: that was where the terrorists tried to cross, and that was where most of our troops were, spread out in small patrols along the wild banks. But it was very difficult for terrorists to cross by the gorges, so our patrols here were fewer, and we covered a larger area. As the sergeant said, we marched our asses off.

The old wooden farmhouse was in a long wide ravine that broke into the southern gorge, about twelve miles below the dam wall. It was dark and rich-damp in the ravine, and it had been a banana farm before the trouble started. The ravine was one of the few points where terrorists could cross easily. Our patrol was lucky to have the farmhouse to live in: further downstream the boys only had tents. And Madara, the old black farm foreman, still lived in the compound behind the homestead with his wives and we hired them to do our cooking and washing. We had hacked a track out of the ravine through the bush, but it was very bad and it took four hours to reach Kariba Township in the jeep.

Willie and I had the first guard duty, from eight to midnight. It was Willie's turn at the boathouse on the river-bank, I had the verandah. From the verandah I had a good view of all sides of the ravine. The rains broke that night. There were great flashes of lightning that lit up the jungle and then great claps of thunder that were so loud and near you started each time, even though you were waiting for it. Then came the rain, first fat slow drops, hitting the corrugated-iron roof of the house like pellets, then down it came in a clatter, then a roar, beating the iron roof, and I could not see the sides of the ravine, nor the boathouse. I thought: I pity those poor bastards in that tent downstream, at number two ravine, they'll be washed out, and I pity Willie in that tin boathouse, he won't be able to hear himself think. The rain settled down to a steady batter on the roof, and there were gurgles and splutters of water running down off the roof and the sides of the ravine, and rolls of thunder. I paced round and round the verandah in the dark, but I could not see anything because of the rain, and I could not hear anything. I found myself again thinking of Suzie, just twelve miles away now, up-river at Kariba Township. Suzie, my Suzie, only twelve miles away from me, married to Jake Jefferson, my Suzanna married to him sleeping in his bed, making love to him, my Suzie *his* wife. At night it was very bad: during the day when we were busy patrolling it was easier, but when I was all alone on night guard duty it was very difficult to stop myself thinking about Suzie. I thought how good it would be to live in this house with Suzie, I thought of her in my bed at night, soft and naked and female and willing, I thought of waking up with her in my bed in New York and Scotland and London and Paris and Madrid, I thought of the fishing and the skating and the skiing and the wine in the sun on Sundays. I thought of all the good things, and I very much regretted all the bad things I had done to her, and I could not feel the way I had felt when I had done them, I only felt longing for her, and much regret. I thought:

if only she had had a child, it would all have worked out, it would have been very good. And I thought of my child born of Suzie's body, Suzie's flesh and mine, I thought of the tiny body, I would hold it in my hands and thrust it aloft in joy and shout, shout that it was marvellous, that I had done something very good. And I could see the thrill on Suzie's face, the happiness, and it felt very bad. And I thought of Suzie trying so hard to have a child, Suzie counting the days on the calendar, Suzie taking her temperature with the thermometer, trying hard to have a baby, and I felt a choking in my throat, and my eyes burned, and I cried inside: *Oh my poor darling Suzie, my poor sweet lovely girl, forgive me, I am very sorry.* I had not seen her for over eight months now, since the day Samson Ndhlovu was hanged. The first time we had gone to Kariba on leave I had tried to find her and at last I had phoned her house: 'I am having a baby now, Joseph, darling Joseph, Jake's baby, Jake's baby, darling, you must forget me, Joseph, as I have forgotten you, because I am carrying another man's child Joseph, you must forget me, you must never try to seek me out Joseph, you must never never phone me again, do not destroy yourself and me and my happiness, Joseph—' Jake Jefferson's child, another man's child in Suzie's belly. Sometimes it was unthinkable, but mostly now it was very real. Sometimes, in the night, I said to myself: it is *your* child she is carrying from the day they hanged Samson – and when I thought that I wanted to crash through the bush to Jake Jefferson's house at Kariba and seize my woman and carry her away. But in the morning I did not believe it, and I thought of Suzie's sad face, Suzie desperately trying to get her baby, Suzie with her baby in her belly at last now, Jake Jefferson's baby, and I did not seek her out again and I did not phone again.

I paced round and round the verandah, the rain beating on the roof, filling the night, thinking about her, trying to think of this war, of what Lazarus had told me. Some Lazarus. Some war. How many of us marching up and down these goddam gorges in small patrols for five months and we had caught nine guerillas? Down in the valley below Chirundu hundreds of soldiers patrolling two hundred miles of Zambezi – how many terrorists slipped through that thin cordon, through that vast jungle? How many soldiers to catch one terrorist? In how many manhours? How many more miles of jungle, how many more terrorists to come? Many many more. Cannon-fodder, undisciplined, untrained, cannon-fodder, yes, but many many more where they came from, an unending supply of them from the vast blackness of Africa north of the Zambezi. And how many soldiers to catch one man? In how many manhours? And for how long? For how many more days, months, years would we be patrolling these vast jungles? For ever? Like Korea and Vietnam? No, not like Korea and Vietnam, worse than that: forever, like Israel.

Oh God if only there was an army to fight against, soldiers to shoot at, something visible to lick, to finish, so that win or lose, we could start again—

The field telephone buzzed, on the verandah. Nine-thirty. I walked over to it and picked it up.

'Number two post. Oi-oi, Willie.'

'Oi-oi, DA. Number one post all clear.'

'Okay, Willie. You enjoying it down there?'

'Lovely. Fucking beautiful down here, it is.'

'Okay. Willie.'

I put the receiver down and continued pacing round the verandah, tramp, tramp, tramp.

Some Barnabas. Big, strong Barnabas. A few clouts and he had talked. I think I had beaten Suzie harder than I had beaten him.

Trembling, face shiny with nervous sweat, he had talked jerkily.

'We were going to Salisbury, Bwana. There we were to find work. We must contact other men of the Party. We would receive our instruction by letter from the big ones in Lusaka, they would tell us to organise the Night of the Long Knives—'

'When is this Night of the Long Knives—?'

'I do not know, Bwana.'

'Your mother-fornicating party has been talking about this Night of the Long Knives for many years, you must know when it will be!'

'I do not know, Bwana.'

I had given him a clout across the face, so his head had jerked and some sweat flew and he hung his head. 'Tell me, Barnabas.'

'I do not know, Bwana.'

Another clout: 'I will have no hesitation in killing you slowly until you talk.'

'I do not know, Bwana.' He did not know.

'How many men were trained in Peking in your group?'

'Twenty-five, Bwana.'

'Who are they?'

He told me, I wrote down their names and particulars. 'Where are they now?'

'I don't know, Bwana, we were to return to Zimbabwe in small groups.'

'When did you last see them?'

'Two days ago, at Lusaka, Bwana.'

'Where in Lusaka?'

'In quarters provided for Freedom Fighters by the Zambia Government.'

'Were you not all sent back to Rhodesia at the same time?'

'We were all told at the same time that we would be returning, but we were to return in small groups.'

'At what places on the Zambezi were the others to cross into Rhodesia?'

'I do not know, Bwana, each group was told separately.'

'When will the others return?'

'I do not know.'

'Why did you cross the Zambezi at the gorges?'

'We were ordered, Bwana. Because it is wild country and the river is difficult to cross here and, therefore, there will be less guards.'

'Will the others cross at the gorges?'

'I do not know, Bwana.'

Another clout.

'I do not know, Bwana.'

I started all over again.

For how much longer would this Godawful war go on? How much longer before we could all go home and take off our goddam uniforms and get down to our jobs and start earning money again, go to work in the morning knowing there was money available for the earning, knowing that hard work and brains were rewarded, knowing there were things in the shops to buy with your money, the nice things you wanted, the things you need, when would we be able to jump into our motor cars again and have the petrol and the money and the freedom and the safety to go on picnics again, holidays again, up to Inyanga and down to this Zambezi valley to catch fish again and drink sundowners in the African sunset again, with the smell of the campfires and the friendly sounds of the cookboy making skoff, when would we stop seeing our people packing up and selling up for a song, and emigrating because they can no longer make a living, when would we stop seeing natives lounging around, out of work because there is no work for them any more, for how much longer must we open the newspaper in the morning and see that there has been another coup in bloodstained Africa, another bloodbath, another dictatorship set-up, more screaming chaos, another hymn of hate, another billion dollars given in exchange for abuse, while we are not even allowed to earn our livings, when would we drive to work in the mornings and feel that hustle-bustle of industry and optimism again, and drive home again at night to our suburbs to wives and children and sleep unafraid for them at night again, without a pistol under our pillows, when would we end opening the papers in the mornings and seeing petrol bombings and murders – *when?* For how much longer? For ever. Like the Israelis.

The field telephone buzzed again. Nine forty-five. I picked it up.

'Number two post.'

'Number one post all clear, DA.'

'Okay, Willie, I'll be down to take over in fifteen minutes.'

Tramp, tramp, tramp, my boots going slowly round the wooden verandah, the rain falling on the roof, the thunder, the splash and gurgle of water. Suzie – a home again – how long will this last?

I looked at my watch. Nearly ten o'clock, time to get into my raincoat and go out into that bloody rain and slip and slide my way down to that boathouse and swap guard with Willie. It was going to be charming in that boathouse for two hours, absolutely bloody charming, with the water pouring in through the holes in the roof and the rain making so much noise on the tin you couldn't hear yourself think. It's all right for Willie, he hasn't got any brains to think with, but me? I unslung my SLR and leaned it against the wall and pulled on my raincoat. It was hot underneath it, sticky and bulky. I buttoned up the flaps and picked up my SLR and slung it under my armpit, muzzle down so rain wouldn't fall down the spout. I walked over to the field telephone and stood by it looking out into the black rain, waiting for Willie's call. Come on, Willie. Ten o'clock, one minutes past. Come on, Willie. I picked up the receiver and whirred the handle, and listened. Nothing. I whirred the handle again and listened. I cursed and put the receiver down. I tramped into the house to the sergeant's room and shook him.

'Sarge, that unprintable telephone has gone on the unprintable blink again.'

'The fookin' thing,' the sergeant blinked.

'I'm going down to relieve Willie, if we can't get it to work again, we'll wake you.'

'Okay,' Sarge said.

I went back to the verandah. I screwed up my eyes and hunched up my shoulders and stepped off the verandah into the rain and mud.

I jumped over the trench and the sandbags we had thrown across the ravine and began to plop and suck my way down the slope to the boathouse alongside the stream that ran down the ravine to the river. We had cleared most of the slope of its bush and banana trees to give the Bren gun behind the sandbags a clear field down the slope to the river-bank, and the earth was churned up and it was sodden mud now. The rain beat down on me and ran down my face, tasting salty. I slipped and staggered down the slope. There was a flash of lightning and the boathouse and the river danced silver and black in front of me and then they were gone again. I squelched on down. I could see the boathouse dimly through the rain now.

'Willie, it's the DA.'

I tramped up to the side of the boathouse. 'Willie, it's the DA.'

I walked to the doorward end of the boathouse and looked in. 'Willie?'

I flicked on my torch and I stifled a cry, Aaar! in my throat.

There was the open end of the boathouse on the river edge and there on his back lay Willie.

There was blood running black from the stab wounds in his chest, and his head and shoulders lay in a pool of black-red blood from the gape across his throat. There was white sinew and cartilage showing in the gape. And there were big black patches around his crotch and his trousers were ripped open, red and raw and still running blood out there, and stuffed in Willie's mouth were his genitals, red and bleeding and blood trickling down his chin.

I spun back out of the doorway and pressed myself against the wall, I fumbled as I unslung my SLR and shoved it against my hip, my hands shaking, and I fumbled as I put it on to automatic fire. My heart was pounding. I stood still for an instant, trying to see, waiting for the bastard to jump out of the boathouse at me. I scurried backwards, doubled up down the wall towards the water. I stopped halfway down the wall and I dropped to my knee amongst the ferns. So the bastards were playing it quiet, going to knock us off one by one as we came down to the boathouse. *Raise the alarm, fire a burst through the bushes that'll wake the sergeant and the boys up top—*

—yes you idiot, and then you'll have given their game away and every goddam terrorist will open up on you—

You've got to wake up the boys up top, you idiot – a noise behind me, a rush of awful fear, terror, blind instinctive self-preservation, I spun round on my knee, a scream in my throat, an animal scream of murder to terrify my enemy, the SLR at my waist, my finger clutched hard on the trigger, da-da-da-da my flesh shaking with the vibration, the acrid smell, a big shape looming dim against the night, a flash of lightning, a big wet black man standing poised big above me, knife raised flashing once in the lightning, a crease of white tooth, shock on his black face, da-da-da-da-da, big form crumbling, darkness again. Then, da-da-da-da-da, two machine-guns flashing in the bush along the banks, I was running doubled up, head down, rain beating my face, the mud skidding and splashing and bullets whistling and beating the air, throwing myself sideways into the stream ditch, splash, scrambling, crouched low, splashing upstream slipping and sliding on the rocks, the mud and the water pulling. Please God please God please God, still the clatter of the machine-guns above the banks of the stream and the bushes ripping, scrambling, panting. Please God—then the heavy angry clatter of the Bren gun mounted at the sandbags up at the house, tears in my eyes, thank you God, thank you, scrambling through the bushes, bullets ripping all above me. Atta boy, Sarge, shoot the bastards, for Chrissake don't shoot me, Sarge, for Chrissake, I mean thank you God, scrambling slipping and sliding and clutching and clawing up the streambed. Then silence.

After the noise, the silence was very loud. Then, in came the sound of the rain again, falling, falling, and the gurgle of the stream and the deafening sound of my boots in the mud and the water. I rested behind a rock, panting. I reckoned I was a third of the way up the slope.

'DA. *You all right!*' The Sarge's shout was muffled by the rain.

My breathing roaring in my ears. Yeah, Sarge, what you want me to do, you idiot, shout hullo and get myself blown to digestible pieces by those ten million savages down there by the boathouse? I didn't answer, I tried to listen above the sound of my panting. I waited, listening, panting. Good, good, let both sides think I'm dead until I get back up this stream to those lovely sandbags. There was a flash of lightning, a long flickering flick-on, flick-on-and-on flash, and I crouched lower, trying to look like a rock, then the crack of thunder and I jerked. Then a short burst of the Bren above me again and then a moment's silence. And then the fizzing sizzle overhead and then the dazzling blue-white light of the overhead spotter-flare, the long dancing shadows of the bush, then the loud heavy clatter of the Bren gun again. Blackness. Silence. Then another sizzle and another long flickering light up in the sky, and then another clatter-clatter from the Bren. Attaboy, Sarge, that'll keep the bastards' heads down. I scrambled up out of the mud, and ran up the steep streambed again, slipping and sliding and cursing and praying. Blackness, silence again but for the roar of my panting in my ears and the thud thud thud thud of my heart in my ears and the din of my boots in the mud and the water – then the mad da-da-da-da-da of the SLRs from the water's edge again, and the Bren's angry answer. I kept running up the stream, praying, crouching, scrambling, bullets going wild all about me. I was nearly at the top, I was nearly crying now, tears of joy and hate and love, keep firing at each other, you bastards, keep firing, just don't shoot me for Chrissake, please God – twenty, fifteen, fourteen, thirteen dark slippery noisy treacherous yards to go, slip and scramble, my fingers raw now, two fingernails screaming and welling and wincing, but I didn't care, my right hand open, a pleasurable reckless pain as I grabbed rocks and branches, mud in my mouth, keep shooting you bastards. Ten seven five four yards, a bush grabbing at my eye, whimpering, slip, grasp pant thud da-da-da clatter-da-clatter-da-da-da, the sandbags in front of me now, one two three slip slide grasp slides strides thud thud thud of the slugs hitting the sandbags. Sarge, Sarge it's me, firing Sarge you lovely bastard. Please God, please God, not one in the back now as I go over. A shout, yes Sarge, it's me, hands clawing up out of the mud, slip back again Jesus Christ. I mean Jesus Christ keep the bullets off my back, slip slide standing up now the bullets thudding the sandbags no lightning, now, please God, one two three up, and struggle and over and da-da-da. And lying in the mud of the ditch behind the sandbags, those sweet sandbags and the roar of the guns and the thud thud of the bullets a sweet cosy sound like the sound of the storm outside your snug lounge windows. And laughing in my throat, tears of laughter.

Chris shaking me.

'You all right, DA?'

'Bloody marvellous.'

'How many of them did you see?'

'About ten million, it seemed.'

'We've seen at least ten.'

'Willie?' the sergeant said.

'Dead.'

I crawled along the ditch till I came to my station in the sandbags. I shoved my SLR through the hole and screwed my eyes up tight, once, and then opened them and I peered out into the wet black. I glanced at my watch. Eight minutes past ten. *Is that all?*

Silence again.

'Ammo,' the sergeant said. 'Chris, fetch some more ammo for the Bren.'

Chris got up and ran doubled up along the trench. Then there was a spotter-flare sizzle overhead, and then our trench was bathed in the blue-white light.

'Well fook me—' the sergeant said. The Bren and our SLRs were chattering da-da-da-da-da. Chris was jumping up out of the trench on to the verandah. A spurt of gunfire came from the black jungled wall of the ravine and raked the side of the house and Chris went down in a heap.

So now we were four.

Blackness again, and silence. Then a long flickering of lightning, on-off-on-off, and gunfire flashed from a dozen places.

'DA, get on to the radio set and call Sunray for reinforcements. And bring a box of ammo back with you—'

I scrambled up and ran doubled up along the trench to the farmhouse.

The rain was beating on the roof and the guns were beating the air da-da-da-da-da and there were long rolls of thunder and the radio bleeped and squealed and crackled.

'Sunray, Sunray, Sunray, Charlie Zero Ten calling Sunray, can you hear me, over—' click.

Bleep squeal crackle, went the radio. There was another roll of thunder.

'Jesus Christ.' Click. 'Sunray, Sunray, Charlie Zero Ten calling Sunray, Charlie Zero Ten calling Sunray, can you hear me, over.' Click.

Da-da-da-da-da went the guns. Ssssh crackle squeal, bloody atmospherics.

'Jesus Christ—' Click. I tried for the eighth time. 'Come in Sunray, please. Over.'

The windows went in a clatter of falling glass, slugs smacked in a row across the wall above me and plaster fell.

'For crying out loud—'

'Sunray speaking, I hear you Charlie Zero Ten, Sunray speaking, I hear you Charlie Zero Ten, over—'

Thank God. Click. 'Sunray sir, Charlie Zero Ten, Private Mahoney reporting engagement number one ravine estimate at least fiften repeat one five terrorists landed armed with machine-guns and spotter flares, they have taken the boathouse, repeat boathouse, not the homestead, we are holding them at the number two post but we've lost two men, repeat lost two men, we are under heavy fire, and we can't see much because of the bloody rain, repeat very heavy rain, visibility bad, consider we can hold them, sir, provided they've got nothing to knock the Bren out with but request reinforcements if possible. Over sir—'

Sssh sssh bleep squeal bleep crack. Da-da-da-da went the guns. – 'Charlie Zero—' bleep bleep crackle 'hear you ...' bleep ... 'Ten'. Click.

'Jesus. Sunray Sunray I'll repeat that—'

I mouthed it into the microphone all over again, the air vibrating with the guns and the thunder and the rain drumming down on the roof.

... bleep 'Zero Ten—' Sunray's voice came back over the crackling radio— '... impossible until morning' bleep 'earliest ...' bleep crackle ... 'landing below the bridge and' bleep 'the lake, repeat extensive attempts at landing below' bleep bleep squeal ssh crackle ... Sunray's voice came back on a wave of atmospherics: 'Night of the Long Knives repeat information indicates tonight is Night of bleep wail crackle ... 'at all cost, repeat hold number one ravine ... Over.'

I flicked the switch.

'Message received Sunray, Sunray's message received, signing off, then, over—' I moved the switch halfway and then I snapped it back: 'Sunray, Sunray, is Kariba town secure, repeat is Kariba town secure? Over.'

I flicked the switch over and listened. Only atmospherics, the long wails and squeals and whines. I snapped the switch back and shouted it again. A voice came back over the atmospherics, but it wasn't the usual voice, it was the Corporal's – Christ things must be a shambles up there. He misheard Kariba town for Kariba dam. 'Okay, I hear ya, DA, I' bleep bleep 'fuggin bastards' bleep squeal 'laid a time charge to' bleep 'the wall' crackle squeal bleep 'OC Police is going over the side' bleep 'demolish' bleep crackle 'Jesus it's pitch black and the' bleep 'rain' bleep squeal 'envy the poor—' I snapped the machine off. My chest was knocking, a thumping in my ears above the clatter of the guns. Jesus – the dam wall! If the black bastards blew that precious wall – Jesus, good Jesus Christ don't let that wall go up, not that wall, God! – the destruction, the unholy havoc, the biggest tidal wave of the world, the destruction, a maniac mountain of water hurtling down the valley on to us, down the hundreds of miles to the sea, the holocaust, the people and the soldiers and the animals and the jungle – the waste the dreadful maniac waste – and Jake Jefferson, oh Jake Jefferson, I hated your guts sometimes but Jesus the bastard had guts, Jefferson going over the side of Christ knows how many hundreds of feet of sheer concrete and the bullets smacking all around – Jesus, Jesus, Jefferson, God surround you, just demolish that charge Jefferson may God help you please God help that brave bastard down that wall – Christ!

I scrambled up from the machine and ran down the passage to the storeroom. The guns were still hammering and the rain was beating down. It was hot and I was cold, and I was shivering now. I unlocked the door and flung it open and seized a case of Bren ammunition. I swung it up on to my shoulder and ran back down the passage at a stagger.

Chapter Sixty-Two

And the rain came down. The trench was deep in mud, we lay in the bloody stuff, firing, waiting, listening, firing again, sending up flares, firing, being fired at. And all the time the rain teeming down. We listened between the hammering of the guns for the faraway roar and thunder of the wave coming crashing down through the gorges. No, not yet. 'Come on you bastards, come and charge us, let's get it over with.' They had good cover in the rocks and bush at the sides of the ravine: it had been impossible to clear all that. At least they'd get smashed to hell by the wave if it came, the bastards, as well as us. And when they heard it coming there would only be only one way for them to run, straight into our guns, the bastards, serve them right the bastards for blowing up the wall – our wall, the fools, it was theirs and Zambia's as well as ours, the fools—a big distant rumble, a jerk, listen, heart pounding, was that the water coming?— But, no, it was only thunder falling on ringing ears. A flash of lightning, a man standing up out of cover, his arm drawn back, poised for the long hard throw of a grenade, four guns swinging on him da-da-da-da, we mowed him down. Luck, next time the lightning wouldn't come at the right time. We sent up flares, hammered the shadows at the sides of the ravine. They had to take us or retreat before light because they would be unable to retreat back across the open river in daylight. And still the noise did not come, the roar of the tidal wave. By Christ he must have done it, Jake Jefferson must have made it by Christ, thank you God thank you, old Jake Jefferson must have done it by God – come on, you bastards, come on! Then at four o'clock the incendiary bomb hit the wooden house from nowhere, and a great ragged yellow light leaped up and flooded the ravine. And our row of sandbags was silhouetted against the fire behind us, and they opened up on us, a dozen guns, but the light also fell on them, the bastards, and there was nothing in the world but the cacophony of guns and the blind blood hate and lust to shoot and shoot and kill kill kill. Then down at the water's edge a man broke cover and ran across towards the boathouse, then another man broke cover and the sergeant swung the Bren on them with a whoop-da-da-da-da and they fell and the sergeant was screaming with glee: 'Reinforcements—Reinforcements—'

And I looked over my shoulder, and a pair of headlights was churning down the track of the ravine behind us, bouncing and skewering and smacking on to the ruts and then surging on, bouncing and splashing.

'Hurrah-hurrah-ha ha ha ha—' the sergeant screamed and his teeth were clenched and his lips were pulled back in glee in the leaping firelight, and the Bren shuddered in his hands and clattered. And a laugh gurgled up in my throat, a welling of triumph, we'd held them we'd held them!

The headlights swung out of sight behind the native compound and then came back into view bouncing and churning and skewering up the track towards the flaming homestead. Then it reached the light of the burning house and it stopped and I looked back again and I saw it wasn't a military vehicle, it was a Ford sedan and the door opened and only one person climbed out and began to run towards us, staggering, a woman in a dress and her belly was big in front of her and she ran with both hands across her belly holding it and she was staggering and she came into the light of the fire and I recognised the long yellow hair flying in the firelight and I recognised the hysterical face weeping.

'Joseph—Joseph—Joseph—' and she fell on her side.

I dropped the SLR in the mud and I ran back to her.

Chapter Sixty-Three

I laid her on the concrete floor of the pumphouse behind the sandbags. Slugs smacked against the outside wall and our Bren was rattling. She was weeping: 'Joseph—Joseph – are you safe are you safe I had to come when I heard of the fighting to warn you about the wall; you'll be drowned Joseph; it's yours, Joseph, it's your baby Joseph—' and the tears were running down her demented face and she was tossing her head from side to side on the concrete and I was trying to hold her still and my heart was pounding in my ears and the sergeant was screaming *Aha! Aha!—run you bastards, die you bastards! Aha! Aha!*—and the Bren was firing again and her words were swimming in my head. She didn't know about Jake going over the side. Then she cried out *'Aah!* and her hands clutched her big belly and she arched her back and she bit into her lip and her eyes screwed up and she cried out – 'Joseph Joseph Joseph hold my hand—' and I grabbed the hem of the dress and ripped it apart up to her belly and felt her swollen belly and I put my hands between her legs and her legs and her pants were warm wet and sodden. And I pulled the pants off her and I tore off my shirt and I was whimpering as I spread it on the concrete between her thighs. And then I was running in the rain, running as fast as I could for the native compound, running and stumbling and falling and scrambling up again, and behind me I could hear the Bren and the sergeant's shouts of glee and then the Bren again.

I ran into the compound shouting: *'Madara,* Madara, call your women to help me – Madara—Madara—' I ran to Madara's hut and kicked the door open. 'Madara!' I bounded to his sleeping mat and kicked it, but I kicked nothing. I ran out of the hut. *'Where are the people, come out of hiding, a woman gives birth—'* I ran to the hut of the junior wife and kicked the door open – *'Woman, woman, come out of hiding, we have won the battle and a woman gives birth—'* But there was no woman in the hut, I ran to the hut of the senior wife and kicked it but it did not open. I kicked it again, and I roared: *'Grandmother open the door, come out—'* I kicked the door again and it crashed open, and there was the old wife of Madara cowering in the corner. *'Grandmother—'* I leaped at her and she raised her spindly old arms to cover her head and I grabbed her thin wrist and pulled her up. 'Do not fear me, Grandmother, it is I, the white soldier, come with me—' I grabbed her blanket off the floor and I dragged her out the door and then I flung my arm around her thin waist and I was running and staggering and dragging her back towards the pumphouse, and I saw that the roof of the homestead had fallen in and the fire was low now and it was raining less and it was beginning to get light.

Chapter Sixty-Four

It was light and it was only drizzling now, a very gentle murmur on the tin roof of the pumphouse. I could hear the squeal and crackle of the two-way radio as the sergeant tried to get it to work again. Suzie was warm and her eyes were open. Outside the boys were standing quietly, hushed, awed, and the wet smoke was rising tiredly from the ashes of the homestead. The noise of the radio stopped and then I heard the sergeant say: 'The wall's okay but the cop got it on the way back,' the boys muttering. I held her head in my lap and I looked down at her, my Suzie, my eyes were dry now and I could feel nothing again, only disbelief. Somebody moved up to the door and blocked the light but I did not look up.

'Nkosi?'

I did not answer the old woman. 'Nkosi, I have washed your child and now he sleeps well in my arms.' I did not look up.

'Take him back to your hut, Grandmother, and tend him well till I come.' The old lady still stood in the doorway. 'Does the Nkosi wish to hold him?'

I did not shake my head. 'No.'

The old lady still stood in the doorway.

'When he awakes he must be fed. The wife of Tarawona beyond the hill has an infant and much milk in her breasts, shall I send for her?'

I nodded, but without looking up.

'Yes, Grandmother. Give him the breast of the wife of Tarawona.'

She half turned and then she stopped and looked back at me.

'I think it will comfort the Nkosi to see his son.'

I turned and looked up at the old woman in the doorway. She held a bundle of grey blanket in her arms.

'No,' I said, 'he killed my woman.'

She looked at me and then she nodded, and she turned away from the doorway holding the bundle and then she stopped again and looked at me.

'Nkosi?'

I looked at her.

'Nkosi. He has a fine body. And much flesh and big bones. I think he was conceived in great love.'

She looked at me and then she turned and shuffled away on her dirty black skinny ankles through the drizzle, back towards the compound and as she shuffled she hunched herself over the bundle to shield it from the rain.

Then the pain returned up my throat, a great erupting stab that shuddered and the tears welled up and I choked and I clutched her head against me and I felt for her hand and I brought her hand up to my chest and I held her hand and I cried:

Suzie Suzie Suzie, hold my hand.

By John Gordon Davis

Leviathan

A compelling novel of adventure and intrigue, 'Leviathan' tells the unadulterated and at times terrible story of whaling, partially from the perspective and mind of a whale. The novel concentrates the senses in terms of willing conservation, whilst entertaining with a varied mixture of characters, some of whom would be classified as eco-terrorists. There are thrills, adventure, battles and heartaches in the story which is taut with human drama, and the author manages to convey the underlying message without preaching, or propaganda.

The Years of the Hungry Tiger

Set in the years of Mao and prior to the handover, 'The Years of the Hungry Tiger' is the story of McAdam, a Hong Kong policeman who is unhappily married. Then he meets Ying-ling, who is a schoolmistress, and he falls headlong for her. This, however, makes him a security risk as she teaches at a communist school, and to make matters worse her father lives on the mainland and so McAdam becomes immediately vulnerable to Chinese pressure. Ying-ling herself is a 'starry-eyed' Marxist with resulting conflicting loyalties. In a novel which contains more than a smattering of realism, the author thrills with a tale of political intrigue, espionage, riots, sex, and the underworld of the island, along with it surviving typhoons, economic crises, and everything a hostile regime can throw at it.

By John Gordon Davis

Taller Than Trees

For many years hunters had tried to kill Dhlulamiti, but he had survived. An elephant some thirteen and a half feet tall – his name translated to 'Taller than trees' – and weighing in at twelve tons he was a giant even amongst the largest species of mammal ever to have inhabited the earth. In his early days, he had roamed the savannah in Africa as a killer, attacking every man that came his way, but now wiser thoughts prevailed. Inevitably, one day Dhlulamiti met up with Jumbo McGuire, a hard hell-raising Irish hunter who was renowned for the number of 'kills' to his credit. As the predators circled with a hope of cashing in on what would seem to be the inevitable outcome and an easy meal, the final epic struggle between elephant and man began.

Cape of Storms

James McQuade, a young handsome marine biologist sails on a whaler into the Antarctic. On board is Victoria Rhodes, one of a number of nurses, and James falls hopelessly in love with her. However, other members of the crew, who range from ordinary as seamen go to very rough personalities, also lust after Victoria. Her origins become the centre of attention and an air of mystery surrounds her. Following a return to port in Cape Town drama ensues and startling facts emerge. The author depicts the brutality of both whaling and human behaviour with no holds barred and undeniable insight in this thrilling novel. It is packed with adventure, sexual frustrations, and mystery.

33897124R00280

Printed in Great Britain
by Amazon